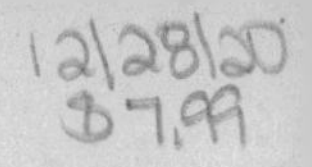


*Praise for*

## *Butterfly Bayou*

"Lila's strength and vulnerability are balanced by Armie's intelligence and humor, making them an easy couple to root for. Blake captures the flavor of her colorful Southern town with a vividly drawn cast. . . . This charming series opener hits all the right notes." —*Publishers Weekly*

"Blake has created a couple to root for, along with memorable supporting characters and story lines with depth. Readers will be eager to visit Papillon again."

—*Library Journal*

*Praise for*

## Lexi Blake

"Lexi Blake is a master!"

—*New York Times* bestselling author Jennifer Probst

"I love Lexi Blake."

—*New York Times* bestselling author Lee Child

"Smart, savvy, clever, and always entertaining."

—*New York Times* bestselling author Steve Berry

"Lexi Blake has set up shop on the intersection of suspenseful and sexy, and I never want to leave."

—*New York Times* bestselling author Laurelin Paige

## *Titles by Lexi Blake*

THE BUTTERFLY BAYOU NOVELS

*Butterfly Bayou*
*Bayou Baby*
*Bayou Dreaming*

THE COURTING JUSTICE NOVELS

*Order of Protection*
*Evidence of Desire*

THE LAWLESS NOVELS

*Ruthless*
*Satisfaction*
*Revenge*

THE PERFECT GENTLEMEN NOVELS
*(with Shayla Black)*

*Scandal Never Sleeps*
*Seduction in Session*
*Big Easy Temptation*

# *Bayou Dreaming*

Lexi Blake

JOVE
New York

A JOVE BOOK
Published by Berkley
An imprint of Penguin Random House LLC
penguinrandomhouse.com

ISBN: 9781984806604

First Edition: December 2020

Printed in the United States of America
1 3 5 7 9 10 8 6 4 2

Cover images by Shutterstock
Cover design and photo illustration by Vikki Chu
Book design by Alison Cnockaert

*To Kori—who loves dogs far more than people . . .*

# *prologue*

**PAPILLON, LOUISIANA**
***Four years ago***

Zep Guidry closed the door to his truck with a grin and wondered if the news he was about to tell his mother would actually give her a heart attack.

After all, she wasn't used to good news about the youngest of her children.

He'd sown a few wild oats in his time, though not nearly as many as his reputation would have people believe. The truth was he'd had something of a wild youth, but that was going to come to an end. Oh, he would still drink and party. After all, what was life without a party?

But he was finally going to get serious about something.

He winced because the thing he was getting serious about was what might cause his mother's coronary. She would laugh at first, thinking he was joking, and then would come that expression that let him know she wasn't sure about this. He was going to get serious about higher education. The big envelope had come today. He'd picked it up at the post office box he'd rented a few years back because as much as he loved his momma, she was nosy about everything. She would open his mail without qualm, and he'd wanted a bit of privacy.

Especially for this.

His momma knew he'd been taking classes at a community college, but she didn't know how serious he'd gotten about it. Half the time the classes were online since they were so remote out here, so he hadn't even needed to leave his apartment over the garage. What she didn't know was he'd applied to finish up his degree at a four-year university, and he had plans that went beyond that.

He knew his small family would have supported him, but he hadn't trusted himself to actually finish. The last thing he'd wanted to do was start something else he didn't complete.

There was a joke around town that the only thing Zep Guidry knew how to finish was a beer.

He was tired of being that guy.

He would complete his associate degree in a few weeks, and that big envelope from LSU had made his hands shake.

He was in. He could work part time and had some money saved up. He'd managed to pay his own way through community college by doing odd jobs. Most of which he had finished. It wasn't his fault that Dean LeRoux's old cypress tree turned out to be full of very aggressive bees.

He would complete his undergraduate degree at LSU and figure out where to go from there. All he knew was that he wanted to work with animals. If he got his degree, he would have choices he hadn't dreamed of before. He might even think about going all the way and becoming a vet.

Was he really going to do this? Was he going to walk in and announce to two women who thought he was mostly a moron that he was going to try to finish college? Would they laugh at him? They wouldn't mean to, but it might slip out. Hell, he knew it sounded like a pipe dream.

But he wanted to try.

It was the right time. Everything seemed to have settled down. His big brother had left the Navy and was happy in his new job in Dallas. Sera wasn't exactly happy, but she was trying to find the right career for herself. She would stay and help out their mother.

Now was the perfect time to try something for himself.

He jogged up the front steps of the house he'd lived in all his life. When he'd been younger, he'd had the room next to his sister's. When Remy had gone into the Navy, he'd moved into the apartment over the garage.

What would it be like to live on his own? He would likely need a roommate. Maybe he could find some gorgeous young lady who could help him through chemistry.

God, he was going to take chemistry. He hoped he could charm the professor.

He was going to college. He would be the first Guidry to get a degree.

He would go to college, get his degree, and then come home because he loved this place. Maybe he could get a job with the park rangers or Wildlife and Fisheries. He could open a shelter close to here because they always had animals that needed help. He could make himself useful.

All of his life he'd loved animals. Probably liked them way more than humans. Animals didn't judge a man on anything but how he treated them. Animals didn't care about a man's past or who his family was. They didn't care that he didn't come from money or didn't seem to have much of a future.

The lights from the house glowed against the velvety night. He would miss this place while he was gone, but there was something deep inside that told him he could do this. He could be something more than the screw-up second son.

He got his key out and opened the door.

A soft sob caught his attention, and he looked to his left. His mother and sister were sitting on the sofa, his momma's hand on Sera's back.

Sera looked up and her face was red, cheeks streaked with tears.

He was going to kill whoever put that expression on his sister's face. His mom looked concerned, but she wasn't crying. If some great tragedy had occurred, his mother would be crying, too, so this was about Sera. And if his sister was crying, it was likely because some asshole had broken her heart.

"What's going on?" He kept his voice soft. He could raise it to the asshole, but he would be gentle with these two women. They'd been the center of his life for so long. Without his father or brother around, they'd been everything to him.

His mom looked at his sister, who nodded.

"You should sit down, Zep." His mom gestured to the seat beside Sera. "Sera's got something she needs to tell you."

Two hours later, Zep still sat on the sofa, his head reeling and all of his plans changed. He should have remembered how quickly the world could turn upside down and leave him in a place he hadn't planned on being. It had happened so often, but he'd forgotten.

His sister was pregnant, and she'd claimed the father wasn't in the picture and likely wouldn't be.

Sera was going to be a single mom.

Sera was going to need help.

His mother walked back in, her expression weary. She

sank down to the couch beside him. "She's cried herself to sleep. I think rest is exactly what she needs right now. Things will look better in the morning."

That was his mother. When his father had passed, she'd been stalwart. She'd gone from a coddled and indulged stay-at-home mom to working every minute of the day to make sure there was food on the table.

"Sera doesn't have any insurance." He stared at the wall ahead, the ramifications crashing down on him.

His mom sniffled. "No, she doesn't. But we can apply for aid. I'm more worried about her car. It's on its last legs. Mine isn't reliable anymore, either. I almost never drive now."

Driving made his mother nervous. He or Sera or one of her friends tended to take her places she needed to go. "The clinic isn't so far, Momma."

"No, but Doc isn't an obstetrician," she pointed out. "We don't have one here. Doc can handle some of the early visits but we'll have to go to Houma later on and we'll have to go to the hospital when the time comes." His mother rubbed her hands together, a sure sign she was worried. "I have to buy a new car. We can't break down. And there will be other expenses. I've been meaning to get a job. I get bored hanging around the house all day."

She didn't. She loved her retirement, loved hanging out with her friends and being one of the town's crazy old ladies, as she put it. That was what her life was supposed to be about now. She'd done her work. She was supposed to rest.

His mind raced, trying to invent a way out of the trap he found himself in. This was his sister's problem, not his. He wasn't the one in trouble. They owned the house. His mother wouldn't need a ton of money, and she might enjoy working at the family restaurant again. His cousin would surely let her take some shifts. They would work out a payment plan for a reliable car and any other expenses. Sera could drive herself. He didn't need to do anything but follow his own path. This was his life. He should live it the way he wanted to.

"Hey, baby, what's that?"

She was looking at the big envelope he'd left facedown on the coffee table.

He picked it up and tucked it between the pillows. "It's nothing. Just some paperwork for my graduation."

His graduation from community college. His only graduation. There would be no LSU in his future. Not for a while.

Because this wasn't merely his life. It was theirs. The Guidrys. His sister's trouble was his trouble. His mother's worries could be halved if he took his part.

She smiled, a weak, watery expression. "Oh, that's so wonderful. It will be good to have something to celebrate . . ."

His mom broke down and he shoved all his plans aside. This woman had been everything when he'd needed her to be.

He couldn't be less for her. He wrapped his arms around her. "It's going to be all right, Momma. You'll see. We'll work something out with Doc Hamet and make sure Sera's taken care of. And you'll have a sweet baby to love on."

"I will love that baby," she said. "But I wanted so much more for my girl. I didn't think it would be like this. I was hoping she could go to college."

His sister had graduated from high school and then drifted around jobs for a few years while most of her friends had gone to college. They would all be graduating next year and looking forward to starting their futures.

Sera's started now.

He took a deep breath and squeezed her tight. "We'll all love that baby and we'll be okay."

He would be okay. After all, it had been a pipe dream to think he could get through college.

But he could be a good son. He could be a good brother. That was all that mattered now.

**MANHATTAN**
*One year later*

Roxanne King-Nelson looked at her husband and felt something inside her break. "What do you mean you buried my complaint?"

Joel Nelson sighed—a long-suffering sound that set her teeth on edge. He'd used that particular sound around her a lot lately. Four years into their marriage and he looked at her like she was more trouble than she was worth. But then they didn't have much of a marriage anymore. Maybe they never had. "I talked to your captain and he's agreed this doesn't have to go any further."

She stood in his well-appointed office and realized there were no pictures of the two of them. Oh, there was a beautifully framed photo of Joel standing with her and her family, but she'd started to suspect that her family and its long ties and reputation with the upper echelon of the NYPD had been far more important than any attraction he'd had to her.

After all, now that she had a problem with her sergeant, he wasn't exactly taking her side. Joel worked directly for the chief and served as a liaison with any number of city agencies. He was perfectly placed to help her but it looked like that wasn't going to happen.

When he'd called and asked her to meet him at his office at One Police Plaza, she'd hoped he'd wanted to talk about how to move forward. She'd known he hadn't agreed with her decision to file a complaint against her sergeant, but she hadn't dreamed he would intercept it and toss it out like it was trash.

She could feel her temper start to boil. It was always simmering these days, a low heat that threatened to become a flash fire at any moment. If she let it go, it might devour her and leave nothing but ash. "Billy Stephens is sexually harassing his female officers, including me."

"I know you feel that way, Roxanne." The words were said with the careful tone of a man who'd done his time in classes on how to handle complaints in the workplace. But then her husband was the kind of man who studied how to manipulate the world to his advantage.

Unfortunately, he apparently had missed the part where he was supposed to take complaints seriously. "I don't merely feel that way. It's true. He sidelined me on two operations I should have been on because I asked him to stop talking about how I fill out my uniform."

Joel's jaw tightened. "I told you I had a long conversation with him about that. He was joking around. You know how guys are. He gives the men in his unit hell, too. While I was there, he told a perfectly fit officer that he was getting tubby. In a weird way, it's a form of affection for these guys."

"I bet he didn't tell Kevin that his ass could be used to distract criminals," she shot back. "He says the same crap about the other women he works with. He also asks me to get him coffee. He doesn't ask the guys."

"Would it be so hard to get him a cup?" Joel asked, clearly exasperated. "It's polite. Look, we all have to put up with things we would rather not put up with. It's like that everywhere."

But it hadn't been. She'd been with the NYPD for almost ten years, and the Army for three before. "I know that I've worked in several units where no one would have joked that way."

"You chose to go into that particular unit. You knew it was a male-dominated unit."

She'd known they were the best, and she'd wanted to be one of them. "I also chose to go into the Army, and guess what, when a guy on my team got handsy, my superior officer took care of it. It was his job to ensure we had a safe working environment and that everyone under his command was supported when they did their job. I am the best sniper on Stephens's team. So why was I stuck back at the station during the bank standoff last week? He looked me right in the eye and told me to monitor the situation and handed Smith my damn job."

"That's his prerogative. Maybe he didn't feel comfortable with you in the sniper's seat. Maybe he was worried you would make the team look bad since that's what you seem to be trying to do with all these complaints." He finally set his pen down and sat back. "This isn't the way to move ahead. You should know that."

Yes, she'd heard that from him for weeks. She was supposed to keep her head down and her mouth shut. Her superiors would appreciate her opinions far more if she rarely ever had them. "I'm not going to move ahead at all since Stephens doesn't like any woman who won't sleep with him. I would think as my husband that you would be offended."

Joel moved in front of her, the first sign that he had any emotions at all concerning this situation. "Has he touched you? Stated plainly that he'll support a promotion if you go to bed with him?"

"It's more insidious than that."

His lips turned down in that way they did when she annoyed him. Lately she'd seen that expression on his face a lot. "So your answer is no and you're causing all this trouble because you didn't get what you wanted. You couldn't take a joke."

She was so sick of this argument. "I'm not some thin-skinned, pearl-clutching lady who can't hear a cuss word without fainting."

Joel loomed over her, but he didn't touch her. "I've talked to some of the officers you work with. They describe you as difficult."

"Because I want them to do their jobs and respect everyone? That makes me difficult?"

"Other words they used to describe you were 'bossy' and 'arrogant.'"

She felt her fists clench. "If I was a man, I would be considered take-charge and confident."

He shrugged as though that argument meant nothing at all to him. "But you're not. Look, Rox, I know it's been hard on you. I know you've struggled since what happened last year."

She didn't want to think about what had happened that summer night. "I did my time with the shrink. I'm fine."

"No, you've changed. Everyone can see it. Losing your partner unsettled you in ways that are only starting to show up now."

She might have nightmares. She might not be as outgoing as she'd been before. But she hadn't suddenly started hating sexual harassment because Ben died. "Or I got a sergeant who's a massive ass. I don't understand why this is about me. Stephens is running that team poorly. He's the problem."

Joel took a step back. He was a handsome man. He took care of himself, from his grooming routine to the discipline he showed at the gym. That detailed care of himself had tricked her into thinking he would pay the same attention to their marriage. "And I've found a solution. You're having trouble with Stephens, so I've used some influence and arranged to transfer you."

She felt her eyes widen. "Transfer me?"

"Yes. I've talked to some people who owe me favors and I'm moving you into a position with Staten Island."

It felt like he'd punched her in the gut. "You're moving me out of ESU?"

Emergency Services Unit had been her dream job. She'd worked her ass off to get in, and it had turned into a nightmare because of her sergeant. She was one of the few women who'd made it to the NYPD's version of SWAT.

"I think you could use a break." He was quiet for a moment, the silence between them lengthening. "I think you're going to take this transfer with grace or we're going to be the ones who need a break."

"What is that supposed to mean?" Roxie asked, though she knew the answer. Hadn't she been waiting for this for a year now? After everything that had happened in the last year, hadn't she known Joel would leave her behind? At least careerwise. This ultimatum had been coming for a long time.

"It means it's time for us to decide if we're going to move forward. I want a family."

"We agreed to wait until my career was solid." She'd bargained with him.

He shook his head. "Your career is never going to be solid. You complain too much. You don't fit in, and that's a real surprise given who your father is. I expected you would play the game far better than you do."

"It's not a game at all." That's what he'd never understood. Joel had moved up the ranks quickly because he didn't mind playing politics. In the beginning, she'd thought she could learn a lot from him. Now she saw his politics for what they truly were—selfishness. He didn't think about doing the best job he could for the people around him. They were supposed to live up to the motto *Protect and Serve.* There was no real "serve" when it came to the people. Joel only served himself.

He nodded as though he'd known that would be her answer. "Everything is a game. I'm beginning to think I miscalculated my play. You've become more of a liability than an asset. I want you to take some time on this new assignment and decide if this is really the career for you. You might do better to emulate your mother."

Her mother was a traditional stay-at-home mom, and there was nothing wrong with that, but since she'd been a kid, she'd known it wasn't for her. "I'm a cop. It's what I've always wanted to be. And I'm a good one."

A low, humorless chuckle filled the office. "Not according to your last review you're not."

"Because Stephens has it in for me." Frustration welled and the need to fight was right there.

"Or because you refuse to get along with anyone."

Because she refused to shut up and take insults and innuendoes? Because she was supposed to accept humiliation from her boss? "I get along quite nicely with most of the guys. You read my complaint. They back me up."

"A few of them do, but most of them will keep their mouths shut because they know how powerful Stephens is," Joel pointed out. "His uncle has the mayor's ear. His father is a circuit court judge, and his mother holds a high position with brass. Big brass. She works right here at One Police Plaza. She's a cop, too. You can't claim misogyny here."

Oh, but she'd met many women who hated other women. "Has she read the complaint?"

"I never let it get to her. If you think she'll be surprised and horrified, you're wrong. She knows her son." Joel looked at her with nauseating sympathy. "She'll protect him. They'll all protect him. Sweetheart, you tried. You got further than most. That's going to have to be good enough. It's time to think about your future."

"This isn't about my future. This is about yours." She wasn't a complete fool. She was well aware that he would see any gossip about her as a reflection on him and his potential. But she'd thought those marriage vows they'd taken had meant something.

"Of course it is. I have to think of my career, but this is for our future. We should talk about that, too." He looked down at his watch. "But it will have to wait. I have a lunch date with our FBI liaison. There's something going on at StratCast and I want our boys in on it."

So the FBI was working a high-profile case and Joel wanted his face on camera making an arrest he hadn't really worked for. "I'm not going to go to Staten Island."

"Then you can choose to quit the force altogether," Joel said without any sympathy. "I told you not to file those complaints. I believe I advised you not to join ESU. I told you that you wouldn't fit in. You ignored my advice and the advice of your father."

Her father had asked her to consider staying at the Precinct she'd served for five years. He'd asked her if working with a high-profile unit like ESU was what she'd truly wanted to do. Of course, her dad would never have had that conversation with her brother. Brian was a detective in Manhattan. He was the perfect cop who never once caused trouble. He was the shining example, and she was still trying to keep up, trying to make her parents see her as something more than the girl who hadn't wanted to wear flouncy dresses and play the part of pretty daughter.

Yet she'd married the man her mother had set her up with. Hadn't that been a mistake. "I quit."

Joel stopped and turned her way. He took a deep breath

and nodded. "I think that's the first mature decision you've made. We can talk about this at home tonight. There are many things you can do that don't involve NYPD. It's time to start a family. It's time for you to come home."

He didn't understand her at all, but he was right about one thing. She wouldn't go anywhere with the NYPD, and she wasn't over what had happened to her partner. It was time to go somewhere different. Maybe Chicago or LA. Boston was close enough that she could see her family.

Or maybe somewhere farther. A place where no one cared that she came from a long-celebrated line of NYPD cops.

Where no one cared that she'd been the one who disappointed them all.

She placed her shield and gun on his desk. "You can give these to Stephens since you're such good friends."

Cool gray eyes rolled. He truly was a gorgeous man, but now she could see the coldness behind those good looks. He was more mannequin than man. "You know I don't like Stephens. I'm simply smart enough to pick my fights carefully. But I do think it's a good idea you don't see him again. You lose your temper so easily."

She hadn't lost her temper nearly enough. "I'm also quitting you, Joel. I'll be out of the apartment before you get home."

She wouldn't take much. They'd been married for four years and she couldn't think of a thing they'd bought together that she wanted to keep. Any memento of him would be a reminder of how she'd lost herself. How she'd settled because her mom had convinced her life couldn't be complete without a marriage and kids.

She'd wanted both, but she'd also wanted a partner, someone who would back her up, who cared about her career as much as he cared about his.

Like Benjy's wife had. Her partner's wife had been endlessly supportive—even when Benjy died. She hadn't blamed Roxie. She'd held her hand as they'd watched the coffin be lowered.

*He adored you, Roxie. He wanted you to be happy. I don't think you're happy, honey.*

She wasn't. Maybe she never had been.

"I should have known you would behave like a child," her soon-to-be ex-husband said. "I'll talk to you when you've taken the time to cool off."

She walked out because she wasn't planning on talking to him again. It was odd. She'd spent the last year worried that her marriage would end, and now all she felt was an odd sense of relief.

It was over. Her career. Her marriage. Any shot at being the daughter her parents had wanted. The last part sparked a sense of sorrow, but she couldn't let that hold her back anymore.

"Roxanne!" Joel shouted her name, finally showing a crack in his calm composure.

But she didn't look back. She got on the elevator and hit the button for the ground floor. Rock bottom. That was where she was going, and it was a freeing idea.

But still, her gut twisted as she thought about finding a new job. Joel's influence went far and wide. Quitting with a bad review and no real references might make the larger city PDs hard to get on.

As the elevator made its way down and she could feel her cell phone vibrating, a thought crossed her mind. She'd recently met a small-town sheriff. Armie LaVigne. They'd met at a conference and he'd talked about making the transition from New Orleans PD to some weird town in Southern Louisiana. Pappy Lon or something like that.

She'd liked him. He was smart and seemed interested in real community policing.

Maybe he could give her some advice. New Orleans would be a change of pace, and Sheriff LaVigne likely still had contacts there.

Yes, another big city. She didn't want too much change, after all.

# *chapter one*

**PAPILLON, LOUISIANA**
***Present day***

Roxanne King stared at the man who'd called her out to his small farm at three in the morning. Archie Johnson was in his late seventies, and he didn't mind running around in the middle of the night in his underwear. The man was wearing nothing but a pair of boxer shorts and a thin white T-shirt. His hair was wild and his glasses threatened to fall off his face.

"I'm confused. Who do you think is in your barn?" She'd gotten the call as she was working the night shift. She worked days, but she took the occasional night shift when the normal guys needed time off. Usually it involved catching up on paperwork and breaking up the occasional bar brawl. It sometimes ended up being a weird therapy session with the participants of the aforementioned brawls. She'd taken more than one person in custody straight from jail to their first AA meeting.

Sometimes the person in jail was merely a dumbass who pushed her until she couldn't ignore him and she tossed him in the back of her cruiser because she couldn't let herself do what she wanted to do with him.

She was not going to think about Zep Guidry. No. She was concentrating on this very important breaking-and-entering call.

"It's the rougarou," Archie said, pointing toward the barn. He'd said the word like it had some magical power and he didn't want to be too loud about it.

"Rouga-what?" She didn't recognize anyone by that name, but then Cajun ways were still a mystery to her and she was several years into this job.

How the hell she'd ended up in a tiny parish in Southern Louisiana she had no idea. To say her new home was a big dose of culture shock would be underplaying the experience.

"Archie! Archie!" The diminutive Caroline Johnson made her way down the steps, a robe in her hand. Unlike her husband, Caroline was dressed from head to toe in a housedress, slippers, and robe, her hair in a silky-looking wrapper. She held the extra robe out. "You put this on."

Archie frowned his wife's way. "It's hot as stink out here, woman."

Caroline shook her head. "No. You're showing off for the ladies. You be a gentleman. You know how I feel about other women appreciating your body."

Roxie was sure Archie was in fine shape for his age, but the sight of his skinny body did not inspire lust.

"You keep your jealousy to yourself," Archie proclaimed. "It's hot and I'm not covering up because the deputy might get the wrong idea. I've never cheated on you in fifty-two years."

They started to argue about the prospect of Archie's skinny body causing the women of Papillon to lose their minds with desire, and Roxie again wondered how she'd gotten here. She'd been on a fast track. She'd been one of the first female snipers ever to serve in ESU. One man who couldn't be a decent human being and here she was refereeing bar fights and calming down tourists who thought Otis was going to eat them—calling a gator by his given name, and somehow that being the most normal part of her day.

This was her life. Her whole life.

A light pierced the darkness of the night around them—a vehicle coming up the long road that led from the highway. The Johnson farm was remote, but then most places in the parish could be considered remote. The Johnson farm was on the north end of town, and there was no ambient light out here. When she'd first moved to Papillon, that darkness had been a foreign thing. A moonless night had felt almost oppressive. Now she appreciated the contrast. There was night here in a way she'd never experienced, and somehow the darkness of the night made the day brighter.

Yeah, she was becoming quite the poet, but one of the things she'd learned was that when she wasn't constantly on the move, she thought way, way too much.

The car turned up the long drive, but she couldn't make out what kind of vehicle it was. The lights weren't the new super-bright kind, but then most of the vehicles around the parish were older. When the Burtons had gotten their brand-new F-150 complete with LED headlights, the number of UFO sightings had gone through the roof. And it wasn't like there hadn't been many before.

"Woman, why are you worried about my naked knees when we've got a rougarou on our land?" Archie asked, pointing to the barn. "You should give me back my shotgun."

"I hid your shotgun because your eyes are going, you paranoid old man," Caroline retorted. "That is probably a poor bunny rabbit running around out there. You don't need to take another shot at it."

"A bunny rabbit wouldn't scare the goats," Archie shouted back.

The lights turned and stopped next to her SUV. They blinked out and she hoped Major hadn't felt the need to follow her out here. Or Armie. She knew the sheriff and her fellow deputy often monitored the radio even on their nights off. Even though she'd promised she would call if she came up against something she couldn't handle alone.

And she would. Probably.

"All right, could someone explain what's going on." She needed to take charge, and that meant getting these two to focus on something other than Archie's ragged shorts. "You said someone was in your barn. I need to know how many people you think are in there."

"It's the rougarou," Archie insisted.

Sometimes she had trouble understanding some of the more rural residents. They often broke into French. She'd learned serviceable Spanish, but French hadn't been important to policing in the city. Especially not the Cajun French a lot of people spoke around here. "Is that a name?"

"That is the imaginings of a crazy old man," Caroline said with a long sigh, and gave Archie a stern look. "Put your robe on."

Roxie bit back a groan. "Is there or is there not someone lurking around the barn?"

"There is." Archie blocked his wife's attempts to cover his body. "It's back and we're all in trouble now."

"It?" She was missing something.

"He's talking about a swamp creature," a deep voice said.

A familiar voice.

"Zéphirin Guidry." Archie breathed the name with a sigh of relief. "Thank you so much for coming. It's the damn rougarou. We thought it was gone, thought your daddy killed the whole nest of them way back in 'eighty-two, but I heard that rustling tonight and knew it was back."

Zep stepped on the porch, his long legs hauling him up with ease. He was dressed in jeans and a T-shirt, worn boots on his feet. It was his usual outfit. Given the time of night, most people would have had to get out of bed to get dressed, but Zep had likely come from a bar. His natural habitat. The only thing that was different from his normal clothes was the bag slung over his chest. "Hey, Rox . . . Deputy King."

She was so glad she'd perfected her poker face at a young age because every time she saw that man, she wanted to sigh and stare for a long time. Zep was a work of art. Six foot three, with broad shoulders and muscles she wasn't sure how he'd earned, Zep was simply the most beautiful man she'd ever met. His jaw was sharp in contrast with the softness of his too-long, dark wavy hair. It had a slight curl to it that made her want to run her fingers through it right before she rubbed her cheek against his and let the scruff she found there tickle her skin.

He was the baddest boy of the parish, and she'd already made her mistake with him.

*You are gorgeous, Roxanne King. I think I could spend some time with you. I think I could spend a lot of time with you.*

Unfortunately, he spent time with a lot of women. And she didn't do bad boys. Well, she didn't do them more than once.

"What are you doing out here, Guidry?"

There was the little frown that hit his face every time she used his last name. If she hadn't been certain she knew the man, she would have thought it was hurt on that handsome face of his. But she knew what it really was. Frustration. Zep was a man used to getting what he wanted. He'd decided he'd wanted a second night with her, and when she'd refused, he'd begun the chase.

He was a man who lived for the chase.

"Archie called me," he replied. "Probably right after he called you."

Archie shook his head. "Oh, no. Before. I knew I would need a hunter, and everyone knows you're just like your daddy was. You have ways. You can see them, talk to them."

Sometimes she wondered if she was in an episode of *The Twilight Zone*. "You think Guidry here can talk to the rag thing?"

"The rougarou," Zep corrected her before turning back to Archie. "You said it was in your barn?"

Archie blinked and then nodded. "Yes. It's in there. I heard something rustling around. The goats were going crazy. I heard it growl and it cursed. I definitely heard it curse in its language. There was a light, too. I saw it under the doors, and then it was all dark."

Zep nodded like that made sense somehow. "I'll go check it out." He gave Caroline Johnson a charming grin. "And you better get your husband dressed, Mrs. Johnson. Women see all that masculinity and they won't know what to do with themselves."

Caroline's eyes lit with righteous fire. "That's what I said. You cover up, old man."

Zep hopped off the porch and started across the big yard, his cell phone lighting the way.

"Hey, you need to hold up." Roxie followed him. The last thing she needed was for him to walk into a dangerous situation and get himself hurt. Her ass would be on the line for letting a civilian take control.

It had nothing to do with the fact that she didn't want to see him injured, that the thought made her stomach ache. Because she didn't care.

"It's nothing," Zep insisted. "Or rather it's not a police

thing, I suspect. The Johnsons don't have anything to steal. They certainly don't have anything in that barn unless someone is trying to steal a goat. I wouldn't recommend doing that. Those damn goats can be mean. They've got horns and don't mind using them."

She fell into step beside him. "I should still go first. I don't understand why they called you. You're not a neighbor."

"We're all neighbors out here," Zep said. "And he didn't call me because I live in town. He called me because I know how to deal with wildlife."

The parish didn't have an animal services department. The sheriff's office had to handle most of the wildlife encounters. She'd had to take a couple of classes from park rangers to teach her how to not freak out. "You think something got in the barn? What about the light he saw?"

"I think Archie likes to get into the whiskey, and he's still got an excellent imagination. Unless we want to have a serious discussion about whether or not a swamp creature is hiding in the Johnson barn."

She sighed as they approached the barn in question. "Swamp creature?"

"The rougarou is our version of a werewolf," Zep explained. "I'm surprised you haven't heard of it yet. We haven't had a sighting in years, but folks love to talk."

Roxie hadn't studied local lore. Of course, she didn't do much of anything beyond work and have the occasional beer with the guys—who treated her like one of the guys. The small group of employees at the Papillon Parish station consisted of herself, Sheriff Armie LaVigne, and four deputies. She was the only female among them, and not one of them looked at her like she was a woman.

It was exactly what she wanted.

But one night, the man beside her had sent the strongest

reminder that she wasn't one of the guys. He'd proven to her she was a woman and she could want everything a woman wanted. Love, affection, passion.

She wouldn't get any of those things from him. Not for longer than a night or two, and then she would be one in the long line of women who pined over the gorgeous . . . what had the town librarian called him? A rakehell. The woman read a whole lot of historical romances.

In this century, they would call Zep Guidry a player.

She wasn't going to get played again.

"Maybe you should stay up on the porch with the Johnsons," she said as they began to approach the barn door. The night around them was eerily quiet, and she was starting to get a little adrenaline pumping. Not because she believed there was a swampy werewolf behind those doors. Rather because she didn't.

"You want to face whatever's in there alone?" Zep asked.

"Do you honestly believe there's some supernatural creature in there?"

"No, of course I don't, but I do know Archie," Zep replied, his voice going low. "I know he sounds like a crazy old man at times, but he does know his livestock. If he says something upset those goats, then something was in there. Might not be now."

"So what you're saying is we might open that door to a goat massacre." It was not a pleasant thought. "I left New York for this."

"I think New York has its share of predators, city girl," Zep replied with a low chuckle she wished she didn't find so sexy. "But I don't think there's one in that barn."

"Why?"

There was that chuckle again. "Because it's so quiet. I assure you if those goats were being attacked, they would not be silent about it. There would be a lot of noise. According to what Archie told me, they were bleating like crazy about twenty minutes ago and then everything went silent. I think whatever was in there is likely gone now."

They'd made it to the barn doors, and sure enough, there was perfect silence coming from inside. She held out a hand to let Zep know she wanted a minute and was surprised when he went still, too.

She should order him back to the house, but the truth was she didn't mind having some company, and he might be able to help. The darkness could be disorienting, and sometimes these old barns could be minefields. "Have you been in this barn? Is it like some of the others I've seen?"

"Do you mean is it full of things that could potentially stab you, and have they been left in places where you could step on them?" Zep proved that he was a perceptive guy, but then she'd never bought his himbo act. "Nah, Archie's pretty neat. But I don't like the thought of you going in alone. It's dark in there and a single flashlight isn't incredibly helpful. I know where the lights are."

"All right, but you do what I tell you to do," Roxie insisted. "If I tell you to run . . ."

His lips quirked up, but there was nothing humorous about the expression on his face. "I'll run and leave you to be eaten by whatever attacks. I promise, Deputy. You know I always protect myself. I'm that guy."

Once again she got that feeling that always hit her when she played the tough cop around him. It was a feeling she hated—like she'd disappointed someone important. Zep Guidry had been a much-regretted mistake. Not someone important. Not someone who should make her feel anything beyond minor irritation.

*But one night he made you feel something you hadn't felt in forever. He made you want something beyond a peaceful day, a cold beer, and a good night's sleep. He reminded you that once you'd wanted something more than a place to hide and lick your wounds.*

Yeah, that was precisely why she was going to stay away from him. The trouble was it was a small town and there wasn't much cover. She ran into him a lot, and often she was irritated enough to shove his cute butt in the back of her squad car because he liked to cause trouble.

Tonight's encounter was different. "All right, I'll open the door and give you cover. You make your way to the light switch."

"I will endeavor to do my best, Deputy," he said, and she could hear that arrogant smirk of his in his tone.

She looked down and pulled open the barn door. It looked like Mr. Johnson didn't lock the place up at night, but then he might not actually lock the door to his house, either. She'd noticed hers was one of the only houses in the area with a security system. She'd had to drive an hour to find one she could buy and had to install it herself.

She opened the door and saw the glow of eyes flash and then disappear.

Like the flash that night right before the bullet had roared through her world, tearing apart something special.

"To your left!" she shouted.

She followed her instinct and leapt toward Zep, tackling him, ready to take that bullet this time.

Zep hit the ground, the wind knocking out of him, but the shock was mostly to his brain. Roxie. What had happened that caused the normally perfect oasis of calm that was Roxanne King to turn into a tidal wave? He'd seen a vague flash of eyes in the darkness, and then she'd yelled at him and launched herself bodily his way.

He went still because he sensed that she'd panicked, and that wasn't something she ever did.

Well, except that morning after she'd made the smart choice to take a chance on him. Then she'd panicked, and when Roxie was panicked, she could be on the mean side.

So he was going to let her take the lead in this very dangerous-to-his-manhood endeavor. He wondered if she understood how close she'd come to her knee shoving his balls back up into his body.

"Are you okay?" He whispered the question.

"Something's in here. I saw something move," she whispered back.

"Okay, uhm, I'm going to tell you something and I want you to stay calm even when I annoy you by pointing out that what you saw was the Johnsons' cat."

As if the cat knew that was its cue, the tabby purred long and loud, tail swinging into view. The cat sat down right next to them and her eyes flashed again, proving his theory.

Roxie cursed and rolled off him, and he missed the slight weight of her body against his. Though he did breathe a sigh of relief that she'd managed not to use his man parts as leverage to get on her feet.

"Hey, Snuggles," he said as the cat rubbed her face against his.

"Seriously?" Roxie groaned in the low light as she picked up the flashlight she'd dropped when she'd attempted to save him from whatever she'd thought was coming after them. "I panicked over a cat named Snuggles?"

"Yeah, it's not an intimidating name, but you should know she's the bane of rats around these parts." He sat up and reached around to find his phone. He found it and flashed the beam around. Ten pairs of eyes flashed back at him. "Don't be too hard on yourself. You're not used to the country. It can be intimidating at night. All the goats are accounted for."

One of them bleated, an annoyed sound.

"Excellent. I saved a bunch of goats from a cat." Roxie sounded equally annoyed.

He got to his feet, Snuggles rubbing herself against his leg. "The goats are used to the cat. She's out here with them all the time. They wouldn't be disturbed by her at all. It had to be something else."

"You know I'm not exactly a newbie," she said. "I've been here a couple of years now."

"You've been in the station house ninety-nine percent of the time. You haven't exactly been hanging out in the woods at night." He moved to the side and found the light switch. In a second, they were in the soft glow of the barn lights. Soft because only one of them was functioning. There were supposed to be five, but it looked like they'd burned out.

He would have to come out tomorrow before his shift at Guidry's and find an excuse to change them or Archie would get the ladder out and likely need his other hip replaced. Or he could slip that bit of information his brother-in-law's way. Harry lived to be helpful. When Zep tried it, people tended to think he was up to something.

But that was what happened when you got a reputation as a bad boy. People never thought you could do something out of the goodness of your heart, and pretty deputies used you for sex and then tossed you aside. Story of his life.

Though he had to admit he'd earned his reputation. He couldn't even lie to himself about that.

"I work a lot. And I'll be honest, I'm not much of a hiker." Roxie slipped her flashlight back onto her utility belt. He didn't know a single other female in the world who could look so damn gorgeous in a set of khakis. Her golden-brown hair was usually in a severe bun, but wisps had escaped and framed her face. There was a brushing of freckles over her cheeks and nose that she almost never hid with makeup. "All right, Guidry. You seem to be the expert here. What do you think happened?"

"Something slipped in, scared the goats, and the cat did her job," he said, walking around the barn, Snuggles at his heels. "Scared it away. That's what she's here for. That and keeping the rodent population down."

"The cat doesn't seem to mind you," she pointed out, sounding disgruntled.

"They all tend to like me."

She made a gagging sound. "Yes, all females fall at your feet."

But then again, she hadn't shoved him into the path of whatever she'd thought was coming their way this evening. She'd done the opposite and actually put her own body over his to save him.

It could mean she was just a really good cop.

Or it could mean something more. He was an optimist at heart, and he chose to believe that meant there was still a connection between them.

God, he had to believe it because it was the only time he'd ever felt that connection in his life, and it had to be with the toughest, most complicated woman he'd ever met. Lucky for them both, he was real simple. And hey, he'd heard opposites attracted.

"I was talking about cats," he corrected as he inspected the west end of the barn. "And dogs. Most small animals, really. I do well with horses. I try my damnedest to stay away from Otis, though. The last thing I need is a gator to decide I'm a friend of his. But cats and dogs are excellent company. Birds, too."

He was good with birds. He'd learned from his father at

a young age how to take care of injured birds or to gently nurse along babies in their shells when they were abandoned. When he thought about his father, he could see him standing over the incubator he'd put together after they'd found a dead swallow and noticed her nest above. He'd climbed up and brought the eggs down, and they'd nursed those birds until they were ready to be on their own.

They'd been tiny things and his father's hand so large and yet gentle.

Roxie stopped. "Do you think Archie sits on the fertilizer a lot? Maybe uses it as a ladder?"

She was standing in front of a bunch of stacked bags of fertilizer Archie likely wouldn't use for months. There was a good-size indention there, as though someone had been sitting on them. The rest of the top bag was coated in dust, so whoever had disturbed it had done it recently.

"I don't think so. He doesn't spend a lot of time out here this time of year. He pretty much only comes in to let the goats in and out of their pens. His sons come through a couple of times a month. They do a lot of the upkeep on this place."

Roxie leaned over and picked up an orange wrapper that had been sitting on the floor. "Do any of the Johnsons eat a lot of flaming-hot chips?"

"Archie sure doesn't. At least not anywhere his wife could see him do it," he replied. "He had a mild heart attack a couple of months back and Lila convinced Caroline that eating a healthy diet might prolong his life." Lila LaVigne ran the town's medical clinic and had lots of thoughts on nutrition.

"Convinced? You know Lila is an expert, right?"

"I'm well acquainted with her skills. I've still got my pinkie finger because of them, but I've seen what Caroline's putting on his plate, and death might be a good alternative," he shot back. "So yeah, that absolutely could have been him sneaking some treats."

He stopped because he heard something in the distance. A whine.

Roxie had gone still, too. "What was that?"

It was coming from outside the barn, to the back. But then he remembered there was a secondary door. Much smaller than the big barn doors that could open up to allow in large livestock, though Archie had given up his cows and horses years before. There was a small door at the back around the size of a normal house door. It was slightly open.

"It's coming from behind the barn," he said, listening again. "From the woods."

Roxie stared at the back door. "It didn't sound human."

He heard it again and recognized it immediately—the low, mournful sound of an animal in pain. "It's not. It's a dog and he's hurt."

He strode through the back door and got his phone out again to turn on the flashlight function. It illuminated the ground in front of him, giving him a safe path to walk.

Roxie was hard on his heels, her light making another appearance, too. "Hey, slow down. You can't be sure it's a dog. What if it's a coyote? Or something dangerous?"

"A dog can be dangerous given the right circumstances, and being injured is definitely one of them," he said, still charging forward. The sound was coming from the woods behind the barn. He moved into the trees. "Watch your step. The ground is soft and there's any number of critters out at this time of night."

She sidestepped a moss-covered log, careful to not rub against it. "You know a lot about them, don't you? Animals, that is."

"Critters," he said, his voice low. "Join the locals, Deputy. And yes, I do. Growing up, I probably spent more time with critters than I did people."

"How far are we from the water?" Roxie asked, and he could hear the slightest trepidation in her tone.

In Papillon, they were never too far from the water, but he doubted there were gators running around here. "The bayou's half a mile to our south. Gators are nocturnal for the most part. They'll be near the water and hunting right now."

"Someone tell Otis," she muttered. "That gator is everywhere at all times of the day."

The town's largest gator often liked to sun himself on the highways. It was easier to go around him than try to get him to move, but Roxie never took the easy way out. More than once he'd seen her trying to shoo Otis off the main road that led into town.

Zep stopped suddenly. He'd lost the sound. The woods could be tricky, and it was easy to get lost if a person didn't know what they were doing. Sounds could bounce off the trees.

Roxie stayed beside him and didn't make a noise.

A whine sounded to his left.

That was definitely a dog. He decided to take a chance. He needed that dog to make some more noise or this could be a long night. "Hey, boy, you out here?"

"I thought we were being quiet," Roxie whispered.

"We were when we thought there might be some intruder waiting to jump us," he replied. "But it's obvious what happened."

"Excellent, then please inform me."

He would have but the dog started barking frantically as though he'd figured out all was not lost. Zep took off at the sound.

"Hey!" Roxie yelled behind him. "I thought we agreed that you would follow my lead."

He would have if there had been something criminal going on out here, but this was the one place he felt like the expert. He knew the woods and he knew how to deal with all creatures great and small and in between. They weren't dealing with a dangerous creature. They were dealing with one who wanted to be saved. The barking kept up, and he could hear rustling as though the dog was stirring up leaves and dirt.

He held up his phone and there was the dog, its whole body wriggling with excitement.

"It's a puppy," Roxie said with a sigh. "Why is it tied up?"

She held up her flashlight so he could slide his phone in his pocket. He dropped to one knee and the puppy immediately started licking his face. The dog was tied to a tree, a choke collar around his throat, but he was practically vibrating with excitement. Archie certainly had not done this, and there weren't any homes out this way where someone might have tied a dog to keep it safe while the owner went hunting or fishing. And he used the word "safe" sarcastically since this puppy hadn't been safe at all. There were predators out here. A whole lot of them, and many would look at this puppy as a nice snack.

"Someone got sick of him." He eased the choke collar off and inspected the dog. "Her. She's a girl. Likely someone bought their kid a pet and then wouldn't put the work in to train it. She's a Lab. They can be rambunctious."

It wasn't the first time he'd found a dog abandoned in the woods, though tying the dog up so she couldn't find her way home was a nasty bit of business. The girl looked like she was in good shape.

"She's gorgeous. Hi, sweetie."

He'd never heard Roxie's voice go so soft before. She got down on the ground with him and put her hand out to let the puppy get her scent. She'd obviously been trained a bit on how to deal with anxious dogs, but he could have told her this little girl did not need time to figure out if she liked the people around her. She was a chocolate Lab. She loved everyone.

"She hasn't been out here long." Her coat looked good, and though she was thin, she certainly wasn't starving. "This might have been her first night. And whoever tied the dog up likely used a flashlight to get back. If he walked near the barn, he could have upset the goats. I think whoever did this is likely our rougarou."

Though he didn't think whoever had done this had been eating chips in the barn, but he could chalk that up to coincidence.

The puppy licked Roxie's face and the smile he caught damn near lit up the forest. "She's so sweet. I hate people. How could anyone leave this little thing to die?"

"I don't know. I haven't heard about anyone getting a puppy lately. A couple of friends of mine recently got some hunting dogs, but they weren't puppies. I'm going to get a leash on her and I'll take her home with me for the night. In the morning I'll take her to Houma and see if she's got a chip. I would bet she doesn't."

Because they didn't have a vet for miles. A lot of people around Papillon treated their own dogs with the exception of vaccines. He moved to reach into his bag.

Roxie ran her hand over the dog's head and down her body. "If you find out who did this, I want to know."

Because she would have a long talk with that unlucky person. Of course, all she could do was talk. He might think about finding that jerk and tying him up overnight in the woods. See how he liked it. "Sure."

He pulled out the leash he kept in his bag and eased it over the puppy's head. It wasn't easy because this was a wriggly pup.

Roxie held her still. "I'm serious, Guidry. I don't want to have to arrest you again."

"Arrest me?"

"Tell me you're not thinking about knocking this guy out and letting him wake up tied to a tree," she shot back as he gently tightened the leash.

At least she knew him. "Fine. I'll let you in on it."

That got him a grin that threatened to take his breath away. "Deal."

He needed to let her know that wasn't likely to happen. "But you should understand that we'll probably never know why this dog was left here. Ninety-nine percent of the time, dogs who are brought into a shelter because they were left like this are never reclaimed, and we just don't know what they've been through. She doesn't have tags. They were taken off so no one could ID her. Whoever did this doesn't want to be found, and that likely means this little pup's past will remain a mystery."

She hugged the puppy close. "What happens if she doesn't have a microchip?"

"She goes into a shelter and we all hope for the best," he replied. "Or more likely I'll get to the shelter, look at her sad puppy face, and bring her home with me until I can find a place for her. I might parade her by Lisa and mention that the shelter is overcrowded and it would be sad if they put her down."

Lisa was his sister-in-law, and she had a tender heart. She would fall for the puppy and then his brother would give him hell because they didn't have time for a dog. His brother ran the local pub and restaurant. It was pretty much a twenty-four-seven job.

Roxie gasped and held the dog closer. "They are not going to put this dog down."

He stood and reached to help her up. "Maybe Armie needs a trained police dog."

It probably wouldn't be a Lab, and certainly not this one from the looks of it. She would likely lick the criminals or beg them for pets.

"Maybe we do." Roxie stared at his hand and started to stand on her own.

She got tangled in the leash because the dog had managed to run a circle around her. She hit the ground with a thud and a curse.

Stubborn woman. "You won't even let me help you up?"

"I don't normally need help," she said with a sigh.

"The ground here is rugged. Hold on to me. I promise I won't try anything. I know how quick you are to arrest an innocent man." She did it to him all the time. At first it was annoying, but lately he'd been wondering if it might not be her version of flirting. Not flirting exactly, but her way of staying close to him even though she thought he was a bad bet. After all, she almost never actually did anything beyond tossing him in a cell and then letting him off with a warning.

"You had unpaid tickets," she shot back as she untangled herself. "Could you give me some light? I think I can manage this on my own if I can see. It's so dark out here. I'm not used to it."

He reached down and picked up her flashlight. It had fallen out of her hands when the dog had created her charming chaos. "Because it never gets dark in New York?"

She chuckled at that. "Trust me, when the power goes out, it gets really dark, and there are things in the city that make the gators look civilized."

She managed to unwind the leash and handed it to him as she started to get to her feet.

Something caught his eye, a slight rustling of leaves and the slither of something moving through them.

"Roxanne, I need you to be very still," he said quietly.

The puppy barked and Roxie stumbled back down.

And that was when the copperhead struck.

# *chapter two*

Roxanne blinked up at the stark light in her eyes and groaned. Everything hurt. An ache went through her like a wave that never actually left the shore and sank back into the ocean. It simply pounded against her. Where was she? She hated this particular feeling. It was why she limited herself to two beers now. No more. After she'd left Joel, she'd gone a little wild and pain had been the outcome.

"Yeah, I bet you feel like hell." Lila LaVigne stared down at her. She was wearing scrubs and not an ounce of her usual makeup. Despite the fact that she ran a tiny clinic in a backwoods parish, Lila had never lost her big-city glam. She wasn't the same woman who'd walked into town a year before. Papillon had softened her up, but she still liked to look chic.

Roxie's head was killing her, and she seemed to be in the clinic. Her night had apparently taken a wrong turn, but then that seemed to be the story of her life. "What the hell happened?"

"Don't close your eyes. I need to make sure you don't have a concussion," Lila said in that no-nonsense fashion that Roxie usually found calming. Lila wasn't a woman who panicked. Ever.

Today, it grated a bit. Wait, today? No, it wasn't day at all. She'd been working the night shift. Yes, she remembered how dark it had been. It had been deep in the night. "How long was I out?"

Lila moved the light over her eyes. "Not long, but long enough for me to worry."

She'd been having the weirdest dream where Zep had taken her out in the woods and they'd found the sweetest dog and then . . .

She sat up and her head throbbed. "I was bitten by a snake. There was a freaking snake."

"There was a snake. This one," Zep said, holding up a bag. She blinked at him in surprise. Had he been there this whole time? "I went back for it. It was hell finding the damn thing again, but I got it. Copperhead. Very venomous. Lucky for you, those boots of yours are tough. Turns out he didn't actually penetrate the leather. So no real snake bite."

"You caught the snake?" The question came out of her mouth on a screech. "Why would you catch the snake?"

"It was nesting close to the barn. If it bites Archie or Caroline, they might not be able to handle it," he replied. "Also, I wasn't sure at the time that it hadn't gotten you. I had to make certain what kind of snake we were dealing with. I already called some friends of mine from a reptile rescue. They'll relocate it to a safer location."

"It's alive?" She stared at the bag, and sure enough, it shifted a bit. A chill went through her. She'd been in a lot of bad positions, places where people were shooting at her. She would take it all over that snake coming her way.

Zep frowned at her like he was deeply disappointed. "The snake was only doing what snakes do. You stepped on him. He bit you. It's perfectly natural." He held the bag out, an oddly prim look on his face. "Would you like to arrest the snake?"

He was so obnoxious.

Lila flicked off the light. "I'm with you, Rox. Don't think too much of his righteous indignation. It's not city versus country on the snake issue. I know lots of people around town who don't like snakes."

"Well, I don't like them," Zep argued. "Hell, if I killed everyone I didn't like, there would be very few people left in this world."

She was likely one of them. After all, it wasn't like she was nice to the man. But it seemed as though he'd been helpful this evening. "Sorry. I'm not used to . . . critters. Especially ones with fangs. So I passed out and I didn't actually get bitten?" It had been at her feet. She could remember the sight in the ghostly light.

Zep brought the bag back down. "Yeah. The boot leather was thick enough to stop this guy's fangs. The problem was you hit your head when you reasonably freaked out over the snake attached to your boot. Hit it real hard." There was a chiming sound and he pulled out his cell with his free hand. "So I had to carry you up to Archie's, and Caroline called 911 and gave you some first aid before I went back out and found the snake. Now, you should know that Archie thinks it was actually the rougarou, and that will get around town."

It was starting to come back to her. Zep had been with her in the woods. He'd held out his hand when she'd gotten all tangled up and fell to the ground in ungraceful glory. She'd looked up at him and he'd been so stunningly beautiful in the low light, like some damn prince from a fairy tale offering her a hand up.

She hadn't taken it. She hadn't been able to. Instead she'd stayed on the ground for a few seconds too long, and she hadn't been alone down there.

"My friend's outside." He slipped the phone back in his pocket. "He's a crazy snake dude. I hope this one doesn't bite him. I'll be back because I still have to figure out what to do with Daisy."

He strode out and she tried not to watch him. His backside was as masculinely perfect as his front.

"I hit my head." It was obvious, but she had to say the words to make them real. She couldn't remember that part. She could remember the way Zep had looked at her when she wouldn't even take his hand. She could remember the rush of fear when the snake had struck, but then it was all black. "And who's Daisy?"

"Daisy is the Lab currently chewing on my dog's favorite toys." Lila stared at the equipment she'd hooked Roxie up to and made a few notes. "Zep says you two found her out in the woods behind Archie's place."

The chocolate Lab. The poor puppy who'd been abandoned. "Yes. We found the dog. That must have been what the goats heard."

At least they'd solved one mystery.

"You know if the copperhead had gotten the dog, she'd be dead," Lila pointed out. "You, on the other hand, are going to be fine because those boots my husband insists are the greatest footwear in the history of time stopped those fangs from sinking in."

She'd always complained about them. She'd wanted to wear something more comfortable like sneakers, but the sheriff insisted on boots. "I will never wear anything else. And I'm glad it got my boot and not the dog."

The dog had been staked out and left to die. The person

who should have cared for the poor puppy had done that—left her in danger because it was more comfortable for the owner.

Yeah, she understood how the pup must have felt.

"I don't like the fact that you blacked out," Lila said. "You were out for longer than I would like."

There was a knock on the door and then her boss walked through. Armie LaVigne was a solid presence in her life. He'd been both boss and big brother to her for the last couple of years. He'd given her a place to go after her ex had made sure none of the big-city departments would take her. "Hey, you're awake. How are you feeling?"

Like a complete moron. "I'm good, sir."

"She likely has a concussion," Lila explained. "I would say, given the CT scan, that it's mild, but I'm not the expert. The neurologist hasn't sent back the report yet."

"Whoa." The parish offered insurance, but a neurologist was expensive and she had a pretty high deductible. "I didn't need a scan. I'm fine. I'll take some ibuprofen and be good to go."

"Don't worry about it," Armie said.

"She needs to worry about it," Lila countered. "It's her brain. It's bruised."

"She's worried about the cost." Armie looked at his wife. "She heard the word 'neurologist' and saw dollar signs. I know I would. It's okay. Lila's brother is a neurologist back in Dallas, and she forces him to work for free. She's mean that way, but it does save the parish a lot of money. The good news for Will is we don't have a ton of head injuries."

Lila shrugged. "My brother makes a godawful amount of money. He can give some back. But he's whiny about being woken in the middle of the night." Her cell trilled. She glanced down. "Ah, and there he is. I'll be right back because he'll yell at me for a little while before he tells me the results. It's the price I pay." She put the phone to her ear as she walked out of the room. "Hey, Will."

Armie looked down at Roxie. "You need to do whatever my wife tells you to do. I'm not joking. We could have lost you tonight if you'd been out there alone."

She started to shake her head, but the pain flared and she lay back. "I wasn't going to call someone in because Archie Johnson's goats got scared by some animal."

"You didn't know it was an animal at the time," Armie replied. "And honestly, you shouldn't be in those woods alone at all. Before you give me hell, I wouldn't let Major go out alone, either. The other officers all grew up around here. They know how to work in the woods and on the water. You need someone who can back you up. I feel damn lucky Archie called in Zep. He might be an idiot most of the time, but he knows how to handle himself out there."

He'd gone back into the woods and tracked down the snake that had bitten her. Well, bitten her boot. He could have been bitten himself. She didn't intend to think too long about that. If there was one thing she'd learned about her neighbors, it was that they took care of each other. Zep might like beer and the ladies a bit too much, but she knew he cared about the people around him. She'd watched him do it, though he tried to ensure no one noticed.

But she watched him far more carefully than she should.

"Why exactly was he out there? Archie treated him like he was some kind of expert." She closed her eyes because the light was too much.

"He's good with animals. His father was, too. His father used to work with the sheriff's office as something of an expert when it came to wild animals," Armie explained. "Especially when it came to animal rehab."

"He was a vet?"

"Nah, we haven't had a vet in town since . . . actually, I don't think we've ever had one. Eddie Guidry always liked animals, and he learned to take care of them. He also knew how to hunt, and that's important out here," Armie continued. "I'm not surprised Archie called Zep if he thought there was a bobcat or something out there in his barn."

"He thought it was some weird swamp thing. Archie, not Zep."

Armie chuckled. "Yeah, I've already heard the term 'rougarou' bandied about. A whole lot of nosy people around town think radios don't work both ways. I figured out what channel they talk on, so I know what the crazies are going to hit me with next. Gene Boudreaux is already trying to call in a cryptozoologist to investigate."

"Zep said it was like the bayou version of a werewolf." She needed to understand. She'd spent way too long keeping to herself in this town. Her grandfather had taught her that the first most important thing a police officer could know was the people he or she protected. She'd forgotten that.

Armie pulled up a chair and sank down. "Only in that it's completely made up by people with way too much imagination and not enough sense. It's kind of a catchall for anything weird that happens out here. Some people think it's a werewolf. I've heard it referred to as a bayou Bigfoot. In other lore it shows up as a bloodsucking bunny rabbit. It's a story to keep Cajun kids in line. Follow the rules or the rougarou will hunt you down."

"Archie isn't a kid."

"Yeah, but he's old school. He still has a priest bless his flock," Armie said with a chuckle. "You should have seen Father Frank's face when we told him he had to pray over a bunch of goats."

This place was strange and mysterious. "Well, I think

the goats got spooked by the asshole who dumped his dog in the middle of the woods."

"Yeah, Zep told me about her. Cute thing." Armie sat back. "Did everything go all right out there? Guidry didn't try anything, did he?"

"Of course not," she said quickly because she wasn't going to reward the man by throwing him under a bus. "He was fine. He was actually pretty helpful."

"So you don't have trouble working with him?"

She snorted. She wished she could sound all delicate and feminine, but that wasn't who she was. "I didn't have trouble with him. I don't know if you've noticed, but I handle him fine."

"You handle him a lot."

"Well, he gets into a lot of trouble."

"A lot of young men get in the kind of trouble he does, and I don't see you hauling them all into jail," he pointed out. "I read your report on the tussle that happened at Dive. You didn't bring any of those men in. You gave them warnings. They got in an actual fight. You brought Zep in the other day for jaywalking."

She had her reasons for that. "Well, I could have given him a ticket, but we all know he won't pay it."

Armie was quiet for a moment. "I've never talked to you about this, but it might be time because I think we're going to need him. I know this sounds silly to you, but there will be some folks out here who get real jumpy if they think there's a rougarou around."

She groaned. "Come on. They can't honestly think there's a werewolf running around the bayou."

"Most of them won't, but there will be some. Especially a couple of the more isolated families. I would expect we'll need to go out and check on them. I think it's also time we had a person on staff who can deal with some of our animal issues. We've got some construction going on, and that means we'll have problems. I know I don't particularly want to deal with them."

A sinking feeling hit the pit of her stomach. "Are you telling me you want to hire Zep Guidry?"

"I'm asking you if you would mind."

This was what got her about Armie. Her boss was always considerate. He cared if she would be uncomfortable having Zep around. Which was precisely why she would lie to him. She didn't want to work with Zep. Being around him was the very definition of uncomfortable since she didn't want to want to be around him. But she did. She wasn't going to explain that to Armie since she couldn't honestly explain it to herself. It wasn't logical. "Of course not. Let him handle the animal stuff."

"Well, he'll be working with us to handle animal-related calls," Armie corrected. "We still have to respond to any and all calls. We'll ask him to join us if we think he can help. I've talked to Remy about it and he's agreed to let Zep go if we get a call and he's working at the restaurant. He can always shift around his staff."

"Like Zep works. He flirts with the women and hopes they leave a big tip." She usually sat in the bar at Guidry's since he worked the main dining room. She would avoid the place altogether, but there weren't a ton of places to eat and Guidry's was excellent. She certainly didn't go to watch him smile at every female in town.

And it really was every female. The man didn't discriminate. Old, young, fat, thin, gorgeous, or homely—they were all charmed by Zep Guidry and his ridiculously bright smile.

"He's not that bad," Armie said. "He's good at playing up his bad reputation, but I don't think he's earned it lately."

"He went to prison, Armie." She admitted the real reason

she worried Zep was a problem. She'd learned about his trouble in Arizona after she'd come to town. It hadn't stopped her from making the mistake of spending the night with him, but it had added to her guilt.

"He was young and not so smart. Has he ever talked to you about it?"

"I read his sheet." She'd been so sick when she'd read his storied history with law enforcement.

"You can read someone's record and not understand the history behind it."

"He wrote a bunch of hot checks. And they weren't his checks."

"Yes, he did something bad and he served a couple of months in jail in Arizona. I think it was actually six weeks with good behavior. I know he sometimes gets in fights or has too much beer or doesn't pay his tickets, but did you ask why he didn't pay those tickets?"

"I don't have to. I'm sure he spent his money on beer."

"Up until a couple of months ago, he was still helping his sister pay her medical bills from his nephew's birth. I only know that because Lila's sister is married to Zep's brother. The family's had a rough couple of years, especially on the monetary front. Zep's put almost everything he's made into paying off those bills. Just remember that when you deal with him. He's not so bad."

She knew he cared about his family. She didn't like to think about him being selfless. It was far easier to view him the way he seemed to want the world to—as a careless, charming player who ambled through life, but Armie's revelations were making her think. What if there was an actual heart under all his good looks? That would make him even more dangerous. "I can work with him."

She wouldn't have to do it often. She could handle it.

The door opened and Lila walked in. "I've got good

news and bad news. You do have a concussion, but it's minor and my brother says the rest of your brain looks great. So you'll be fine, but I either need to send you to the hospital for observation for the day or someone needs to stay with you."

"I'll be fine." She wasn't about to go to the hospital. No way. "Just give me some instructions and I'll be out of your hair."

"No, you won't. You'll be completely in my hair because, like I said, I need to know someone is watching you for the next twelve hours," Lila explained. "I can do that by driving you an hour and a half to the hospital, checking you in, and then having someone pick you up late in the evening. Or you can have a friend stay with you today. I would tell you to hang out here at the clinic, but we're closed this morning. I'm going to Noelle's science fair. If we can ever trick another NP to come down here, well, we'll still be closed sometimes."

It was weird since hospitals didn't close in New York, but this clinic was the nearest thing they had to a hospital in Papillon. Lila would definitely insist on driving her since she wasn't even letting her lie on the couch by herself. There was no way Lila would let her get behind the wheel.

"I swear I'll be cool," she promised. "I'll sign one of those forms and everything will be okay. I don't mind signing it."

"You want to sign an AMA?" Lila's eyes had widened slightly but not in a surprised way. Nope. Roxie knew that look. It was the "dumbass said what" look.

"You're not leaving against medical advice," Armie declared with a frown.

She didn't have anyone to call. She quickly went through the short list of people she knew well enough to ask for a favor. She pretty much only knew the guys she worked with. She worked and then went home. She got the occasional beer, and sometimes she hung out with Lila. That was the sum of who she might be able to ask.

Major was working. He would have been called in to take over the rest of her shift and his own. Armie would be at his daughter's school event. Vince would be working with Major, and the fourth deputy, Chris, had recently hired on and was moving today.

The door opened and Zep walked in, Daisy on a leash, though she obviously wasn't trained. She squirmed and strained against the leash the minute she got in the room.

"Sorry, I wanted to make sure you were all right before I head into Houma," he said. "Also wanted to give you the chance to say good-bye to Daisy."

If she didn't find someone to "watch" over her, Armie would likely do it himself. Or they would have to spend their whole day driving back and forth to the hospital. He would miss his daughter's science fair, and it wasn't some elementary event where they showed off homemade volcanoes. Noelle was in her senior year of high school and competing for scholarships.

Also, she might save the puppy from having to go to some horrible shelter.

She looked at Zep. She knew what she was about to say was a mistake, but she didn't see that she had any other choice. She was desperate. "I need someone to make sure I can wake up every couple of hours."

Zep stopped and looked around as though trying to make sure she was talking to him. "You want me to call my sister or something?"

His sister and her husband, Harrison Jefferys, owned a B and B, the nicest one in town. That could be the solution. She could check in for the day and sleep on the couch in the great room. She'd heard their family dog was almost like a nanny to their little boy. Maybe he could be a nurse, too. "Does she have any rooms open?"

Armie huffed and Lila started shaking her head as though they both knew she planned to ask a dog to help her out before she'd ask the human male in the room.

Zep nodded as though that was what he'd expected. "Sorry. I was talking to Sera and Harry last night and they're completely booked. They've got a big family coming down for the week. From somewhere back East."

Then she didn't have a choice. She closed her eyes and wished the ground would swallow her up. It would be easier than doing what she had to do now. She sighed and opened her eyes because the ground was still firm beneath her. "Would you do it?"

The slowest, sexiest smile crossed his face. "I can definitely wake you up, darlin'. Though I'm more used to putting pretty ladies to sleep. Wait. That came out wrong. Never mind. I can do it."

She already regretted the choice. It might have been better to let the snake have her.

"You don't actually have to stay, you know," Roxie said as Zep eased into the driver's seat of his truck.

Well, he should have known she would say that, but it still disappointed him. He also couldn't let her get around Lila's dictates. "It's all right. I don't mind."

Daisy was in the back of the cab. It wasn't one of those big cabs that could fit three people. It was cramped, but Daisy treated it like a dog run. She took three steps to one side and then turned to race the whole small bench to get to the other side. Yipping all the way.

The dog was excited.

Zep was kind of excited, too, but he wasn't allowed to

show his excitement by getting a case of the zoomies. He was going to get to spend time with her that didn't involve being thrown in a jail cell.

Most men would have given up by now. Most men would have walked away and found someone easier to deal with, someone who would actually admit she liked said man in question. It wasn't like he hadn't dated since they'd spent that one fateful night together, but none of it had been more than casual. He hadn't even had sex since he'd been with Roxie.

Not that anyone would believe him. Even though he hadn't even made out with a woman in a year, it hadn't seemed to have made a dent in repairing the town's view of him. One day he would sit his own son down and have a long conversation about the importance of male chastity and how once a man is established as a horndog, it's almost impossible to get rid of the stain.

Zep knew he should believe her when she said she didn't want to see him again. The trouble was she went out of her way to be around him.

It wasn't the first time he'd had some beautiful creature snarl his way even though it was obvious she needed some affection.

He had to find a way to prove to her that his affection wasn't merely sexual. He could take care of her in other ways.

He winced because Daisy didn't have the same issues Roxie had. She was boundless in her need for love. As in she knew absolutely no boundaries. She had her paws on the back of his seat and licked the side of his face with enthusiasm.

Roxie giggled. He'd never heard her laugh in a way that was pure joy. "She likes you, Guidry."

"I need her to like me a little less until she's had a bath."

He put the truck in reverse and eased out of the space. He wanted to tell her this was the most loving he'd gotten since he'd been with her, but he was smart enough to know she wouldn't want to hear it. Nor would she likely believe it. "You need anything before we go back to your place? Lila said you might not feel like eating, but if you do, it's all right. I could stop by Dixie's and get something to go."

He'd been given a full set of instructions on how to ensure Roxanne didn't die in the next twelve hours. He'd been given a list of things to watch for. Vomiting was one of them.

He could handle it. He wasn't some fancy guy who'd never had a baby throw up in his mouth. He knew way too much about babies for a dude who wasn't a dad.

He'd made the decision to put his family first several years before, and he'd kept the promise. His nephew was a bright light in the world. But he could be gross on occasion.

"I couldn't eat right now," Roxie said.

"Are you feeling nauseous?" If she was, he would turn the truck around and take her straight back to the clinic. If she needed to go to the hospital, he would go with her. She didn't have anyone who could take care of her.

Her chin came up in that stubborn expression he'd come to know so well. "Zep, you don't have to worry about me. I'm fine. I never meant for you to actually come to my place. I needed to let Armie and Lila off the hook, if you know what I mean."

"I don't."

She frowned his way. "They take their responsibilities seriously, and they view me as a responsibility. I needed to make them feel good about letting me leave the clinic so they could go and do their family stuff."

"I don't think they see you as a responsibility. I think they see you as a friend." He was always surprised by her pessimism. She had a whole lot of walls for him to climb, and they were high.

She turned in her seat and stared out the front windshield as he put the truck in drive and started out of the parking lot. “I like them a lot. I think I might fit in with them because they both spent so much time in cities.”

Armie had been a detective in New Orleans for years, and Lila had lived in Dallas until she’d decided to make her home close to her sister Lisa. But it pointed out one of the walls between them. “You don’t like it much here, do you?”

“I don’t know. I guess I don’t understand it. It was a culture shock.”

“You can’t get over it if you never go out.” Her habit of never going to town functions unless she was working had thwarted many a plan to get her to see him as more than a way to pad her monthly arrests.

“I go out,” she protested.

He knew her habits far too well. “You go to Guidry’s and the bar at the edge of town. You sometimes get breakfast at Dixie’s. That’s not getting to know the parish.”

“I see a lot of the parish. I’ve pretty much driven over every inch of it.”

“For your job. That’s not the same,” he replied. “You see people at their worst and never give them a chance to show you who they really are.”

“That’s not true,” she replied. “I have seen them at their best. I see a lot of drunks and jerks who need to use their words instead of their fists. But I’ve also been there when there’s a storm or an accident. I’ve seen them take care of each other. I’ve seen them make way too many casseroles when someone’s sick. It’s not about the people around me. I like them for the most part.”

He finally figured it out. “You’re worried they won’t like you.”

"Small towns can be hard on a newcomer. They all look at me funny."

They probably looked at her because she was gorgeous and mysterious, and when she smiled, he felt the whole world light up. The one good thing about the last year was that she hadn't started dating some super nice guy who could give her everything—who he couldn't compete with. "What's funny about it?"

She shrugged. "Nothing, really. I guess I'm not used to standing out like a sore thumb. Where I come from, it's different. A newcomer can blend in easily. It's not that people don't care. They do. The culture is different."

"You're not used to people being all up in your business. You're used to people having a lot to do and not noticing most of what goes on around them."

"That's a good way to put it. I'm not used to people being so interested in me. Or having such weird notions," she admitted. "Did you know there are people here who think if you go to New York, you'll immediately be murdered or sold into some form of servitude? When I first got here, Helena from the church laid hands on me and thanked the Good Lord for delivering me from hell. I told her I wasn't from hell. I was from Brooklyn."

"In their defense they think the same thing about any big city. It's not merely New York. They worry the big metropolis of Baton Rouge will swallow up their precious babies," he replied. "And how many of your New York friends found out you were moving to Southern Louisiana and recommended you watch *Deliverance*."

Her smile told him everything he needed to know.

"I know they seem backward and dumb, but they're not," he said softly.

She shook her head. "I didn't say that. I don't think anyone's dumb. Just different from what I'm used to. It's not like everyone in New York is intellectual. There are plenty of weirdos walking the streets of the city. People are people wherever you go. But the weird is usually different. Although back after Hurricane Sandy, everyone thought we had super-rats coming up from the tunnels. So maybe not so different."

He liked it when she smiled unselfconsciously. "Well, I saw a video of the one with the pizza. He looked pretty super to me. You know what I've never once seen?"

"A rougarou?" She asked the question with a hint of expectation, almost like she hoped he would deny it.

Unfortunately, he couldn't. "I thought I saw one once, but it was a couple of guys who'd gone mudding and taken it way too far."

She pointed his way. "See. There. I don't understand mudding."

Mudding had been the entertainment of his youth. These days, he pretty much liked to stay clean. But he understood. "It's fun. It's like our version of an amusement ride, though we have some carnivals come through town, too. It's even fun to get stuck and have to figure out how to get out. I don't know. It's kind of freeing. I could take you sometime. It would be a good way to get to know the area. Outside of the best places to arrest people. I know you're deeply acquainted with all of those. You live on Rose, right?"

"Yeah," she replied, her eyes on the road. "It's not far from here. It's a duplex. My landlady lives next door. Maybe we should rethink this. If you walk in with me . . ."

He thought he knew what she was worried about. "You live next to Darlene Cooper?"

She nodded.

"She's one of the biggest gossips in town." Though it wouldn't be bad for him to be seen with Roxie. Especially if he could follow that up with more sightings around town that did not involve the gorgeous deputy putting handcuffs on him. More than once he'd seen parish gossip work its magic and suddenly two people who weren't dating decided they might as well since no one would stop talking about them.

"She's a nice lady, but she does like to talk." Roxie hid a yawn behind her hand. "I could ask her to watch me. I didn't think about her."

"It's six in the morning," he pointed out because he wasn't about to give up his chance to spend time with her. "And doesn't she have a doctor's appointment to get to? I have to assume that because every time I talk to her, she mentions some horrible ailment. In great detail. I know way too much about her regularity."

That got another brilliant smile from her. "She does that when she doesn't want to talk to someone. Usually someone she thinks is annoying."

He was always nice to Darlene. "I am not annoying. I'm considered quite charming."

"You flirt. A lot. You flirt like most people breathe."

"See, this is another one of those cultural differences."

She crossed her arms over her chest and leaned against the door. "Yeah, like we don't have players in New York. I assure you the accent might be different, but the result is the same. You tell everyone exactly what they want to hear—especially women—and a whole lot of them give you a pass on everything. You're pretty and smooth-talking, and you get away with working less than the rest of us."

"First of all, I do not sweet-talk my way into . . ." If he ever wanted her to look at him like someone she could actually talk to, he had to start being honest with her. "Fine. I learned at a young age that if I was charming, I didn't have to be smart."

A single brow rose over her eyes. "You don't think you're smart?"

"Come on. You don't think I'm smart, either."

"I've never said that. I've said you're a douchebag player, but not that you aren't smart."

"I'm not a player."

She snorted. It was wrong that he found it so cute.

"I don't like that word. I'm not playing with people." This was an old frustration. "I don't tell Dixie she looks pretty to get her to give me free coffee."

"Yet she does."

"She does that because I take care of her cats when she goes out of town. One of them is old and needs a bunch of meds, and not all of them go into food, if you know what I mean. She's a lot like Darlene in that way." He wasn't sure he could make her understand. "What you call flirting, I think of it as my way to show the people around me that I see them."

"It makes you less honest," she said, an odd primness to her tone.

"Honesty? What about me telling Dixie she looks nice isn't honest? She does look nice. Maybe your version of nice and mine are completely different."

"You told Caroline that she should have Archie cover up or all the women would be on him. You cannot tell me that the women of Papillon would lose their minds if they saw Archie in his boxers."

He grinned her way. "Nah, that was all about you. See, I happen to know that Caroline firmly believes all women want her husband. Especially younger women. She also thinks gold diggers will come after him for their spectacular farm. I don't think Caroline sees the world the same way we do."

"You think she's crazy? Like she needs help?"

They definitely had two different definitions of crazy. Or maybe it was just that he didn't think it was all that bad to be some kinds of crazy. "I think when you look at that old man, you see wrinkles and knobby knees, and she sees the man who carried her over the threshold more than fifty years ago. I think when you look at that farm, you see stinky goats and a barn that needs a coat of paint. Caroline sees everything they built together. She sees years of love and work, the place where she raised her boys. I don't know there's anything crazy about that. I hope my eyes work the same way when I'm her age."

"I didn't think about it like that." She leaned against the door. "No, that's not crazy at all. But this place is strange."

"Strange can be good."

"Or it can get you bitten by a snake."

"Thank the Good Lord that Armie makes you wear proper boots. And don't worry about gossip from Caroline. I promise no one is going to think you're after Archie for his body or his goats. They'll be far too busy asking you how you managed to survive the rougarou and if you think it will come after them next."

She groaned. "You really think they're going to ask me about this thing?"

"Oh, yeah. I think we live for drama like this."

"And you think it's going to be fun? You're not the one who's going to have to answer all those calls. Unless you took the job."

He was kind of surprised she didn't sound like that was a distasteful thing. When Armie had asked if he would do some contract work with the parish, he'd been shocked. He'd expected Armie was going to tell him to leave the clinic and let Roxie alone. Instead, the sheriff had thanked him profusely for taking care of her and offered him a job. A job he wanted. "Would you be upset if I did? I don't have to."

If he was being honest with himself, he didn't like to

work at the restaurant. Guidry's was his brother's dream, not his. His brother had left his job in Dallas to take over the family restaurant and he was happy now. This job with the sheriff's office was the first work-related thing to excite Zep in a long time. But he couldn't make her uncomfortable. If it had been anyone else, he would have told them to deal with it, but she was his weak spot.

"If Armie says you're the best for the job, I believe him," she replied. "I also believe you might be the only candidate. Are you really good with animals? I don't mean making them like you. I'm talking about taking care of them, knowing how to deal with them."

Sometimes he thought it was the only thing he was good at. "Yeah. I've been taking care of animals since I was a kid. My father learned from his father. Back when he was growing up, my father's family kept livestock around and he took care of them. Since we didn't have a vet in these parts, people would call him out and he would help. If it was something he couldn't handle, he would call someone in. My dad learned from him, and he taught me since Remy had zero interest in anything beyond baseball and food, and Sera was not thrilled at the thought of getting bit or clawed up. The first time a chicken pecked her, she ran away and never came with us again when my daddy would do his rounds."

"I used to walk around the neighborhood with my grandpa," Roxie said, her eyes closing. "He was a street cop all his life. He walked the same beat for thirty years. They tried to promote him but he liked where he was. He knew the people who lived in the neighborhood. He lived there, too."

"Your granddad took you to work?"

"No. He wasn't uniformed when he took me. Although it was part of his work," she said, not opening her eyes. "He would go and check on people. If someone was sick and he knew about it, he would check in. This was a long time ago, when Brooklyn wasn't Manhattan lite. We were working class. We needed each other. That's something I do understand, something we have in common."

Her whole body had relaxed. Normally that would be a good sign, but he'd listened to everything Lila had told him. He needed to make sure this was normal weariness. "You feeling okay?"

"Just tired. Didn't sleep much this week. So it sucks that you have to watch over me. I can take a nap, right?"

"I can let you sleep for a while as long as you're not nauseous or dizzy." He had a list of what to look for. He wasn't going to get much sleep between checking on Roxie and making sure Daisy didn't wreck her apartment.

"I like your truck," she said on a yawn she covered with her hand. "It's soothing. Reminds me of being a kid. When we would go see my uncle, we would drive out in Granddad's truck and I would sleep on the way. I could feel the road and he would drive and I would know I was safe."

It had been so long since she'd really talked to him. He didn't want it to end. "Sounds like you're close to your granddad."

The sun was coming up, and the light hit her face. Instead of moving away from it, she turned her cheeks up as though soaking in the warmth. "Was. He died when I was twenty. I was in the Army. I still miss him. You were close to your dad?"

His heart clenched the way it did every time he thought about his dad. "Very. I miss him, too. I only got ten years with him, but they were great years."

"I'm sorry about your dad," she said quietly.

"I'm sorry about your granddad."

She was quiet, and after a moment he realized she'd fallen asleep.

He got the feeling Roxie didn't fall asleep so easily. She was a careful woman. Even though she wasn't ready to admit it, she trusted him on some level. Or she was dying. It was one of the two. "Rox?"

"I'm fine," she murmured. "Just tired. No nausea. Like I said, I haven't slept much lately. I never do this time of year."

"What about this time of year makes you not sleep?"

"It's almost my birthday. I hate my birthday."

That was something he definitely didn't know about her. He had no idea when her birthday was. Birthdays were a big thing around town, but he couldn't remember hearing anything about Roxie celebrating. That meant Armie—who would know—was respecting her choices. "What happened?"

She shifted so she could look at him. "That's not the usual response. Most people think I hate my birthday because I'm grumpy or I'm being overly dramatic about getting older."

"You don't mind getting older. You're not vain. If you hate something, it's for a reason, and it wouldn't be a trivial one. It's not that you ate bad cake once or a boyfriend broke up with you on that day."

She was quiet for a moment. "My partner got killed. It wasn't on my actual birthday, but we'd just had a party. Nothing big. Just cake and ice cream. His wife sent them up with him. Then we got a call and an hour later he was dead. So I don't like this week much. Bad stuff happens this week, as we learned from the snake."

"Ah, but you could have been wearing different shoes," he pointed out. "And you got to save this little thing. That's a positive."

Daisy bounced up and down like she knew they were talking about her.

Roxie reached out and gave the dog a pet. "She's sweet. I'm just going to close my eyes until we get to my place. Okay?"

Lila had told him it was okay for her to sleep a bit. He was tired, too, but he could set an alarm and wake up in a few hours to make sure Roxie was all right. "Okay."

He drove toward her place and couldn't help but think the night had changed something between them.

# *chapter three*

Roxie stirred and glanced at the clock. Two. And it was light enough in her bedroom that she knew it was day. The barking outside reminded her that it wasn't her usual day.

She felt way better having gotten some sleep, and would feel even better after a shower.

Her cell buzzed. Someone had plugged it in and set it on the nightstand.

Someone? Zep had done it. Zep had driven her home, made sure she could walk up the stairs, and put her in bed with only a few snarky innuendos. Of course, if he hadn't made them, she would have been worried.

She yawned and looked down at her phone. Her mom had called three times. Probably something about her birthday. Her mother insisted that her birthday wasn't merely hers. It also belonged to her family, and that was why she should get over the whole "my best friend in the world died" and celebrate. But then her mother wasn't one to dwell on anything dark. Life was too short, her mother would say.

Her mother also reminded her regularly that her eggs were shriveling up in her ovaries and all her shots at grandchildren were going with them. It didn't matter that her brother would likely procreate at some point. All that mattered was Roxie was the daughter and should have already produced another kid for her mom to dote on and screw up with her insistence on perfection.

She took a deep breath and turned the phone over. She couldn't deal with this now. In a couple of hours she would call back and explain again that she didn't want to go home to celebrate something she didn't have any real part in beyond being expelled from her mother's womb. As her mom would point out, she'd even gotten that wrong since she'd been an emergency C-section and had ruined her mother's ability to wear a much smaller bikini than anyone should wear.

Nope. She couldn't handle all that judgment right this moment.

There was a loud bark and she moved to the window, drawing back the utilitarian curtains that had come with the place. Zep was in her backyard, wearing nothing but a pair of jeans. He hadn't even put on his shoes. Daisy was bouncing around the yard and generally being super cute. Zep had a frown on his face and his hair was tousled in a way that should have been messy, but simply made him all the sexier.

She opened the window, ready to call out to him, to let him know she was awake, and his duty was done.

"Come on, girl. I can't go back in until you do your business," Zep said with a yawn of his own. "And she's going to wake up and toss us both out. We have to get back in there and prove our worth. Your job is to look adorable and not leave gifts on her floor."

He wanted to stay? When would he get that she wasn't some conquest? That's what it had to be. Zep Guidry wasn't used to women saying no to him. He'd wanted a second night with her and she'd refused. He was going to get that night even if he had to charm it out of her.

Would it be so wrong? Maybe they could keep it quiet. If they didn't cause a bunch of gossip, why would it be wrong to see him again? Not see him. That would imply they were dating. Sleep with him again. Have sex with him again because he was good at it and she wasn't seeing anyone and she was a healthy female with needs.

Yes, that was a good reason. It was practical when she thought about it. Her job was stressful. She needed to let off some steam every now and then, and the gym wasn't cutting it anymore. There wasn't anyone else in town she was attracted to. She'd seen Zep and couldn't think about anyone else.

He wasn't good for her. He was too charming, too good looking, too smooth. He was an ex-con, though doing a couple of months in county years before wasn't exactly hardened criminal material. Armie was willing to hire him.

She shook her head. She wasn't going that far. But she might think about a mutually satisfying arrangement. It was clear to her that this odd fascination with him wasn't going to go away.

And hey, if she was right and he had no interest in her if she was actually interested in him, then all her problems would be solved.

Well, all the ones that revolved around him. Her family was another story entirely.

Her cell buzzed again.

"Daisy, come on, girl. She's never going to like us if you poop on her carpet. It's a very clean carpet," Zep cajoled. "I don't know if you noticed, but she's kind of a clean freak. We have to respect that. Clean is good. You've been some of the places I've been and you come to realize clean is way better than dirty."

The puppy merely dropped down in that playful way puppies did and gave a cheerful bark.

Daisy was a lot like the man she was currently running circles around. She was going to do her thing, and despite all the trauma she'd been through, she obviously expected the sun to shine on her no matter what. She was adorable and she knew it. Just like Zep.

The cell kept buzzing.

He'd been so good with both the dog and her the night before. She'd seen a different side to him. So often she saw him at his worst. He had a bad habit of getting in fights. It seemed to be a form of entertainment out here.

He was so gentle with Daisy, and apparently he'd risked his life on the off chance they needed the snake that had bitten her. Now he was pleading with the puppy not to pee on her carpet. Most people she knew would have left the dog outside.

Instead, Zep was outside with the dog. And it looked like he'd taken a nap on the comfy chair she sometimes read in at night. His boots were beside it and his shirt draped over the back. He would have been ridiculously uncomfortable. She'd told him he could leave, but he wouldn't. He'd told her he would be right there in case she needed him.

How many times had he taken the puppy out? Had he gotten any sleep at all?

The phone buzzed and she sighed.

She turned away and retrieved the phone. Her mother had obviously decided whatever she had to say was important, and she wouldn't give up. She would simply call until Roxie answered.

She would way rather watch Zep try to deal with a puppy version of himself, but she slid her finger across the surface of the phone to accept the call. "Hello, Mom."

"Roxanne, I've been trying to get hold of you all morning. I was starting to worry something had gone terribly wrong. You can't not answer when your mother calls and you're a cop. I was about to dial that station house of yours and demand answers."

"I'm fine. I worked the night shift." She wasn't about to admit that something had actually gone wrong. Especially not that she'd nearly been taken out by a snake while searching for a Cajun werewolf. To say that her mother had been against her moving to Louisiana would be an understatement, like calling a Cat 5 hurricane a gentle breeze with a smattering of rain.

Hurricanes had been one of the reasons her mother had listed for not moving to Papillon. Along with alligators, lack of potential for advancement, and yes, she'd mentioned *Deliverance*. She was every bit as scared of this place as Hallie Rayburn's mom was of New York City.

"The night shift? You're not some newbie." Her mother sounded like she was in a car. "Why would they treat you like that? Your boyfriend allows this? I would think he could control your schedule."

She winced because that was a reminder of the white lie she'd told when she'd first moved down here. It had been all about self-preservation. "It's a small department. We all work nights from time to time. I was taking my shift."

Hopefully that would be the end of it. She didn't want to get into her imaginary dating life with her mother. The only reason she had an imaginary dating life was to keep her mother out of any kind of real dating life she might have. In some distant future.

"Well, I still think he should take better care of you," her mother insisted. "Say what you like about him, but Joel always made sure you had good assignments even though he wasn't in your unit. He used his position to better his family. He took care of you."

"He did not do that in any way." Her mother was excellent at rewriting history to fit her worldview. She was starting to get a headache that had nothing to do with her minor concussion. "In fact, he went out of his way to not help me. The only time he ever got involved in my career was to stop me from attempting to save myself from sexual harassment."

A long sigh came over the line. "I don't want to have this argument again. He was doing what he thought would help you. He loved you. I hope this Armie person cares about you half as much as Joel did. He hasn't been dating, you know. He did right after the divorce, but he says he needs a break now. I think it's because he knows he's not over you."

How exactly would her mother know? "You've talked to him? Seriously?"

"I had a perfectly innocent lunch with him the other day. I happened to be in the city and he was free. You know he's friends with your brother. You can't expect all of us to cut him off completely. Your brother works with him."

And work was the most important thing. Nothing mattered more than moving up the ladder.

"Will you stop harping on her, Pamela? You promised this would be a good trip for all of us. All of us includes Roxanne."

She stopped because that had been her father's voice. "Is Dad in the car with you?"

Her father should be golfing. He'd retired a few years back, but he kept up a game with some of his friends from the precinct. They golfed every Tuesday morning without fail and then spent the afternoon at the club. He'd done it for years, and her father didn't like to change a schedule.

She heard the door to the backyard open and then close and Zep saying something about Daisy being a good girl. At least one thing had gone right.

"Yes, your father's in the car, but don't worry. Your brother's driving. I wouldn't let your father drive here. It's very frightening, and his reflexes aren't what they used to be," her mother was saying.

"Where are you going?" They hadn't taken a family trip in years.

"It's a surprise," her mother replied in a smug tone.

Oh, she'd heard that tone before. It always accompanied something terrible. A cold chill crept up her spine. "Mother, where are you?"

She rushed to the opposite window, the one that looked out over the front yard. She watched as a minivan pulled into the small driveway she shared with Darlene.

Her brother was behind the steering wheel, and there was a dark-haired woman next to him.

Yep, there was the nausea Lila had warned her about.

"We're here," her brother said in a cheerful voice. "All of us. Happy birthday, sis. I'm excited to meet this boyfriend of yours."

The boyfriend she'd made up. Except she hadn't really. It would have been far better if she'd completely made up a boyfriend. But no, her imagination sucked, so she went for something halfway real. When her mother had threatened to start trying to match her up to men in town, she'd casually tossed out that she was dating Armie LaVigne. Who was now married. Who probably wasn't willing to give her some cover.

Panic threatened to well up inside her. They were here. If her mother found out she'd lied, she would never hear the end of it. Her mother would bring it up in every conversation, tell everyone she knew. Her psychologist cousin would be brought in to attempt to put them all in family counseling. And when she got over the lying part, her mother would be on her to find a partner. She would send man after man her way.

Her life would be a living hell.

And there was no stopping her mother unless she was willing to finally cut off the relationship.

Was she ready to do that? Did she honestly want to not see her family again? She'd spent the last few years pondering that very question.

There was a knock on the door, and she started to shout as she grabbed her robe. "Zep, don't—"

"Hello," her mother said, striding in. "You must be the reason my daughter is here in this town thousands of miles away from her home. I get it now. You're gorgeous. You are a very good reason for her to stay here. And she never told me she had a dog. Oh, hello, puppy."

"I'm sorry. Roxie is sleeping," Zep started to say, clearly confused.

"I'm here." She rushed down the stairs.

"Hey, baby, go slow." Zep met her at the bottom, a concerned look on his face that rapidly turned into a wince. "I'm sorry . . ."

He was about to apologize for calling her baby, but she had way bigger problems than his use of affectionate nicknames. It was stupid. She should fess up, but looking at her perfect family currently snobbishly judging her living space and pretty much her whole life sent her right over the edge. She threw herself into the arms of the hottest man she'd ever met and planted a kiss on him.

Zep's hands came up and steadied her, not pulling away from the kiss at all.

She drew back slightly and whispered, "Please follow my lead."

"Uhm, sis, your dog seems to need to go out," her brother said. "She peed right on my shoe."

Zep groaned. "I'm so sorry. I just took her out."

But Roxie decided to keep that dog right then and there.

* * *

Zep was beyond confused, but she'd kissed him. She'd planted those gorgeous lips right on his. Oh, it hadn't been the world's most passionate kiss, but it was a kiss and he was going to take it. It was the absolute closest he'd gotten to her in a solid year, and he'd wanted more.

And then the puppy had decided the guy in the collared shirt who looked a little like Roxie was a fire hydrant.

"Daisy, outside," he said in a firm voice. He went and scooped the dog up. "Sorry, we're training the puppy. Have to teach her to go outside. Excuse me for a moment."

He hustled Daisy into the backyard and hoped Roxie took the opportunity to fill him in. He was a little sleep-deprived, and not everything was making sense. He set Daisy down as the door came open behind him.

"I'm sorry," she said in a hushed voice. "I need you to follow my lead. That's my family in there. I have no idea why they're here, but I need you to help me. It's nothing big. It was a little white lie to ease my mother's mind and keep her off my back."

Ah, now he was getting the picture. "Momma thinks you have a man in your life and you don't want her to know you lied so she'll stay off your back."

"Precisely. Also, she thinks you're Armie."

"What?"

"Like I said, go with it. I'll make sure they don't even come close to the station house," she said, talking as fast as she had the first day she'd gone on the job. She'd taken on slower tones as she'd gotten comfortable in Papillon, though the state of her apartment made him question if she'd gotten comfy at all. There was nothing of herself in the apartment. He wouldn't be surprised if she'd simply taken the whole thing as is and not altered it in any way.

There were no pictures on the walls, no mementos. It wasn't a home. It was a way station. "I'll tell them you're about to go to a conference and you won't be back for a couple of days. Do this for me and I swear I'll pay your next parking ticket."

He didn't want her to pay his parking tickets. The only reason—beyond forgetting them—that he didn't pay them was to get to see her. Somehow she was the only one who ever arrested him. Major would roll his eyes and tell him to get to city hall or the fine would go up. Armie would set Zep's brother, Remy, on him, but Roxie got personal about it.

"You want me to pretend to be your boyfriend while your parents are here?" He needed to make certain he understood what she was trying to do. He didn't mention pretending to be Armie since he wasn't about to do that. It wouldn't work. This wasn't some city where she could take them to a restaurant where no one knew who they were. She had like four choices in the whole parish, and every single one of them would be filled with nosy people who would ask way too many questions. But he could explain that later.

"Yes." She looked soft with her hair tousled. She usually kept it in a severe bun, and he understood why she styled it that way for work, but he'd only ever once seen her with it down, with all that silk falling around her shoulders and brushing the tops of her breasts. "I know it sounds stupid, but I need you."

It wasn't anything he would have expected from her, but family could drive a person to do things they normally wouldn't.

Daisy finished her business and bounced their way. He fished a treat out of his pocket. "Good girl. And yes, I'll help you out."

A long sigh came from Roxie. "Thank you. I promise it'll be quick."

The back door had come open and Roxie's mother strode out. Mrs. King wore slacks and a crisp white button-down shirt, her hair cut in a sensible but stylish bob that hit right at her chin line. She was a woman who took excellent care of herself. "Roxanne, your brother is cleaning up. I told him he couldn't treat dogs around here like New York dogs. They're here for different reasons. Dogs down here have to fight off wild animals."

And she obviously rarely left the city. "Mrs. King, it's a pleasure to meet you." He held out a hand, which she shook. A little too long. "I'm sorry about Daisy here. She's new to our little family and she's just getting trained."

Daisy was trying to climb up Roxie's body. Roxie stared down at the dog and the puppy sat.

Oh, that puppy knew who her momma was. Now it was merely a question of fitting himself in there. And it would start with this fabrication of Roxie's that he was about to take to a whole other level.

"I'm Zéphirin Guidry, Mrs. King," he said before Roxie could introduce him. "It's a pleasure to meet you. I hope our little Daisy here didn't cause too much trouble."

Mrs. King looked at her daughter. "I thought you said his name was Armie. I thought that was an odd name, but it certainly didn't start with a Z."

For once in the whole time he'd known her, Roxie looked like she had no idea what to do.

Luckily, he did. He slid an arm around her shoulders. "Baby, you didn't tell her what that mean old Armie did to you?"

"No, I didn't," she said in a tight voice. "But I guess you're going to."

It was all the permission he needed. "It's no big thing. You know how it goes. They thought it could work but it kind of fizzled out. No real chemistry there. And then Lila Daley waltzed into town and stole that man right out from under Roxie's nose. They got married real quick. But have no fear. I swooped in and dried all her tears."

"I didn't cry. Like you said, we didn't have any chemistry. It didn't last long," Roxie replied, letting a little of her irritation flow.

"Why didn't you tell me?" Roxie's mother asked. "I mean it's not like you can be ashamed of him. He's an attractive man."

"It's not that serious," Roxie tried.

But he was going to block her. "We recently moved in together. She's a cautious one, your daughter. She likes to go slow. A lot of people around here didn't even know we were dating at all until recently. She wanted to make sure I wasn't going to leave her for the first big-city chick who waltzed in and opened a clinic. I told her she was the only big-city first responder I was interested in, but it took her a couple of months to understand I'm a one-woman man."

"And such a handsome one at that," Mrs. King said. "You should call me Pamela. I want to know everything there is to know about you."

"I think Zep should go in and put on a shirt." Roxie gave her mother one of her patented stern looks. It was the kind that got even him standing up a little taller and hoping she didn't carry through with the threat in her eyes. "Mother, you don't have to stare at his chest."

"But it's a nice chest. Your father never looked this good, and honestly your brother is getting a little pudgy in the middle. I've told Shawna she needs to fix that. Since he moved up to lieutenant, he's let himself go," her mother said, giving Zep a bright smile. "It's obvious you're not going to do the same, sweetie."

"Why don't you tell me why you're here," Roxie said.

"For your birthday, of course. We haven't seen you in two years, Roxanne. You never come home anymore so we came to you. We have a whole celebration planned at the bed-and-breakfast. It's so quaint, and there's a man there who is almost as handsome as this one," Pamela said with a nod.

"You're out at the B and B?" Zep asked. Sera had mentioned someone had rented all the rooms they had ready. "My sister runs the place. And Harry is definitely not as handsome as me."

"Is everything all right?" The man who had to be Roxanne's dad stepped out. He had silver hair and looked to be on the thin side. He was dressed almost like his wife, though his slacks were dark and he'd tucked his button-down in. His shirtsleeves were rolled up. "You must be Armie. Somehow I thought you would be older. You're the sheriff around here?"

"No, I am not." That was another reason why he couldn't pretend to be Armie. He was far too young and pretty to be a grizzled sheriff. Why the hell had she told her parents she was dating Armie? Armie was too old for her. Armie was too much like her in some ways. They would never be compatible.

Did she have a thing for Armie?

"This is Zéphir—" Pamela began.

"You can call me Zep." He held out his hand and shook Mr. King's. "I was explaining that Roxie hasn't dated Armie in a while. He's gotten married and we're together now."

"He's living with her, Tony," Pamela explained. "Living together and she didn't even mention it to her parents. She's gone wild since she moved down here. I told you. But he seems like a fine young man."

Roxie stepped in front of her father. "Dad, it's nice to see you, but I'm a little unprepared. I had no idea you were coming."

"Because we wanted it to be a surprise," her father replied. "Though we did try to call."

"I was working the late shift. I turned off my ringer." She directed the comment to her father as though she knew her mother wouldn't care.

"Sorry. We don't know your schedule," Tony King replied, though his tone was a bit disappointed. "You don't talk to us much. You haven't even congratulated Brian on his engagement."

"I sent him a text," Roxie shot back.

Oh, she needed someone to smooth the way or this whole visit was going to go poorly. "We hadn't decided on what to get them yet. We were debating on what to send them as a couple."

"A coupon for a good lawyer," Roxie said under her breath.

His fake girlfriend was a little overstimulated. It was time for some honesty. "Mr. and Mrs. King, we're so thrilled you're here, but Roxie and I were working late last night and she took a little tumble. Hit her head pretty hard. She needs some more rest. Why don't you let me take you all out to dinner at my family's restaurant tonight?"

"She hit her head?" Pamela's eyes had gone wide.

Roxie sent him a death stare. "It's fine. I've already seen a medical pro. Lila says I'm good. I just need a little rest."

"Isn't that the woman who stole your boyfriend?" Pamela asked. "I don't think we should trust her. She might let you die so you can never get him back. I saw it on *Dateline*. The same thing happened to a woman in Yonkers, though the other woman was a dental assistant. I don't trust them. They're always young. Why are there no older dental assistants? Because they marry the dentists. That's why."

"Mom, Lila isn't trying to kill me," Roxie said with a sigh. "But I do need to rest and I'm not even dressed and Zep isn't dressed. I wasn't ready for any of this."

"Well, you would have been if you—" Pamela began.

Her husband put a hand on her shoulder. "We'll head back to the B and B, sweetheart, but we will take your boyfriend up on his dinner invitation. Will you be all right by then? Or would you like me to drive you into a bigger city to see a doctor who didn't marry your ex?"

"Lila's solid," Zep explained. "She's connected to my family. See, her sister married my brother, so we're all good. It's a small town. Everyone's connected, but Lila's excellent at her job. Roxie's fine, but I stayed up so I could make sure she didn't get sick. I could use a nap before we all get together."

Tony nodded as though he'd made his decision. "Come along, Pamela. It wasn't fair to ambush her like this. Roxie, give your boyfriend my number so he can text me where and when to meet you for dinner tonight while you get some rest. We'll take Brian and Shawna back to the B and B with us. I think we could all use a nap. It was a long trip to get here. Don't forget that, Roxanne. We came a long way to see you. We went to a lot of trouble, and we expect you to spend some time with us. We'll talk at dinner tonight. Zep, it's good to meet you. I intend to get to know you while I'm here."

"But I—" Pamela stopped when her husband took her hand. "Fine. I'll see you tonight, dear."

Zep followed behind Roxie as she showed her parents the door. It did not escape his notice that the brother's fiancée stayed far from Daisy. So did the brother. Apparently he was once peed on, twice shy.

The place was deadly quiet as she shut the door behind them and took a moment before she turned around.

He was prepared for the death stare she sent his way. "Now, Roxie, let me explain."

"You live with me? You had one job, Guidry. One. All you had to do was answer to Armie's name, explain you've got to go to work, and leave."

"That's actually three things, and you know I can get confused." He sighed and shook his head because he had a shot with her now, and he wasn't going to play around with the truth. Charm hadn't worked on her. It was time to see if being real would. "It wouldn't have worked."

"How do you know?"

"Because Seraphina told me the B and B is booked for the whole week," he replied. "They aren't simply here for the afternoon and they'll be gone tomorrow. You have to deal with them for a full week. Do you honestly believe they won't talk to people around town?"

Her jaw tightened, a sure sign that she was frustrated and on the edge. "They could have been handled. And they'll still talk. What happens when they casually mention you're my boyfriend? People will laugh."

Had she learned nothing? Papillon residents stuck together. They had to because they didn't have anyone else. He pulled his cell out of his back pocket and dialed his sister's number. "Sera, I need you to do me a favor. I'm putting you on speaker. I'm here with Roxie."

"Of course." Sera's voice came over the line. His sister always sounded chipper these days thanks to her marriage to Harrison Jefferys. "Is she okay? I heard she nearly got kidnapped by a rougarou. You should know that particular rumor has already gotten to Gene, and he will be watching her the next full moon."

Roxie's eyes had gone wide. "What? It was a snake. And

it only got my boot. Does Gene actually think I'm going to turn into a werewolf?"

"Yes. Harry told me there was a spirited discussion about your fate at Dixie's this morning. Gene argued his werewolf position, but Herve and his brother claim a witch sent the rougarou so she can take control of Roxanne's body and arrest whoever she wants, even innocent people. Now, I think Herve is setting that whole scenario up in case anyone finds out that he and his brother set up a fight club in his garage. Don't worry about that, Roxie. No one is dumb enough to actually join in, so it ends up with Herve and Louis punching each other a couple of times and then everyone drinking some sketchy wine. But Herve's girlfriend is worried about witchcraft ever since they got Wi-Fi out there and they started using Louis's Netflix account. So he's setting himself up an alibi. Harry, did anyone mention a snake? No. The snake must have gotten lost somewhere in there. But I will tell you there's a rumor going around that Caroline caught Roxie trying to get Archie alone in the barn in the middle of the night."

Roxie groaned. "I did not. I was investigating a call. I checked out the barn but Archie wasn't with me. Zep was. We heard something out back and found a dog tied to a tree, and then I fell and got bitten by a snake. I also hit my head on a log and have a minor concussion."

His sister sighed over the line. "Poor puppy. Is he okay?"

"He's a she," Zep corrected. "And her name is Daisy, and Roxie is okay, too."

"Oh, sorry. I knew that, though," Sera admitted. "I saw Lisa earlier and she'd already talked to her sister. She said Lila said Roxie was okay and that you had taken it on yourself to make sure she stays that way. Roxie, is he bugging you?"

"No," he said.

"Yes," Roxie replied at the same time.

"Do you want me to help you?" he asked.

"I wanted you to help me when I thought you were going to help me the way I wanted you to help me. You went rogue," Roxie accused.

"No, I pivoted," he explained. "Listen, Sera, I need your help. Those folks who checked in today are Roxie's family, and her mother is a lot to handle."

"Don't I know it," Sera replied. "She's already had me change the sheets, ensure all the bathroom equipment is functioning properly, and prove we have Internet out here. She asked if I knew what the Internet was. But the dad seems pretty nice."

"I'm sorry," Roxie said with a wince. "My mom is a lot. And she caught me unaware."

"See, Roxie has been telling her momma she has a boyfriend so she wouldn't worry." He didn't completely understand, but he thought that was the gist of it.

"Oh, I bet worry was the least of her problems. I bet that woman would matchmake." Sera proved she understood far better than he did because Roxie was nodding as his sister continued. "I get it. If I hadn't been living with my momma when I was single, I would have tried the same thing. I would have totally made up a spectacular . . . Oh, no. Her momma's going to want to meet the boyfriend. Who doesn't exist."

"Well, see, I'm not so great at making stuff up." Roxie bit her bottom lip.

"She told her mom she was dating Armie." It was best to put it all out there. "So when Momma King showed up this afternoon, she got me instead of Armie. Luckily I wasn't wearing a shirt at the time and I distracted her with my manly chest, but we need a plan in place now."

"Does Armie know you fake dated him?" Sera asked.

"No." Roxie had gone the sweetest shade of pink. "So if we can leave that out, it would be great."

"Do you honestly believe your mother won't mention him? She won't complain about how he treated you even though she has no real idea about how he treated you?" Her silence was his answer. "So here's the play. Sera, I need you to get on the emergency line and let everyone know we've got a citizen in extreme trouble. Here's the story we're putting out. She and Armie dated for a while. It fizzled out because he's obviously too old for her, and then he married Lila, who he is perfect for."

"I don't think Armie will like that," Roxie interrupted.

But he wasn't about to stop now. They were on a timeline and it was short. All that had to happen was the Kings deciding to stop at the local convenience store where Effie Charles would ask for their whole life story and inevitably blow their cover. "Roxie and I fell for each other a couple of months ago, and we recently moved in together and adopted a dog we named Daisy. We're very happy and I consult with the Papillon Parish Sheriff's Department on situations involving animals. So we live together and work together."

"Does Armie know that?" his sister asked. "The working at the station part, or are you just planning on hanging around there?"

His sister didn't always have faith in his work ethic. "I'll have you know Armie did ask me to be on call. So there."

Sera was quiet for a moment. "Just like Dad?"

"Yeah." He straightened up because he couldn't get emotional right now. "So you'll do it?"

"Roxie, you want me to do this?" Sera asked because she had some girl power thing going.

"I don't even know what you're doing but I'm kind of at a loss here, so yeah," Roxie admitted.

"Then I'm on it. I'll text you when it's done." His sister hung up.

"What did I agree to do?" Roxie was still looking at him like she wasn't sure if she was going to murder him.

"Sera will call Dixie and our sister-in-law Lisa. She'll tell them our cover story. Dixie and Lisa will then call two others each, and before the hour is up, everyone will know the story we want them to tell. Don't worry. Whoever calls Gene will go over the story ten times to make sure he doesn't shove something weird in there. In a few minutes we'll be bulletproof." It was not the first time the town had come together to protect one of their own. "I think you should call and talk to Armie, though."

"Yeah, I'll call him in a minute." She looked a little shocked. "Why would they do that for me?"

He shrugged. "Why wouldn't they? Everyone's told a little lie from time to time. Especially to keep a momma calm. In the beginning they'll do it because we asked them to, but you'll get some lectures about being honest with your momma. Then they'll meet your momma. Unless you think your momma will come off better in public."

Roxie shook her head. "She won't. She'll be awful."

He'd been planning on that. "Then they'll do it because you're one of us and we protect our own."

"But I'm not from here. I don't even have many friends here."

"So? Do you think anyone really likes Celeste Beaumont? She's mean. Nicer in the last few months but mean, and yet the whole town came out to help her when her husband died. I'm sure she tossed every casserole brought to her door, but they were brought." Did she think people around town didn't like her? She always seemed so confident, but he knew that could often hide insecurity. "Roxie, the people here know what you do for them."

She waved that off. "I break up bar fights. I hand out tickets."

"And you risked your own life to save three people caught in a flash flood a few months ago. No one's forgotten that." It had been the night his sister had gotten trapped on the other side of the highway with Harry. The storm had been sudden, and the sheriff and his deputies had done heroic things that evening. Roxie had risked getting swept away by fast-moving flood waters. She'd put herself out there and gotten all three of the passengers in that car to safety.

"It's my job."

He shook his head and moved in. "It's more than that. It's who you are. You're the one who runs in when everyone else is running out. You put yourself between people and danger, and you don't think twice about it. You might be a little standoffish, but that's the only thing keeping you from having a bunch of friends. How many people in town have invited you to supper?"

"A lot. I thought maybe they wanted me to not give them tickets or something."

He should have found a way to get in her life earlier. It would have saved her so much trouble. "No. They're trying to offer you hospitality. And some of the mommas are probably trying to see if you would do for their sons."

She groaned. "Well, then I'm glad I didn't go. It's weird, right? Inviting someone you don't know to dinner."

She only thought that way because she hadn't gotten used to small-town life yet. The odd thing was, this current crisis might force her to face some of the good things that could come from living in Papillon. "Not around here it isn't. After all, how would you get to know a person? All I'm trying to say is they'll help you. You don't have to worry. It's already in motion."

"I know I should thank you."

He wanted her to rely on him. "You don't have to. I would do this for you no matter what."

She stood there as the moment lengthened. He could practically feel the air crackle between them. He knew what chemistry felt like, and this went far beyond the mere physical. They worked on so many levels. He had to find a way to make her understand.

She huffed suddenly. "You know you didn't have to live here. The story works perfectly fine without you living here. In fact, it would have worked best if you'd been a guy I just started dating. That would have been a good scenario."

But then she would be able to keep her distance. "How would you have explained me being at your place with you in your PJs and me without a shirt on? We'd obviously spent the night together."

One side of her mouth tugged up in an adorable smirk. "Since you outed me for the concussion, we could have been coworkers who are barely dating and you did me a favor."

"Wouldn't have worked. There's no way your parents would've believed that."

She frowned suddenly. "Well, we could have said anything at all since my mom couldn't see past your chest. Do you ever wear a shirt?"

Sweet jealousy. He could work with that. "I'm more comfortable this way. And you need to follow my lead on this one. I'm excellent at crafting a fiction. I've got the whole thing down. See, in my head, we're real close. We're definitely a very affectionate couple."

"No, we're not. We're super casual. Almost like bros."

He moved in again and noticed she didn't move away. "Nah, we're definitely in that 'crazy in love, can't keep our hands off each other' stage."

She turned her face up and put her hand out. She touched his chest, her palm open. She didn't push him away, merely kept her hand there, right over his heart. "Is that what we are? Fake us, that is?"

His whole body started to hum. That was what being close to her did to him. He felt parts of him that had been dead so long come to life. It was about far more than his body. "Absolutely. And think of all the benefits."

"Oh, there are benefits to you getting your hands on me?"

"Yes. So many benefits, the chief one being you can't talk to your mother if you're too busy kissing me." He leaned over, coming close. "We'll be that couple everyone avoids because we can put on a show, if you know what I mean."

"I'm going to regret this, but I've been thinking about us."

He liked the sound of that. He hoped. "What have you been thinking about?"

Her hand came down, but she moved toward him. "I've been thinking about that night."

"Are you ready to talk about it?" He reached up and smoothed back her hair, his arousal tamping down a bit because the emotional stuff was more important. And even thinking that made him wince inwardly, but he soldiered on. "Because I think about that night a whole lot."

"I don't know there's all that much to talk about, but it was good," she started before her phone rang. She reached into her pocket and then she was walking away from him. "Hey, boss. I'm glad you called because I have something I need to . . . Oh, so you've heard. Yeah, I can explain . . ."

She moved around him, walking back to the stairs.

So close and yet so far away.

Daisy whined. Zep looked down and the dog was staring up at him. He fished a treat out of his pocket. He would have to grab some things from his place if they were going to stay here for the week.

"She was talking about sex." He sank down to Roxie's couch. Daisy was immediately on top of him, snuggling down and turning over for a belly rub. At least one female in his life was paying attention to him. "I think we're going to have to work on this, girl. You like it here?"

Daisy's eyes had closed and her body had gone still as though she would do absolutely nothing that might disrupt her belly rub.

"Yeah, I do, too, but it's not going to be easy to get her to let us stay." He was talking to a dog, but then he'd spent an enormous amount of his life talking to animals. Luckily none of them had talked back, except that one time he'd tried Herve's wine. "You do your thing. Look real cute and give her completely unconditional love. I'll handle the rest."

They were going to finish that conversation. Tonight.

# *chapter four*

"Do you think Daisy's okay?" Roxie asked as Zep pulled into the parking space. The lot in front of Guidry's Bar and Grill didn't have actual lines on it. Spaces were more suggestions, which meant people parked like hell, and there wasn't a thing she could do about it. But then it was about more than the crazy parking. She kind of wanted to ticket the golf cart that was parked on the grass in front of the playground. That thing couldn't possibly be street legal.

"I think she's miserable in her crate because she wants to be with people all the time, but she'll get used to it," Zep said, putting the truck in park.

She really did like his truck. She also liked Guidry's, but her family was in there and she was about to find out if this insane plan of Zep's was going to work. "She'll get used to being miserable?"

He turned in his seat. "No. She's not miserable in the crate. The crate is way more luxurious than your apartment. You basically bought out the pet department. She's comfy."

They'd driven into Houma and found a big-box store. Zep had tried to tell her Daisy didn't need much, but it had been a long time since she'd had anyone to spend money on. It had felt good to buy Daisy a crate, a fluffy bed, way too many squeaky toys, and some cute bowls. And treats and food. And a collar, and then she'd had to make one of those little engraved dog tags.

"The reason she's miserable," Zep continued, "is that she's worried we won't come back."

Well, the poor puppy had been staked out and left for dead. Of course she was worried. At the store they'd been able to scan Daisy for a microchip. She hadn't had one. They'd stopped by a vet and had her checked out. Beyond being a bit underweight, she was healthy.

"Once she realizes we'll come back, she'll calm down and she won't howl like that. Eventually she'll see her crate as a nice place to rest," Zep promised. "The important thing is we always come home and let her out. It will take time, but she'll learn to trust."

Maybe she and Daisy had a few things in common. "I don't know if I should keep her. I work long hours."

"Do you want to keep her? If you don't, then you just spent a ton of money on a dog you don't want. Are you worried the owner is going to show up and want her back?"

"If that asshole shows up, I'll arrest him," she declared. "It's illegal to tie a dog up in any way that threatens the dog's life and health. I'd love for him to show up and try to take Daisy."

"I don't think he will, warrior princess. But that wasn't the question. Do you want to keep her? It's okay if you don't. I can take her and I'll find someone. I won't take her to a shelter. I'll keep her with me until the right family comes along. I'm pretty good at matching people and pets."

She was already in love with the dog. Even though the little Lab had already started chewing on the furniture. Luckily she was pretty neat and organized. There wasn't much for Daisy to mess with, which was likely why the toys she'd bought had been a huge hit. She'd spent the hour before they had to go to dinner playing tug with the dog.

It had been a nice day after her parents had gone back to the B and B. The conversation with Armie had been awkward. He'd laughed his ass off and teased her about their failed love affair. Then she'd been left with Zep, who she'd worried would press her.

Instead he'd made her some toast and coffee and offered to drive into Houma to get the supplies they would need for the dog. They'd gotten Daisy in the back and spent the nicest afternoon she could remember. They'd wandered through the store and she'd watched as Zep had patiently started teaching Daisy to walk on a leash. He never once lost his cool, never seemed to get frustrated with the puppy. When she misbehaved, he used a firm voice. When she was good, he gave her a treat. That bag he'd shown up with the night before contained a bunch of treats, as though he would try to make friends with any creature he came upon. He'd taken Roxie to a tiny place that sold sandwiches, and she'd discovered she liked shrimp po'boys. They'd eaten them in a park and he'd told her more about his dad.

He hadn't pushed her. He hadn't tried to get her into a position where they got physical. It was odd because knowing that everyone thought they were pretending had helped her relax around him. She hadn't been scared someone would judge her for being with him or laugh for thinking she might be able to keep him. She'd simply let herself be, and it had been lovely.

But she knew this couldn't last. "I work twelve-hour shifts sometimes. I don't think that's fair to a dog."

"So? Take her with you. As long as she's properly trained, no one is going to mind having a dog up at the station house.

Hell, Lila has Peanut at the clinic with her most days. We'll get Daisy a police dog vest and then you can put her on the payroll."

Sometimes Peanut came in with Armie. Peanut was a sweet golden retriever mix who usually slept at the sheriff's feet. Would anyone care if she brought her dog to work? In the past it would have been wholly unprofessional, but professional meant something different here.

What would happen if she decided to try to get on in New Orleans again? She definitely wouldn't be able to take Daisy to work with her there. Was she being hasty?

"Hey, how about we consider you her foster mom for now?" Zep offered. "We'll keep her at your place until your parents leave and then we'll decide. Like I said, she can always come with me."

"Shouldn't you ask your mom?"

He sat up a little straighter. "I do not live with my mother."

She stared at him.

"I live in an apartment above the garage, thank you very much."

It was good to remember he was a manchild. He had no ambition beyond where he was going to grab his next beer and find a woman for the night. "Yeah, well, I still think you should probably ask your mom."

"I've been keeping animals for a long time. My momma is used to it." He stared at her for a moment, studying her. "Is that why you wouldn't go out with me again? You think I live with my mother because I can't afford anything else?"

"I didn't go out with you in the first place. Drinking a lot and falling into bed together isn't a date. Not in my world. Also, you didn't actually ask me on a date. I believe you said, 'Hey, Roxie, let's do this again sometime,'" she replied simply.

It was likely what he said to every single woman he slept

with. She often wondered if she'd told him, "Yeah, sure," would he have spent the last year pursuing her? Or would he have drifted on to the next woman without another thought to her?

"Huh. I guess I did say that, but that wasn't what I meant." He sighed. "I haven't spent a lot of time dating in the last couple of years. I know you think I'm living at home because I'm some kind of loser, but I did it because my sister needed help. Now I do it because my mother's getting older. She hasn't lived alone in fifty years, and the house is a lot to keep up. I stay over the garage because I need my space. It's why I haven't gotten serious about anyone. No one wants a boyfriend who has to drop everything because his sister needs someone to babysit for her."

"I didn't say you were a loser." But she'd thought it. And of course, she had to think about what he considered helping. She could see a world where Zep put everything on hold so he could "help" out. If she was going to have any kind of relationship with him, she had to accept the fact that he wasn't a man like the ones she'd known. He was unfocused, unambitious, and maybe unreliable.

Though she had to admit he was helping her out now, and he hadn't drowned her in judgment. He'd accepted her explanation easily and done everything he could to help her out.

A wistful look came over his face and she wanted so badly to reach out and touch him. "You wouldn't be the first."

She unbuckled her belt, and despite all the alarm bells going off, she moved closer to him. "I didn't want to date anyone at the time. And you said it yourself, you don't date much at all, so let's call it what it is. You wanted to know why I didn't hook up with you again. As it so happens, I've been wondering that myself."

She'd thought about it all day. Why shouldn't she indulge herself every now and then? They could keep it quiet. It wasn't anyone's business but their own, and from what she could tell, Zep wasn't bad at keeping secrets. She hadn't heard about his conquests in a long time.

"Wondering what?" he asked.

"If we shouldn't use this time to decide if we can make it work. I'm not seeing anyone. I assume you're not seeing anyone."

His smile went from wistful to wolfish in a heartbeat. "I'm not seeing anyone, Roxanne."

She should run because just the way he said her name made her shiver. She wasn't the type of woman who shivered with desire. Nope. Sex was a bodily function and it was good, but it shouldn't make her go all gooey on the inside at the thought.

It had been too long. That was the problem. When she'd slept with him before, she'd been overly emotional. It had been the anniversary of her divorce, and that had colored her view. This time she could put the experience where she should have that night. It would be sex and nothing more. A booty call. A mutually beneficial experience.

The fact that his truck was so old made it easy to move closer to him. It had an old-school bench as the front seat. There was nothing there to stop him from sliding her way. Nothing to stop her from doing the same until they met in the middle.

"You want to give us a shot?" His hand moved to cup the side of her face.

It was taking a chance on her part. "I think it could work. We don't even have to be discreet right now. Why don't you kiss me? It's part of our cover. I think you promised me if I was kissing you, I didn't have to talk to my mother."

He was so close, she could feel the warmth of his body. He leaned in, his mouth hovering over hers. "I did promise you that. I don't want to be known as a man who doesn't keep his promises."

His hand moved to the nape of her neck, sending a spark of arousal down her spine right before he kissed her.

His lips brushed hers and a soft warmth spread through her body. It had been so long since anyone had touched her in an affectionate way. Not since the last time this man had taken her into his arms. That was the only reason her body seemed electric. That was the only reason her heart seemed to soften. He kissed her slowly at first, as though he was willing to take all the time in the world because nothing was more important than this moment and this kiss. His fingers threaded through her hair. She'd left it down because if she didn't, her mother would talk endlessly about how she would never attract a man if she didn't look feminine. But now she was glad because she loved the way he lightly gripped her, using her hair to gently move her the way he wanted.

She let her hands drift to his chest, that gorgeous chest she'd seen a hundred times because he didn't like to wear a shirt. Especially when it was hot, and it almost always was hot. She would drive by the house he'd grown up in and he would be mowing the yard wearing nothing but jeans and boots.

He was wearing a button-down now. He'd dressed up for dinner. She hadn't even known he owned a pair of slacks, but they'd been in the duffel bag he'd brought to her place earlier this afternoon. She felt the soft material under her hands, but it wasn't a substitute for skin. She could still remember the way his skin felt against hers. She wanted to feel that heat again.

"Do you have any idea how long I've wanted to kiss you

again?" Zep whispered against her lips. "I've been thinking about this for over a year. It's even better than I remembered."

He deepened the kiss, his tongue surging into her mouth, and the kiss went from sweet to sinful in a heartbeat.

She forgot where she was. All that mattered was getting more. More kisses. More touches. More of him.

No one in all her life could make her forget the world the way this man could, and for that reason alone she knew she should stop, should run as fast as she could, but denial hadn't worked.

She could have her cake and eat it, too. Everyone thought they were pretending. No one had to know that at least part of it was real.

"One week," she said. "We can have a whole week to work this out."

Work him out of her system. Maybe if she could get over this crazy desire for him, she could move on.

"We will," he promised. "We will work this out, Rox. You'll see."

A little warning bell went off in the back of her head, but he was kissing her again and any doubt flew straight out of her brain. He started to press her against the seat.

Before she could go any further, there was a knock on the window, and it was like the whole world stopped.

Zep sat back with a frown. "We've got company."

She turned and her mother was standing there waving her hand, a wild look in her eyes. "Roxanne! Roxanne! There's an alligator. It's in the parking lot. We can't get Shawna out of the car. Does your boyfriend have a gun? Everyone has a gun down here, right? Your father is calling 911."

She rolled her eyes even as she opened the window. "It's

just Otis. He suns himself on the big rock. He fell asleep and forgot to go back out into the water. Please don't call 911."

She could hear the guys ribbing her over dealing with an Otis sighting. Or they would all be horrified at her family because the minute the police got involved, her father would criticize everything. Nothing would be up to his standards, and he would let them know.

"I've got to deal with this," she said, straightening her shirt.

"It's okay." Zep opened the door. "I can handle this one." He slid out and walked toward her mother. "Now, Mrs. King, don't you worry about that old gator. That's Otis and he's a sweetheart, but I know he can be scary. I'll go get my brother and we'll move him so you can have a nice dinner."

Her mother had visibly calmed the minute Zep stepped out of the truck.

Roxie climbed out, her only halfway feminine shoes hitting the gravel of the parking lot and reminding her why not a lot of people wore heels to go to Guidry's. "You know I've dealt with Otis, too."

He looked back and winked her way. "Baby, you direct traffic around Otis. I have to actually physically move that sucker. I should probably take off my shirt. Wouldn't want to get sweaty."

"You're such a nice man," her mother said as she followed Zep. "But aren't you worried? That is a very large reptile."

"It's all part of the service, ma'am." The charm oozed off him.

Roxie nearly turned an ankle in her heels.

"Call me Pamela," her mother said, putting a hand on his arm. "I'm not so old, you know. Roxanne, come on. We need to go tell Shawna the men can handle this. I need a drink. Please tell me they have vodka here. It's not one of those dry places, is it? I've heard they have those down here because they're religious. I don't understand that. If God didn't want us to drink, why would Jesus make all that wine?"

Roxie watched as Zep escorted her mother in and she was left to make her way across the lot. This was what Zep did, and it was so good to get a reminder. That charm wasn't simply for her. It was for every woman he met. He was a flirt, a player of the highest order, and just because he was willing to spend a week with her didn't mean he would be hers.

Yes, one week. She could get him out of her system in a week.

She had to.

Zep glanced back at the patio of Guidry's. The sun was starting to go down, the dimming light shimmering over the water. The restaurant overlooked the small bay where his great-grandfather had built a marina complete with a bait store and mechanic shop. The restaurant had come later. He'd spent a lot of time in those shops when he was a kid. Remy had always loved working the restaurant, but Zep had preferred the laid-back boat repair business. He could fix a lot of things as long as they had engines.

That was him. Jack-of-all-trades. Master of none.

"Okay, so I'm trying to wrap my brain around this," his big brother said as he joined him. He'd been working in the back office when Zep had explained they needed to move Otis so the out-of-towners wouldn't freak. No one from Papillon would pay the big gator any mind. If anything, they would be happy to see him because if he was hanging out at Guidry's, he wasn't blocking the damn highway. "Roxie King, who is one of the toughest, most no-nonsense women I've ever met in my life, convinced you to be her new fake boyfriend because her old fake boyfriend—who also happens to be her boss—got married in real life. Did Armie know he was her fake boyfriend?"

Remy approached the big gator, whose head came up.

"Well, he does now." Zep got into position. It wasn't the first time they'd had to convince Otis to sun himself somewhere else. The sun was going down and Otis would move on, but he couldn't explain to Roxie's parents that the reptile had a schedule and was polite enough to keep it.

He was expecting a pretty severe lecture from his brother. Remy viewed him the way everyone else did. He was a joke. Charming and attractive and fairly useless unless one was having a party, and then he was the life of it. "Armie took it pretty well. Lila told Rox that there are days she'll loan him back to her. That woman doesn't get fazed by anything."

"No, she doesn't, but I'm a little surprised." Remy gave him that look, the one that let him know the lecture was about to begin.

This was his life. He was standing at a big gator's tail end waiting to get yelled at by his brother. If Otis chose to be stubborn, he would have to grab that gator tail and drag him away. He'd gotten all prettied up, and if he got muddy, he would be the one giving a lecture. To a gator.

Was it any surprise no one took him seriously?

"What was I supposed to do? She doesn't want her mother to think she's single. You met Pamela. She's a lot to take. You're right. Roxie is a steady woman. If she's rattled by this, if she thinks her mother could disrupt her life, then I'm going to believe her."

Remy sent him a stare he would likely one day use on

whatever kiddos he and Lisa had. It was the look that told anyone on the receiving end that they should start telling the truth. "I want to know why she had to turn to you in the first place. Tell me why you were still at her house at two in the afternoon. You could have left. You could have had her neighbor look in on her. Darlene has a key to her place."

He hadn't even considered it. Even when he'd realized he would have to catch any rest he would get in that too-small chair she had in her too-small bedroom. "Lila told me to stay with her. Even if she hadn't, I would have stayed. I wanted to make sure she was okay."

Otis's big mouth came open as if he was yawning. Yep, he was right on time.

"You wanted to get close to her any way you possibly could." Remy managed to make the statement as accusatory as possible. "You've been chasing that woman for over a year. I want to make sure you're not manipulating the situation to trick her into giving you what you want."

That was a kick to the gut. "And what do I want, Remy? You think I want to trick her into bed with me? I'm trying to think of some other nefarious purpose I could have for upending my life, adopting a dog, and looking like a fool in front of the whole town."

Otis lifted his big body up. At least one thing was going right.

"Why would you look like a fool?" Remy started to follow Otis down the path that would take him into the bayou.

Zep could think of a hundred reasons why. He almost always looked like the fool, but most of the time people didn't look at him with pity. "Because I'm chasing a woman who tells everyone she meets that she doesn't want me. Maybe I'm looking for revenge."

Remy's gaze softened. "Stop, little brother. I know what you want and it's not revenge. You want her. You're crazy about her. You think I don't know how long it's been since you spent the night with a woman?"

Otis picked up the pace as they neared the place where the bayou and bay merged. "You keep track of me?"

"There are only a couple of places close by where you can get a drink. I know you go to that bar at the edge of town a lot," Remy admitted. "I asked Cain to keep an eye on you."

Cain Cunningham was the bartender at The Back Porch, Zep's bar of choice lately. Mostly because he worked at the other place to get a beer close to town. "It's good to know I always have eyes on me. A little like a kid, huh?"

"I'm worried about you, and I definitely worry about that bar. Zep, you're drifting. You don't want to spend the rest of your life taking shifts here. It's not what you love. I want you to consider working down at the shop for a while. Willie's planning on retiring in a few years. You work under him for a while and learn how to run the shop and the marina. How does that sound?"

It sounded awful. He liked working on cars and boats, but only as a hobby. He liked keeping up his truck, but it wasn't what he wanted to do with his life. And yet his brother would erupt in laughter if he told him what he'd been thinking about doing.

He'd been thinking about going back to school. Try to get his degree so he might have a shot at working with animals. Becoming a park ranger required a surprising amount of school.

He hadn't cracked a book in forever. Worst of all, he didn't have the money to afford it.

"I'm working with the parish," he said quietly. "Armie wants someone to help with animal calls."

"That's great, but it's not a career. Unless he's going to put you on full time," Remy prompted.

That wasn't about to happen, and they hadn't even talked

about pay. He might be volunteering. "Nah. He'll call me when he needs me."

Like now. He might get called in to calm down tourists who didn't realize Otis was far too lazy to eat either them or their small pets. Not unless the pet lay down in front of him and didn't fight. He'd once watched Otis stare down a ferocious Chihuahua and then run as fast as his four legs would take him.

"That works perfectly with a job at the shop," Remy pointed out. "If you need to go, you can go. That's the beauty of working here. In a couple of years, you'll be your own boss."

Well, it wasn't like he was the world's greatest server. He didn't have a passion for it or anything. Maybe he should take his brother's advice and help out. "Sure. Have Willie put me on the schedule for the week after next."

They watched Otis amble off.

"You don't have to look like it's the end of the world. Zep, you have to settle down and find a job. I know how much you've helped out at home. Sera was lucky you didn't want to leave here like most kids do, but she's fine now. You need to be more like her. You need to settle on something."

Sera hadn't settled at all. Sera was living her dream, and it had been handed to her on a silver platter. Not that she hadn't deserved it, but it had come out of nowhere. She'd inherited the gorgeous mansion of a house she now ran as a bed and breakfast, and she'd married a man who was more than happy to work on it with her. His siblings were building something for their futures.

Zep would be what everyone always thought he would be. He would be the burden. He would be the one who was lucky his brother could give him a job. "Sure. I'll try to be more like you and Sera."

"I think Roxie might look at you differently if she

thought you were serious. You can't coast on your looks for the rest of your life."

"You know I did pretty well in community college." The words were out of his mouth before he could think about it.

Remy's brow rose. "You want to go back to school?"

Yes, he did, but he couldn't figure out how to pay for it at this point. Everything he'd saved before, he'd used to help pay the medical bills for Luc's birth. Not that he'd ever mentioned that to Remy. "Nah. Wouldn't know what to do with an education anyway. I'll work at the shop. But you should know that Roxie and I are going to explore this thing between us. She told me that's what she wanted."

His brother turned back to him, his body shadowed as the sun went down, and for a moment he could see his father standing there. "She said she wants to date you?"

He shook off the odd feeling.

"She said we should take this week and see if we work." Except that wasn't exactly what she'd said. "She said we should see if it could work. But I assume she means the relationship. Then she let me kiss her in the parking lot. That's practically a declaration of intent since everyone knows how nosy people are. It's not like people will politely avert their eyes." The public display of affection had done a lot to ease his mind. If she didn't care about someone seeing them kissing, she was getting used to the idea of being with him.

Otis seemed to be well on his way to whatever nighttime plans he had, so it was time to get back to Roxie. He turned and started up the drive.

Remy was right on his heels. "You're sure she wasn't talking about her fake boyfriend plan? Her parents are here for a week. She's giving it a week to see if it can work. How do you know she wasn't talking about you taking over for Armie as her cover?"

That wasn't what she'd meant at all. Was it? She couldn't kiss him the way she had and have been talking about anything but giving them a real shot. "I don't think so." He hadn't talked to his brother about his relationship with Roxie. Remy had been happily married for a while. Maybe he could help. "You know we've been together before."

"The rumor around town is that you hooked up with her and then moved on like you always do, and she gets a little revenge on you by arresting you for everything under the sun. I think you push her to arrest you because you know you made a mistake by treating her like every other woman you hooked up with."

He should have known that was the rumor. He wouldn't be surprised if Roxie had heard that one, too. "It isn't true. I asked her out the next morning. Hell, I'm pretty sure I told her I was serious before she went to sleep that night. With me. I spent all night with her, and I don't normally do that. I made a connection with her that night, one I never felt before. She turned me down and ignored me every time I asked her out. The arrests are the only thing that gave me hope, and yes, I know how stupid that sounds. But she never actually presses charges. She's a careful woman. She knows I'm a bad bet, but I'm going to show her that I can take care of her."

"In bed," his brother said.

Frustration welled inside Zep. "And out of it. Do you have any idea how hard it is to keep her mother's attention? The minute I let it go, she's all over Roxie. In the brief time before I came out here, that woman complained about Roxie's hair, questioned her skin care regime, asked why she wore those shoes, and if there was a place to buy clothes here. Like we don't have clothes."

"You know how people who've never been out of the city can be," Remy said with a chuckle. "Though people who've never been out of Papillon are just as bad. Give her some time and she'll settle down. From what I heard, Roxie hasn't been home to see her family in a couple of years."

"What do you know about why she moved down here?" He was curious about what stories had gotten around town.

"The usual," Remy said with a grin. "There were all sorts of stories flying around when she moved here. She fled the city because she was looking for the Lord. She's hiding from the mob. That's my favorite. I've heard some city man broke her heart."

They made it back to the restaurant, but Zep paused outside the door. "The way I heard it, a couple of things happened. I know she lost her partner on the job. That's got to be tough. She got divorced. She doesn't talk about it much. She told me he was a cop, too, and it would have been hard to stay on the job after they broke up."

"Have you thought about the fact that she might not belong here?" Remy asked, sympathy plain in his tone. "That she might be using this job and this place as a way to lick her wounds? What she went through with her partner is hard. I know because when I was in the Navy, we lost a man, and I've never truly gotten over it. Still, she was on a highly specialized team in the NYPD. It's the kind of job only the most focused and ambitious people go for. I worry there's not much to be ambitious about here."

He'd thought about it a lot, but he couldn't believe she would walk away. "You're worried she's going to wake up one day and realize it's time to get back to her real life. But you're wrong. She'll settle in."

His brother was staring at him. "Now I'm really worried."

"What did I do?" Zep seemed to be pushing all of his brother's buttons today.

"You're more invested in this than I thought."

Had his brother not been listening? "I told you. I'm

crazy about her. I want this to work. You're right. It is time to settle down. Some people settle down around a job, a career. Maybe I want to settle down with a woman. Maybe I want her to be the center of my world, and I'll do whatever I have to do to make that happen. Maybe making Roxie happy is my reason for living."

His brother went silent, and it was a moment before he reached for the door. "I hope she lets you, brother. I think you should take this week to talk to her about what you want, what she wants. Don't assume you know what a woman wants deep down. I did and it cost me and Lisa a lot of time we could have spent together."

He knew his brother's story. He'd made assumptions about the woman who would become his wife, and he'd been so wrong. But Zep had made a careful study of Roxanne King. His problem was the opposite of what Remy and Lisa faced in the beginning. "You're worried she doesn't truly want me."

"I'm worried she doesn't understand you yet," Remy explained. "You don't let anyone in. I know you get frustrated because you think no one sees you, but you're the one who hides behind a mask. You're the one who smiles and charms and never gets real with anyone. Until you do, you can't expect her to pick you because she doesn't know you."

"Everyone knows me." It wasn't like he was an introvert.

"No. I don't think anyone truly knows you, little brother. I'm going to give you some advice, and then I promise I will let you be. If you care about Roxie, be vulnerable with her. Show her all the places where you ache. It's the only way you'll know if she's the one who can ease you."

Remy walked inside, but Zep stayed for a moment, his brother's words looming over him.

The thought of being vulnerable made him nearly ill. If he was vulnerable, he would have to be honest with her.

Honest about his hopes and dreams. Honest about why he let them all go.

He wasn't sure he could do it.

He walked in and past the kitchen. When he got to the dining room floor, she was there at a big table, surrounded by her family. Her mother was talking a mile a minute about everything that had happened in New York since Roxie had left. The future sister-in-law nodded and agreed with everything Pamela said. Her father and brother were in a deep conversation, and Roxie turned his way. Her eyes lit up and he was struck by how much he loved looking at her. It wasn't merely about how gorgeous she was. There was something about this woman that comforted him, an inner light within her that spoke to him, focused him.

*Save me*, she mouthed, and then a brilliant smile came over her face.

He practically ran to get to her, sliding into the seat next to hers. "Now that old gator is off for the night and out of our hair." He wasn't going to mention that Sera and Harry saw Otis out by the B and B most nights. Nope. That could be his sister's problem. "We can settle down and I can tell you all about the amazing things your daughter's been doing for the parish. Did she tell you about saving a bunch of people when the clinic was on fire? The old clinic, not the new one."

Pamela's eyes had gone wide. "You were in a fire?"

Roxie shook her head. "It was fine."

"It blew a bunch of oxygen tanks, and she managed to save Armie and Lila." No one ever said he didn't have an excellent imagination, though he was sure Armie would agree Roxie had been intensely helpful that night. Again, she'd run in when everyone else had been running out. "She helped save her ex and his new girlfriend."

"She didn't mention that," Tony said.

"That sounds a lot like the time I chased a perp into a burning warehouse," her brother, Brian, began.

Pamela put out a hand. "Yes, dear, we all know about that. I want to hear about my daughter."

Roxie's hand slid over Zep's and she inched closer to him. "I don't know about that. Zep here has been known to embellish."

He didn't think of it as embellishment. He thought of it as being able to tell a good story, and she'd been at the center of a bunch of them since she'd taken the job here. "Roxie is a hero around these parts."

He leaned in. It was time to save his lady in his own unique fashion.

# chapter five

Roxie sat on the sofa of her living room in the dark, waiting for the front door to open, when her cell phone rang. She sighed and looked down. It wasn't so late that it would be a surprise if someone called her, but she'd had a lot of socializing for the evening. The dinner had gone on and on, with Zep telling story after story about her heroics and how much the town loved her.

She wished it were all true.

Was it even somewhat true? Did she fit in here better than she thought she did?

All evening long she'd had people come up and say hello. She rather thought that had been about Zep. It wasn't like people ignored her, but they flocked to him. They adored him for his shiny good looks and charming personality. He was the center of any gathering he was at, and it hadn't changed because he was new to her family. They'd all hung on his every word. Even her brother, after he'd realized he wasn't going to be allowed to take over the conversation like he normally would. He'd actually seemed a bit impressed at what she'd managed to do in her time here.

If she'd been left to her own devices, she probably would

have gotten annoyed with her mom and started a fight. Instead, she'd had a pleasant evening, and she wanted that to continue. She wanted that kiss to follow through to its natural end.

She glanced down at her cell and realized she would have to answer. She slid her finger across the screen to accept the call. "Hello, Lila. I promise, I'm feeling great."

"No residual nausea?"

Oh, she had a bit but only because her parents weren't leaving anytime soon. "I'm good. And thanks again for letting me tell that dumb story about Armie. I know it seems weird."

"We've all said or done dumb stuff to try to avoid nosy family members from causing trouble. Believe me, I've done it. My siblings are always in each other's business. I've told many a story so I didn't have to hear a lecture. But I was surprised you picked Zep as your new fake boyfriend."

"I didn't," she admitted. "My brilliant plan was to have Zep say he was Armie, shake hands, and then disappear for the remainder of their stay. Sheriffs have lots of work to do."

But then she would have been alone with them this evening. She wouldn't have had someone who talked like she was the sun in the sky. She wouldn't have felt like the center of the universe for once in her life.

Lila whistled. "I don't think that would have worked. It's a small town. It's far too easy to run into people here."

"That's what Zep decided. Without consulting me, he changed up the plan and now we're living together for the next week." She managed to make the words sound desultory even though she knew she was . . . *happy* wasn't the word. *Satisfied. Content.* Ready to exploit the current situation in order to release some sexual tension.

"How is that going to work? Is he there now?"

"No, he's out walking the dog." Daisy had been beyond happy when they'd walked in the door. She'd nearly managed to knock her crate over in her abundant joy.

"You decided to keep the dog? No one told me you were keeping her." Lila gasped as though the important headline had been buried under the irrelevant family drama. Beyond her own family, Lila tended to prefer the company of four-footed creatures to people.

"Yeah, no one's looking for her so I'm going to keep her for now."

"I'm so glad to hear that. She's a sweetheart. I thought Zep would do what he normally does."

Roxie was way too interested in talking about Zep. He was supposed to be the equivalent of a warm male blow-up doll, but she was getting way too invested and she couldn't seem to stop herself. "What do you mean, '*normally* does'?"

"You know he works over at the parish animal shelter, right? He volunteers there a lot, and if he finds strays, he brings them over in hopes of finding the right family for them. The rumor is that he does it because it helps him meet a lot of ladies, but I happen to know he doesn't ever work the front desk. He only works with the animals and the vet from New Orleans when she's there to visit."

He worked at a shelter? He hadn't mentioned that. Or maybe he had. It was clear that he loved animals from the way he handled Daisy. She could also vaguely remember him talking about how much he enjoyed working with animals that night when they'd first hooked up. She'd blown it off as one of those charming things he said to make every woman in a two-mile radius sigh and ignore what a player he was.

She had to remember that. She had to remember that this was what he did. He made everyone feel like he heard them, like he cared about them. Like he made her feel.

That was precisely why she wasn't getting serious about a man like Zep Guidry. But she could have a little fun and break out of this horrible cage she'd been in since the divorce.

Not the divorce. Since her partner died.

"That's cool. I didn't know he worked there. I've met the vet. She seems nice." She was a lovely woman who lived and practiced in New Orleans. She helped out in some of the more rural parishes a couple of times a month.

Was she the reason Zep volunteered his time?

"She is. She's also married and happily so," Lila said.

She was glad Lila couldn't see her because she could feel herself flush. "Why would that matter to me?"

"Because you should know Zep doesn't have a thing for her. From what I can tell, he doesn't have a thing for anyone but you. I see Zep a lot, you know. His brother is married to my sister. Zep's much smarter than anyone—including his family—gives him credit for. Sometimes it takes an outsider to see past, well, to see past a person's past."

Roxie was confused. "What does that mean?"

"It means Zep likes to project a certain image. Okay, not *likes*. He's used to being the hot guy, the cool guy. Remy was the athlete, the solid one. Sera was the pretty, popular girl. Zep learned from a young age that his place was to make people laugh, to make them feel good. After his father died, from what I can tell, he made everyone comfortable. I've had some conversations with my sister and brother-in-law and Remy says he doesn't once remember his brother crying even though he was incredibly close to his dad. But he would hear him at night. He wouldn't cry in front of anyone because he didn't want to upset his mother. He was ten, Roxie. Imagine a ten-year-old boy who is willing to check his own emotions to spare someone he thought needed him to be strong. There's a depth to him that most people miss."

She heard him talking outside and moved to the door. She'd been sitting here wondering how to get what she wanted out of him with the least amount of embarrassment, and that included not directly asking him for what she wanted. She lifted one of the blinds, and sure enough, there was Zep still dressed the way he'd been for dinner. He held Daisy's new leash, which was attached to the red collar Roxie had picked for her earlier in the day, and he was talking to Cal Beaumont, who was in town visiting his mother. Cal was in his car, the window rolled down. Her house was on the way to Beaumont House so it must have been good timing. Cal had been Zep's closest friend for a long time, but he'd recently moved to Dallas for a new job.

Was Zep lonely without his friend?

Well, he'd definitely made another. Daisy was looking up at Zep like he was the most beautiful thing in the world, her head tilted up and her dark eyes filled with puppy love.

"It's not a real relationship," she murmured to Lila. Though she intended it to be real in a physical sense. At least for a while. She could practically feel his lips on hers. She'd thought she remembered everything about that night, thought the experience was branded onto her soul.

That kiss in the parking lot had proven her wrong because that kiss had been even better. That kiss had promised a place for her to forget the world.

"I know you had one briefly."

"We had a one-night stand." Damn the rumor mills. She'd known there had been people who'd seen her with him that night and that the bartender might have talked, but Lila hadn't even been in town back then. The fact that the story was still circulating brought heat to her cheeks.

This was precisely why she hadn't taken him up on his offer of more. Once could be written off as a test drive. From what she could tell, most of the women in Southern

Louisiana had slept with Zep at one time or another. She'd seen them sigh as he walked in a room and giggle behind their hands, likely comparing their nights in his bed.

Jealousy sucked. She had to let go of it because he wasn't a man who settled down.

"All I'm saying is maybe you should consider giving him a real chance," Lila replied.

She wasn't sure she had the choice. Not unless she was willing to come clean with her parents. That would be the only way she could see to avoid the inevitable fact that they would wind up in bed together. If she was honest with herself, she didn't even want to consider letting Zep go. Everyone knew why she was hanging out with him. They understood why he was staying at her place. Would they talk regardless? Yes, but she could face those rumors. "I'm grateful he's helping me."

Outside, Zep stepped back and gave Cal a wave. His shoulders were ridiculously broad but his body was lean. He had a swimmer's build, with long arms that wrapped around her and made her feel oddly safe.

"He's good at helping," Lila said over the line. "I know he's got this terrible reputation, but he didn't earn it. Watch him. Helping is how he shows he cares."

She barely heard the words because he'd turned and was walking up the path that led to her half of the duplex. Daisy walked alongside him, far more sedate than she'd been on the way out. She trotted without the crazed pulling she'd done when he'd first started around the block. He stopped and she tried to keep going, but after a moment she calmed and came back to his side. He reached into his pocket and gave the dog a treat before resuming the walk.

"Well, I would like to see you for a follow-up tomorrow." Lila's voice reminded her that she was supposed to be doing something beyond staring at the gorgeous man who was about to come through her door. "If you don't stop by, I'll track you down, and I won't be in a good mood. Have a nice night."

The line went dead. Sometimes Lila's big-city, no-nonsense, take-no-prisoners attitude was soothing. More and more lately, it was kind of annoying. If anyone else wanted to bend her to their will, they showed up with cookies or a casserole, and only then did they make their very polite demands.

Lila got straight to the point and threatened. She really would show up. Lila LaVigne took her job seriously, and was especially serious about her husband's employees.

The door opened and Zep and Daisy walked in. Daisy took one look at Roxie and acted like they'd been separated for days instead of the fifteen minutes it had taken for Zep to walk her around the neighborhood. Her whole body shook and she barked, trying to get into Roxie's arms.

She got to one knee and gave the puppy some enthusiastic pets. "Hey, sweet girl."

Zep groaned. "She's never going to calm down if you give her attention when she's all riled up."

She frowned at him, narrowly avoiding Daisy's sloppy kisses. "You want me to ignore her when she's happy to see me?"

Zep got to one knee beside her. "I want her to behave, but I like that you don't mind she's hyperactive. But seriously, we've got to train her and part of that is training you. She'll modify her behavior to please you."

She ran her hands over the puppy's body and up to her ears, looking into those deeply trusting eyes. "I don't mind her being happy to see me. But hopefully you'll work with me this week on the potty training. She already seems to be walking on a leash better."

"Oh, she'll forget it all by morning, but then we start it

over again," he said, his lips in a wistful smile. "I can teach you how to train her over the next couple of days. If you've decided you want to foster her for a while."

She really wanted to keep her. But she shouldn't. She shouldn't get attached to anything here. Armie was trying to get her on at New Orleans PD or one of the bigger suburbs. She'd told him she would do three years here to help him get his deputies trained, and then she would get serious about hiring on at a bigger department.

She wouldn't be allowed to keep Daisy with her. Daisy would be in a crate or she would need a pet sitter. That was an option. But she had a plan and it was almost time to put the plan in place. Papillon was a bump in the road.

"Yeah," she heard herself saying. "I mean, unless you don't think it's a good idea. Like I said, I work a lot."

Maybe he would save her from herself. If he told her she could be bad for Daisy, she would let the puppy go.

"And like I said, you can take her with you," Zep reassured her. "Or have someone watch her. Once she's trained, she can be on her own for a while. Dogs sleep a ton during the day, too. All she wants from you is love and food. Dogs don't require much more." His voice had gone husky, as though he'd been talking about something other than Daisy. "Now that we're done with the evening, you want to tell me how you think it went? I hope I held up my end of the bargain."

They had a bargain? From what she could tell, he'd done all the work and gotten nothing out of it but trouble. He'd upended his whole life to help her for a week.

What had Lila said? Zep showed he cared by helping. But shouldn't he get something out of it, too? She could think of a few things she would like to give him.

But first she would tell him what she really thought.

"You were amazing. I think my family is kind of in love with you. Please tell me my mother didn't hit on you more when I wasn't looking. She doesn't actually mean it. She likes to flirt. I think it makes her feel young."

"Your mother was fine." He moved up to the couch and sat back. "She talks real fast, though. I had to pay attention to keep up. Your brother and father seem nice. I couldn't tell much about the fiancée. She just seemed scared of alligators. And pretty much everything else. She didn't eat much."

"Shawna doesn't eat at all." Her brother and Shawna had been dating off and on for five years and not once had she seen that woman eat a full meal. She knew there were women out there who were naturally on the slender side, but Shawna worked hard to keep skinny. It looked good on her and she seemed perfectly content to push her food around. It would likely save her brother a ton of money, and he was always concerned with that. Roxie sank down on the couch with him. "She missed out. The étouffée was delicious tonight. I'm sorry my parents were fussy about the food."

They'd looked over the menu and found something wrong with every single thing, from the fact that the chicken was fried to not understanding what a grit was and what it had to do with shrimp. Remy had offered to grill some chicken and shrimp for them. He'd made some baked potatoes and rice that wasn't dirty since her mother couldn't handle that.

Zep's brows rose. "Oh, I seem to remember a newcomer from the city a while back who didn't know what jambalaya was."

She hadn't been as bad as her mom, but in the beginning she hadn't been familiar with most of the dishes here. "I grew up mostly eating white food. Like literally white food, and really bland, too. My mom was good with chicken breasts and white rice and mashed potatoes. Canned green beans. She wasn't the most imaginative cook."

"Sometimes you have to be open to new experiences." There it was again, that deep tone that made her breath catch because he wasn't merely talking about rice and beans or a muffuletta. "You love jambalaya now."

She loved a lot of things about Papillon now. She shook off that word because she wasn't going to even come close to associating it with Zep Guidry. It would be dangerous to love someone like him, and she didn't do that kind of danger anymore. "It's good. I like it a lot. I like it at Guidry's."

She could like him, too. But only for a little while.

"I know," he replied with a slow, sexy smile. "You like it so much, I even started giving you the local heat."

She gasped because she hadn't changed the way she ordered. She hadn't known there was more than one. "There's only one on the menu. I thought I was already on the local heat. Is that why I had the blandest bowl last Tuesday?"

"I wasn't in that day. I left a note, but if your server wasn't Lisa, then they probably ignored it," he explained, his hand stroking down Daisy's body. The puppy looked perfectly content to be sitting between the two of them. "And I would like to point out that bowl you had on Tuesday was the same recipe you started out on."

She shook her head. "No. It was so bland. Have you been sneaking cayenne pepper in?"

"No. I would go into the kitchen and mix the tourist jambalaya with the one Remy makes for locals. It wasn't much at first. Just half a scoop. You seemed to like it. You're now eating the local stuff exclusively."

It was weird but she was kind of proud of that since she'd always been told she wouldn't like spicy food. Her father talked about how it gave him heartburn and her mother wouldn't touch it. "Why would you do that? Were you trying to see if you could get me to lose my cool?"

He frowned as though the idea had never occurred to him. "No. I thought you would like it, but I would never give the local stuff to an out-of-towner unless I knew for a fact they could handle it. Remy believes firmly in an amount of cayenne it takes a while to build up to. I got the idea because when Lila first came to town, Lisa started cutting her normal coffee with chicory, and Lila eventually came to love it. Sometimes it's all that's available in some homes. I know it seems sneaky, and if you hadn't liked it the first time, I would have told you what I did and had you try it without any pepper."

He'd tried to ease her way. "So you do this for everyone? Is it a Guidry's tradition?"

"Not at all. Remy gave me hell when he caught me doing it. I just thought you would like it. We sometimes run out of the other, but we always have the local stuff. At first that bland jambalaya was the only thing you were willing to try. That changed over time, but in the beginning, I wanted to make sure you could always have something to eat."

There were not tears pulsing behind her eyes. Nope. She was having some kind of allergic reaction to something in the air and that was all there was to it. It wasn't that he'd done something incredibly sweet with absolutely no thought to getting anything out of it for himself.

"I think you should kiss me now." She suddenly realized she'd been waiting to say those words all night, ever since that first kiss had been interrupted. She had a chance to get herself out of this, but she wasn't going to take it. What she was going to take was this week. She would take it and enjoy it. It could be her reward for surviving.

Something like relief went across his face and his hand

came out, touching her hair. "I'm glad. My brother had me . . . well, it doesn't matter."

She was going to ask him what had happened with his brother tonight, but then his lips were on hers and she stopped thinking about anything but how well that man could kiss.

Zep always seemed to take things so lightly, but there was nothing light about the way he kissed. He focused in on her, his lips moving over hers like he was memorizing the way she felt against him. His hands were gentle on her, fingers tangling in her hair. She found herself following the lead he offered her, moving her head this way or that, anything to keep those lips on hers.

Then there was something between them as Daisy whined and tried to get in on the action.

Zep groaned and backed away. "I'm going to have to teach her some manners and how to not block her momma's friends. Come on, sweet girl. It's time for bed. I'll put her in her crate for the night."

He got up and started moving toward the kitchen/dining room area where Daisy's crate was sitting until Roxie decided where to put it.

What was she doing? She was trying her hardest not to have feelings, but they were there. They always had been. Something about this man moved her, and she couldn't shove it away. She'd tried her hardest, but she couldn't ignore him. And she couldn't be with him. Not the way she wanted to be. He wasn't that guy. He was the guy you had a good time with, the one who still wanted to be buddies long after he'd moved on to the next woman.

Could she do that? Could she sleep with him tonight and be his friend in the morning? Or would she be devastated when she saw him with another woman next week?

"Hey, nothing has to happen between us that you don't

want." Zep stood in the doorway staring at her in a way that made her wonder how long she'd been standing there thinking. There was a soft look on his face and all of his usual charm was gone. "Roxanne, I'll help you no matter what. I don't need anything more than a thank-you. Don't get me wrong. I want you. I want you so badly, I stay awake at night thinking about you, but the last thing I would ever do is to take something you aren't happy to give. So I'm going to borrow your shower and then I'll sleep on the couch."

"You won't fit on the couch." There were two bathrooms in her place, but the one downstairs didn't have a shower. She'd thought seriously the other day about looking for a little house she could start fixing up. There were a couple around town that would work. Then she'd reminded herself she wouldn't be here forever.

He stopped in front of her, but didn't touch her, choosing instead to give her a sad smile. "I've slept in far worse places, sweet . . . Roxie. I can handle it." He moved to the stairs, grabbing his small bag. "I'll take a quick shower. Gator wrangling is rough business."

She frowned. "You didn't wrangle Otis. You just waited until he left."

He winked and his grin was heartbreaking. "Don't tell your momma. She thinks I'm a superhero."

He strode up the stairs.

Her phone chimed and she glanced down. It was a text from her mother.

Loved meeting your guy. He's so sweet and you looked beautiful! I'm so glad to see you happy. I was very worried.

Her mother being worried usually led to terrible things. But Zep had put her at ease. Zep had made sure everything ran smoothly. For once in her adult life, she'd been able to pretend they were a happy family, that she hadn't screwed up and ruined all her parents' expectations. They'd had a good time and it had been all Zep since she would have taken every word out of her mom's mouth as some kind of passive-aggressive bull and countered it with her own aggression.

Instead, she'd had a nice meal and listened to Zep's stories and heard about how her brother's wedding plans were going. She'd found out her father was the new champion of his golf club and that her mom had planned the social event of the year.

So often when she was with her family, it felt like an intervention, like she was the one everyone was worried about because she hadn't gotten her life together. It had been good to feel like she was an accepted part of the family.

Zep had given her that.

She quickly texted back and promised her mom she would see her tomorrow.

Up above, she heard the shower come on.

Daisy whined from the crate, but she didn't bark. After a few tries, she seemed to settle down.

Was that what she was doing? She'd boxed herself in but not in the cozy way Daisy was. Daisy had a comfy bed to sleep on and a couple of toys. Zep had taken one of Roxie's shirts and put it in so the puppy could have her new mom's scent around her.

Roxie's crate did nothing but keep people out. It wasn't a place to sleep and rest for the next day. It was a cage of her own making, and it was going to cost her the week she could have with the sexiest man she'd ever met.

Or she could be brave and walk in there and ask for what she wanted. She could offer herself to him because she knew he wasn't going to turn her down. At the end of the week, they would both be better because they would have gotten this ridiculous longing out of their systems. Or rather she would have gotten it out of hers and he would be good because she would let him walk away this time. He seemed to need that control and she would give it to him. When the time came and he explained that he'd had fun, but it was time to get back to real life, she would let him go and she would be friendly with him.

She would stop arresting him at every given opportunity just so she could be close to him. The need to be close to him would wane.

All she had to do was take that first step. Up the stairs.

To her room. To the bathroom.

Somehow she found herself there, and without another thought she pulled off her dress and tossed it to the side. The hum of the shower was soothing as she made short work of her bra and undies.

This was what she wanted. Time with him.

She opened the door, happy he hadn't locked it, but then maybe this was what he'd hoped for, too.

She stepped in and up to the shower. It wasn't huge but they could both fit. She stared at him for a moment, the mist from the shower making him look almost unreal. His back was to her, every inch of his glorious skin on display, but his head was down in a way that made her ache to soothe him.

She knew that look. Weary. Lonely.

She rather thought she looked a lot like that most days of her life.

Maybe they could ease each other.

His head turned and he was suddenly staring at her, the hungriest look in his eyes. He didn't say anything, but the heat in the room had spiked and her whole body went taut with that one look.

It was like every inch of her skin came alive.

He turned and she could see his body. Muscle after muscle, each one masculine perfection. His hair was slicked back, making his face look starker. He always had that devil-may-care look in his eyes, but it was replaced with something primal.

"Are you sure?" The question came out of his mouth deeper than his usual tone. "I need you to be very sure, Roxanne."

She was sure she couldn't walk away. "I'm sure."

He held out a hand. "Then join me."

She placed her hand in his. So often she felt unfeminine and she was fine with that, but there were moments when she needed to feel like she was a woman. His big hand surrounding hers was all the reminder she needed. The worry fell away and she was left in the moment. Nothing mattered except being close to him for a while.

The warm water hit her skin, but it had nothing on the heat his hands made. He pulled her close and his mouth was on hers like he was a starving man and she was the sweetest treat he'd had in years. He kissed her over and over, his tongue surging in to dance with hers.

His hands moved down her back, tracing the line of her spine.

She shuddered and let her body brush against his, chest to chest. Her breasts got crushed in the most delicious way when he pulled her in snugly against him.

"Do you know how long I've waited for you to let me back in?"

"Over a year." She didn't doubt the fact that he'd probably had ten women or more since the night they'd spent together, but he'd wanted her. She believed that. She was the one who'd gotten away.

"It felt like forever," he whispered against her lips. "I've been waiting forever. I have no idea how you do this to me, but I can't deny it."

She couldn't, either, and she no longer had any desire to. All her desire was focused on him and the way his hands explored her body. She let herself explore, too. The night they'd spent before had felt rushed, and her senses had been dulled. There was nothing to keep her from focusing on the feel of him, how soft skin covered hard muscle, how his jawline had a light scruff across it though she knew he'd shaved earlier in the day. It whispered against her cheeks and tickled her neck.

She could feel exactly how much he wanted her. He pressed against her belly and she could feel herself softening, every muscle in her body getting ready to accept him.

"I want to remember every part of you. I can't stop thinking about you. Ever since that night, you're everywhere. I have to see if you taste as good as I remember." He dropped to his knees and then she was holding on to his shoulders because the heat had gone off the charts. He put his mouth on her, exploring her sex like his hands had discovered her skin. Pure pleasure shot through her like a rocket, and she heard herself groan his name.

She loved his name. Zéphirin. It was as unique as the man himself. It felt good to say it. So often she hid behind his last name, calling him Guidry to distance herself. But it was good and right to say his name in this place. It was intimate.

His hands cupped her backside, holding her there for his mouth and tongue. She held on for dear life while he gave her more pleasure than she'd had in forever. Maybe never. He was open and honest when he was making love. He was focused on nothing but her, and when they were together, she was the center of the universe.

It was an addicting experience. This was what she craved every bit as much as the pleasure he could give her.

She let the thought drift away as the peak hit her and she was left shaking.

Zep stood and kissed her, the taste of her own pleasure still on his lips. He was breathing like he'd run a race when he rested his head against hers. "Don't go anywhere."

He stepped outside the shower and she took a long breath as warm water sluiced down her back. It hadn't been enough. He'd given her the first orgasm she'd had in a year, but it wasn't enough because he hadn't been with her.

That was the danger of Zep. She wanted more than mere pleasure from him. She ached for the connection she'd found that went beyond any other man she'd ever known.

He strode back in and she realized why he'd left. He had a condom in his hand.

He'd taken such good care of her. She wanted to do the same for him. She took the condom out of his hand and opened it.

A low groan came from his throat and his head dropped back. "You're going to kill me, baby."

She gripped him and stroked, enjoying the fact that he was under her power for a moment. His eyes had closed and his hips moved, pushing himself into her hand over and over. She watched his gorgeous face and thrilled because she was doing this for him, making this connection with him.

She wanted to watch him, wanted to see him take the same pleasure she had, but not more than she wanted him inside her. She rolled the condom on and moved into his arms then realized they had a problem. "We should take this out to the bed."

"No time," he said as he picked her up, pressed her against

the side of the shower, and then he was inside her with one long thrust.

She wrapped her arms around him, wound her legs around his waist, and let him take control.

He kissed her, turning what was innately carnal into something sweet. He kissed her forehead and her cheeks, her lips and her chin.

"You feel so good," he whispered. "You feel so right."

Being with him felt right. Too right. She had to try to distance from him, but it was impossible in the moment. It was impossible when she felt like they'd torn down all the barriers between them and had managed to find this third thing. There was Roxanne. There was Zep. But in that moment she felt like she'd become something different, the Roxanne she could be exclusively with him. The part she could show only to him.

Her whole body tensed and then released as the orgasm hit her, stronger this time because he was with her. His arms were tight around her, his body merging with hers until she couldn't tell where she ended and he began.

He held her for a moment more as she started to come down.

"You have no idea how much I needed that, baby," he whispered before kissing her cheek.

She took a deep breath as he eased her to her feet. Her whole body felt languid, but her heart was racing. "Me, too. I figured as long as you're here, we should take advantage of the stress relief possibilities."

She meant it as a joke, something to break this horrible vulnerability she suddenly felt. She wasn't good at talking out her problems, and she certainly wasn't going to start with him. Zep liked kidding around. Joking and sarcasm were pretty much the languages he spoke.

He stopped and stared down at her. "Stress relief? That was stress relief for you?"

Somehow even though the water was still hot, she'd gone cold. "What was it supposed to be?"

He turned and stalked out of the shower, leaving her alone.

What had she done? What should she do? Should she apologize? All the warmth of the moment was gone and she was left exactly where she'd been before.

Alone.

# *chapter six*

Stress relief.

Those two words had been pounding through his head ever since the moment they'd come out of her mouth.

Stress relief.

Zep stopped at the stop sign, but only briefly because it was damn near midnight and no one was on the roads. He'd gotten the call shortly after exiting the shower that should have ended in . . . well, it should have ended in a shower. It should have ended with him running the soap all over her body and having her do the same to him. He would have washed her hair, running his fingers over her scalp and getting her to purr for him. And then they would have gotten dirty all over again.

But no. It had ended the minute she'd said those two words.

Stress relief.

He didn't feel relieved now. He felt like a fool. His brother had been right about everything. Roxie didn't take him seriously. She viewed him as some kind of sex toy.

"That was a stop sign, you know," she pointed out from the passenger seat.

And despite the fact that she viewed him as a warm, living blow-up doll, she didn't trust him enough to do his job. Or maybe that was exactly the problem. "If you wanted to drive, you should have taken your own car. And this is an emergency."

He'd gotten the call as she'd walked into the bedroom from the shower. His cell had trilled, and for a moment his heart had stopped because it had been so late, he'd worried something had gone terribly wrong.

Then he'd realized it was the police department. Major Blanchard was apparently on nights this week and he'd taken the call about another animal problem, this one out at Dixie's place. Since Roxie had walked out with that "we should talk" look on her face, he'd figured he'd been saved by the bell because talking would likely lead to fighting, and fighting would get his butt kicked to the curb.

He didn't want that. He needed more time. He needed to figure out how to deal with this turn of events. He'd misread her, but that didn't mean they had to break up.

The fact that he would consider it a breakup when she obviously didn't even think they were dating proved that Remy had been right all along.

"It's not an emergency," she said. When she'd offered to drive him to the site, he'd refused and told her to go to bed since he was the one being called out, not her. Naturally she'd been sitting in his truck by the time he'd gotten ready. She'd simply put her damp hair up in a bun, tossed on some clothes, and been ready to go. "Major said everyone is fine, but he wants you to take a look around the area and see if you can figure out what Dixie saw."

"Which is probably why they called me out and not you," he grumbled.

"I thought I could help. That light is red. You know street signs aren't suggestions."

He stopped and sat. No one was around but here he was, waiting for something that wasn't going to happen because it was after midnight and no one was out. But wasn't that a metaphor for his relationship with her? He was sitting at a red light, and even if it turned green, it wouldn't make a difference. The road would be exactly the same.

It would go nowhere.

So why couldn't he walk away?

"I wasn't trying to make you mad," she said softly. "I'm talking about what I said in the shower. Not getting in the truck. I didn't care if I pissed you off then. I would have come with you whether you liked it or not."

"Because you can't trust me to do the job Armie hired me for?" He turned down the street that Dixie lived on. Luckily they weren't far away. Maybe there really was a rougarou out there, and if there was any good in the universe, he could be murdered by it and avoid this conversation completely.

"No, because I started this case with you and I want to continue it." She stared out the window. "We both know she thinks she saw that rou thing. Everyone's talking about it, and I want to make sure we didn't miss something. Maybe it wasn't Daisy the goats heard out at Archie's. Maybe it was something else."

"It's most likely a mistake. She heard something. Everyone's talking about the rougarou, and even though Dixie isn't superstitious, her mind made connections and now she's scared. I've seen it happen a lot." Up ahead he could see the outline of a familiar vehicle. Major drove the same type of parish SUV that Roxie drove. His lights weren't on, though it looked like Dixie had put on every light in her ranch house. It glowed like a beacon against the dark night.

"That makes sense, but I want to check it out," she said. "I don't have anything else to do."

"You could have dried your hair. You'll catch a cold."

She turned his way, her lips curling up. "It's warm out. I think I'll be okay, but it's nice to know you care. Maybe I also wanted to come with you because I wanted to make sure you're okay."

Sure she did. He pulled up behind Major's SUV. "Let's get this done so we can get some sleep."

She put a hand on his arm. "I didn't mean to upset you. Come on, Zep. Don't be mad at me. It was good. I was happy."

"Because I relieved your stress."

She sighed. "Because I liked being with you. I didn't say things right. I don't know if you've noticed, but I'm not good at this kind of thing. I'm awkward and weird."

She wasn't weird. Or rather everyone was weird, and he had a high tolerance for oddness. Sometimes he thought his attraction for her began because she was unlike anyone he'd ever met. She didn't come on to him, didn't try to tell him her life story in the first ten minutes. There was something deep about the woman that made him want to solve all her mysteries, that made him think she might want to do the same with him.

But once again he'd found someone who didn't think he was worth knowing. Who could blame her? She was a serious woman. He needed to remember that. "It's all right. We should go and see what's happening."

"Zep," she began and then opened the door. "All right. You got called out and you need to do your job."

"Is it a job?" Zep slid out and grabbed his bag. It contained most of the things he would need if he was dealing with an animal. He would let the deputy shoot something if they needed to. He was more of a lover than a fighter. "I didn't exactly negotiate anything with Armie. He asked if I would do it and I said yes. I end up doing an awful lot of work for no money."

Only to get a reputation for being lazy for it.

She moved in step beside him as they started for Dixie's front door. "I'll check for you. Armie can procrastinate about paperwork. If you let him, he'll put it off and you won't get paid for a month. I'll make sure it goes through and that you get paid the normal contractor rate."

"Thank you. I appreciate it."

She stopped him. "You're doing the job. You should get the pay. I know I'm grateful you were with me the other night. Did I say thank you?"

"Not exactly."

She put a hand on his arm and her eyes were steady on his. "Thank you, Zep. For everything. We're going to talk when this is done. Like I said, I'm not good at this. I don't think we work long term, but I can't deny that I want to have this week with you."

He was about to argue when the front door opened and Major stepped out. He was a fit man only slightly shorter than Zep himself. Major was the all-American hero type, and Zep had to wonder if he had any interest in Roxie. Was this the kind of man who would work for her long term? Major practically had a halo.

Major stepped up, relief obvious on his face. "Rox, I'm so glad you're here. We're having a night. I've got a freaked-out mom. Patsy Howell checked in on her son and he wasn't in his bed. She's sure he's been kidnapped. I have no idea why anyone would want to kidnap a sixteen-year-old boy who never shuts up, but I gotta check it out."

"He's likely out drinking," Roxie said. "But stranger things have happened."

"I've got someone checking the teen hangout spots, but

I need to go and calm Patsy down." Major was already off the porch steps and walking past them. "I'll let you know if this turns into something serious, and then we need to be all hands on deck."

Roxie nodded. "I've got my cell. Zep and I can handle this."

Major turned and his brows had risen, his lips curved up. "You and Zep? You know I only called him."

Roxie's hands went to her hips. "He's new. I thought I should be here to make sure it all goes smoothly."

"Uh-huh, we'll talk later," Major promised. "Again, thanks for coming out."

He jogged down the path to his SUV.

"Zep, is that you?"

He looked up and his momma was standing at the entrance of Dixie's porch wearing her bathrobe, her hair up in her nighttime turban. It was a brilliant yellow that, combined with the black velvet robe, made her look a little like a giant bumblebee, but then that was his mom. She lived three doors down. *They* lived three doors down from Dixie. It wasn't like he was moving in with Rox. Hell, he wasn't sure he would even be staying with her after tonight.

"Hey, Mom. You remember Deputy King, right?"

His mother moved down the steps, her arms open. "Of course I do. Roxanne, we're so glad you're here. And so glad you're all right after coming so close to the monster last night."

He sighed. "Mom, you know there's no monster."

Roxie looked a little surprised but she gamely gave his mom a hug. It made him think about the fact that she hadn't hugged her own mother or father at dinner.

His mom let her go and turned his way. "Now you hush, disbeliever. I'm already on it. Marcelle and I are working on a spell that will keep the rougarou away."

He couldn't help it. His eyes rolled whenever his mother started in on the woo-woo. "How much you going to charge for that, Momma?"

His mother drew herself up, her shoulders straightening. "Just a nominal fee, of course. Though not for the tourists. We have to upcharge them a bit. Mysticism isn't free, you know."

"It is," he replied. "It is absolutely free. Now, where is Dixie and how did you get involved?"

"I called over to the house." Dixie stepped outside. She was a person he'd known all his life. Dixie's family had owned the diner in town since she was a child. It had been named after her. Dixie's had been the place his dad had taken him every Saturday morning. He and Remy and Seraphina would eat pancakes while his dad let his mom have the morning to herself. Dixie's very presence was practically comfort food. "I was trying to get hold of you. I misplaced your cell phone number. I know I was supposed to put it in my phone, but I'm better about writing things down."

And then losing them. "I'll put it in for you before I leave. So tell me what's going on. You saw something?"

She nodded and waved for them to come inside. "Yes, it was out back. I got up for a glass of water. I didn't turn on the lights because there was enough moonlight that I could find my way. I was standing in front of the kitchen sink and that's when I saw something moving out in the oleander bushes."

He moved through Dixie's small home, through the living room and into the kitchen. Her husband was standing there, a shotgun in his hand.

Roxanne merely sighed. "Tell me you didn't take a shot at something, Gary."

Gary Halford hadn't been born in Papillon, but he'd

moved here after he fell in love with Dixie. It hadn't taken him long to get used to the culture. "Naw, but I let that thing see I'm not unarmed."

Zep wasn't sure how some animal looking for food was going to understand the whole armed versus unarmed thing, but he let it go. "So all that happened was some bushes shook?"

"Of course not." Dixie sounded offended. "I wouldn't call the police about some possum rummaging for food. It was bigger than a possum. Way bigger. I thought it was a possum at first, and I went out to shoo it off. They like to eat up my strawberries, and I have an important pie competition coming up," Dixie explained.

"Your strawberry pie is the best in the world," her husband assured her.

"That's because I grow my own berries." Dixie had an air of authority about her whenever it came to cooking. "Anyway, despite the fact that I have a small fence around the garden, our possums can climb."

"They couldn't if you would let me shoot them," Gary argued.

Dixie turned on him. "You are not shooting possums in our backyard. You could miss and hit one of the cats. I just want to keep them out of the strawberries."

"I think we probably shouldn't shoot anything in the backyard." Roxie seemed determined to get back to the story at hand. "So you walked out of the house. What happened next?"

"I started toward the back fence. That's where the oleander bushes are. I got about halfway there when I realized it wasn't a possum." Dixie shivered, clutching the lapels of her robe. "I got this real bad feeling. It came over me like a breeze, and I knew something was watching me. That's when I focused in on it. I couldn't see it very well, but I'm sure it was up on two legs and it was staring back at me, Zep. I saw its eyes flash like a cat's in the dark and I heard whispering. I couldn't make out what it was saying but I think it was talking. Something about sound."

That was creepier than what had happened out at Archie's. "Did the cats act weird?"

"They were all sleeping," Dixie said. "I don't let them out much. They're indoor kitties. There are too many things that can hurt them out in the world. Anyway, I ran back in and woke up Gary and then I called you. Well, I called Delphine and she told me you were working for the sheriff now."

"Only part time on cases involving animals," he explained.

"Like your daddy and his daddy before him," Dixie said with a smile.

"My baby has always been good with animals," his mother said. "So gentle. Growing up, he would bring in the saddest-looking little things and help them get back to good health. I loved watching him with those sweet creatures. Except that raccoon he took in. It would throw food at me."

"Only after he reached puberty." He'd loved that raccoon. "And that was when he returned to the wild. He was abandoned, or probably his mother was killed. Now let's get back to the potential werewolf out in Dixie's backyard."

"We're going to go take a look," Roxie announced. "Please wait in here. We'll be right back."

Dixie put an arm through her husband's, cuddling up against him. "All right."

His mother put a hand on his shoulder. "Baby boy, are you sure you should go out there? I could make you a charm."

"I got all the charm I need, Momma. Why don't you make some coffee? It looks like we might have a long night if I have to drive Roxie over to the Howells'." If Major called an all hands on deck because they couldn't find the teen, he would have to take her over.

His mother nodded. "I hope the two aren't connected. It would be terrible if it turned out that Austin is the rougarou, but I did hear him spouting off to his momma at the Piggly Wiggly the other day, so it wouldn't surprise me. That boy has a mouth on him."

Roxie pulled the flashlight out of the bag she carried and opened the door. Like most of the homes in this particular neighborhood, Dixie's backyard was large, far bigger than the house itself. It had once been her parents' home, and she'd kept up the garden. To the right there were rows of vegetables and herbs coming in.

"Does your mom believe this stuff?" Roxie asked the question with a small smile on her face.

"My mother believes in anything that can make her and Miss Marcelle a buck," he replied. His mother could be a menace. "Remind me sometime to tell you about her ghost-busting days. It was not pretty, but surprisingly profitable."

Roxie grinned, a heart-stopping expression. "I'll be honest. I find your mom amusing. I know I should shut that stuff down, but no one ever complains."

It was the Dellacourt charm. That's what his mother called it. "Oh, they might complain, but then they're worried Miss Marcelle might actually have some hoodoo and everyone shuts up. The oleanders are in the back. They're up against the fence she shares with . . . I can't remember who lives right behind her."

"I can find out. Are you worried it was a person and they might have jumped the fence?" Roxie started moving to the back, passing the small firepit and chairs.

"Yeah. The only thing I can think of that would walk on two legs would be a bear. We don't have bears this far south.

I'm worried someone was creeping along back here." He had his own flashlight out.

That was when he heard a whisper.

Roxanne had obviously heard something as well because she held up a hand, fist closed. He'd seen his brother do the same thing, a military gesture requesting quiet. She pointed her flashlight down and nodded his way.

There were multiple footprints in the dirt, and it was easy to see that some of the bushes had been disturbed. A couple of branches were bent or broken.

"Shhh."

He frowned because that had come from behind the fence.

"You're squishing me," a feminine voice said.

Roxie pushed through the bushes and hopped up to the middle brace of the wooden fence. "Hello, girls. How is it going tonight?"

Zep pressed through the branches to join her, the fence creaking only slightly at their combined weight. He looked over the top of the fence, and sure enough, there were two teen girls huddled behind a small shed. They were dressed in pajama bottoms and hoodies, each looking like they were ready for bed but also not. He would bet anything the parents in the house had no idea that the slumber party they were hosting wasn't slumbering at all.

"All right, kids, it's time to talk," he said.

The trouble was they hadn't had any time to talk. Roxanne reflected on her problem twenty minutes later as they stood in Hannah Belton's family kitchen, her parents frowning the whole time. Hannah and another teenage girl sat across the table, the light from the overhead lamp reminding her of a spotlight in some overdramatic interrogation scene. Hannah and Ashlyn Travers were supposed to have been working on a class project.

"How are you going to give your report in the morning?" Mrs. Belton pointed a finger her daughter's way. "You'll be far too tired from playing around all night. I knew this was a mistake. This is why you're not allowed to have sleepovers on weeknights. Ashlyn, what is your mother going to think when I tell her that you were out in the middle of the night?"

She kind of wished she could have conducted this interview without all the parental help, but that's what happened when dealing with teens. The parents were always more freaked out than they should be.

She'd snuck out several times when she was a teen. It was a minor rebellion that usually led to uneventful nights. But she did have some questions. "How long were you out in the backyard?"

Hannah had been crying since the moment they'd looked over the top of the fence. "Not long. I needed some fresh air and we were actually doing part of this project for school."

Ashlyn hadn't shed a tear. She was definitely the tough girl of the two of them. "I was getting some footage for a multimedia project we're working on. I needed some video of the moon, and it wasn't out tonight until later. I dragged Hannah into it. Mrs. Belton, we finished everything we needed to do. The report is one hundred percent ready to go. You can read it if you like. It's all my fault. I should have waited, but the full moon only lasts three nights."

She was a cool customer. But there was something missing. "How long had you been out there?"

"I don't know." Hannah answered between sniffles. "Not long."

"You were supposed to be in bed." Mr. Belton decided

to get in on the action. "Not getting into trouble with the cops."

"I didn't think I would get in trouble with the cops." Hannah started to weep again.

"I don't think the deputy is going to haul you to jail. Mr. and Mrs. Belton, Hannah's not in real trouble. She didn't do anything illegal, right?" Zep was sitting to the side, but his voice oozed calm and reason.

If only he could be as reasonable about their relationship. Their non-relationship.

She'd hurt him and she hadn't meant to do that. She hadn't once considered the idea that she *could* hurt him. Zep Guidry let the world and all its problems slide off his back one hundred percent of the time. She should know since most of the time she was there when Zep got in trouble. Other people would fight her and call her names as she was arresting them. They would argue and give her hell. Not Zep. He would simply slide her a sexy smile and ask if she needed to frisk him. Or something equally obnoxious.

Or he would be calm and quiet. When she thought about it, he'd only said the obnoxious stuff once right after their night together. Had he been flirting with her? It had been two nights after they'd slept together, and she remembered he'd had the sweetest smile on his face when she'd walked into the bar where the fight had taken place. According to the witnesses, Zep hadn't started it, but they'd decided to take everyone down to the station.

He'd had that smile that threatened to melt her. It was the moment she'd decided to be as professional as possible, to not let him get away with anything or people would know. They would know she hadn't been able to stop thinking about him, that she couldn't get him out of her head.

The smile had died that night, and he hadn't smiled at her that way again until today.

Then she'd ruined things. Again.

"It's not illegal to be in your own backyard, right?" Hannah seemed ready to jump on anything that could save her.

"It's not your backyard, young lady," her father replied. "I paid for this house and I say you can't be out there at midnight playing around with your friends. I should let the deputy arrest you."

Yep, parents could be rough on a girl. "I'm not going to arrest her. I only want to know if she went over the fence."

Hannah's eyes went super wide, and Roxie worried she was about to get another round of crying.

Ashlyn held up her hand. "That was me, too. I got up on the fence to get a better shot and I dropped my phone and then the café lady came out and everyone around here has a gun, so I froze. I know I should have let her know I was getting my phone, but I was trying to keep Hannah out of trouble."

It was a good story, but there was something about the young lady she didn't quite believe. "You dropped your phone?"

She nodded. "Yes. I was trying to get up on the shed so I could get a better shot. I was using the camera on my phone."

"Can I see the picture?"

A hint of pink flushed her cheeks. "I didn't get one. I was trying but I dropped the phone and then everything went crazy."

Something was not adding up.

"But that was at least twenty minutes before we found you standing there." Zep seemed to be thinking along the same lines she was.

The timing was off. Most kids she knew would have fled back into the house. So what had kept them standing there?

"Well, first I had to wait until I was sure the dude with

the gun wasn't going to shoot me," Ashlyn replied, her chin up. "I wasn't able to get back over the fence until he went inside when the first police showed up. The hot guy. Deputy Major. It's a terrible name for a hot guy."

"You should not be objectifying young men," Mrs. Belton pointed out before turning to her daughter. "I told you she was a bad influence."

"She's my friend." Hannah sniffled again.

"I thought the boyfriend was the bad influence," her father muttered.

"Who's the boyfriend?" There had been more than one set of footprints in those bushes. If it had all happened like Ashlyn said, there shouldn't have been all those footprints. Roxie could write it off as Dixie's or her husband's, but there had been an overly large set right by the fence. Dixie and Joe were both on the smaller side.

And they did have a missing teen.

Hannah's eyes had gone wide, and her mouth opened and closed again.

"Austin Howell," her father said with a shake of his head. "He lives a couple of blocks over. He's a bad influence. Her grades were perfect until she started dating that moron."

"He's not a moron," Hannah yelled with all the teen-in-love angst she could muster. "He's going to be an artist. He's going to make great films someday and you are so unfair."

Roxie sighed and turned to the rational one as the Beltons began arguing about young love. "So the boyfriend showed up?"

Ashlyn stood and moved to where Roxie was. "Yeah. We're working on this project together, but then mostly they made out and I had to do all the work. Typical. And he is so not the artist I am. Look, I'm sorry we scared the old folks."

"And where's Austin?" Roxie got the feeling she could close two cases with one simple answer.

"He's hiding in the shed," Ashlyn admitted. "Scaredy cat didn't want to get caught. He walked over from his house. But could we not tell his mom? She knows my mom and she's a bit overprotective."

"Oh, his mom knows," she said, pulling her cell out. At the very least she could tell Major they could all stand down on the missing teen. "Zep, could you go and talk to the teenage boy currently hiding in the shed? I suspect you'll relate to him better than an angry dad."

"What do you mean he's in my shed?" Mr. Belton asked.

It was going to be a long night.

Hours later Roxie was fairly certain no one was going to be shot, though there were three grounded teens. She got into the truck and slid in beside Zep. "You were good with the parents."

He started up the truck. "I've had to be over the years. That wasn't my first rodeo."

She suspected it wasn't. "You were probably the bane of all the high school girls' parents."

He went quiet, driving down the road, the silence lengthening between them.

It was already light outside, and Papillon was up and at work. It was the second night in a row he'd gotten next to no sleep because he was helping her. He was upset and she wasn't sure how to reach him. All she knew was that she really wanted to. She didn't like this feeling in the pit of her gut that she'd done something wrong and hurt him.

"At least we can put the rougarou rumors to rest." She couldn't take the silence another moment. It was odd since she liked quiet. She didn't talk a lot, but she liked it when he did.

"Don't count those rumors out yet," he muttered. "People here like a good story, and a tied-up dog and young love gone wrong aren't as good as a Cajun werewolf running wild. I assure you, there will still be talk. Don't worry about it. We've got the big crawfish festival in a few weeks. I'm sure something will happen at it that will get people talking."

"The last festival I worked, your sister-in-law had a catfight with Josette Trahan after she drank way too much strawberry wine." People still called it the Great Hair Pull Incident. Josette had come out on the losing end of that one.

"I think it was more about Josette putting hands on my brother," Zep replied. "Lisa's a little possessive. And yes, something like that will happen and we won't hear more about the rougarou. Hopefully before my mother sets herself up as the rougarou whisperer. She will charge for that. I wouldn't want you to arrest my momma."

"I wouldn't arrest your mother," she shot back.

He fell back into silence. Not so easy this time.

She decided to try again. "I'm sorry."

"Nothing to be sorry about," he replied, his eyes steady on the road.

She hated this feeling. This was the time when she should shut down and let it go. He would either get over it or he wouldn't, and that would tell her a lot about how her week was going to go. "I feel like there is because you're mad at me and I don't really understand what I did wrong."

Somehow she couldn't do what she'd done in the past. She couldn't simply let this emotion sit between them.

He sighed. "You didn't do anything wrong. I'm afraid your honesty hurt my feelings. But it wasn't wrong for you to feel the way you do."

"About you? I wasn't saying anything bad about you, Zep. I made a dumb joke about stress relief."

"Yes, that's what it was and that's why I got my feelings hurt."

"What?"

"It was a joke to you," he said. "It meant something to me. You're not wrong, Rox. *I* was. I should have listened to my brother. He told me we weren't on the same page, but I didn't believe him."

"Okay, now I'm the one who doesn't understand."

"I thought you really liked me. I thought you'd finally figured out that I was serious about you and wanted to be more than . . . well, than stress relief. I wanted to be more than a one-night stand. I get it. I'm too old to be some young stud. I'm the one who gets in trouble. That was fine when I was a boy. Everyone loves a bad boy. It's pathetic on a man. It's a joke. You made the joke, but I *am* the joke. I'm the walking, talking joke of the parish."

"No, you're not." Except wasn't that why she'd stayed away from him in the first place? She had never once considered that he thought of himself as a joke. "I think every man in town would like to be you. You get all the ladies."

He stopped the truck at a red light and turned her way. "What is that supposed to mean? Are you talking about the fact that I can get a woman to dance with me? Hell, honey, I'm at bars most nights. Of course the women there want to dance. Not one of them wants to do anything more than have a good time. That's what I am. I'm a good time. I'm stress relief. I'm not the guy you call when you need to talk. I'm the guy you get in bed with and forget about the next day."

"I didn't forget about you."

"We'll have to agree to disagree about that." The light had changed and he sighed as he started to drive again.

"I'm sorry. I don't view you as stress relief." She'd never considered the fact that the reason Zep didn't date was anything but preference. It hadn't been hard to think about him preferring quick hookups to taking women out. She'd heard the stories of love-'em-and-leave-'em Guidry, but not once had she asked herself if they were true. She'd listened to every rumor about Zep without considering that he might be different, that there might be a private side to the man.

Had she viewed him the same way everyone did? As a gorgeous face with no real soul behind it?

"I'm sorry I hurt you," she said quietly.

"I suspect I'll survive."

"Hey, I'm trying here, Zep. I'm sorry I hurt you. I hope that you can accept my apology. I don't know what your brother said, but I do appreciate everything you've done for me."

A long moment passed. "I accept your apology and you're welcome. Remy just told me we weren't on the same page. He said you probably weren't thinking long term when it came to me, and he knew that I was definitely considering it."

The words floored her. He was thinking about them in some kind of long-term relationship? In a relationship at all? "You want me to be your girlfriend?"

He was quiet for a moment. "You don't have to say it like it's an insane idea."

"You don't have girlfriends."

"Yes, I believe I pointed that out."

She was so confused. "You could get a girlfriend if you wanted one. You're not exactly hard on the eyes."

"You would be surprised. Most women around here don't view me as anything they would want to bring home to their mommas. And yes, it might be because in my youth I slept with a bunch of their mommas, but I've changed over the last couple of years. I'm not the same man I was."

"You slept with their mothers?" She shouldn't be shocked but there it was.

"I didn't discriminate when I was younger," Zep admitted. "A beautiful woman was a beautiful woman. I know I sound like an idiot. I know I deserve the reputation I got, but I've grown up in the last couple of years. I've had to. Sera . . . well, Sera needed a lot of help in the beginning. She needed me and Momma. And then we had to take care of Luc. I took a bunch of odd jobs because we needed the money, but someone needed to watch after Luc, too. Sera was trying to find stable work. She tried out a lot of stuff. I had to back her up so that meant being flexible. Also, there's not a lot to do around here unless you want to work on a rig."

And then he would have been gone for months at a time. Had his choices not been as selfish as everyone suspected? She knew his sister had been through a lot of jobs. But she hadn't thought about Zep doing more than the occasional babysitting gig. "I'm sorry. I didn't mean to treat you like a joke, but you're right. I'm not thinking long term. Staying here long term was never in my plans. I know everyone thinks I came down here because of what happened to my partner, but that's not the truth. I will miss Ben every day, but he's not the reason I left New York. I came here because after my divorce, my ex made it impossible for me to stay. I was happy where I was."

Had she been? After Ben had been killed, she'd closed herself off to anything but doing her job and rising up the ranks. Ambition had been far easier than self-reflection. It still was, but Zep was forcing her to think. Or maybe it was all about her current situation with her family.

"You're going to leave?"

"The plan was always that I would come here for a couple of years, and when the right position opened, I would take it. Armie has contacts in New Orleans."

"You should talk to my brother, too. He knows a bunch of people in Dallas." Someone honked behind them and he looked up, cursing softly under his breath as he realized the light had gone green. "Sorry. I need to pay more attention. But if you're interested in living in Dallas, Remy could help you."

She put a hand on his arm. "It's not about you. It's about my career. This is what I've always wanted. Most of my friends wanted to be models or doctors. I know. I had an eclectic group of friends. I wanted to be a cop like my granddad."

But hadn't she moved into a career that resembled her father's more than her granddad's?

"I understand that your career is important." He turned down her street. "I'll go back to my place and let you alone. If you need me again, give me a call."

"I thought you were staying with me for the week." A bit of panic welled inside her and she realized how much she'd been counting on having this time with him. She wanted to be around him even though she knew it would end when her family left. "I still don't know how to take care of Daisy."

"Sure you do," he said, weariness in his tone. "You take her on a couple of walks. Feed her. Pet her. She'll be fine. If you get in trouble, you can call me."

She wanted to argue with him, but how could she? She'd put him in this position, and she couldn't give him what he wanted. "All right."

"After we get some sleep, I'll come by and pick you up for dinner. We're supposed to meet your parents out at the B and B."

They'd made the arrangements the night before. Since it was her day off, she was supposed to call her mother when she got up. She would have to text and let her know it would be later in the afternoon. "You would still go? I can make something up."

"I'm not going back on my word. I'm going to be wherever you need me to be, but I need some sleep and I can't do it on your couch. Maybe I'll feel better if I can get some rest."

He was so tired. She could see it in every move he made. He was tired because he'd spent every minute of the last two days taking care of her. No one had taken care of him.

"I don't think you should drive," she said quietly.

"It's not far."

"Please stay."

His mouth tightened and he turned into her driveway. "All right. If that's what you need, I'll stay."

He parked the car and was quiet as they walked inside. He let Daisy out of her crate and the puppy went a little crazy, but he was patient.

She watched him, truly watched him. She saw how patient he was as he dealt with the dog. He even knocked on Darlene's back door and talked to her for a few moments. Her neighbor smiled at him and then she was letting Daisy into her house.

"I got a dog sitter for a couple of hours," he said as he walked in. "She's been in that crate for way too long. Darlene's got a dog. It's good for Daisy to get socialized."

Darlene's golden retriever was a sweet-natured dog. She would be as patient with Daisy as Zep had been with her.

Maybe it was time she showed some patience and kindness, too. "Thank you. Do you want some food or do you want to go to bed?"

"I'm beat. I don't think I can stay awake to eat," he admitted.

She didn't want anything but rest either, and she wanted to rest with him. She couldn't promise him more, but she needed him to understand she didn't think he was a joke.

"Can I get a pillow?" He looked down at the couch.

She threaded her fingers through his. "Please come upstairs with me. My bed is big enough. We don't have to do anything, but I want to sleep with you. I want to wake up later and make you a breakfast that won't be anywhere near as good as what you would normally make. Please. I need to take care of you today."

She meant every word. It was a need deep inside her. She would have lost something if he'd gotten in his truck and driven away. He might have come back, would almost certainly have honored his promises to her. But something fundamental would have changed between them. There would be a distance.

He brought her hand up and put it over his heart. "But you'll still dump me at the end of this."

"I . . . I don't know what happens when this week is over, Zep. I thought I did, but maybe I don't. I do know that I'm planning on leaving. Maybe not in the next few months, but definitely in the next year. I don't want to hurt you, but I also don't want you to leave." It might be selfish of her, but it was true.

He brought her hand up and kissed it. "All right."

She led him upstairs to the bed she'd never shared with anyone. She pulled off his shirt and helped him out of his boots. She unbuckled his belt and got him down to his boxers before tucking him in. There was nothing sexual about it, but the emotion she felt went deeper. Intimacy. This was even more intimate than the shower they'd shared because she wasn't trying to get anything from him. She wanted to give.

She texted her mom and turned off her ringer before getting herself ready. When she got into bed beside him, she rolled to her side.

"Is this a friendly sleepover or can we cuddle?" Zep asked.

She moved against him, wrapping her arms around him and laying her head on his chest. "I would like a good cuddle. I didn't mean to treat you like a joke. I don't think you're a joke."

His hand smoothed over her hair. "You're the only one who matters. That's what I figured out. I don't care what anyone else thinks of me. But you're different."

"I'm different?"

She heard him yawn. "Knew it the minute I saw you. Knew you would change things for me."

She was about to ask him how, but she felt his breathing settle into the rhythm of sleep. She lay there for the longest time wondering if she'd changed things for the better or the worse.

# chapter seven

Zep woke up to the smell of bacon.

All in all, it wasn't a horrible way to start the morning, but then he remembered what had happened the night before.

He forced himself to sit up.

He was in Roxanne's bed, but it wasn't a forever thing. It was a "Hey, we're here for a week, why not work out some stress?" thing.

It still hurt and he wished it didn't. He wished he could take what she'd said, process it, and move on.

She was going to leave and he would be left alone to figure out what to do with the rest of his life, which would probably involve hanging out with friends who were all getting married and being that weird guy who's always around but doesn't truly have a place.

The funny thing was this general sense of discontent hadn't hit him until he'd met her. He'd been content that he'd done what he needed to do and helped out his family. But then he'd met Roxanne and realized what not making something of himself was going to cost him. It was going to cost him her.

He slid out of bed and checked his phone. He had a couple of texts from his friends wondering where he was since he hadn't been at The Back Porch for two nights in a row. It reminded him that he had a schedule and it wasn't exactly filled with stuff to do.

He missed Luc. For the first years of his nephew's life, he'd seen that kiddo every single day. Then Sera and Harry had gotten married and they'd moved out to the B and B. Now he was lucky to see him once or twice a week. He hadn't realized how much being around Luc had made him feel like he was doing something important.

The phone rang and his mother's number came up. It was past noon, so at least she'd waited awhile before making the call that had been utterly inevitable. He'd managed to duck her when he'd gotten his stuff the day before, and she hadn't said anything last night since they'd been in front of Roxanne, but he'd known this was coming. "Hey, Momma."

"Zéphirin, you naughty boy. What is going on between you and that sweet deputy?"

"Momma, she's not exactly sweet." Except she'd felt that way the night before when she'd wrapped herself around him. They'd nestled together like puzzle pieces and he'd slept better than he had in ages.

"Oh, she is in her own way," his mother insisted. "Now, what are you doing with her? I heard a rumor that you're tricking her mother and father into thinking she has a boyfriend because her mother meddles. I can't imagine what that's like. The poor girl."

Sure she couldn't. "Anyway, I'm staying here for a few days. It's not a big deal. I'll be back by Monday, if not sooner. If you need anything, all you have to do is call."

"Baby, wait. I want to talk to you. Your brother is worried

about you. He talked to me this morning because he heard you went on a call last night. I told him that I was there and you were with the deputy. She wasn't on duty. She wasn't supposed to be there, was she? Remy thinks you two might be getting in pretty deep."

Well, of course his brother was worried. Remy was always worried about him. But that was what happened when big brother had to go halfway across the country to get little brother out of jail the one time he'd decided to follow his heart. His heart? It was more like his dick, though it had been his heart that really got him in trouble. "I'm fine. I'm doing a friend a favor. Everything's going back to normal next week."

Normal and boring. His days were dull, and his nights seemed to drag on until they mixed together and he couldn't tell one from the other.

"She's never been your friend, Zep. Do you think I don't know that you spent the night with her and then she started arresting you at all turns?"

No one ever said his momma didn't lay it on the line. "All right, I'm helping out a woman I like."

"How much do you like her? You've never said anything about her to me. I always thought you were more the free-love type."

He could point out to his mother that love was rarely free. Everyone paid for it one way or another. He worried what he felt for Roxie was going to cost him a lot. Not in money, but then he'd learned there were far more precious things than cash. But he wasn't about to tell his mother that. She would get with Miss Marcelle and start working on a love spell or some nonsense. "Roxie and I are friends, nothing more. I know we don't hang out a lot, but we understand each other."

It had felt that way to him. He had to consider the fact that they could click, could have an amazing connection, and yet want such different things that they couldn't work.

"I think this is about more than liking a woman. I know you've changed a lot in the last year. Was it because of her?"

He sighed. "I like her. That's all. And maybe I'm finally growing up. Maybe watching my sister and brother get married and settle down made me think."

"Oh, honey, Remy's right. You do have a thing for her."

He sighed in frustration. "I just told you I didn't."

"Yes, but I know you lie to me a lot. You don't talk to me about a lot of the things you want because you don't think you honestly deserve them," she said quietly. "Sweetie, you should talk to me. I can tell you what an amazing man you've become. Maybe if I talk to your deputy, she'll see it, too."

That nearly made his heart stop. "Absolutely not. That is the last thing I need. Like I said, it's a favor for a friend, and we'll go back to normal at the end of the week. I'm asking you not to get involved."

"How uninvolved do you want me to be?" she asked. "Because I might know things. But if you don't want me involved, I can keep it all to myself."

His mother was tuned in to the gossip mill that flowed through Papillon. If she knew something, he might as well know it, too. "What have you got?"

"Well, I happen to know that Roxie's parents aren't merely here for her birthday. You should know that Seraphina heard her parents talking and she thinks they've got some plans up their sleeves. They might be smiling, but they don't like the fact that Roxanne isn't in New York anymore."

"Sera's been eavesdropping?" He hadn't even thought about the fact that Sera was literally Roxie's parents' landlord for the week. She would have seen a bunch of things no one else would. They'd rented out all five rooms at the

B and B despite the fact that they should only need two. Or perhaps three, since he'd been told the previous night that Shawna required extra closet space and apparently Brian snored, so she liked to sleep by herself. All of which would change after they got married, according to Pamela.

"Of course not. She would never do that, but she had been almost ready to serve breakfast when she heard something that made her stop. Just out of sight. And wait there until they were done talking. That's nothing more than proper hospitality."

Sera could be nosy, but this time it might work to his advantage. "She heard anything else? Anything I should know?"

"Her parents are planning a surprise for her. I don't know what it is, but they're flying it in from New York," his mother confided. "According to Sera, they talk a lot about the upcoming wedding and how they want Roxie back home before it happens."

She wanted to go home. He wasn't going to be able to keep her.

The only question was how to distance himself.

Or if he should take whatever time he had with her.

The bedroom door came open and she was standing there. She was in pajama bottoms and a tank top, her hair piled on the top of her head, and all he wanted to do was sink his fingers into all that soft stuff and see her the way no one else got to.

Wasn't he the guy who lived day to day? Hadn't he learned that was all the universe had for him? Why was he even hesitating? She wanted him for the week? Well, she could have him.

And he could have her.

"Mom, I need to go."

"Are you sure you don't want to talk about—"

He hung up and turned the phone off before putting it on the nightstand. He stared at her for a moment, taking her in. She was so gorgeous, and he loved seeing her out of uniform. "Good morning, Roxanne."

A slight pink stained her cheeks, letting him know she wasn't unaffected by his presence. "I made some breakfast. Don't be too impressed. It's bacon and frozen waffles. I haven't toasted them yet. Are you hungry?"

Such a silly question. He was always hungry around her. So damn hungry. "Come here."

She took a deep breath and her gaze held his. "I thought you were mad at me."

"There's nothing to be mad about, baby. You don't want the same things I do. That doesn't mean we can't find a short-term compromise. I believe you said something about being together for the week."

She moved to him. Her bare feet crossed the carpet until they were between his. Such small feet, and he loved the pink polish on her toes. "I don't know, Zep. We should talk about this. I don't want to hurt you."

It would hurt like hell when she walked away from him, but he was starting to think it might hurt more if he never tried at all. "Do you want me?"

She bit her bottom lip, and her answer came out on a breathy sigh. "You know I do."

"Why did you stay away?"

She hesitated before answering. "Because we can't work. But I also couldn't really stay away. I know I've been harder on you than anyone else."

It was time to give her some honesty. "Do you know why you always find me in the middle of fights? Because I knew what shifts you worked, and I would get into the middle of the trouble just so I could see you. I knew it was the only way to get close to you. I had the money to pay those tickets. Hell, I knew I would get the tickets. I actually do know how and where to park. But if I didn't get in trouble, I wouldn't ever get to see you."

It was a stupid thing to admit, but it was true.

She put her hands on his shoulders, and her palms smoothed over his skin. She let her hands trace his shoulders and neck. "You have to stop that. You work for the sheriff's department now. You can see me a lot. I'll have to see you a lot. I won't have to arrest you for stupid stuff anymore."

His hands found her hips, and he tilted his head up to look into her eyes. "Oh, I think you could still arrest me from time to time. I like watching you work. Come here. Let me help you out of those clothes."

He cupped her hips and snagged the hem of her tank top, dragging it up and unveiling her lovely breasts. He wanted to see her in the early morning light, wanted to enjoy every single moment of time he had with her. Her arms came up, making it easy to pull the shirt over her head. He tossed it to the side and stared at her for a moment. "You're the most beautiful woman I've ever seen."

She snorted lightly. "You must not have had your eyes open most of the time, then, Guidry."

His hands found her hips again and he held her tight, looking up into her eyes. "Don't. Don't joke right now. I'm serious."

Her face fell. "I'm not beautiful. I'm not awful, but I'm not gorgeous or anything."

"You are to me, and I'm not saying that to get you in bed. I can get you in bed without another word. You want an orgasm and I can give it to you. But you have to take my words, too. Remember what I said about Archie and his wife? How she doesn't see the same thing you do?"

"Yes."

He loosened his hold and ran his hands up her body, cupping her breasts. "You are the sexiest woman I've ever met. I don't know why. I think sometimes people simply click, like they're meant to be together. I know you don't believe that. It doesn't have to be forever. It can be that we came into each other's lives for some reason, and fighting it hasn't made either one of us happy. So listen and believe me when I tell you that I saw you and I knew I had to know you. You and Armie walked into Guidry's and I couldn't take my eyes off you."

Her shoulders had relaxed, and she leaned toward his hand, giving him full access to her breasts. "All I knew was you were the one everyone warned me about, and I still couldn't stay away. I love it when you touch me."

He was going to do so much more than touch her, but he could start there. He moved his hands down and eased his fingers under the waistband of her pajama bottoms. She wasn't wearing underwear. All he felt was warm, smooth skin. He cupped her backside and brought her close. He leaned over to kiss her breasts. He lavished each one with affection, pulling her nipples into his mouth and teasing them with his teeth and tongue. He held her close, offering her no release from the sweet torture.

"You'll sleep with me while I'm here?" He needed to make sure they were on the same page this time.

"Yes. I want that." Her hands had come up, rubbing along his back. "I haven't wanted anyone like I want you. Not any other boyfriend. Not my ex-husband."

He pulled back and looked up at her. He loved the almost desperate look in her eyes. He wondered if this was what she'd meant before. "No one's ever made love to you like me? How do you mean? Because I can't imagine a man who doesn't want to spend his every waking breath looking at you, loving you."

Her fingers scraped gently over his scalp and she laughed, but this time it was a genuinely amused sound. "We've already talked about your lack of imagination, babe. But you're on the right track. No one's ever taken me out of my head before, made me care about nothing but his next kiss, his next caress. I don't know how you do it, but it's addictive."

And maybe it might be a way to stay close to her. The idea that he might bind her up tight, so tight she couldn't leave him behind when she went, started to bubble in the back of his head.

Did he want to leave Papillon? His home, his family?

He shoved the thought away because all that mattered in the moment was giving her as much pleasure as he could, showing her exactly how well he could take care of her. He needed to prove how right she was about this being different from her every other experience. "I want to take my time with you, baby. I want to make sure there isn't an inch of you left unloved."

"Then shouldn't we get you out of those boxers?"

He would, but in his own sweet time. For now he wanted to concentrate on her. It didn't matter that his whole body was taut and ready. She was all that mattered. Making her forget that anything existed outside of this room was his only job right now. "Nope. We're slowing down. The first couple of times I got you in bed went way too fast for me."

"You didn't get me in bed yesterday. You threw me up against the shower wall."

He loved the intimacy of being alone with her, of having memories that didn't involve handcuffs with her. "Like I said, I was hungry. I was a starving man. But now I can take my time and enjoy my meal."

She leaned over and he let instinct take hold. His fingers tangled in her hair and he dragged her down on top of him as their mouths met. He kissed her even as he turned her over on the bed and covered her with his body. He pressed himself against her, loving the feel of her. He kissed her over and over again.

"Tell me what you like," he said as he dropped his head to kiss her neck.

"I like you," she replied. "I like everything you do to me. It drives me crazy when you kiss me."

He moved to her mouth again, kissing her lightly before plunging his tongue deep. Her arms tightened around him and she met him kiss for kiss, touch for touch. This was what he'd missed the first two nights he'd spent with her. He'd missed taking his time. He'd been so greedy for her that he hadn't allowed himself to simply sink into the experience. He'd wanted to please her, and he thought he had, but this time, he was confident in his ability and that let him enjoy the experience of being with her.

"Have I told you how gorgeous you are to me?" He stared into her eyes, memorizing how blue they were.

Her lips quirked up. "Yes, you have."

"Do you believe me yet?"

The grin faded and he saw how vulnerable she was in that moment. "I don't know."

"Then I'll have to say it until you do. Or show you." He kissed her again. "I'll make you believe, Roxanne King. I'll make you believe that you're the loveliest thing in the world."

And maybe along the way she would start to believe in him, too.

He kissed a path across her torso and made his way down, easing off the bed at some point so he could be close to that part of her he loved to taste. He adored the whimpers that came from her as he lavished her with affection. Her hands fisted in the comforter as she held herself in place.

"You're supposed to tell me what you like. How will I know if I should keep doing it?"

"I freaking love it, Guidry," she ground out. "Don't stop. Don't ever stop. You're killing me here."

And that was exactly the response he wanted. His whole body was tight with desire, his heart thudding in his chest as he settled back down to his task.

It wasn't long before she was quaking and calling out his name.

He let himself off the leash. It was his time. He stood and shoved the boxers off his hips, reached for the condom, and managed to get it on before he fell on her.

"I want you. I want you every minute of the day," he groaned before making a place for himself between her legs.

She wound her body around his, holding on to him like he was a life preserver.

"Then you should take me," she growled. Her nails dug into the skin of his back, the minor pain making him feel savage and wildly possessive.

He thrust up, joining their bodies and sending a thrill of pure bliss through him.

"Yes, I definitely like that." She tightened around him, drawing him in deeper. "You should do that a lot."

He meant to do it as often as he could. He surged inside her again and then he wasn't thinking of anything except how good it felt to be connected to her. Heat overwhelmed him and he found a rhythm that had her moaning. When she went over the edge, she took him with her. He went careening, losing himself in her.

He pressed her into the bed as he started to come down from the high of the orgasm, pleasure giving way to comfort and warmth.

"I like that," she whispered. "I liked that quite a lot. I like you, Zep."

He held her close. It would have to do.

For now.

Roxie watched as Daisy ran around and around Harry Jefferys's big German shepherd on the back porch of the Butterfly Bayou Bed and Breakfast. The dog named Shep simply watched with almost amused indulgence as the puppy barked and jumped and then chased a bug. The whole time her tail wagged as though her joy couldn't possibly be contained and needed an outlet.

Roxie was falling madly in love with that dog.

She had to make sure she wasn't doing the same with Zep Guidry.

It was hours after he'd made love to her. She couldn't call it anything else. What they'd done in that bed for most of the afternoon had been making love. After that first time, they'd lain in bed and talked about nothing in particular. He'd told her some stories about his childhood, and she'd talked about what it had been like to be a cop in New York. He'd laid his head on her chest and listened to her while his hands had moved over her body.

Then he'd made love to her again.

It had been hard to get out of bed and get ready for the dinner at the B and B with her parents.

She glanced over to where he stood next to Harry at the barbecue. He was smiling at his brother-in-law, a beer in his hand and the late-evening light shining down on him.

He looked so right here. This was his natural home. He

fit in with the lifestyle. Laid-back, concentrating on family and friends instead of climbing a ladder he wasn't sure where it went to.

What did Zep want out of life?

"He's real cute." Shawna stared at the padded chair next to Roxanne.

They were by the pool in the outdoor living area that included a backyard kitchen and plenty of dining space. The pool was lagoon style and had a slide she was sure Luc had fun with. She hadn't been out here since the pool had been finished. Of course, she'd barely been out here at all. She worked and slept and occasionally had a beer with the guys. Lather, rinse, repeat.

"Yeah, he is," she replied because Shawna was talking about Zep. Or maybe Harry. "They both are."

Shawna was wearing a far too short dress, but she managed to sit with perfect grace. "Yeah, they are, but I was talking about your guy. I'm surprised he is your guy. He's not your usual type."

"Turns out my usual type is asshole." Not that she'd dated a ton. She'd had a couple of boyfriends in high school and then she'd gone into the military. When she'd come out on the other side, she'd dated very little, and when Joel showed up, he'd made sense to her.

Zep didn't make a lick of sense. Not even one. He wasn't her type at all. She liked serious. She liked ambitious.

She didn't go out with men who spent their time drinking and partying with friends. She didn't date men who danced the night away and charmed everyone in their path.

"Oh, yeah, that's what Brian says about your ex. I knew Joel was terrible the minute I met him. He's one of those cops who's only worried about his career."

She was surprised Brian wasn't all Team Joel. "Some people say Brian is, too."

Shawna shrugged one shoulder. "Mostly, but I can handle that. I could have told you it wouldn't work for you. Brian can definitely pay more attention to moving up than doing a good job, but I've found a lot of men treat careers that way. He's doing it for us, though. For our future. It's a future I want, so it's okay. Like your mom and dad."

It was odd. Shawna had been around for a long time but Roxie had never sat down and had a talk with the woman. It just went to show her that she shouldn't judge a book by its fairly shallow-looking cover. "My mom was concerned with my father's career. Supporting him was kind of her career. That's what Brian's going to want."

"I know. He doesn't hide it or anything. He pretty much told me what he wanted when we started dating," Shawna explained. "I don't have anything I want to do besides have a family and stuff like that, so it works for me. It was never going to work for you. I know that Joel told you he was fine with the two-career thing, but I knew he was lying. At first I thought maybe he was lying to himself, but then I realized what he really wanted."

"To get close to my dad." She'd figured that out, too.

"Your dad helped him move up quickly." Shawna crossed her legs, one ridiculously high heel bouncing. She glanced over to the table where Roxie's parents were sitting with Brian and then lowered her voice. "Did you ever wonder why your dad didn't use those favors for you?"

"What do you mean?"

"I mean a man only has so many favors he can call in. He's the reason Brian got transferred. He wasn't going to move up with the captain he was under. So your dad pulled some strings to get him moved to a precinct where he could have more upward mobility. Why didn't he do the same for you?"

She hadn't known her father had been behind Brian's move. She'd been told he'd earned it by breaking a couple of major cases. The trouble was she'd also heard rumors that her brother had merely been there when the cases resolved. It wasn't too strange a story. It happened a lot. Some beat cop did the work and a detective took the credit.

But why should credit matter? It didn't here. They helped each other here because there were so few of them. She hadn't thought a thing about taking Major's call the night before so he could handle the potentially much more important call. There wasn't credit to be taken here. There was merely the job to do, partners to take care of.

However, she could think of a few reasons why her father wouldn't use his precious capital. "I didn't want to leave my team. I wanted my CO to be fired because he was a sexually harassing jerk of a man who didn't deserve his badge. In fact, it was a transfer that got me to walk out."

Shawna's eyes focused on her. "But what would you have said if you could have moved to Brooklyn? To your granddad's precinct?"

"That wasn't what they offered me. Not they. Joel. He transferred me to Staten Island. No disrespect to them, but my talents would have been wasted there."

"And they're not here?" Shawna waved that off. "All I'm saying is I wonder if you would have had a different reaction if they'd offered to move you to the place you always wanted to be. I happen to know a couple of cops from that precinct, and they would have killed to have you. But Joel wanted to live in Manhattan."

Plenty of people commuted. "What you're saying is Joel wanted a wife who wouldn't hurt his career. It doesn't matter. I can't go back and change things. I can't tell my younger self, *Don't marry the douchebag who'll have far more contact with your family after your divorce than you will.*"

Shawna leaned forward. "It might be hard for you to believe, but Brian isn't friendly with him. I know it looks like he abandoned you, but he didn't want to. You didn't even tell him you were quitting."

She glanced over at her brother. Should she have talked to him?

"Roxanne, Shawna," her mother called out. "Come over here. Seraphina made appetizers and they're delicious. The shrimp here is excellent."

Shawna's nose wrinkled. "I don't like the food here. It's so spicy. All I want is a Frappuccino."

Still, she got up and dutifully walked over to the outdoor dining table. Roxanne looked over to where Zep was laughing at something Harry said. Could she go join them instead? She sighed and followed her soon-to-be sister-in-law.

"That's because they were swimming in the Gulf a couple of hours ago," she told her mother as she sat down.

"Well, all the food here so far has been very good," her father said.

Her mother took a sip of her wine. "I don't know. It's spicy. Roxanne, how did you cope with it?"

She'd coped because she'd had Zep slowly introducing her to it. *I wanted to make sure you could always have something to eat.* "I got used to it over time. It doesn't hurt that Zep's family owns a restaurant. I got to try a lot of things."

Her mother's eyes strayed Zep's way. "Yes, his family seems interesting. His mother is definitely a character. She was here earlier to see her grandson, and she told me all about the two of you."

Dear lord. What had Delphine said? She would only have been trying to help, but Delphine had a vivid imagination.

"She definitely talked her son up," her father said. "According to her, Zep is practically a national hero. How long have you worked with him? Is the office where you met him?"

She wasn't about to tell her dad that she'd met him briefly

at Guidry's before she'd found him in a bar, taken him to a cheap motel room, and forgotten all about her troubles for a night. She wasn't going to tell him that she'd run as fast as she could when she'd remembered who he was.

"No, he's only started working for the parish recently."

"And he handles stray dogs?" Brian asked. "Why doesn't he work for animal services?"

"Because we don't have an animal services department," she explained. "We've got a lot of land, but our population is spread out, so central services are hard to handle out here. It's why we've got a sheriff but no police. We have to serve the whole parish, not merely a city."

"Well, if you would come home, all you would have to serve is a neighborhood," her mother interjected. "Don't you miss home? I can't imagine living in this place. I mean the B and B is nice, but there's no Broadway."

Yes, she'd heard this before. She would reply the same way she always did. "When was the last time you saw a Broadway show?"

Her mother waved that off. "They're too expensive and most of them are depressing, but I like to know I could go if I wanted to."

"Well, we have Miss Alma's drama and dance school, and they put on a killer production of *Cats* last year and the only admission was donations to the food bank." The production had been done with actual cats onstage and a children's chorus doing all the singing offstage. Miss Alma had called it avant-garde theater. Mostly the cats had rolled around and slept while the kiddos sang their hearts out. Except Dixie's tabby, who'd been in heat at the time. Yeah, she was fixed now and there had been many a birds-and-bees discussion later.

Shawna stared at her. "What about shopping? I didn't even see a Sephora in town."

"We get all our makeup from either the Walmart in Houma or Graceline Touk sells Mary Kay. I would be careful around her, though. She'll upsell you hard because she's working on a new pink Caddy." She sat back, kind of enjoying the horror in her mother and Shawna's eyes. "We might not have lots of clothes shopping, but we have a store where you can buy bait for fishing and Bibles. But not any of the weird Bibles. Only the King James Version. That's what the owner says at least. He will also bless your fishing gear, but I don't think he's a real priest."

The lack of shopping didn't bother her. She wasn't a high-maintenance chick. She didn't do regular spa visits, or even her makeup most days she was working. She got her hair cut twice a year and hadn't started going gray yet. She wore a uniform to work, and every place else was pretty casual. Armie kept a workout room at the station house, and jogging in the park was free.

And peaceful.

"I have a hard time thinking you're happy here. I don't see it on your face," her mother said.

How many times had she been told she would be prettier if she smiled? "Mom, I was born with resting bitch face. It's served me well in both the military and as a cop. I don't smile a lot. It doesn't mean I'm not content."

"I think if you smiled more, you might get further in life. Shawna always smiles."

Shawna gave her the biggest grin. One that she never had on her face unless her future mother-in-law or men were around.

Her mother gestured Shawna's way. "See. Smile and the world smiles with you."

There was one problem with that. "I don't care if the world smiles."

Her mother frowned. "That's another problem. You have

to care about what people think more or you're never getting out of here."

"What if she doesn't want to get out of here, Mom?" Brian sat up straighter. "What if she's happy here? From what I've seen, she's got a boyfriend she cares about, a nice place to live, and a steady job. I thought we were coming down here to make sure she's okay. She seems to be okay. Can't we enjoy some time together? I was thinking about going fishing. Zep and I talked about it earlier. He said there's a lot of good fishing to be had out here."

Did she want her brother and Zep to go fishing together?

"Of course she wants to get out of here." Her mother had at least had the courtesy of lowering her voice. Seraphina had walked out onto the deck, Luc following close behind. She joined the men at the grill and had the glow of a woman who was well loved.

"I'm looking into some options," Roxie admitted. "I've got some feelers out for departments in some larger cities. Hopefully I'm not being blackballed."

Her mother's lips pursed. "You were never blackballed."

"Then explain to me why I couldn't get a job." She was so sick of her mother pretending nothing had gone wrong.

"I don't know, Roxanne," her mother said with a long-suffering sigh. "I only know that everything went wrong when you divorced Joel. I like this new boy. I do, but he's obviously not cut out for what you're going to need."

Zep had given her a lot of stuff she hadn't even known she'd needed. She hadn't known she needed a dog. She hadn't known she'd needed long hours spent in bed with nothing to do but touch and caress another person.

She forced the images away. He was in her head way too much. "What do you think I need, Mom?"

Her mother's expression became overly serious. "You need to come home and get serious about your life. You're not getting any younger. How long do you think your eggs are going to last? I read an article about infertility, and half your eggs are dead."

She was going to need so much liquor.

"I'm going to get a drink." Roxie pushed the chair back and stood.

"You shouldn't drink when you're trying to get pregnant," her mother chided. "Not that you should try right now. You need a serious man. I know he's good looking and charming, but is he father material?"

She walked away, praying her mother didn't follow.

The great room of the B and B had a small but elegantly appointed bar in one corner. This was where Seraphina and Harry hosted nightly wine hours for their guests. Tonight's selection included a bottle of Scotch, likely in deference to her father's preferences. She passed up the bottles of Pinot Grigio and Cabernet and went straight for that eighteen-year-old Highland single malt.

She'd just taken a drink when she heard a familiar voice.

"You have to forgive her. She's under a lot of stress." Her brother walked up and poured himself a glass, too.

Sera was going to be surprised by how much Scotch her family could go through. "Do I? I can think of so many reasons to not forgive her. Talking openly about the state of my eggs is the latest."

"She's worried about grandkids."

"Yeah, I got that. Why is she down here bugging me about it? You're getting married. Shouldn't she bug you? Shawna apparently smiles more than I do. I'm sure that means she'll make better babies."

Brian was quiet for a moment. "Shawna can't have kids."

That made her stop. "What?"

"She's not fertile. Do you remember when we broke up?"

They'd dated off and on for the last few years. The truth

was she'd been surprised when they'd announced they were engaged. She'd always thought that Shawna wasn't serious enough for him.

And she hated that she'd had that thought because her mother had said the same thing about Zep.

"You broke up a lot."

"Yeah, I guess we did. Well, I'm talking about the major breakup. You know I asked her to marry me on Christmas Eve this year."

"Yes. I heard all about it." She'd decided to work through the holidays. She hadn't gone home. She'd told herself she was taking one for the team since her working gave the others a chance to be with their families. Now she mostly thought she'd been avoiding her own.

She'd missed her brother's engagement.

"That wasn't the first time I asked her to marry me," Brian admitted. "I asked her six months before and she turned me down."

"I hadn't heard that. Mom mentioned something about you two having a fight, but she didn't tell me what it was about." And Roxie hadn't asked because she hadn't wanted to know anything about her family for years.

"I was pretty vague about it with her. I know she loves me but she can be difficult to deal with. I didn't tell her we'd broken up because Shawna had told me she couldn't marry me. I didn't tell her that I'd ignored the way the woman I was supposed to love had cried. She rarely cries. It's pretty much dogs dying in movies and me asking her to marry me that first time. That's when I've seen her cry. Did I stop and ask what was wrong? Nope. I heard that no and flew into a selfish rage. I walked out. It took a month for me to finally go to her and ask her why."

"I'm sorry. I didn't know."

He shrugged and poured her another glass. "We haven't

been close in years. Maybe never. Some siblings are like that. Anyway, Shawna told me what she hadn't before. Her mother died at thirty-nine of uterine cancer. When she was younger, she took a genetic test. She had the gene for it and made the decision to have a hysterectomy. She didn't save her eggs because she'd decided to not have kids and didn't want to deal with the cost. But then she met me and realized she wanted a family."

Her brother had always wanted that perfect life. A wife and two point five kids, a job everyone respected. "Had you not talked about it before? How could she not tell you?"

"She was afraid. I know she should have been upfront about it, but I also know her. She was afraid of losing me. She thought I would walk away, and who knows. Maybe I would have in the beginning. I took some time to think about it because I really did want kids."

"You can still have kids."

He shook his head, but it was a rueful expression. "I wanted my kids. I wanted kids who looked like me and her. I thought a long time about this because we could still have biological kids. We could have them with a surrogate. But I wanted our kid. That was when I realized I was a moron and I looked around. I see kids who need parents every day. It doesn't matter how they come into our home. All that matters is that when they grow up, they will have a piece of me and a piece of her. They'll be ours. We're getting married and we've decided to adopt. Shawna has been taking classes for how to deal with special-needs kids."

She stared at him, the idea almost unbelievable. Shawna did not seem deep enough to do something like that.

He frowned her way as though he knew exactly what she'd been thinking. "You don't know her. I know you think she's an airhead, but when she cares about something, she takes it seriously." He took a long breath and seemed to shake something off. "Anyway, I'm telling you all of this because our mother hasn't completely accepted it yet."

She was actually shocked she hadn't heard about this from her mother. Her mom wasn't known for keeping secrets. "The idea of you adopting?"

"She's still pushing for us to have a baby using a surrogate. She can't wrap her head around the idea that her grandkids might not look like her."

This was exactly what bugged her about her mother. She didn't understand why Brian put up with it. "Doesn't that make you mad?"

"It's how Mom is," he replied with a sigh. "It takes time for her to change her thinking. Do you remember how Mom used to talk all the time about how marriage is between a man and a woman and it shouldn't be any other way?"

She vaguely remembered it. Mostly she remembered the rest of the family giving her mom hell about how she'd changed. They teased her, but her mother simply said she didn't recall saying anything like it. "She came around on that. The last I remember she was going to a Pride Parade. I don't remember how that happened."

"Her sister finally came out. Mom doesn't get it until it personally affects her. Then she's on floats waving pro-lesbian signs and rewriting history. Once she meets that first kid, she'll love him or her and she'll tell everyone it was her idea."

It was typical. Right out of her mother's playbook. "How can that not bother you?"

"Because love is love and I don't question how we get there. Just so we do get there. Probably because I'm far more like Mom than I want to admit. Because in some ways I understand her. Because Shawna managed to forgive me." He took a sip of his drink. "When are you going to forgive us and come home, Roxanne? When are you going to stop punishing us?"

"I'm not punishing anyone. I didn't have a job anymore. And don't say it was all my doing. I quit because I had to. Joel had taken over my career. He was pushing me to a place I didn't want to go."

"But you didn't come to me. You didn't talk to Dad."

"I talked to Mom." That might have been her biggest mistake. "She told me I should take the Staten Island position and work on my marriage."

He groaned. "I worried it was something like that. She gives the only advice she knows. If you had come to me, I would have tried to help. I probably could have gotten you on somewhere, but you wouldn't even pick up the phone when I called."

A little guilt bubbled up inside her. She didn't like the feeling. "You were friends with Joel."

Brian stared at her as though he could will her to believe what he said next. "But I'm your brother. I'm your family. Again, I know we're not close, but damn, Roxie, I wish you would have trusted me even a little."

She hadn't even thought about it. She'd only talked to her mother because she'd needed a place to stay when she'd left Joel. She'd spent a single night before she'd moved in with a friend while she waited to hear back about a job.

"I'm sorry. I assumed you and Dad would take Joel's side. I know he talked to Dad about it. Dad didn't think I should have made that report."

"I didn't think it would do what you hoped it would, either. No one was willing to listen at the time. But I would have backed you. I don't know what Dad would have done. He's pretty old school."

"I didn't want to know." She still didn't. "But me moving here wasn't punishment. It was the only job I could find."

"Then why haven't you come home to visit?"

She hated the feeling in the pit of her stomach that she'd done something wrong. She hadn't. She'd done what she needed to do. "Because I've been busy."

His eyes rolled. "All right. Well, I hope your busy schedule opens up in time for my wedding, and I hope you can be patient with our mom. You're not serious about this guy. You can't be angry with her for something that's true."

"Why would you think I'm not serious about him?"

"Because you're already thinking of your next job," he pointed out. "Because you'll eventually find one in a big department where you can move up, even if you don't come back to NYPD. Because he's got a record and you wouldn't ever get serious about a criminal."

Her heart threatened to stop. "You ran a trace on him?"

"Of course. Don't worry. I told Dad he was clean but only because I know you're not serious about him. Is he for show? I never actually bought that you were seeing the sheriff, either. You don't date people you work with. Definitely not your boss. You wouldn't have dated Joel if you'd been in the same precinct."

She wasn't about to tell her brother that he was right on all counts. Maybe he was a better detective than she thought he was. "I don't have to justify myself to you or anyone else. And I would appreciate it if you kept Zep's record to yourself. You had no right to look into his past. It was a long time ago and he was a kid. Whether you think I'm serious about him or not, he's . . . he's my friend and I don't want Dad giving him trouble."

"Or maybe I'm wrong about you not being serious about him. You should think about that. If you want to get anywhere in our world, you can't do it with him. He'll drag you down." He finished off his drink. "I'll go and see if I can get Mom to talk about something other than your maturing reproductive system during dinner. You think about what I said. I know you don't think you're punishing us, but that's what it feels like. And I hope like hell you aren't punishing yourself."

Her brother walked away, and she was left with a sinking feeling in her gut.

# *chapter eight*

Zep wondered what the hell had happened with her parents. He'd thought it had gone fairly smoothly, but now he realized she'd been silent most of the night. "Your mom seemed to be in a good mood."

"She's good at putting on a show." Roxie sat in the passenger seat with Daisy in her lap. The dog had promptly fallen asleep the minute the truck had started down the paved drive that led to the highway.

Roxie wasn't good at putting on a show. She wasn't good at hiding her emotions at all. He'd always thought that she had a spectacular poker face, but spending all this time with her had taught him that when she was really emotional, she shut down.

She'd shut down on everything tonight and he needed to know why.

Direct questioning wouldn't help. She would reply with one-word answers, and they might lose all the intimacy he'd fought so hard to win.

Luckily he knew exactly what to do. When he'd realized that she'd barely eaten all night, he'd known what had to be done.

"Hey, you missed the turn." She didn't sound like she cared all that much.

"We're not going home." He liked saying the word *home* and associating it with her.

She finally turned toward him. "Zep, I'm tired."

"You barely ate."

"I wasn't hungry. And honestly, I wasn't in the mood for steak."

"How about some gumbo?"

A brow rose over her eyes. "You're going to make gumbo at this time of night? I thought that was one of those things that takes hours to make."

A good gumbo could take all day, but he wasn't going to be cooking. "I texted my brother two hours ago. He left a pot on the stove for us. Guidry's is closed, but I have a key. I wasn't much in the mood for steak, either."

He turned down the road that led to the marina. There was a glorious full moon hanging over the bay.

"You're hungry?" She asked the question with a hint of anticipation. Like she could be hungry if he was.

"I'm starving. Your dad grilled me way longer than Harry grilled those steaks," he said, pulling into the parking lot. At this time of night it was completely empty. He pulled up to the back of the building.

"Then I could eat. I don't think we have much back at home."

"You have lots of ramen noodles and cereal."

She shrugged. "I eat out a lot, either here or at Dixie's."

"Well, let's get some food. I think we were both too afraid to eat at the B and B. I know I was worried I would screw up and give away the game. Your father is an excellent interrogator. I didn't realize what he was doing until he sprang the 'what are your intentions toward my daughter' part."

Her eyes widened. "He did what?"

Daisy's head came up as he opened the door and eased out of the truck. She got to her feet and jumped out with him. "He didn't say it in those words, but I got a lot of questions about my job and my prospects. Lucky for me, my brother recently gave me an out there."

She followed behind him as he used his keys and opened the door that led to the backroom and kitchen. "Gave you an out?"

The smell of gumbo hit his nose, and his stomach growled in pleasant anticipation. "He wants me to take over managing the boatyard, and more specifically the shop. I'm pretty handy with engines."

"That smells good." She walked into the kitchen. His brother had done a great job of modernizing. The space was clean and glistening, every pot and pan in place with the exception of one. There was a small covered pot on the counter, and Remy had left out two bowls and spoons. "I've never seen you work on an engine. No one talks about you being a mechanic."

"I'm not really. I dabble. And I think for the most part no one talks about me being good at anything but drinking beer. I should get more credit for my dancing abilities. I move well." The gumbo was still warm as he poured out two bowls.

"I'm serious." She took the bowl from him. "Why didn't you mention you're taking a new job? Does it have any effect on the job at the station?"

He nabbed two beers from the fridge. "It will definitely be easier to mesh the two than the server job, and the paycheck will be more steady. Come on. I want to show you something. Come on, girl."

"Do you mean me or Daisy?"

He winked her way. "Daisy's the girl. You're obviously a woman, baby."

She groaned but followed anyway. "Ah, there's the Zep I know. For a minute I thought you were going to get serious with me."

"You should know I'm not serious about much." He started to lead her out into the dining room, but that wasn't his destination.

She stopped and he heard her gasp. "Oh, that's amazing."

Guidry's back wall was all heavy hurricane glass that gave a spectacular view of the bay. She was likely used to how pretty the water was and being able to watch the boats go by, but she'd never been here after hours to see it like this. The moon was full and hung over the bay, casting a soft glow to the ocean.

"Remy, Sera, and I would help out during the summers, and after hours we would turn off all the lights and sit out here and watch the moon and the water. I love this place. I know it's my brother's and it's his passion, but I do love it, too."

"Is that why you want to take over the shop?" She walked through the door, followed by Daisy, who seemed perfectly content to simply follow her new mom.

"I don't want to take it over at all. It sounds awful." He walked to the bench at the far end of the patio. There were tons of tables, but he wanted to sit on that bench with her, wanted their legs to brush against each other, and he wanted to be able to ease his arm around her shoulders when they were finished.

He sank down on the bench and she found a place beside him.

"Then why would you take it?"

He sighed. He shouldn't have gotten into this. "I figure I don't have anything better to do. You know me. I kind of go with the flow. But don't worry. I told your dad it was a way better job than it is. I made myself sound pretty important."

He was good at deflecting. It was a skill he'd developed over many years.

"It won't work with my dad," she said between spoonfuls. "You're not important unless you're some kind of law enforcement, and he won't think the fact that you're a wildlife expert who works for the parish is impressive, either."

Well, he never said she sugarcoated things. "I suppose that's why you initially told him you were seeing Armie."

"Armie has credentials in my dad's world, and if my father approves, then my mother doesn't give me holy hell for still being single at thirty. I know it sounds dumb, but I really was trying to keep the peace. I worry at some point I won't even be able to talk to her anymore."

She went quiet again, simply sitting and eating her gumbo, her eyes on the bay.

"I didn't talk to my brother for a couple of years. When he went into the Navy, he would write us all letters, but I tossed them out. After a few, he just wrote Mom and Sera."

"Why didn't you write to your brother? You two seem close."

"We're closer now, though I wouldn't say we're super tight," he admitted. "He's seven years older than me. We didn't hang out much as kids. I was closer to Sera."

"That's like Brian and me. There's six years between us. He was in school by the time I was born. He had friends and this whole life. He didn't need a toddler hanging around. I was surprised he came down with my mom and dad."

"I noticed you two disappeared for a little while."

She nodded. She'd polished off her bowl and set it on the table next to the bench, picking up the longneck he'd brought for her. "Yeah, he was trying to play peacekeeper between me and my mom. Sometimes I wonder why she tries, you know. If I'm such a damn disappointment, why even keep trying to fix me."

"Because you're her daughter. Not that I agree with the idea that you need to be fixed, but it's my experience that mommas always need to be needed. When was the last time you asked her advice about something?"

Her nose wrinkled. "Never. At least not since I was a kid."

"There you go. See, I ask my mom for advice on everything and she doesn't bug me about getting married and having kids. She's constantly planting hints to Remy and Sera that she needs more little ones running around. Me? She leaves condoms in my apartment."

That brought a smile to her face. "She knows you well."

Naturally, that's what she would think. At least she'd smiled. "Yeah, I guess so."

Her eyes narrowed on him. "There it is. You have a tell when you get your feelings hurt. Your lips purse slightly and you look away. What did I say? You were the one who joked about needing condoms."

He frowned. "I wasn't hurt."

She looked back at the water. "Okay. My mistake."

She went silent, one hand on her beer and the other on Daisy's head as the puppy settled down beside her.

He'd lost his appetite. He set the bowl down. "All right. What did I do wrong?"

"Nothing."

Another moment of silence passed between them. "Damn it, Rox. We were fine and then I made a joke and . . ." What had his brother said? He had to be vulnerable. He didn't want to be vulnerable with anyone. That wasn't his place. He was the good-time guy. He was the guy you partied with and looked to for fun. Did he want to be that guy for her? It was what she thought of him, but maybe that was because he'd never once shown her another side. "I hate it when my mom leaves condoms around because it makes me feel like she doesn't want grandkids from me. I know it's stupid because that's not her intention and it's not like I'm ready to give her any, but it hurts all the same."

"Seriously?" she snorted, a derisive sound. "I'll trade you for mine. I'll take free condoms over her talking about the maturity of my eggs any day."

Yes, that was why he didn't talk about feelings. They were surprisingly delicate things. "Yeah, I'm sure that's easier. And you know I'll use them. Well, I'm going to go clean up and we can head home."

Her hand came over his, stopping him from standing up. "There's that tell. Zep, I'm sorry. I'm not good at the feelings thing. It's been pointed out to me on occasion that I'm not particularly sensitive and I'm not one to talk about anything important. But I kind of think not talking hasn't worked for me. It's hard when everyone views you as the not successful sibling. I've only got one. It must be hard to have to deal with two. I think that's part of what got to me. In my mother's head, the only way I can have any value is to have kids. She's never cared about my career. She cried when I told her I was joining the Army. Not because she was scared for me. She was upset because it meant I would put off having a family. She thought I should try becoming a teacher or a nurse because it was a good way to find a husband. I asked her if she understood it wasn't the freaking fifties anymore, and I promptly left the country to shoot things."

It was so much easier to talk about her. "You always knew you wanted to be a cop, right?"

"I just knew I loved what my grandfather did. It was noble. We had a whole family of cops. It was tradition. For the men. My dad seemed proud at the time, but now I wonder."

"Have you ever asked him?"

"Do you remember the part about me not being great with my feelings?" She turned his way, her eyes on him now. "And I'm proving it because I didn't mean to talk about me. Why are you taking a job you don't want?"

Yeah, this was way harder. But there was expectation in her eyes. She wanted to know, and it wasn't a polite question. She wanted something real from him. "Because I don't have anything else to do. I can take over the shop and help my brother out, or I can keep on taking shifts from people who are way better at serving than I am. Not everyone knows what they want to do in life. Not everyone has this grand plan and perfect job for them."

"But most people have things they're interested in. You like working with animals."

"Yeah, that doesn't actually pay. We're too small a town to have a dog training school." He took a deep breath and decided to go all in. "I guess I was kind of lying, though. I wanted to do something like work with the park rangers or with the wildlife department. I was even going to finish my four-year degree. I got into school . . . well, the preliminary part. But it didn't work out."

Her eyes had widened. "Are you serious? I didn't take you for the college type, Guid . . . Zep."

He so preferred it when she called him by his nickname. His last name put distance between them. "No one did. My mom was shocked when I decided to go to community college. She was even more shocked when I actually finished. Or she would have been if she hadn't been dealing with the fact that her daughter was pregnant with no insurance and no man in the picture. I didn't actually make it to graduation."

She stared at him for a moment. "You didn't go to college because your sister was pregnant."

Well, it hadn't taken her long to figure that out. Her

detective skills were in fine working order. "Doctors are expensive. Remy helped out, but he wasn't around much, and for my mother, having me around was comforting. I was the one who did all the late-night stuff. Why do babies always get sick in the middle of the night?"

"I don't know much about babies."

"I know way too much about them for a man who isn't even close to being ready to have one of his own."

She leaned over, putting her head on his shoulder. "But you want your mom to want you to have kids."

It was stupid, but there it was. "Yeah. I guess I want to be like my brother and my sister. I want her to see me as something other than a burden."

"You're not a burden." Her arm wound through his and she seemed to settle in. "Have you ever thought about going back? To school, that is. Sera and Luc are good. The restaurant is good. It might be time to give it another go."

"I think that time is gone. It probably wasn't a realistic dream in the first place. It kind of was a miracle I survived those two years of community college."

"Don't."

He looked down at her.

Her head was tilted up, a stern expression on her face. "Don't negate yourself like that. You got through it. Have you ever considered the idea that the reason people don't take you seriously is that you don't take yourself seriously?"

He didn't think about that at all. He was who he was, and it was how it had always been.

Or had it? Had he bought into this version of himself somewhere along the way? Had he allowed himself to be put in a corner, told what his role was, and not even thought about challenging it? "I guess I haven't."

She settled back down, and he loved the way she sighed against him. "Well, you should. You're not such a bad guy.

You're actually pretty solid. And you can find the best gumbo."

She was relaxed again, and all it had cost him was a little honesty. Maybe his brother had been right and what she needed was for him to open up. Of course there was something else he knew all the girls liked. "I happen to know there's bread pudding in the fridge."

"See, I knew there was a reason I liked you."

Roxie sat across from Zep, pleasantly full from the ridiculously rich bread pudding he'd heated up for them. They'd sat outside for a while, and the whole time she'd thought about what he'd told her. "So when are you taking over the shop?"

"Not until Willie retires. He runs it right now." He tipped back his beer.

She was surprised by how little he'd drunk. Once again, maybe she'd listened to too many rumors about the baddest boy on the bayou. According to the pearl clutchers of the town, Zep Guidry spent his nights drinking and seducing every woman in sight. She'd certainly caught him out at bars, but now she wondered about how frequent that was.

How many bad boys gave up their hopes and dreams to take care of a sister and nephew? She'd thought he was a selfish ass, but she had to consider that she'd had preconceived notions of the man and she hadn't allowed herself to get to know him.

Had that been fear?

"But you're going to start soon?" She had an idea brewing in her head. It wasn't formed yet. It was nothing more than a cloud of thought pinging around in her brain.

"I'm not on a timer or anything. Remy wants me in place when Willie does decide to finally buy the camper of his dreams. I suspect I'll start in a few weeks. I'm doing some volunteer work at the shelter a couple of towns over. It's the closest one, but it's a drive so I usually spend most of the day there when I work. I sometimes think the distance is why pups like Daisy end up in the woods."

"Because there's no place close to take her." She doubted that would change some people's minds, but it could encourage others to help rescue abandoned animals.

"Not unless you want to drive an hour down the highway," Zep replied. "I know the guy who runs the shelter. He doesn't have a lot of help and he definitely doesn't have a ton of money, so I volunteer a couple of days a month."

He seemed to volunteer a lot. For a man who everybody treated like a joke, there were a whole bunch of people who depended on him. Or maybe she was the one who didn't understand. She was viewing everything through her own filter, her experiences. She'd put up a barrier to protect herself, but she was starting to wonder if she needed it.

"Why did you write those hot checks?" It was time she asked. She could look at his record all day long, but it wouldn't tell her the whys. When she thought about it, she'd started to feel differently. Yes, a crime was a crime, but it didn't necessarily make up the whole of a person. There were reasons behind most crimes, especially when the "criminal" hadn't repeated his mistakes. She couldn't count the bar fights. They were kind of one of the only things for young men to do on Saturday nights besides church socials.

"It was one check. Not checks." His eyes had flared and then he shook his head and sat back. "I guess I should have figured you would know all about my mistakes. It explains a few things."

"What?"

"Did you find out about it before or after you decided you didn't want to have anything to do with me?"

She had to tell him the truth. It seemed like it was a night for honesty no matter how much it hurt. "I knew about it before we spent the night together."

"Then why would you spend the night with me? You weren't drunk. I made sure you'd only had two beers before I approached you. I didn't want to take advantage of you."

"I did it because I knew I wouldn't have a relationship with you. Because weirdly, I thought you were safe."

His lips pursed slightly, and his eyes were on the table. "Well, I guess that's honest."

One of the things she'd learned about him was how he could look unaffected even when he was hurting. "I was honest with you that night. I told you it was about sex and nothing more."

He nodded her way. "You were very honest with me that night. You didn't do anything wrong. I'm the one who lied since I knew I wanted more from you and told you I was okay with it."

"I was honest with you, but I wasn't honest with myself. I was attracted to you from the moment I met you, but I didn't want to be. It wasn't you. I didn't want to be attracted to anyone. The divorce was harder on me than I like to say." It was one of the reasons dinner had put her on edge. She'd had to sit there with her parents, who'd been married for almost forty years, and her brother and her future sister-in-law, who'd turned out to have some real depth to them. And she'd known they were all disappointed in her. "I don't like to fail and that's what divorce felt like to me."

"I fail all the time," he replied softly. "I sure as hell failed at being a proper criminal."

"What were you doing in Arizona?" She was curious. She'd asked Armie, but he hadn't been sheriff at the time. She certainly hadn't asked any of the Guidrys.

"I was making a fool of myself," he replied. "I had a

friend who got some work on film sets. He convinced me I should come out and try to be an actor. He had an agent who'd seen my picture and convinced him he could find me some work. I didn't want to be an actor or a model, but at the time I did want to get out of Papillon. I got in my car and got as far as Phoenix before it broke down. Naturally I met a girl. She was in college. I was in Phoenix for about a month when it happened. I'd found a job and was living in this crappy motel while I saved up to fix my car."

"You wrote that check to fix your car?" According to the reports she'd read, he'd cashed a check for two thousand dollars written to himself.

"I didn't write the check at all," he said with a sigh. "The girl I was seeing, she wrote it and convinced me to cash it. She said she couldn't cash it herself because she was in trouble with the bank, so she had her mom write it out to me. I know. I was stupid."

"You didn't get the money?" It was worse than she'd imagined. Not on the guilt side. On the naïve idiot side. He could have done serious time for forgery and he hadn't even gotten the money? He'd been trying to help someone, and he'd been burned hard.

He shook his head. "Nope. I did what she asked and turned the money over to her. When the police showed up, I was arrested and my girlfriend's mom bought her story that I'd stolen the check and she had no idea I was doing it. I got a public defender, and lucky for me, he was actually pretty decent both at his job and as a human being. He made a deal with the DA. If I pled out, they reduced the charges. I would get six months and likely would do about half if I behaved. My brother actually came and picked me up when I got out. He's the only one who knows what really happened. I don't know if he believes me or not. Probably not, but at least he trusts me now."

She believed him. He'd been barely eighteen. "They didn't want to bring in a handwriting expert?"

"I couldn't make bail, Roxie. If I'd fought it, I would have sat there for maybe longer than the actual sentence," he explained. "I know I could have called my mother, but that seemed worse than jail. As soon as I got out, I went home and I actually got my priorities in line. That was when I went to community college and I met the vet who runs the shelter in Houma."

That was when he'd started to dream. Then he'd sacrificed to help his family, the same one he wanted so desperately to hide his mistakes from. He should be hard with a hundred walls up. That time in jail should have taught him to protect himself, yet here he was every day giving to the people around him. Why hadn't she seen past his gorgeous looks and bad reputation to the real man inside? "You don't owe your brother your entire future."

She had the most insane urge to sit on his lap and wrap her arms around him. Seeing him like this was softening her up in ways she hadn't imagined. Or perhaps she had, and it was exactly why she'd stayed away from him.

"It's not like I'm doing anything with it."

But he was. He was helping a lot of people. He was kind. Wasn't that something? He was right. Not everyone got their dream job. Not everyone's dream was a job. It was hard to imagine because she'd always wrapped up her own self-worth in her job. She followed her instinct now and got up, moving toward him. He looked a bit surprised as she eased onto his lap, but his arm went around her waist.

"I was fooling myself about you." She put her hands on his cheeks and looked him right in the eyes, willing him to believe her. "I felt something when I met you, and it wasn't lust. It was more. I told myself I could have one night and then walk away. The same way I'm telling myself I can have a week with you and walk away."

"I don't want you to walk away."

"But, Zep, you have to understand that I never meant to stay here. I always meant for this place to be temporary for me."

He hugged her tight and let his forehead rest against hers. "I understand. Whatever we have is not going to last."

Hearing him say the words hurt her heart. "Can we not make a decision right this second? The truth is, I don't have any interviews coming up. Who knows? I might be here for another year or two. We don't know what could happen. I've tried to control whatever this thing is between us. What if I didn't? What if I just let it be for now?"

His free hand moved over her thigh, turning the moment into anticipation for her.

"So even after your parents are gone, you'll still see me? You won't try to hide it?"

It was one thing to be seen with him when everyone thought they were simply tricking her parents. If she was seen with him after her parents went home, she would be one more of Zep Guidry's conquests. She would be talked about, gossiped over.

She shook her head. "No, I won't hide it."

She wouldn't treat him like something she was ashamed of. The more she got to know him, the more she liked the man behind that gorgeous mask he wore.

He kissed her and for the first time in hours she felt herself relax.

"It wasn't a failure," he whispered. "Your marriage, that is. It just wasn't meant to be, baby. If I know you, you put everything you had into it."

She felt tears pulse behind her eyes. She never cried, but

he brought out something soft inside her. "I don't think I did. I married him because I thought it was time to get started. I married him because he was the right kind of man for me. I married him because I didn't think I would ever fall in love. I thought it was nothing but a Hollywood myth, and that good sense was a better bet than lust and hormones. But I was wrong. I feel something for you. I don't know what that is, and I don't know if it can work. But I feel it."

"Then we have a deal. We're together for however long it lasts, and we're going to be good to each other." He kissed her cheek, a deeply affectionate gesture that somehow he also made so damn sexy. "I won't ever hold you back, Roxanne. I promise that."

Before she could say another thing, his mouth was on hers and she wasn't thinking about anything beyond his next kiss.

Then she felt another warm tongue on her ear.

"Daisy," Zep said in a deep voice. "Off the table."

She laughed because Daisy was trying desperately to get in on all the hugs and kisses.

"I'm going to train that dog," Zep vowed. "But lucky for me, I know where the office is and there's a comfy couch."

He picked her up, hauling her close and making her feel so feminine.

She had some time with him. She was going to make the most of it.

# *chapter nine*

Zep followed Roxie inside the station house. Usually he was pushed in front of her and tossed into a cell. This was a totally new experience. He wasn't being locked up. He was going to work.

"Aw, hey, who is this beauty?" Major stood up from his desk and went down to one knee as Daisy made her station house debut. She proved she'd never met a stranger as she immediately went to the deputy and started trying to lick him all over.

In that way, Daisy wasn't unlike some of the other females of the town. Every momma in Papillon with a single daughter had tried to get the man over for Sunday supper.

A tiny voice inside Zep's head kept saying that Major was probably the right kind of man for Roxie.

But Major wasn't the one who'd spent last night in her bed, and Zep was going to try to ensure he kept it that way. If he stayed in her bed, he could keep everyone else out of it.

"This is Daisy," Roxie was saying. "Armie told me I could bring her in. I hate the idea of her being in a crate all day, and she's not exactly housebroken yet."

"She's getting there," Zep added. "She's a smart girl. She'll settle in. It's been a while since the sheriff's department had a mascot."

"Do not tell my daughter I was enthusiastic about this." Armie LaVigne came out of his office and gave the puppy a pet. "The old sheriff used to keep his big bloodhound in the station house. He said it was because the dog helped with tracking down dangerous criminals. I told Noelle no when she wanted to bring her hamster up here. She swore she could train it to sniff out drugs."

Major stood. "The old sheriff's hound didn't do much more than sleep. Kind of like the sheriff himself. I, for one, am happy to have a dog around. She can go for a jog with me later on. I'm pretty good with the puppies."

Roxie smiled, something he'd noticed she did more and more these days. "That would be great. She needs tons of exercise. We had her with us last night and she was still hyper at midnight. She seems to have two speeds—dead asleep or a hundred miles an hour."

"Well, she's a Lab, so expect that to continue for at least the next year and a half," Armie said. "She's welcome here. You brought bags, right? If you didn't, I have some for when I bring Peanut to the station. We enforce sanitation laws for everyone."

"Yes, we will clean up after the dog. Can't have the po-po getting mixed up with a poo-poo scandal," Zep replied.

Roxie groaned. "He's been waiting to use that one for a while, I bet. Stop with the bad puns, babe. You work here now. Armie's the only one who's allowed to make dad jokes."

Armie gestured back to his office. "Major, can you watch the dog while I take these two back to visit with the mayor and my lovely wife? And I don't make dad jokes. I make jokes. Funny jokes."

This was why he'd come into the office with her today.

Armie had called him in this morning. The mayor and Lila had requested a quick meeting with him and Roxie concerning some problems they were having around the parish.

With the damn rougarou.

That didn't exist.

He followed Roxie into the small conference room, where Lila LaVigne sat talking to the mayor of Papillon. Sylvie Martine gave him a big smile as he walked in. The mayor's mother was his mother's most frequent coconspirator. They'd grown up together, and Sylvie was the most reasonable of his sister's closest friends.

"Hey, Zep. It's good to see you." She was dressed in a stylish blouse, slacks, and heels he wasn't sure how the woman walked in. Like his older brother, Sylvie had spent time in big cities before returning to the bayou to help out her hometown. She'd taken over the mayor's office when the previous mayor had died suddenly.

"And Roxie," Lila said pointedly, her eyes like laser beams on the deputy. "It's good to see you. Especially since I was supposed to see you yesterday."

He saw Roxie wince and decided to try to play the knight. "I kept her busy all day. You know how my shenanigans can go. It was entirely my fault, Lila."

Lila shook her head. "Nope. It was hers."

"See, I kept her out late with my partying and terrible social ways," he tried.

"Still her fault." Lila obviously wasn't buying it.

"Her family is in town." He wasn't going to give up.

Roxie put a hand on his arm. "Stop. It was one hundred percent my fault. I got busy and I forgot to come see you. I'm sorry. I'll do whatever tests you want this afternoon. I promise."

Lila gave her a once-over with a frown. "You feeling okay? No headaches or dizzy spells?"

"I'm feeling great," Roxie said. "No nausea. Well, until Zep made a dog-doo joke, but that had nothing to do with the concussion and everything to do with his terrible sense of humor."

"I thought it was kind of funny. It was a word play. That's not dad-joke territory." He took a seat across from Sylvie and was beyond pleased when Roxie sat down beside him.

"It was kind of funny," Armie agreed as he sat at the head of the table.

Lila's eyes rolled. "You love a good dad joke."

"I don't do dad jokes," the sheriff argued.

Lila turned to the other women at the table. "Noelle has a social media page devoted to the awful jokes her dad comes up with. It's got ten thousand followers." Armie started to say something but his wife held him off, obviously ready to get on to the point of the meeting. "Now, Armie has explained a bit of this to me, but I have been fielding questions about what to do if bitten by some sort of mythical creature."

Zep should have seen that coming. "It's called a rougarou. Or that's what we would call it if it was actually real."

Sylvie sighed. "It's been years since we had a rougarou sighting."

"I looked it up on the Internet." Lila sat back, her frustration obvious. "Why? I have dealt with some crazy stuff in this town. I have a whole list of protocols on how to handle golf cart injuries because someone recently screened *The Fast and the Furious* at our senior center and then encouraged our elderly to treat their carts like racing cars."

It was Zep's turn to wince. "It seemed like a good idea at the time. They were having trouble setting up the new system and I went down there to help. They had terrible movies. All old people stuff."

"They are old people," Lila pointed out.

"Don't have to act like it. They're old, not dead." He wasn't about to mention that he'd helped a couple of the old guys juice their golf cart engines.

"My point is, I have to deal with weird stuff all the time because the people of this town are all crazy and stubborn, but I am not supposed to have to deal with werewolves," Lila explained.

"According to my mom, it's actually a witch," Sylvie added. "You see, only a witch can turn a person into a rougarou, so until we find the witch, we'll have the problem. But then my mom is one of the crazies, so we should probably talk about how to put down the rumors. It's not like anyone actually thinks there's something roaming the bayou with the head of a wolf and the body of a man looking to suck someone's blood. Cajuns can be on the superstitious side. They don't really believe it, but it makes them nervous that the story is going around. I'm getting calls about people hearing things at night."

Armie nodded. "My guys responded to two calls last night about something prowling around backyards. They couldn't find any evidence of even animals running around, though I think we've found a new make-out spot. We're going to put the lot behind Gene's store back on the patrol list. I don't care about kids making out as much as I want to make sure they're not doing anything else."

Roxie had her phone out, making notes to herself. "I find that when I come across a couple of teens hanging out, offering them condoms makes them run as fast as they can. Of course, I tell them what I'm really going to do is have a talk with their mothers about safe-sex practices. That was how I shut down the party spot out by the B and B."

Sylvie nodded. "That is brilliant."

Well, it would have worked on Zep when he was a kid. Though now that he was an adult, he got a lot of talk about condoms still.

He wondered if his momma would be all about the safe sex if he and Roxie were truly living together.

He was still going there. Even after everything she'd said the night before, he was still thinking about how to keep her. Or go with her if she left.

"Did either one of you see any evidence that we've got a loose animal running around?" Armie asked.

It was so odd to have everyone looking to him for answers that didn't include how a fight started. "I think the only thing running around out at Archie's was Daisy and whatever asshole dumped her in the woods. As for Dixie's, that was a bunch of kids who say they were working on a project but were probably making out."

"And at least two of those kids are grounded," Roxie added. "I don't know about Ashlyn, but the other two won't be seeing the light of day outside of school for a while."

"Why didn't anyone call me last night?" Zep had had his phone with him.

"Both of the calls were here in town, and given the stories going around, I expected nothing would come of them. Also, I knew you were at dinner with Roxie's parents," Armie explained. "Having talked to Roxie's dad this morning, I'm glad I didn't call you out and leave her alone with them. I now understand why you came up with that story about having a boyfriend," he said to Roxie. "You needed the backup."

Her face went a flaming red and her whole body tensed. "When did you talk to my dad?"

"Your mom and dad were at Dixie's this morning," Armie admitted. "He came over to our table. He wanted to introduce himself."

"Why would they leave the B and B?" Roxie looked a little panicked. "It's literally in the name. Bed. Breakfast. They didn't have to go out into the town."

"Oh, they've been all over the place," Sylvie admitted. "I saw them outside the library. Your mother wanted to know where the mall was. She was surprised when I explained there wasn't one for fifty miles."

Zep needed to get Sera to text him whenever they left so he could keep Roxie updated.

"I think they were trying to get a feel for where you live now. I can imagine it's a culture shock." Armie looked entirely amused by Roxie's embarrassment. If he was anything like Zep, he likely hadn't thought she could be embarrassed at all. "Your mom didn't talk to me. I think she was snubbing me."

Lila's eyes lit up. "Oh, she was definitely snubbing us. She actually turned her nose up at me. It's been a long time since I got treated like I'd done something terrible."

"I'm so sorry." Roxie's eyes had gone huge, and Zep got the feeling she apologized for her mother a lot.

It was an interesting relationship, and one he'd thought about last night.

Lila shrugged. "I probably have done some of those things. Ask my siblings. I'm not known for my Southern charm. But this is the first time I got in trouble for breaking up a couple that never dated. Miranda Jossart had too much fun with it, though. I heard her telling your mom that once I got my claws into Armie, I wouldn't let go. I believe the term 'gold digger' was used. Has she seen Armie's place? There is no gold there. None."

Armie chuckled. "I never worried about you wanting my extreme wealth. You were always after my manly body."

"It is pretty nice," Lila admitted.

Armie winked his wife's way before turning back to

Roxie. "Don't worry about a thing. It was all smooth sailing at Dixie's this morning. Your dad asked a bunch of questions about how I run the department. He's never worked for a small town before so he's curious about the difference in how we handle things. And don't worry. I totally lied about Zep. I said he was an upstanding citizen and scholar."

He frowned Armie's way, but Roxie put a hand on his arm as though lending him her support.

"I'm sorry if my dad bugged you, Sheriff," she said. "And Sylvie, I assure you they won't be at all interested in city hall. They'll be out of here Saturday and my life can go back to mostly normal."

The *mostly* part gave him hope. Also, the fact that she was treating him with some affection in front of people who were important to her job was a good sign that he might get the time he needed with her.

"He didn't bother me at all," Armie replied. "I assure you I'm going to want to meet all of Noelle's friends and coworkers when she heads off to the community college. I intend to drive her back and forth."

"I thought Noelle was applying to UT Austin," Sylvie said.

Lila sighed and shook her head. "Don't listen to him. She's already been accepted into UT Austin's bio chem program. He's in complete denial. It's okay since he's going to soon turn all his paternal paranoia the new baby's way. I pray this child is a boy."

Armie reached out and held his wife's hand. "And I want another girl to spoil, but we'll be happy with either."

Lila's eyes softened and she squeezed his hand. "We will. But this is another reason why we have to get this town to chill out about werewolves. And bunnies. I got a call asking about the rougarou and if it's possible to spread lycanthropy through the rougarou eating carrots and then bunnies eating the carrots. There's someone out there who is worried we're about to have rabid bunnies. Or maybe the bunny was the rougarou. I don't know. I think it was Herve's girlfriend, and she was a little drunk. She called the hotline to ask that question."

"My office is getting those calls, too," Sylvie said. "I think the only thing we can do is the one thing I don't want to do."

Armie's brows rose. "I don't think we should do that. I . . . we don't need that."

Oh, but it would be so fun. "I think we do."

"What are we talking about?" Roxie asked.

"The best entertainment in the whole world," he replied. "Town hall meeting. Open to the public. Dixie has a popcorn machine she sets up outside of town hall. She makes a killing off of it."

"I'm glad you think it's going to be fun, Zep," Armie said, sitting back.

Suddenly he realized every eye was on him. It was disconcerting because they all had that "we know something you don't" look in their eyes. "What?"

"You're the expert." Sylvie actually looked sympathetic. "So you're running that part of the meeting. You'll be giving everyone updates."

His stomach dropped. "What?"

Armie's face split in a wide grin. "Yeah, that makes it all worthwhile. That look right there. It's been a good day."

"You're mean," Lila said, but she was smiling, too.

"So everyone in town is going to view Zep as the expert, and they'll all call him." Roxie seemed to understand the horror of the situation. "Which means they will all call me if they can't find him because they will probably figure out that we're real dating instead of fake dating."

"Now, hey, baby, I will answer my phone. I promise." He wasn't giving her an easy out.

"I knew it." Lila held out a hand. "Pay up, Madam Mayor."

Sylvie rolled her eyes but fished a five out of her purse. "I'm glad I went stingy on that bet. She wanted me to put twenty on the line, but I thought her insider tips might be better than mine. Sera can be oblivious."

"Remy is not, and my sister likes to gossip as much as she likes to breathe." Lila took her five. "And of course they were going to come out of this together."

"Uhm, I mean we're . . ." Roxie seemed to fumble.

She wasn't a woman used to being the center of attention.

"What she's saying is we're not really dating. But we're going to try to be more polite to each other at the end of this." He was used to smoothing things over and making less of what should be more. "We're friends. That's all. You should give Sylvie back her five."

Lila's gaze could turn piercing at times, and this was one of them.

"Keep the five," Roxie said with a sigh. "He's lying. We're dating and it's okay because he's not going to start fistfights anymore. He's going to be a perfectly respectable boyfriend."

He was her boyfriend? "I am. I mean I will be. Starting now. And I will answer my phone so they don't call you asking where I am."

"You better." She laughed suddenly. "Because watching you deal with the great rougarou crisis is going to be so funny. I've gone to a town hall before. It's crazy. I'm definitely getting some of Dixie's popcorn."

She was going to be a terrible girlfriend. And he was going to enjoy every moment of it. Well, except the whole "run the town hall and answer everyone's utterly insane questions" part of it.

Lila stood up, grabbing her bag and gesturing toward the windows that separated the conference room from the main part of the station house. "You might want to put a hold on that popcorn order because your dad asked if he could come in, and my husband, while good at making terrible jokes, is awful at coming up with excuses on the fly. He's here to see where you work."

Roxie's face went sheet white as she turned and saw her dad standing in the middle of the station house, talking to Major and petting Daisy. "He's here."

The good news was Zep had a date with a whole bunch of dogs. "Good luck, baby."

She growled his way.

He would definitely have to make up for that later. Lucky for him, he'd figured out exactly how to make her relax.

Mr. King waved their way.

She was going to need so much relaxing.

Two hours later, Roxie sat in the cruiser and wished Armie had taken a single one of her cues. If he had, then she wouldn't be sitting here with her dad on a ride-along. If Armie had been even the slightest bit good at deflection, her dad would have asked a couple of questions and gone on his way.

Instead, he was spending all day with her.

All day.

"How often do you go out on your own?" her father asked from the seat beside her.

He'd been fairly quiet since they'd left the station. She'd done her routine tour of the town, ensuring everything looked normal. Lila had been out walking her dog outside the clinic and probably coming up with ways to spend that five bucks she'd won from betting on a love life that shouldn't be hers to bet on.

Roxie had waved to a couple of people she knew and had stopped briefly to talk to Dixie. The diner owner had been crossing the street to enter town hall. It was on the square that always reminded Roxie of the set of a fifties movie. Dixie had been jaywalking.

But she owned the only place in town that served waffles, so she had merely suggested Dixie use the crosswalk next time.

Now they were stopped off the square, waiting for something to happen. Anything, really. She was right back to wishing for some kind of natural disaster.

"I'm on patrol duty this afternoon. I can catch speeders on my own. There are often only two of us on duty at any given time, although most of us monitor the radio when we're home, and we can show up pretty quickly if someone needs backup."

She needed time to think about what Zep had said the night before, time to process what had happened. She'd hoped a good eight hours of driving around the parish would give her that, but no. Her father had different plans. First he'd wanted a tour of the station house. That had taken all of five minutes. He'd sat in Armie's office while she'd filled out reports. She'd heard him asking all sorts of questions about policy and procedure. Armie seemed to be taking it all in stride. She'd tried to explain that she had a lot to do and would love to have lunch or something later on in the week.

Armie had agreed heartily when her father suggested the ride-along. Hence the not being able to think about important subjects.

When had Zep become important? He was supposed to be fluff. Icing on the cake.

She'd liked teasing him in the meeting. Hell, she'd liked sitting next to him in the meeting. He'd been awfully sweet, trying to save her not once but twice. She probably should have taken the second out he'd given her, the one where not everyone in the world knew they were dating, but all she'd been able to remember was him asking if she planned to hide the fact. Like he was something shameful, something to keep locked away even while she enjoyed him.

"Well, it's definitely a different way of policing."

Good. If she argued with her father, she didn't have to think about how nice it had felt to wake up next to Zep this morning, how right it had felt to make coffee while he and Daisy walked around the block. Something sweet had settled inside her as she'd poured two cups and waited for him, something she'd never once felt for her ex-husband.

Now that she thought about it, it was a good thing to avoid. "Different doesn't mean worse. This town may seem quaint and out of touch to you, but there are solid people here."

"I didn't say it was worse." Her father's voice was steady. If she'd irritated him in any way, she couldn't tell. "What you do here reminds me a bit of your grandfather. I noticed it the other night at your boyfriend's restaurant. Everyone knew your name and you seemed to know them. By the time I joined, that kind of policing in the city was much harder to do. I moved precincts a lot. It makes getting to know people less of a priority, but you have to if you're going to move up."

He didn't have to point out that there was no moving up in Papillon Parish. She could run against Armie, but she had no grand desire to take control of the sheriff's office. The truth was she liked her job.

Would she miss it when she was in a bigger city? It had been hard to settle in at first since this place didn't have all the things she was used to. There weren't a lot of choices in Papillon, but there was a beauty to the simplicity that she hadn't counted on.

"But this is a much slower pace," her father continued. "I can certainly see the appeal, though I wouldn't think it would be for you. You were always my adrenaline junkie."

"Hey, there are things that happen out here that can get your heart pumping. Being a deputy here is not that different from where I was. We would wait around for something to go wrong and then hold on for dear life." As if to put a point on her statement, a black cat strolled out from behind the café. The cat sat at the edge of the road, yawning as though the world was far too boring to deal with. That cat would likely be the most interesting thing in her day. However, she'd had days when buildings went up in flames or storms threatened to take out half the town. "The difference is when someone is in trouble here, I usually know who they are and I know how many kids they have, or that if I lose someone, I'll have to look into that mom's face and explain."

"I can understand how hard that would be. Tell me something, Roxanne. Are you happy here? Or are you only staying around for that boy?"

This was not a conversation she wanted to have with her father, but she felt the need to defend Zep. "He isn't a boy. He's a man."

Her father chuckled. "You'll have to forgive me. At my age, you all look like boys and girls. It's hard to remember that at your age your mother and I already had Brian and she was pregnant with you."

Yes, what she needed was a lecture on how her generation was immature. "I'm a late bloomer, I guess."

Did she and Zep have more in common than she realized? They both seemed to struggle with expectation versus reality, and she'd been guilty in that with him, too.

"You're not. You always knew what you wanted. You were focused and centered until the last few years," he replied as though he'd given this subject a lot of thought. "You were excellent at your job. The divorce threw you off. I was surprised you acted so emotionally."

Why wasn't there a hurricane? Maybe a robbery. She wouldn't want anyone hurt, but a nice, potentially violent distraction would be good around now. "Divorce is hard on a person. You and Mom are lucky."

Another chuckle. "I don't know about that. You make it as long as your mother and I have and you just kind of keep going." He sobered and stared out over the town square. "I know you struggle with your mother sometimes, but she loves you."

Her heart constricted because it could be easy to forget that her mom had been the one who packed her school lunches and included little notes about how much she was loved. Her mom could be obnoxious, but she'd been a good mother. "I know. I didn't turn out the way she hoped I would. You would think somewhere around the time I joined the military, she would have figured out I wasn't going to settle down and be some good wife."

"Would that have been so bad?"

"Would it have been so bad for Brian?"

He held a hand up. "Understood. I'm sorry. I know it's not very modern of me, but it's different to send your daughter out. And you are good at your job. Your boss speaks highly of you. He seems to be a solid guy. He was a detective in New Orleans."

Her father often liked to point out the obvious. "Yes, I know that."

"Are you sure that things can't work out between the two of you? He seems much more like a man who I could see you with."

Since her dad had thought her ex-husband was the perfect man, she wasn't giving great credence to his thoughts concerning her love life. He also was forgetting one important fact. "He's married. You met his wife."

"She wasn't very friendly. Well, we both know marriages don't have to be forever." Her father finally glanced her way, a concerned expression on his face. "I want to talk to you about that Guidry boy. Man. Whatever you want to call him. I know your mother likes him, but we both have grave concerns. Do you honestly believe he would make a good husband? Don't get me wrong. He's a charming, attractive young man, but he belongs here. You don't."

"What's that supposed to mean?" It didn't matter that she'd thought the same thing before. She didn't like her father judging her relationship with Zep. It was something between the two of them.

Zep had been judged enough.

"It means it's time for you to come home, and I don't think he's going to fit in," her father said bluntly. "You have to know he's got a record."

Well, naturally her father had run a trace on him, too. She should have known he would do it, but she'd hoped he would understand that they weren't too serious. "Of course I know. I'm not planning on marrying him. I like him. His offense wasn't violent."

She watched as a sedan passed them, making its way toward the stop sign ahead. Why wouldn't it speed by and instigate a chase? A chase might get her out of this uncomfortable conversation.

Her father wasn't saying anything she hadn't thought before. He was giving her back all the reasons Zep was a bad bet. But the night before had changed something between them. She'd seen the hurt in his eyes, a hurt she would have sworn she couldn't ever cause him.

"It doesn't matter if it was violent or not," her father continued. "A cop can't have an ex-con as a partner."

She rolled her eyes and watched as the sedan came to a stop because the cat had decided to leave that side of the street for better prospects. The cat sauntered across the road. Yeah, it was jaywalking, too, and like Dixie, she couldn't even give the cat a ticket. "You're acting like he spent years in a federal prison. It was six weeks in minimum security because he was a dumbass."

"I don't care if he wasn't guilty," her dad argued. "You're not going to get back to NYPD with him at your side."

She stopped and turned his way. "What?"

"One of the reasons I wanted to come here in person was to discuss your future. I've talked to Joel. He knows now that what he did was wrong. At the time he thought it was best for your career if he didn't let you file that report."

"You thought I shouldn't file that report, either. Do you know you were wrong?" The old anger threatened to bubble to the surface. God, she'd thought she'd gotten over this.

Her father sighed, a long-suffering sound, and he pinched the place where his nose met his eyes. It was his "I'm getting a headache" expression. "We're all trying to keep up with what's acceptable and what's not, Roxanne. Women officers back in my day wouldn't have had a problem with what your supervisor did."

"Yes, they did. They were just too scared to talk about it. They knew damn well they would lose their jobs. Those women had to go through what they did so I don't. I get that you think the world has changed, that suddenly this generation is less tough than the one before. I'm not. I simply will not allow myself to be treated that way. The funny thing is you're the one who taught me that. You taught me how to stand up for myself and then betrayed me when I did it."

Her father's eyes flared but she was saved by the fact that the sedan was now backing down the street.

"I did not betray you," her father was saying.

But she was getting out of the car. Unlike the current driver of the slowly reversing sedan, she wasn't going to chase a car down in reverse, nor would she make a crazy U-turn on this fairly narrow street.

Besides, she didn't even have to walk fast to catch up to the creeping sedan. Karen Travers was the one behind the wheel, and it looked like her daughter was sitting in the passenger seat. Ah, she remembered Ashlyn Travers well from the other night. Karen was roughly forty-five, and she was a stalwart presence at most town functions. She was famous for her pecan pie.

And apparently her bad driving skills.

"Mrs. Travers." Roxie raised her voice and patted the hood of the car.

"Mom!" Ashlyn yelled as she pointed Roxie's way. "It's the police. Great. You are a freak who got the po-po on us. What is wrong with you?"

Karen's eyes were wide as she turned and caught sight of Roxie. She stopped the car and the window came down. "I'm so sorry, Deputy. Was I doing something wrong?"

This was one of those moments where she brought out the "dumbass said what" face she'd perfected over the years. "On this particular street, we usually drive our cars in a forward motion, Mrs. Travers. And by usually, I mean always. It's illegal to drive backward down the street."

Karen shook her head. "No. Sometimes you have to do that. Did you see that cat?"

Ashlyn's eyes rolled so far in the back of her head, Roxie

was surprised they didn't simply make their way back around. "Oh, my god. Please don't say it. Please don't humiliate me like this."

Roxie looked back up the street and the cat was on the other side of the road, licking one paw like she didn't have a care in the world. "Is there something wrong with the cat?"

If there was, she might need to call Zep and they would have to work together. That wouldn't be such a bad idea. Maybe the cat was attacking people and they would have to chase it down.

Although the cat didn't look like it had a problem. The cat was still sitting at the end of the street, licking her paws and looking at them like she knew she'd caused a ruckus and was perfectly fine with that.

Karen nodded and sighed like she was satisfied that Roxie understood. "Yes, it's black. It's got totally black fur."

"And that means you have to drive backward?" Roxie looked in the car, hoping she didn't find any liquor. She might have to ask Lila what prescriptions Karen Travers was on. She didn't see anything illegal. There was a bunch of what looked like cameras in the back. Video cameras and equipment. Ashlyn had mentioned something about a school project the other night. It looked like she was using better equipment than her phone.

"Yes, ma'am," Karen replied as though the answer should have been easy to understand. "Now I have to get going because Ashlyn's due at her AV Club meeting and I have to make my way around, if you don't mind."

She realized her dad had gotten out of the car and was watching the situation.

"Do you intend to continue backing down the road?" Roxie asked, trying to come up with some reason for Karen to decide to forgo forward.

"Of course," Karen said, pointing down the street. "The cat is black."

Ashlyn beat her head against the dashboard before turning Roxie's way. "She won't go forward because the black cat crossed the path she was going to take. I'm not kidding, Deputy Roxie. She's insane. You should take me into protective custody because she's going to humiliate me on every level. There has to be a law or something."

Roxie was getting the bad feeling she totally didn't understand the situation going on here, and that often meant one thing. "Is this a Cajun thing?"

Karen had a helmet of blond hair that didn't move an inch when she shook it. "It's an everyone thing. Don't you know that you can't ever keep walking down a path a black cat crossed?"

"Yes, it's a weird old Cajun thing." Ashlyn talked right over her mother. "No one is freaked by it anymore except my mother."

"Well, your grandmother didn't believe it. She laughed and sashayed right through that cat's path and she got hit by a car," Karen said, her voice filled with pure righteousness.

"Pawpaw hit her with a car because he caught her cheating on him with their dry cleaner," Ashlyn shot back.

"Yes, but maybe she would have gotten away with it if she hadn't crossed that path," Karen argued. She turned back to Roxie. "Sorry, Deputy. My family has a scandalous past."

"How about present. Grammy is the bane of the nursing home. She's the reason they had to do that class on safe sex practices. I'm doomed," Ashlyn was saying. "One day I will make a film about how weird my family is."

"I thought you wanted to make horror films," Karen pointed out.

"Yes, that's what I said." Ashlyn crossed her arms over

her chest in a show of teenage stubbornness. "My life is a horror movie."

Karen wrinkled her nose. "Don't mind her. She's got all those hormones. I think her daddy letting her watch all those movies about weird animals that got irritated and killed people affected her brain."

"Irradiated, Mom," Ashlyn corrected. "Trust me, if an irritated animal is going to take you out, it will be me. And I'm going to be late. If I didn't have to carry everything, I would walk. Thanks a lot."

Boy, Roxie was glad she didn't have teens. Her dad had a smile on his face. Had she been that bad as a teen? She'd definitely had a mouth on her, and she'd absolutely fought with her mom.

Karen tilted her head her daughter's way. "There's a reason we get them as babies. So, I should go. I'm going to back up to Florence Street and make my way back around to Main. I promise I'll put her in drive as soon as I can."

Roxie had some questions since the route Karen was planning was to the west and the cat had come from the west. "How do you know the cat didn't already cross that path? When is it okay for the cat to cross? Because when you think about it, the cat's been running all over town. We don't know exactly where she's been. I think it's a she. She has a kind of feminine wile about her."

Karen frowned. "I don't know how I would know. You're right. That cat could have gone anywhere, come from anywhere. How would I know where the cat's been?"

Oh, dear. "I was joking. I've been watching that cat all day. Definitely, you can feel safe going down and around to Main. You're good. You know what? I'll even make sure you can back up safely."

She hadn't forgotten what it was like to direct traffic. She could do it. The last thing she needed was Karen Travers to take up residence right here on the middle of Elm Street because she was too worried about where that damn cat had been.

"Are you sure?" Karen asked.

An SUV pulled up alongside Karen and Janice Herbert rolled her window down. "Karen, is everything okay? Deputy, whatever she did, it was probably because her husband is a dumbass."

Roxie shook her head. "She's not in trouble."

"That cat walked right across the road in front of me." Karen pointed to the end of the road, where the cat had gotten up and twitched her tail.

Would there be a voice of reason? Roxie wasn't holding any hope. Janice was known for her strongly worded opinions and her strongly brewed tea. She wasn't known for reason.

"Oh, no," Janice said in a totally unreasonable tone. "I got my grandbaby in the car. I can't go through that. She just got over the crud, and honestly her hair isn't coming in the way I want it to. I think she got Johnny's family hair. This baby doesn't need any more bad luck."

"Deputy pointed out that we don't know where the cat's been," Karen said, anxiety in her voice.

"Mom, it only works if you see the cat and then purposefully cross the path." Ashlyn leaned over to look Roxie's way. "I don't believe this crap. It's a cat. It's a kitty who is only trying to live its life. But I do study up on urban legends and superstitions. They make good horror films. Kind of like my family. Hey, could you give me a ride? I'll sit in the back and everything. You could turn the lights on and I might make it in time."

Roxie wasn't going to set that precedent. If she did, every kid in the parish would treat her like Uber but without the tips. Besides, she now had two cars that wouldn't drive the direction they should. If she let them, they might set up a camp here so Janice's grandbaby got better hair or something. It was a typical day in Papillon. "Nope, I'm going to get you all on the right path. There's no way to make a U-turn so we're going to do this your way. Just go slow. I'm going to make sure no one plows into you."

She jogged down to the intersection and motioned for Karen to back up first. After all, her daughter needed somewhere to put all that teen angst, and the AV Club was better than partying. She held out her other hand to stop a truck coming down the intersecting road.

The man behind the wheel stopped and hung his head out. Jerry Nichols. He ran a business on the other side of the square. "Everything all right? Is there an accident?"

Normally she would think this was an example of rubbernecking, but not here. People here knew everyone, so she viewed the question the way Jerry likely intended it—does someone need help?

What if that had been what most people in New York were really asking? It was the way her grandfather had viewed people. It was odd how being down here had made her question all the assumptions she'd made about her life in the city. She'd learned that the people here weren't so different despite their accents and food and weird superstitions. What if, despite their fast-paced lives, the people she'd known then had cared every bit as much?

"A black cat crossed Karen's path and Janice is worried about her granddaughter's hair coming from her son-in-law." It sounded ridiculous even to her own ears, but it was apparently a big problem. Her job was to help fix problems. Oh, she'd thought it was combatting crime, but she'd learned. Sometimes it was all about containing the crazy.

Jerry nodded sagely. "Oh, I get it. That black cat is everywhere these days. Nobody's claiming it. I was hoping the rougarou would eat the sucker. Bad luck. You're doing a good job, Deputy."

"Thanks." She watched as Karen and then Janice made their way around the path to bad luck and got on their way. Jerry nodded as he, too, avoided the cat.

She walked back to her SUV under the watchful gaze of her father.

"You should have given them both tickets," her father said. "They were breaking the law."

"Everything was fine. They didn't hurt anyone." If she hadn't been around, someone else would have come along. Janice would have helped Karen, or she would have made it to the end of the street and Jerry would have made sure she got through the intersection safely. The worst that would have happened was a fender bender, and honestly, Herve could use the work. He got pranky when he didn't have enough to do.

"If this is how you work now, maybe we should reconsider you coming back," her father said gravely as he got back into the SUV.

She heard a purring sound and the cat was rubbing against her leg, looking up at her with big dark eyes.

She reached down and picked up the cat, who immediately settled down in her arms. The cat was on the thin side.

Zep would know what to do with it.

"Has word gotten out that the deputy can't resist an animal sob story?" she asked. Yep. She was talking to cats now.

It was far better than talking to her dad.

She had a chance to go back to New York? To start her career again?

She walked to the SUV with the cat in her arms. Hopefully Daisy liked cats. It wasn't like she would keep the cat.

She would make sure it ate something, and when her shift was over, she would drive out to the shelter Zep was volunteering at today and drop the cat off.

She wouldn't keep it because she wasn't staying.

One way or another, she was going to leave.

# *chapter ten*

The smell of popcorn didn't make him hungry the way it used to. It made him nervous. He wasn't a public speaker.

"You okay?" Roxie was still in her uniform. No one else in the world could wear khakis the way his baby could. She managed to make that uniform sexy.

He was in one of two pairs of slacks he owned and his very best button-down. It was what he wore when he got dragged to church on Christmas, Easter, and funerals.

This could be his funeral if he couldn't handle the crowd.

"You are not okay." Roxie put her hands on his cheeks and forced him to look her in the eyes. "Zep, this is all going to be fine. They'll ask you some questions and they will be weird, but you answer them with science and reason and everything will be cool."

"Yeah, I don't know that science and reason work with some of our neighbors." He took a deep breath because she was right. It was going to be okay. What was the worst that could happen? It wasn't like the town was going to fire him. They hadn't really hired him in the first place. "Hey, do you think this counts as overtime?"

"I think you weren't smart enough to negotiate with

Armie in the first place, so getting more out of him now could be hard," she pointed out. "Though I've been thinking a lot since I found Sunny. She probably wouldn't have been wandering around and scaring superstitious people if we had our own department of animal services. The sheriff's department can't handle lost animals. If we find them, we have to send them to a shelter an hour away. No one's looking that far away for a pet. I don't think most people even know that place exists."

That had been her excuse for not taking the cat she'd named Sunny to the shelter. It was too long a drive, and he'd just come from there and they had to get ready for the meeting. Except her version of getting ready for the meeting had mostly been playing with the pets. So now Sunny and Daisy were getting acquainted. Or rather Daisy was likely howling in her crate and Sunny was yawning and showing the dog that cats were way cooler because she didn't need a crate.

Roxie had told him he could take the cat in the next time he went to the shelter.

Next month. There was no way that would stick.

So now they had a dog and a cat. He'd gone from being single with no responsibilities to having a girlfriend and two pets to take care of. He was good at this relationship thing. If he didn't watch out, he might wake up next week with a wife and two point five kids.

Maybe his momma was right about the condoms.

"Well, I could start a page on the county website and list the animals we've found." He'd done it for the shelter he volunteered at. It shouldn't be too hard here in Papillon, though he wasn't sure what the parish's infrastructure was like when it came to the website. "Maybe I can convince Sylvie to open up the town website and let me upload a page explaining what to do if you've lost a pet or found one."

"You could do that," she said in a way that made him think she had a better idea.

Before she could say anything more, his brother was walking up the steps with Lisa Guidry at his side.

"What are you doing here?" Zep asked. Remy never came to town meetings. "You said town halls were nothing but slightly contained chaos."

His brother slapped him on the arm in a sign of fraternal affection. "Oh, but this time you're the one trying to contain it, and that is one show I wouldn't miss for the world."

His sister-in-law grinned. "Besides, we have to find that rougarou and fast. I think you'll discover that there's a citizen's posse forming. They were talking about it at lunch today. We live in interesting times."

Dear lord. "I get to deal with that. Yay."

"Oh, if there's a posse running around, I'll deal with it," Roxie promised. "You handle the talking and I'll be the muscle. You're really too pretty to put in the line of fire." She went on her toes and kissed him. "I'm getting some popcorn. See you inside."

"I'll go with Roxie," Lisa offered, stepping away from her husband. "Your sister is already in there with Harry and Luc."

Roxie frowned. "If Harry and Sera are in there, who's keeping watch over my parents?"

"Uhm, I'm pretty sure they don't need someone watching them twenty-four-seven," Lisa was saying as they walked into the small building that served as town hall and sometimes a banquet hall. Or a concert hall. Really all the halls a town could need were right in there.

"We will have to agree to disagree on that point," Roxie replied, opening the door. "I would like to know where they are at all times while they're here. My parents slipped away for breakfast and that ended up costing me a whole afternoon of listening to my dad tell me everything I'm doing wrong with my life. I'm sure my mom would love a shot at that, too. Hey, I heard Remy used to be a bodyguard. Maybe he could be like a reverse bodyguard."

Lisa walked through. "I think he's got a lot to do at the restaurant, but we know some folks."

"I'm not calling anyone down to track Roxie's parents," Remy called out.

"Way to help a friend, Guidry." Roxie let the door go but not before Zep got a look inside the building. There were people milling about in the lobby, and Dixie had a line formed for popcorn. Then the scent wafted out. It was supposed to be a snack, but he'd always known it was a symbol that entertainment was coming.

There were a lot of people in there.

"You've turned a nice shade of green." Remy was staring at him, an amused expression on his face.

"I'm not big on public speaking," he admitted. "I don't know how I got roped into this. One minute I was making some extra cash helping the sheriff with animal calls, and the next I'm some sort of expert at mythical creatures in our midst. You know what this town can do to experts."

"Drive them utterly crazy," Remy said with a laugh, but he sobered quickly. "You know you really are kind of an expert when it comes to this."

Had his brother lost his mind? "To rougarous? I assure you I am not. I am distinctly a disbeliever in werewolves."

"I wasn't talking about the rougarou. I meant you're an expert at handling the people of Papillon. You've been doing it all of your life."

He snorted because that was a lie. "I don't handle anyone. I just try to get by."

Remy nodded as though Zep had just made his point. "See, there you go. You're making less of yourself again.

You are an insanely likable person. You put people at ease, and if you would act like you cared at all, they would listen to you."

"Act like I care?" Zep asked.

"You have a mask on," Remy explained. "All the time. It's a mask of indifference that you think is going to save you from getting hurt. If you never look like you're trying, then you never have to fail. But I know you do care and that what you're going to figure out is that it's the not trying that's really failure. No one is going to care that you fall on your face. We've all done it."

"If I fail, everyone is watching." He wasn't even going to fight his brother on the problem. He knew he was avoiding making big decisions because he didn't trust himself enough to make the right choice. Because he couldn't have that dream he'd had when he was a kid. Did that mean he didn't dream at all? Or that he should find a new one? "I wonder if it's easier in a big city."

"I have been all over the world, brother, and I can tell you that if one thing is easier someplace else, then they got something harder, too. You think everyone would see you failing here, think about a place where no one would see you at all," Remy said. "In the end, people are people and no one gets out of this life without pain. Being alone is hard. Being with someone is hard. So pick which struggle you want."

He knew exactly what he wanted. And it might mean he had to choose between her or his family. If he got the choice at all.

Remy glanced back toward where the ladies had disappeared. "It looks like you made some headway with Roxie. Her parents aren't around and she's still playing the part."

"I think your gumbo did the trick," he said, and then realized he was doing exactly what his brother had accused him of. He was making something important into something less. "I really talked to her last night when we got back from the B and B. I came clean on a lot of things, including my time in Arizona."

His brother's eyes widened. "You never talk about that."

"She's special." That was what he'd figured out. The key to getting Roxanne to understand he was serious was to treat her like she was special. Because she was. "She's important, and that means she gets more of me than anyone else. I love my family, but if I'm going to be Roxie's partner, she's got to come first."

It had been so good to open up to her the night before. Something had eased inside him when she'd sat on his lap. He'd always dreaded the idea of pity. But sympathy and empathy were beautiful things, and he needed to change his mindset. If Roxie was his girlfriend, if they were partners, then he needed her to truly know him, and that meant opening the dark, sad places of his soul and offering those up, too.

His brother was quiet for a moment as though considering what he'd said. A soft look hit his eyes. "Then you're good and I take back everything I said before. You can put her first and that means you're ready for this relationship."

His brother was looking at him like he was proud. Remy looked so much like their dad.

He was not going to tear up. He was not going to.

The sound of crunching saved him from doing something silly. He looked to the street and saw a golf cart on the sidewalk and one of the town hall's trash cans slightly dented from the encounter.

An elderly couple immediately started arguing about the man's driving.

He might be ready for a relationship, but he was so not ready for this.

* * *

Roxie settled in beside Lisa Guidry and watched as Armie took his place at the table on the stage. Normally she would sit to the side, but the truth was, despite the uniform she wore, she wasn't actually working. She'd attended these meetings but she'd never been a part of them. She'd always watched from the side of the stage, telling herself it was just in case something went wrong and she was needed.

Now she could see her actions for what they were. She'd distanced herself from the people around her, not wanting to make friends or become one of them because she wasn't going to let herself stay here.

But even if it wasn't forever, why shouldn't she make some friends? She was never going to find a place like this again. Why not let herself have this experience? It seemed like she put off everything because she wasn't in her perfect future.

But the future never actually came. It was always something in the distance, and she was wasting the now.

"Seraphina!" Lisa stood up and waved Zep's sister over.

Sera stood beside her massive wall-of-muscle husband. Harrison Jefferys had a little boy in his arms. His stepson, Luc, though he never called him that. To Harry, Luc was simply his son.

Sera sank down into the seat beside Lisa and gave them all a brilliant smile. "Hey, Roxie. Good to see you, girl. Is it true Zep is running a part of this meeting? Hallie called to tell me about her momma and this black cat thing she's got going, and she mentioned that Zep would be talking at the meeting tonight. I didn't believe it, but I called Sylvie and she said it was true. She's the mayor. She can't lie. Has anyone checked the water fountain to make sure he hasn't figured out a way to put vodka in it?"

Lisa laughed. "I'm more worried that he's going to tell everyone to go hunt for this thing and we'll have chaos in the streets."

Roxie felt her brow rise. This kind of joking was what got Zep in trouble in the first place. She was sure they didn't mean anything by it, but she had to make them understand what it did to Zep. "I assure you he's taking this job seriously. He's been out most nights this week trying to calm people down. He's not going to rile them up because he would be out there on the front lines dealing with the crazy."

Lisa's mouth had dropped open slightly. "Oh, I wasn't saying anything bad about him. I was joking around."

"He's sensitive about the whole bad-boy thing." She'd figured that out this week. "But he won't tell you. He's smarter than he's given credit for. I think it would be best if we didn't joke about him screwing up. He's genuinely nervous about this and wants to do a good job. Let's all try to support him."

Harry had taken the seat beside his wife and leaned over. "You tell her, Rox. I've been saying for months that Zep is way deeper than anyone gives him credit for."

"I love Zep. I wasn't . . ." Lisa stopped. "I guess I was."

"It's hard to think of Zep as serious," Sera said with a frown on her face.

"Really?" Roxie had given a whole lot of thought to Zep's family situation. "He seems pretty good with Luc."

"They're practically playmates," Sera replied.

"Not really. He puts in a lot of time and effort with Luc. He truly wants what's best for him. I know Zep makes it easy to think he's not serious, but how many other young men do you know who would stay home and help pay off his sister's medical bills? That feels like real love to me, and that means he's serious. He's definitely serious about the people he cares about."

Sera's face had fallen. "I always thought he stayed home because he didn't have anything else to do."

Oh, she hoped she wasn't saying something that would upset Zep, but Sera should know that her brother had loved her enough to sacrifice for her. "He'd been in college. Why do you think he didn't want to continue?"

Lisa's eyes had widened. "Zep went to college?"

Did the man tell people nothing of his own accomplishments? She'd managed to go from a husband who made it sound like making himself a sandwich should get him a Nobel Prize to a boyfriend who refused to tell anyone how amazing he was.

"Community college," Sera replied. "But I thought he only went to check out the girls. That's what he always said."

"I'm sure that's what he told you, but you can't believe he drove an hour to and from class to check out the chicks?" She wasn't going to tell them his story. That was his to reveal, but she could lead them down a path to a place where they at least asked the questions they should have. "He graduated. I don't know many men who do that so they can try to get laid. Zep can pretty much do that without an associate degree."

"Zep has a degree?" Lisa looked dumbfounded.

Did any of these people know him? Probably not any better than her family knew her. But oddly, seeing it from another side—from a side where she knew these people loved him—was starting to make her rethink her own. So much of life was about point of view. If Zep never offered them his true point of view, how could they take him for anything but what he presented? Had she done that with her family, too?

"He did. He graduated, but it didn't seem important to him," Sera argued. "He didn't even go to the graduation."

"Was anything going on that might have distracted him from that?" Roxie asked. It was clear to her that someone needed to give Zep's family a jolt when it came to him. Maybe she would be that someone.

"She'll get there," Harry said, watching as Luc climbed on the chair beside him and waved at everyone walking in.

Sera teared up. "I was pregnant and scared, and he didn't go to his graduation because he wasn't going to rub it in my face."

"There she is." Harry pulled his wife close and kissed her head. "Your brother has quietly done more for this town and this family than anyone realizes." Harry leaned over and caught Roxie's gaze. "It's good he has someone who sees him. I'm happy for the both of you."

Up ahead, Sylvie Martine was taking her place at the long table onstage, and Armie greeted her. There were three microphones. One of those was for Zep.

They didn't really need the microphones. It was a small hall, but Sylvie had told her once it made them seem more professional.

Roxie stared straight ahead because she was worried if she didn't, she might get emotional. "And Zep would never replace water with vodka. He's a whiskey man. Or rum when he wants to dance."

Harry nodded. "She's right about that. He is not into the clear liquors. Speaking of the man. Hey, brother. How's it going?"

Zep looked surprisingly respectable in his church clothes, but she couldn't help but think about how he'd looked without the shirt on. She'd sat on the bed with Daisy and Sunny and watched him get dressed. He'd been nervous, but he had nothing to worry about. Not looks-wise. He was a gorgeous man dressed up or dressed down.

He had a notepad in his hand. She'd helped him carefully craft his statement, and they'd gone over a few of the questions he would likely be asked.

He deserved to be taken seriously.

"Good," Zep said, his eyes finding hers. "I think it's going to go . . . it's going to go as well as it can."

His brother had followed him in. "It's going to go great. He's ready."

At least she didn't have to go up against Remy. "He is."

"Hey, Zep. Haven't seen you in a while," a feminine voice said. Debbie Griffiths worked at the courthouse. She was a pretty woman in her early thirties, and Roxie had always gotten along with her. Sure, she sometimes got drunk off her ass and liked to pit men against each other, but who didn't have a hobby? "You look good, boy."

Zep nodded her way. "Debbie."

Remy settled in on the other side of the chair Luc was currently bouncing his body up and down on. He was talking to the kid behind him about his dog. Remy formed a secondary barrier to keep Luc from straying off.

"I hear you're practically on the force now," Debbie said, giving Zep a long once-over.

If Zep noticed, he didn't show it. He merely shook his head. "I'm just helping out. I should go—"

Debbie put a hand on his chest. "Hey, maybe after this meeting, you want to go grab a—"

"Move along, Debra."

Every head in earshot swiveled Roxie's way because she'd used her cop voice. And not her happy, "let's not scare the kiddos" cop voice. She had one of those, too, but she'd used her "let's scare the crap out of everyone and force them to comply" voice. It had served her well over the years.

Debbie's eyes had gone wide, and her hand had moved

right back to her side, where it should have been all along. "I . . . I was going to ask Zep if he wanted . . ."

"He doesn't have the time to party tonight. And he's got things to do for the foreseeable future. You should take your seat." Roxie didn't move from hers, merely stared at the woman, who should know better than to touch a man who didn't belong to her.

Debbie nodded. "Yes, of course. I'll go join my friends. It's about to start."

She hurried off.

"Damn, Deputy," Lisa said with a whistle. "I need to work on that. There are women in this town who think my husband is on the menu, if you know what I mean."

Zep grinned at Roxie. "Thanks. She can get handsy."

She better not. Was she already possessive? That was a stupid question, given the fact that she'd run a woman off and had already thought about ensuring the lady parked properly. Every single time. Nope. That was petty and she wasn't going there. She'd done her duty and warned Debbie off her man.

"You're welcome," she said with a wink. "You should get up there. Armie's got his frowny face on."

"Doesn't he frown most of the time?" Zep asked.

He needed to get to know the boss. "He has twenty different frowns. That one is his 'I want to get this over with and get home to my wife' frown. It's one of his fiercest expressions."

"She's right about that look," Lisa agreed. She gave Zep a thumbs-up. "You look great. You're going to do so well."

Sera had gotten up and worked her way to her brother. She smoothed down the collar of his shirt. "You are going to be so good at this, Zep. You were always good at talking."

"No, I'm not," he replied with a grimace.

"You are," she insisted. "So go up there and convince this town that they won't be eaten by a werewolf."

"Wolf?" Luc was staring at his mom. "I don't want a wolf to eat me."

Harry immediately picked the kiddo up. "You won't because Uncle Zep is on the case."

Zep reached over and tousled his nephew's hair. "There are no werewolves. I promise, buddy. You're okay."

Sera sniffled. "I'm so proud of you."

Zep looked over at Roxie like she could explain why his sister seemed to have gotten so emotional.

Roxie merely gestured toward the stage. "That frown is getting frownier."

Zep sighed and accepted a hug from his sister. "Okay. I'm going. You're all weirdos and somebody needs to explain what this is about later."

"I think your sister simply realizes how much you do around here and she's grateful," Harry said.

Sera stepped back. "Very much so. Go on, Zep. Don't let Armie scare you."

There was a puzzled look on Zep's face as he stepped back. "I won't. I'll be far too busy being scared of the audience." He looked her way. "I'll see you after."

"I'll be here ensuring no other Debbies decide to get handsy with the sexy expert animal guy." And she would be enjoying the show. He was definitely nice to look at. If Zep was always talking at the town halls, they might be more fun.

Of course, for him to be present and giving reports, he would have to have a place with the parish government.

"You like my brother." Sera had switched seats with Lisa. "I always thought you hated him."

"No one can hate Zep." He was too charming, too smooth. Except he'd shown her he could be something more than a player. When she'd brought the cat home, he'd simply shaken his head and made arrangements to pick up all the things a cat would need. She didn't think he believed her about taking Sunny to the shelter. She probably shouldn't have named her. Or watched her completely ignore Daisy, only to get irritated when Daisy stopped paying attention to her.

"You really like him." Sera was suddenly all up in her business, giving her a hug.

She was getting random hugs from his family members now? Still, no one could resist Seraphina, either. She was too bright and full of life. She hugged her back. "I do. I like him. But it's still early, so we don't have to get too emotional about it."

She kept saying the words because she needed to hear them.

Sera sat back, but she shook her head. "Nope. This is right. This is it. I have a feeling about this. You're going to get married and we'll be complete."

"Whoa," she said because no one had said anything about marrying anyone.

Lisa leaned over. "Don't scare off the new girl."

Zep had made it to the stage, and he took his seat. His eyes caught hers, and he gave her a smile.

God, that smile went straight into her like a lightning bolt. She could get in way too deep with this man.

Or she could realize what was best for her career and go back to New York. Go back home.

Was New York still home?

"My baby!" Delphine Dellacourt Guidry made her entrance with her usual aplomb. She wore a floor-length flowy dress and some chunky jewelry, her hair up in its normal turban, though there was a rhinestone pin in this one. "Look, Marcelle. My baby is up there with your baby."

Sure enough, Marcelle Martine was standing there with Delphine. She was dressed similarly to her best friend, though her dress was a sunny yellow. And she was carrying a thermos of something, which she passed to Delphine as they reached their row of chairs. She waved at her daughter. "Hi, baby. You can start the meeting now."

"Zep, honey, you look so handsome!" Delphine said as she sat down and took her place next to Remy. "You look just as smart as Sylvie does. Oh, my."

Zep's head hit the desk.

Sylvie simply sighed. "All right, my momma's here so we can start."

"That better be coffee in the thermos, Delphine," Armie said.

Delphine stood, the thermos in her hand. "You hush, Armie LaVigne. I used to change your smelly pants when you were a baby. This is champagne because it's my baby's big day. Are you telling me a momma can't celebrate her baby's big day?"

"He's giving us an update on a werewolf that doesn't exist," Armie said.

"Oh, that's how they get you," Delphine promised. "They make you think they don't exist, and then what do you think comes out of the dark to bite you in the butt? Only thing standing between this town and the rougarou is my baby."

Marcelle stood. "Although we can help, you know. Delphine and I have been talking about a spell."

It was Sylvie's turn to face-palm. "Momma, sit down and drink your champagne."

Marcelle shrugged. "Well, I was going to give you a discount."

Delphine winked and pulled out some red plastic cups

from her bag. "Works every time. And it's not really champagne. It's rum punch. Champagne sounds classier."

"Hey, maybe we shouldn't around the deputy," Marcelle said under her breath. "She's the mean one."

Roxie sat up straighter. She wasn't the mean one. Mostly. "Give me some." Damn it. She could really use a drink, but she hadn't been smart enough to change. She'd done what she always did when she went out in public. She'd used her job like a shield against everything. "Actually, save some for me. I'm still in uniform."

Delphine gave her an approving smile. "I'll do that for you, baby girl. You don't talk bad about my new baby, Marcelle. She's only going to be mean to the other people now."

"She's not mean, Momma," Sera argued.

Roxie was genuinely amused. Being a part of the Guidrys would be a complete change from her own family.

Who were still here, lurking about in the shadows, waiting to bite her in the ass.

"All right, everyone get settled," Sylvie announced. "We need to get down to business at this emergency meeting. I'm going to open the meeting with a statement from our task force leader, Zéphirin Guidry."

"That's my baby," Delphine shouted with pride.

"Momma, please," Zep begged quietly.

She couldn't help but giggle a bit at the sight of his gorgeous face twisted in pure agony as his momma told him to keep going.

Out of the corner of her eye she caught sight of another child who was totally embarrassed by a parental unit.

Ashlyn Travers wasn't sitting with her mother. She wasn't sitting at all. She was standing at the back of the auditorium with a handheld camera.

Roxie leaned over to whisper a question Lisa's way. "Do

you know if they always film these things? I hadn't noticed it before."

Lisa glanced up as Sylvie was talking about the rash of calls the government was getting. "Not that I ever noticed. Must be a school project. I heard they had an AV Club going at the high school. They're learning how to edit and put together films. Some of the kids were in a couple of days ago talking about how you can even record whole movies with your phone these days."

Wasn't that interesting?

She settled back as her mind started putting pieces together.

She might be able to make this meeting work in all their favors. And Delphine might actually need that champagne because she intended to give Zep some real choices tonight. All she had to do was make her move.

# *chapter eleven*

Zep wished he'd thought to change out the water bottles with beer. Or rum. He was going to need it to get through this meeting. Not only was his mother out there treating him like he was graduating from preschool, but he had to deal with the Q and A portion of the evening.

"Has anyone considered that this could be the government? We all know they have some crazy experiments going on." Herve owned the auto repair shop and way too many trucker hats. The one he had on today proclaimed that *Shrimpers Do It With Grit.*

Armie snorted and sat back, leaving it all to Zep.

He'd made his statement. That had been the easy part. His prewritten speech had been plain and clear. There was no mystical predator running around. Yet he was still answering the rumors. "There are no experiments going on. There is no rougarou. At Archie's place, the goats got spooked by a dog in the woods. What happened at Dixie's place was kids fooling around. There is absolutely nothing to be worried about."

Sue Nelson, who worked for the post office, moved to the microphone. "That's easy for you to say. You weren't at my place last night. Something was watching me. I was in my backyard and I saw a flash of light from the woods behind the shed. And I could hear something moving."

"I looked at the police reports from last night," he offered, deeply aware that he was being filmed for some kind of high school film project. He'd questioned Sylvie when he'd seen the blond girl from the other night with a camera. He definitely didn't want to fumble this and end up as a meme. "The deputy who handled the complaint saw no evidence of any large animal in the area."

"But that deputy isn't even from here," Sue argued. "Deputy Blanchard is good at all the normal police stuff, and he is very nice to look at."

"Sue, we have talked about this," Armie interrupted. "You cannot objectify my deputies."

"Well, I'm only doing it to the really good-looking ones," Sue shot back. "Maybe you should hire some less attractive men. And I would like you to know I don't objectify you at all, Armie LaVigne. Not since you gave me that ticket for parking in a perfectly fine spot."

"That perfectly fine spot was a fire zone," Armie pointed out.

She waved that off. "And the fire wasn't occupying it at the time, so there. And also, you would be far more attractive if you smiled more. But to my point, Deputy Blanchard doesn't know all the critters from around here yet. And I watched that documentary on crazy people who raise zoo animals in their backyards. How do we know they didn't let a few out and we've suddenly got a tiger problem?"

Sometimes Zep wished the Internet had never come to Papillon. "We don't have any big cat rescues close to us. And there are no private zoos, so I don't believe that we're dealing with a tiger."

"How do you know?" a voice shouted from the back of the audience. A familiar voice.

He looked out over the crowd and Roxie was standing up. "I know because tigers leave behind evidence that they're here."

"That's not what I meant." Roxie stepped out of her row and started to walk toward the front. "I meant how do you know we don't have any private zoos or private citizens who own dangerous animals?"

What was she doing? He leaned forward so the mike would pick him up. "I know most of the people in the parish. I haven't heard anything about illegal animals."

"And if you did, what would you do about it?" She eased up to the public mike, standing in front of him with that authoritative stance that got his motor running every time. It didn't work with anyone else. Only her. There was something so . . . Roxie about the way she stood.

"Well, I guess I would tell the sheriff." It was really all he could do. There wasn't anyone else to tell. He could call Wildlife and Fisheries but that could move slowly, and people around the parish would deal better with someone local. "We don't have an animal services department. That's precisely why the sheriff hired me. I'm a subject matter . . . I hesitate to use the word 'expert.' I'm a guy who knows a lot about local wildlife."

"But you weren't the guy who was on my property last night," Sue interjected. "Major was. He didn't even look in the trees to see if the tiger was up there. He just glanced around and then said I should pick up my chip bags or it would be littering. I don't even eat chips. My body is a temple."

Roxie's expression had turned distinctly thoughtful and she stepped back for a moment.

Herve took the chance to make his move. "Don't be ridiculous. It's not a tiger. It's a rougarou. We used to have them all over the bayou in the old days. They're coming back. My pop-pop always said they would rise again. I think we should hire Miss Marcelle and Miss Delphine to take care of this problem."

"Hallelujah," could be heard from the audience. From Zep's mom.

He shook his head. He knew exactly what was going on here. "I know she promised you ten percent, but ten percent of nothing is going to be nothing. Now, listen up, everyone. There is no rougarou. There is no tiger. There was an asshole who dumped a puppy he didn't want, and some teens who didn't know when to go to bed. I don't know exactly what went on last night. But I promise, I will come out to your place, Sue, and I will check for tracks. I'll check into every single incident until I prove to you that this is nothing more than Archie having an active imagination."

"No you will not." Roxie had her hands on her hips and was sending him that stare she got when she wasn't going to be moved.

He wasn't sure what he'd done wrong, but he caught sight of the girl with the camera coming in closer like she knew something dramatic was about to happen. At least this time she wasn't climbing on top of the shed and losing her camera in someone else's yard. "I thought you wanted me to be more involved."

Roxie shook her head. "You are already far too involved for very little pay. Armie, are you going to pay him to answer every citizen's call?"

"I was planning on seeing if I could pay him in beer, actually," Armie admitted.

Zep turned toward the sheriff. "I am not being paid in beer."

"You used to," the sheriff pointed out.

"No, I was never paid in beer. And we're going to talk about my rates because I'm not doing the work of an entire department for fun. I'm good at this and I deserve to be paid." He was getting a headache, and that camera was on him. "Ashlyn, could you put that thing away?"

The teen didn't flinch. "Sorry, it's a school project. Could you talk more about the animal attacks?"

A gasp rippled across the audience, and he needed to get ahead of that. "There have been no attacks. None. We can negotiate my pay later. For now, I assure you all that I will help get us through this . . . is it really a crisis?"

"No, but it points out a problem the parish has," Roxie said. "Mayor Martine, when are we going to deal with our animal issues? The sheriff's department is not equipped to handle animal calls, and we don't do a good job of it. What happened when the Nichols family found that nest of possums under their porch?"

LaTonya Nichols stood, her bag of popcorn in one hand. "My dad wouldn't listen to anyone, and he went under the house himself to get them and got himself stuck. It took six hours to get him out, and he needed a rabies shot."

Zep sighed. "The possum was likely only under the house to have her babies, and she would have been gone in a few weeks. If it really bothered you, I could have relocated them. Possums are also incredibly helpful animals."

Another man stood. "Yes, they help themselves to my trash."

He knew exactly how the man dealt with his trash since he had to pass it most mornings on his way to the restaurant. "You have to cover the cans, Lewis. You can't toss bags in a can without using the lid the parish provided. I've told you a thousand times that's how you attract animals. And the only reason we're not overrun with ticks is the possum population. You start taking them out and everyone in this county is getting Lyme disease. There is a balance that must be kept."

"You tell 'em, baby!"

He would love to blame his mother's enthusiasm on inebriation, but she didn't drink to excess, and she could be obnoxiously peppy fully sober.

"It's good we have someone around who understands the balance," Roxie pointed out. "Mayor, who answers questions about animal issues in city hall?"

Sylvie's gaze had narrowed. "I believe I know what you're hinting at, and we would need funding for that."

"Funding for what?" Zep asked.

Roxie turned his way. "How serious are you about a career working with animals?"

Was she doing what he thought she was doing? "It would be my dream job."

Roxie went back to staring at Sylvie like they were caught in important negotiations. "If I can find the funding, would you be open to it? There are numerous federal grants available to aid rural governments across the country."

Armie leaned forward. "My wife knows a lot about that. She could be helpful."

Sylvie's lips turned up. "If we can find the funding, he's got the job, and I will not attempt to pay him in beer. But it wouldn't be the easiest job in the world."

"I think you'll find between his associate degree and his work experience, that he's highly qualified to run Papillon Parish's Department of Animal Services," Roxie said, triumph plain in her voice.

Zep froze. He'd thought she was trying to convince Sylvie to make his consultant position permanent. "What?"

Armie leaned over. "I believe your girl is setting you up to start a whole new department at city hall. If you don't want it, you should speak up now because let me tell you, once you get into that office, you probably will work there the rest of your life."

He would have a place. That was what Roxie was offering him. He looked out at the audience because he'd promised his brother he would take over that shop. He didn't want to upset his brother, but damn, he wanted the job Roxie was trying to create for him.

His brother had a big smile on his face and gave him a thumbs-up even as Luc was climbing all over him.

"I'll do it." He turned his gaze to Roxie.

"Excellent," she said.

"Well, that is great, but it doesn't explain what happened in my backyard last night, and I'm going to hold the sheriff's department responsible if my kids turn into werewolves," Sue said.

"Oh, you hush, Sue. Your children are already little hooligans. Getting them to only misbehave on full moon nights would be a blessing," Gene said. He owned the grocery store and was the resident conspiracy theorist, though he tended to believe deep state conspiracies, not supernatural ones. "And they do leave their trash everywhere. I told the sheriff your kids have been playing around in the parking lot, leaving those fiery chip things around."

Something sparked in his brain.

He turned to Armie. "Is that what you meant earlier? You said something about chip bags and finding a new teen hangout spot?"

"Yeah, they didn't throw their stuff away even though there was a trash can ten feet away," Armie grumbled.

It was all coming together in his head. "And Sue, you said you saw a flash of something. A flash of light? Dixie said she saw something similar."

Sue nodded. "Yes. I did. But it could have been one of

Gene's lights flickering. I wish I'd picked a different house because it's terrible to have to watch his back parking lot from my yard."

"You thinking what I'm thinking?" Roxie asked.

"I would very much like to know what either one of you is thinking." Armie's brow had risen. "You seem to have figured something out."

He looked out and Ashlyn finally had her camera down. "What's the name of your project?"

Roxie turned and stared at the teen, too. "You can talk here or we can do it at the station house. And you three in the back, do not think you can sneak out. I can find you, and when I do, it will be so much worse because I'll bring your mommas in."

He noticed what he hadn't before. A row of teens had gotten to their feet, trying to sneak out of the hall. Two girls and a boy, including the young lovers from earlier in the week.

"Ashlyn, you should answer Mr. Guidry," Roxie said with a steely look in her eyes.

Mrs. Travers stood up and walked to her daughter. "Ashlyn is working on a project for her school, and her friends are helping her. That's all. Why are you harassing her?"

"What's the name of your project?" Roxie moved closer, reminding him a bit of a cougar seeking prey.

Ashlyn swallowed nervously. "Uhm, it's a short film about what happens in a small town."

"What happens in small towns?" Roxie prodded.

"Uh . . . stuff. It's about how boring towns are," the teen said, seeming to get some of her stubbornness back.

"You told me you were making one of those scary movies." Her mother's hands went to her hips. "That's why you've been out so late. You said you needed nighttime shots to get the mood right." She pointed a finger her daughter's way. "If you were out playing around with boys, I'll have your hide. I knew that Hannah was going to be a bad influence on you."

Hannah stood up. "I am not a bad influence, and Austin and I were only making out in Miss Dixie's backyard because we're supposed to be the heroes of the film. It was supposed to be romantic, but then Ashlyn said she had to kill one of us off or it would be too mainstream. What does that even mean?"

Ashlyn's eyes had rolled. "It means I'm an artist, Hannah. No one wants a happy-ending horror film."

"And what kills the lovers in your film?" Roxie asked as righteously as any whodunnit sleuth ever had before.

Ashlyn's lips closed.

He was so right about this. "What's the name of the film, Ashlyn? I'm going to find out. Do you know what I think happened? I think you decided to make a film about a mythical creature, and how do you make a film on a shoestring budget these days? Your characters film the footage themselves. Like *Blair Witch*."

"It's called found footage and it's an art form," Ashlyn argued.

Zep stood up because she'd forgotten something. "How many of your actors knew they were acting?"

Her mother had a horrified look on her face. "Is that why you had your phone up when I was making breakfast this morning? You said you were playing around. I didn't even have any makeup on. You were going to put it in a film?"

"I find your reactions are better if you don't know you're being filmed," Ashlyn admitted. "And I got great footage of the old dude and the goats freaking out. Sorry, I didn't know about the dog. I totally would have saved the dog."

Zep went to the edge of the stage. "You were still in the woods when we got there, and you were definitely not looking for your phone at Dixie's. You were purposefully scaring people so you could get their reactions on film?"

"It's called *The Rougarou's Revenge*, and I'm putting it in a contest for found-footage horror," Ashlyn declared. "Though Hannah and Austin were actually pretty terrible. How about you and the deputy become my romantic interests? You two have great chemistry on film."

Roxie's eyes narrowed. "You filmed us?"

He needed to get down there or his honey was going to get in trouble. He jumped off the stage and rushed to join her. "I don't think this is how found footage works. You're going to need releases from everyone. Signed releases."

"She's going to need a long talking-to." Armie stared down from the stage. "You were sneaking around in people's yards hoping they would think you were some kind of crazed killer werewolf. This is Louisiana. You're lucky you weren't shot."

Ashlyn's eyes lit up. "Oh, the old dude totally took a shot, but his aim wasn't good. It's the best scene in the whole film so far. Very exciting."

Her mother looked like she might pass out. "Oh, my lord."

The crowd started to argue about how to deal with the teenage wannabe auteur, but Sylvie stood with the microphone in her hand. "All right. We can now safely say we caught the rougarou and move on with life. We hope to have the animal services department up and going as soon as possible, and until then, if you have questions about any animal issues, contact the sheriff's department and talk to Mr. Guidry. Momma, you better still have some booze because I've had a day."

The meeting was over and Zep had survived. Survived and thrived since apparently he was going to have a job at the end of all this. A low-paying civil service job.

A job he might love.

Sometimes life flooded in, obliterating everything in its path, but what he'd come to learn was that dreams could change. Life wasn't some concrete thing that became useless if it lost a piece. It wasn't a puzzle that couldn't be complete without one specific thing.

He could have a new dream. A good job where he could make a difference. A happy home. A family.

Simple dreams, but ones that would make him whole.

Roxie turned to him with a brilliant smile on her face. "And she would have gotten away with it if wasn't for this meddling deputy. We solved the case."

"Yes, and that means you get to do the paperwork," Armie said with a shake of his head as he joined them. "I'm going to have such a talk with those kids. Every single one of them is having the lecture of a lifetime tonight." He looked toward the back of the building. "Don't you leave, Austin. Yeah, I'm talking to you, son. I've already called your dad."

He stalked away, and Zep did not envy those kids. They were about to be treated to a whole lot of Armie's frowns.

Roxie was still grinning. "I don't even care about the paperwork. That was fun."

"Oh, my new baby is so smart," his mother said, joining them.

"I helped," he said, though he didn't really mind giving Roxie all the credit.

"Yeah, what I saw was Roxie here saving your butt from having to spend every night prowling around looking for werewolves," his brother said, reaching a hand out.

He started to shake Remy's hand, but his brother pulled him in for a hug. "You're not upset I'm not taking over the shop?"

"I'm happy you're going to get to do something you love,

brother. That's all that matters. And you should never let that one go. She's good for you," Remy said before stepping back.

"Uncle Zep, is there tigers out there?" Luc stared up at him, his eyes wide.

He reached down and lifted his nephew up. He'd given up one dream for his sister, and this kid had been the product. Luc was healthy and happy and so sweet, it hurt his heart sometimes.

It had been worth it. It had all been worth it.

"Nah, but even if there were, Roxie here would track 'em down, and I would make sure they got someplace safe," he promised. "You're in good hands, buddy."

Luc leaned over and put his arms around Zep's neck and sighed like he had when he was just a baby. It was a sigh of comfort, of trust.

It made him look over at Roxie, who was talking to his mother.

All he needed was time and she might discover she could find her dreams here, too. With him.

"Zep, did you hear what they said?" Archie was dressed in his Sunday best, slacks and a short-sleeved button-down, a bow tie around his neck. "I'm going to be in a movie."

"You are not going to be in a movie," his wife insisted. "I'm going to sue that girl. She took pictures of you in your shorts."

"I want to be in the movie," Herve said. "How do I get in on that?"

Roxie strode over to him and held out a hand. "I'm sorry. I'm going to need Mr. Guidry here to help me with some paperwork. He's a very important member of our department."

He passed Luc off and let her lead him out.

She'd saved him again since Archie was arguing with his wife.

He walked with her toward the door to the auditorium, perfectly happy with how the day had gone.

Roxie held Zep's hand and started to drag him through the crowd. If they stayed, they would inevitably be pulled into some big family thing where they all went back to Guidry's for dinner, and she wanted him to herself.

All to herself.

Like right now.

Her heart thudded in her chest. It had been a weird high to figure out how to handle all her problems in one go. Maybe not all her problems, but a couple of them.

"When did you figure out it was Ashlyn?" Zep asked as they made their way through the crowd.

"When she looked excited about filming a town meeting," she admitted. "That is not a young woman who is interested in civics. You came to the same conclusion."

It had been cool that they'd been on the same page. In sync.

"Hey, Zep, now that you're the animal man, can we talk about the snake population out near my place?" A man in overalls tried to stop them before they hit the doors that led out of the main auditorium.

"He's got paperwork to do," Roxie insisted. "You can call him during his office hours."

"I have office hours?" Zep asked.

"You're going to. I assume you're going to accept the job? I didn't want to speak for you back there." She was restless, and a million questions were going through her head.

She'd ensured that he had a good job, one that he would enjoy, one that would fulfill him, and she was happy about it.

But didn't it ensure that when she left, he would want to stay here?

The conversation with her dad weighed on her, and she couldn't stay behind and pretend like her head wasn't going a million miles a minute.

She could go back to New York. She could potentially have her old job again. Well, her dad hadn't said that in so many words, but she could work toward it. She could basically erase the last couple of years and start over.

But the idea of not being with Zep made her ache inside. She didn't want to ache. She didn't want to hurt. She wanted this to be simple, and sex was simple.

She would get him in bed and not let up until she could breathe again. In the morning, things would be clearer. She wouldn't be thinking about how nice it had felt to sit with his family and feel perfectly comfortable, like she was one of them. She wouldn't think about how much fun she'd had solving a stupid case and standing in the middle of the town hall and feeling like she belonged.

"Hey." He tugged on her hand, stopping her. "I thought we were supposed to do paperwork."

"I don't want to do paperwork right now, Guidry."

His jaw tightened. "I don't like it when you call me that. My name is Zep."

She felt her eyes roll because the last thing she wanted to do was fight with him or be reminded of how she disappointed him. "Zep, I would like to go home now. I would like to go to bed."

"I think we should probably talk about this. A whole lot of crazy stuff happened in there."

He didn't want to go to bed? He wanted to bask in the approval of the town? God, did she have a right to keep him from that? But she couldn't. She stopped because she was doing what he'd accused her of before—using him for stress relief, and he would be upset to find that out again. She schooled her expression before replying. "It's cool. You probably should go back in there and be with your family. I'm going to head home. I can walk."

The last thing she wanted to do was walk. Walking would lead to thinking, and she didn't want to think at all. If she walked, she would have to pass Dixie's, where she had coffee most mornings, and consider the fact that the coffee in New York wasn't going to taste the same and she'd just gotten to where she liked the coffee here, and where would she find jambalaya the way Remy made it and . . .

"Hey." Zep was suddenly standing over her, his deep blue eyes staring down. "What's the matter?"

"Nothing." She'd played this all wrong. She should have followed her rule book and stayed backstage. She shouldn't have followed her stupid heart and pretended like she was one of them. "Like I said, go back to your family."

He glanced around. "Come with me. I know a way out."

She knew one, too. It was the door. The one he was leading her away from. "I can find my way home."

He turned down a hall and his grip was strong enough that if she wanted to break it, she would have to fight. That would draw a crowd, and then she would be the subject of gossip yet again. Maybe he knew a back way out, but he didn't have to come with her.

"I told you, I can make it on my own, Guidry."

He stopped in the middle of the empty hall, the voices from the meeting now hushed by distance. "And I told you not to call me Guidry."

He pressed her against the wall and loomed over her, and just like that, she was back to wanting to get in his pants and forget about the rest of the world.

But there was a problem with that. She put her hands up, meeting his chest and keeping a careful distance between them. "Guidry's your name."

"No. That's my family name, and you could call my brother the same thing. My name is Zep, and you don't call anyone else that. Don't think I don't know what you're doing. I'm not going to let you distance yourself from me. Not if you want me to give you what you need."

"What do I need?"

"Me. This." He pressed closer and her hands fell away. "Tell me what you need, Roxanne. You don't have to tell me the whys. You don't have to talk to me at all, but you have to look me in the eyes and tell me you need me."

Heat flashed through her system, and she was so aware of him. Aware of how close he was and how warm his skin was. Aware of how he smelled like her soap, and how all it would take to press her lips to his would be to go up on her toes. Still, she shook her head. "No. I promised I wouldn't use you."

His hands gripped her wrists, and he brought them up and over her head, pinning them to the wall. "It's not using if you ask me. Something set you off. Something got you all wound up, and you need to relax. This isn't the same as before."

"How?"

"Because you're not trying to get me out of your system. I don't think you are."

She had to be honest with him. "But I don't know if I can keep you."

"I'm willing to take that chance. I'm willing to do everything I need to take care of you as long as you're willing to let me be your man while you're here."

Tears . . . freaking tears . . . pulsed behind her eyes. "And if I won't be here for long?"

Things were happening so fast. It felt like she'd spent almost two years with nothing changing at all, like she'd been in limbo, and now that she'd finally started to find her way out of the weeds, her life had sped up again. All she wanted to do now was slow it down, spend this time with him, freeze a moment, and stay there. No future. No past. Just him. Just her.

His gaze softened and then he released her. "Then we should make whatever time we have count. You just gave me a gift and I want to show you how much I appreciate it, how much I appreciate you. I am definitely taking the job."

"Even though it's not your dream job?"

"Dreams change. They don't have to stay the same all our lives," Zep replied. "Sometimes we don't know what our real dreams are until they walk into our lives."

She felt the loss of his touch but only for a moment because he leaned over and picked her up, his arm going under her legs and hauling her close. "Zep, what are you doing?"

"Taking care of you," he vowed as he strode down the hall like she didn't weigh a thing. "Taking care of me."

She thought he would take her out the door and put her in the truck. Instead, he turned at the door to a conference room and managed to get it open. "I thought we were going home."

"Where you would get distracted by an overly excited puppy and a cat who wants to pretend she doesn't need your attention?" He set her on her feet, found the light switches, and turned one set of lights on, flooding the room with a dim glow that showed off a very utilitarian conference table. She'd been in this room before. They used it when they updated city hall on the budgetary needs of the sheriff's office. "No. You're wound up and I don't understand why because you seemed fine before."

She shook her head. “I’m good at shoving things down.”

“Be good at taking things off.” He pressed the button that locked the door.

He wanted to do that here? “I don’t think that’s a good idea.”

Anyone could try to come in. There were people all over this building because of the meeting. That little lock wouldn’t keep anyone out. Not really.

“Don’t think.” He moved in, advancing until she felt the edge of the table. “Just feel. Let me take over. No one’s coming in here. They’ll mill around the hall for a bit and then everyone will head to Guidry’s or home. And it wouldn’t matter if they did. I would tell them to get out and I’d go right back to loving you. Nothing would keep me from that.”

Because he would make her the center of his world. Because he wanted her more than any man had ever wanted her before, and that did something for her. The feeling wasn’t merely sexual. Zep’s want went beyond the physical. It was what she hadn’t understood before. He needed her for far more than sex. He needed her to ground him, to help him find purpose, to teach him how worthy he was.

That was what made her gut roll at the idea of leaving him.

He picked her up and set her on the table, shoving a chair out of the way. His hands sank into her hair. “Don’t. Don’t pull in on yourself. Share it with me.”

Somehow it was easier to talk with his hands moving over her scalp, his hips shifting her knees apart and making a place for himself there. “Talking to my dad was rough. He wants me to think about coming back to New York. I might have a job there.”

He stilled, but only for a moment, as though he had to absorb the blow before he moved on. “Okay. You need to think about that. But not now. Now, concentrate on this.”

He leaned over and his mouth covered hers in a long, luxurious kiss. He held her still for a moment before her hands came up to find his hips, and she let go of anything but the feel of him.

Her body went liquid. His hands stroked over her and suddenly her shirt was open, the tops of her breasts exposed to his touch. He quickly found the front clasp of her bra and freed them. Cool air brushed her skin, making a contrast to the fire that licked everywhere he touched.

She would never get enough of this man. Not enough of his touch or his kiss. Not enough of cuddling with him and working beside him.

It no longer mattered that someone could walk in. He was right about that. She would tell them to shut the door and get back to loving him.

His tongue slid inside her mouth, gliding against hers in a lush approximation of what he would soon do with another part of his body. She could feel his desire pressing to her core even as his kiss stayed patient. He seemed willing to override his needs to give her time to enjoy every moment they had together. Sex for Zep Guidry was something to be indulged in, to revel in.

Because it was his way of telling her how he felt. Because he wasn't sure how to say it in words.

Because he might love her.

His arms tightened around her. "Lean back."

She would do anything he asked of her. She'd come to trust him so much. He wouldn't willingly hurt her. Her heart might get torn asunder, but it wouldn't be his fault. It would be hers. She put her palms down flat on the table behind her and offered herself up to him.

"Have I told you how beautiful you are?"

He told her so often, she almost believed it. "Yes, but I haven't told you how beautiful you are, Zéphirin. Inside and out. I always knew you had a gorgeous face, but it was that beautiful soul that got to me. Touch me or I won't be able to breathe."

His hand came out, big palm covering her breast. "I think about touching you all day. You should understand that even if I'm not around, I'm still touching you in my head. You're so soft."

No one had ever called her soft before. She was hard. She'd always had to be, but maybe she'd found the one place where she could let her guard down and let that softness that was always there inside come out.

He pulled her blouse and bra off, dropping them to the side, and then worked the buckle of her belt. It clanged to the table, the sound reminding her she was still in uniform, and that meant still carrying a gun.

"Damn it. I don't guess Armie would consider allowing you to wear a skirt?" Zep asked.

He always made her smile. He would have her in a miniskirt chasing down the bad guys if he could. But there was a simple solution. "Back up a minute. I'm not letting you out of this until you give me everything you promised, but it won't work if I'm in these pants, and you need to get out of yours, too."

He stepped back. "Nah, I can do what I need to do just by shoving them down a little, baby."

She kicked off her boots and worked her way out of her pants, and before they hit the floor, he was on her again. He turned her so her back was pressed to the front of his body. She was naked while he still had all his clothes on, and there was something sexy about it. She could be vulnerable with him. He would only give her pleasure.

His hands found her breasts again, but this time he cupped and fondled them while he whispered in her ear, telling her how much he wanted her, how beautiful she was, how lonely he'd been without her all day.

When his hand trailed down her torso and found her feminine core, she gasped and went still against him, not wanting to miss a minute of his talented fingers. He stroked her, taking her higher and higher with every touch, every sweet word he gave her.

Her whole body shook as the pleasure washed over her, and even the air around them seemed soft and warm, cocooning them in intimacy.

"I don't want you to think about anything but me," he said as he lifted her up again and set her on the conference table. His hands went to the buckle of his belt.

She watched as he freed himself, protected her by rolling a condom on. He was so beautiful. Her guy.

She wouldn't be able to think about anything but him from now on. Certainly not in this room. This was the room where she fought to stay awake while she backed up Armie as he fought over budget projections.

Now every time she sat in this room, she would see Zep as he gathered her into his arms, as he connected them in the most intimate way possible.

She held on to him as he thrust inside, pushing her again to find that peak he seemed to take her to so often. He leaned over and kissed her, connecting them in every way he could.

This. This was what she would miss. This wild connection. When she was with him, she felt more alive than she did when she was alone or with anyone else.

The orgasm rolled over her even as she felt him shudder in her arms.

He fell forward, giving him her weight. She loved this moment, the one where he sighed and laid his head against hers.

"Better?"

She felt a chuckle go through her. "Yeah."

He kissed her cheek. "I'm glad because this was a good day for me. Did I thank you for getting me a whole department?"

She rubbed her cheek against his. If the somewhat awkward position was bothering him, he didn't show it. "You might curse me one day when you're sitting in this room taking meeting after meeting. But, Zep, you're going to be great."

He kissed her and the world faded away all over again. Whatever would come, she would face it.

Tomorrow.

# *chapter twelve*

"So a bunch of teens were trying to make a horror movie and they thought it was a good idea to hide in people's bushes to get shots of them being scared?" Major asked as he set his stuff down on the desk next to hers.

It was time for shift change. Normally Roxie would hang out for at least an hour or so, but this afternoon she was anxious to get home. Anxious to get through the evening because, after tonight, she might be able to breathe again.

"Has the story made it around town already?"

"Yeah, it was all my dad could talk about when I visited him today," Major replied, his handsome face set in curious lines.

She wished she could be as focused as Major's dad. All she seemed to be able to think about was Zep. She hadn't been able to get him out of her head all day. It hadn't helped that he'd come in at lunchtime with BLT sandwiches and fries from Dixie's. He'd sat with her and eaten and talked about how his morning had gone. He and Daisy had been working on training in the backyard while Sunny had watched through the window.

"That's the long and short of it," she replied. They stood in the big room of the station house. Armie's office was off to the left, and the rest of the department all had desks dotting the office space. Zep was currently closed off in the conference room filling out forms on the laptop she'd given him. Despite Armie's status as a small-town sheriff, he did not stint on the paperwork.

She'd done her own when she'd gotten in this morning, but Zep was just learning the joys of filing reports.

"This is Ashlyn Travers?" Major pulled out his chair. "Karen's kid? I saw her last week up at the nursing home where Karen works. She had a camera out. I wonder if the residents know they might be movie stars soon."

"I don't think she understands the idea of release forms. Nor does she understand trespassing laws and plain old consequences."

"And she didn't think about the fact that she could get shot?" Major sat at his desk, his feet up on the edge as though he was ready for a quiet second shift.

"I'm pretty sure she thought it would make the movie better."

Major shook his head. "Did Armie's head explode when he heard about this?"

Roxie had to chuckle. "From what I can tell, he's still yelling. He started as we left the hall last night, and he told me he was meeting with the AV teacher at the high school this afternoon. Those kids might never pick up a camera again. Or maybe they will since I heard a couple of people asking when the film would be out and were they in it."

That brought a big smile to Major's face. "It was all the people at the assisted living facility could talk about. If she did manage to make a movie, it would be the biggest thing to hit this town in a long time."

She leaned against her own desk. Despite the way she'd

spent the night and the peaceful lunch she'd had with Zep, she still had questions running through her head. She'd been able to shove them aside when she was wrapped up in his arms. After they'd left the town hall, they'd picked up dinner and headed back to her place, where they'd spent a pleasant evening watching a movie with the dog and the cat in their laps, her head drifting to his shoulder when she'd gotten sleepy. And yet today, she was restless again. Every hour that brought her closer to the dinner plans her family had made seemed to ratchet up her tension. "Does that ever bother you?"

"The fact that not a lot happens here?" Major sighed and sat back. "I think every place on earth has its problems. I did my stint in the Army. I know what it feels like to have way too much thrown my way. You do, too. Life is a little like pick your poison. I could have gotten on at a bigger department. I could have gone into private security. I would have had all the adrenaline I wanted, but what I wouldn't have is my dad. My mom died when I was in high school, and while I was in the military, my dad met and married a woman from here. I don't know how long I'll have with him. So I made that choice. I moved here to be close to him. My life is here. That means the most exciting case I'll get to handle will likely be figuring out who stole the mailboxes. You got to bust open the case of the fake rougarou, so you're already going to be legendary in this town. Is it true you managed to get the mayor to promise to open an animal services department?"

And she'd handed her own boyfriend a job. She was sure they were talking about that, too. "You know we need one."

"We absolutely do. I kind of thought you were going to open your own since you've adopted two pets this week."

"I did not." She huffed because she was lying to herself. "Okay, Daisy is too cute to leave, and I feel bad for the cat.

She didn't ask to be born with all black fur. She's not bad luck. I'm worried if I send her to a shelter, no one will take her because you're all crazy superstitious down here." She held a hand up. "I know. I know. We're all crazy at heart, but I don't want Sunny to get put down because someone thinks she's bad luck."

Major considered her for a moment. "Wow, you're finally settling in. I didn't think it would happen, since this was only temporary."

"I don't know. Lately, I've been wondering if I could maybe handle this for a couple more months. A year maybe. Or more."

"Are you serious?" Major's feet had come down and he was staring at her with an incredulous expression.

Why was it so surprising? "It's not a bad job. And it's not like I have anywhere to go. You know it looks sketchy on a résumé if you move around too much. No one likes to have to train and retrain all the time."

"I thought you were looking."

"I was. Maybe it's time to stop." But the idea her father had dangled in front of her was still in the back of her mind.

"You understand that if you spend too much time here, it might be hard to find a job where you want. Bigger offices don't think much of rural cops. I always thought you would go back to the city." Major glanced toward the conference room. "Is this because of Zep?"

The question made her stop. How did she answer that? "Yes" would be accurate, but it would also start rumors. "He's a nice guy."

Yeah, that answered the question.

"I know he's a nice guy, but I'm surprised you would give up your career for a guy at all. You didn't seem the type."

"Who said I'm giving up anything?" She wasn't. There

wasn't anything at all concrete about her father's plan for her in New York. Likely they would make her jump through hoops she wasn't ready to jump through, or make her work her way back up the ladder, and she wasn't directing traffic again. Not unless it had to do with a cat.

"Come on. We all know you're not going to stay," Major argued.

She didn't like the sound of that. Being a member of a team meant you counted on the people on the team. And yet she'd been the one to walk in and tell her coworkers she wasn't staying. How hard had that been on them? To know she'd walked in and viewed a job they enjoyed as nothing more than a way station on the road to much better things? Was that why there was always a careful distance between her and her fellow deputies?

"I never meant to make any of you feel like this job isn't worthy."

He stopped for a moment as if he had no idea what to say to that.

As if he didn't believe her. "I didn't mean to make you feel that way, Major. I'll admit that when I first came here, it was a big transition. It took me a while to finally understand that this job can be every bit as hard as my old one in New York."

"Somehow I doubt that," he said wistfully.

What had Major wanted to do with his life? She'd never asked because she hadn't gotten to know him very well.

It was funny how opening herself up to one person led to her wanting to do it more.

The door to the station came open and Armie strode in, his face set in its frowniest of frowns. It was the one that told her the boss was in a mood. Usually it meant he'd had a fight with his wife, but Roxie didn't think that was the case this time. Armie was the only one she'd really gotten to know, and that had been because she worked with him the most. "You okay, boss?"

He stopped and seemed to realize he was frowning. His expression shuttered. "I'm fine. I have never in my life been so happy my daughter wants to be a scientist. Yes, she talks over my head most of the time, but I'll take it. The artistic teen would drive me insane. Did you get that paperwork done?"

"Yes." That was an odd statement coming from him. While Armie ran a tight ship, he didn't normally require paperwork be done immediately. "And Zep's doing his. He's not a great typist, though, so we could be here for a while."

Armie nodded and grunted in a way that let her know something was definitely wrong, and it wasn't about his wife.

It was odd how well she'd gotten to know Armie. She liked him. She would miss working with him if she left. Maybe that was why she hadn't gotten close to anyone else. She followed him to his office, closing the door behind her. "What's going on? You wouldn't be this upset about the kids. Did one of the parents give you hell?"

He sighed and sank into his chair. "I need a better poker face."

His poker face was fine. She'd watched him stare down any number of intimidating people without breaking a sweat, which told her that whatever was bugging him was something he was emotional about. And that worried her.

"Is everything okay at home? Are Noelle and Lila all right?"

His eyes flared. "Of course. They're fine, Rox." He sat back and seemed to come to some decision. "I got a call about you."

"What did I do? If this is about me giving out too many tickets again, all I can say is people around here should drive better. It's really unsafe, Armie." And she was way slower on writing tickets these days. She hadn't even given Karen one.

"I got a call from someone at NYPD and they asked about you."

Her stomach threatened to drop. "Why?"

"He wanted to know some things about your employment. It sounded very much like you've been interviewing."

"I haven't had an interview. I would have told you. My father mentioned to me yesterday that there might be a place for me, but I haven't talked to anyone who could hire me."

"But you would go."

"I don't know. I mean . . . I would have to think about it, but it's not as simple as it was in the beginning." Her chest felt tight again. All the work Zep had done the night before and this morning washed away. She was going to have to make a decision and she wasn't even close to being ready. "You always knew I didn't mean to stay. When I mentioned I was even thinking about it, Major was surprised."

"Yes, well, what you didn't know is that I never intended for you to leave," Armie admitted. "Yes, I was going to make those calls for you. I have and I've got feelers out both in New Orleans and Dallas, where I have contacts. But I was going to try to talk you out of it because I think this place has been good for you. And I think you're good for Papillon."

"I don't know about that."

"Having a woman in the department has changed a lot of things for us. I know you were one of a few women on your team, and that was a big deal. You were a role model for other women in New York, but here in Papillon, you're a role model for every girl who would have grown up never seeing a woman with a badge. You are the only woman officer we've ever had, and it's made a huge difference."

"I'm the first? You never told me that. Maybe that's why I had to explain to several people that I wasn't a stripper the first couple of months I was here." It had been an odd transition.

"Do you know what it meant for me to bring you here? A smart, tough woman for our girls to look up to? For our women to feel comfortable talking about their problems with?" Armie's face was set in grim lines. "I understand that you need to do what's best for you, and I can't offer you the kind of money they will. I can't offer you the type of career you'll get there, but I promise you that you'll make a difference here that no one else can."

"Are you asking me to stay?"

He nodded. "Yes. Shamelessly. I don't want to lose you."

Her heart actually hurt. "God, that's not fair, Armie. I never promised I would stay."

"And yet I want you to." He sat back. "But know that I'll support you no matter what you decide."

"As I haven't been offered anything but my father's hints, I can't say there's a decision to be made yet." But if there were rumors running through the precincts, then it was likely someone would contact her. It wouldn't be her father. It would be someone from One Police Plaza.

Wouldn't she be the stupidest woman in the world if she turned down an offer to return in a blaze of glory in order to stay in Papillon and play house with her boyfriend?

Wasn't that what she'd tried to avoid all her life? Becoming her mom? Giving up all her hopes and dreams for some guy.

But what had Zep said yesterday? Sometimes dreams

changed. Sometimes life opened a path a person hadn't thought of as viable before.

Was staying in Papillon a viable life for her?

There was a knock on the door, and she looked through the window. Zep stood there, the laptop she'd given him in his hand.

"Just remember you're wanted here. Even if you leave, you'll always have a place with this department, and I think you'll find you have a place with that man standing there," Armie said before he raised a hand. "Come on in, Zep."

He opened the door and walked in. It was as if the sun had come with him. That smile of his worked wonders on her mood. "Hey, bab . . . I mean, good afternoon, Deputy. I did that report you wanted me to do and I didn't even answer sarcastically."

Armie's eyes rolled. "Like I don't know you're basically living together, and it's gone way further than you needed to hide the fact that Roxie's been pining for you since she met you."

She felt heat flood her face. She never got embarrassed, but then maybe that was because she rarely truly cared. Her feelings for Zep were real, and that made her vulnerable.

"Pining. That word gets tossed around a lot." Zep didn't make a big deal out of it. He simply set the laptop on Armie's desk and gave her a wink. "My brother used it talking about me the other day. In that scenario, I was the one pining for you. What the hell does pining mean? It's weird."

She had no idea why they called this longing she felt and had for months and months pining, but Armie was right. She'd spent all this time with an ache in her chest, and it had only gone away when she was with him.

Would she spend the rest of her life pining for this man?

"So when I take over the animal services department, I'll be like the sheriff of animals," Zep began.

Armie's lips kicked up in a grin. "Sure. You be the sheriff of all the mangy dogs and restless cats. And Otis. You get Otis, my friend."

Zep groaned. "I swear that gator knows he's causing trouble and he loves it."

Armie seemed genuinely amused. "Well, I'm happy he's your trouble now, and you should know that Herve found a baby raccoon whose momma got hit by a car and he thinks he can raise it."

Zep shrugged. "He can until that sucker hits puberty, and then all bets are off. Damn it. I'm going to have to deal with that. Seriously, you think a teenage boy is rough. Teenage raccoon is way worse." His hand brushed against hers as he looked at Armie. "I talked to a couple of people over at the mayor's office, and they said this might be the best place for me to find a space. I've got a couple of projects I need to work on."

"You haven't gotten hired yet," Armie pointed out.

But that was the beauty of Papillon. Unlike a big city or even a larger town, they could move quickly. "I've already talked to enough of the city council to know they won't fight Sylvie. No one is going to fight him for the job, either, so it's all about finding the money. I've already found a good portion of the funding we're going to need. I filled out the paperwork this morning. I have ideas on the rest."

Armie looked at Roxie, a fierce expression on his face. Although this was his fake angry face. "You did city business when you're working for the department?"

She shrugged. "It was a slow morning. It was fill out grant applications or play solitaire."

It had been a nice morning. She'd liked knowing Zep was in another room working on something.

Armie gave up with his fake anger and smiled. "You are

always good with paperwork. It's one of the reasons . . . well, one of the reasons I'm so happy you're around."

His smile had faded halfway through—the moment he'd started to say, *one of the reasons I don't want to lose you.*

She wasn't going to feel guilty. She hadn't promised to stay.

Armie seemed to shake off his emotions. "And Zep can use the empty desk at the back. Feel free to come in whenever."

"Thanks," Zep said. "I want to start working on a page on the city website and start putting together a shelter. I'm going to get the kids involved. I've got plans for a fund-raiser."

Oh, she might have made a Leslie Knope–style monster. "You know we're still months away, right?"

Months away. Would she even be here to watch him get his department started?

"I know, but I want to hit the ground running," Zep said with a sparkle of pure enthusiasm in his eyes. "And we should go or you won't have time to get ready for our dinner."

Armie pushed back from his desk and stood. "That's right. You're having a birthday dinner with your parents tonight. I heard Seraphina's planning something nice."

She breathed a sigh of relief. "If I get through tonight, they leave tomorrow and my life can go back to mostly normal."

"Yeah, it'll be good to get back to normal." Zep's voice was light, but there was something about the way his jaw had tightened.

He was worried she meant something she didn't—that they would go back to the way they were. Did she have a right to reach out and comfort him? Would it be a lie to say they would find a new normal, one that included their relationship?

Even though it might not be fair, she couldn't stop herself from reaching for his hand. Maybe things would go back to normal once her parents left. No one from the force was calling her, so any offer of work was still up in the air, and if there was one thing she'd learned while living here, it was not to borrow trouble, as Dixie would say.

She was better at finding some peace because of this place.

"You ready?" He was staring down at her. "I promised your momma I would have you there at seven, and you're supposed to wear a dress."

"You own a dress?" Armie asked.

Sarcastic man. "I have a dress. You've seen me wear a dress." She sighed and put her hand fully in Zep's. "Okay, let's get this over with."

"Happy birthday," Armie said with a mysterious smile. "I hope you have a good night."

Okay, that was weird, but she let it go.

"Hey, and you two should remember that last year the town hall put security cameras in all the hallways," he called out. "I really hope you cleaned that conference room after you were finished."

She gasped and it was far more than just her face that flushed.

Zep merely grinned that shining god of the world grin of his. "I assure you we were just talking. Nothing more."

"How did talking muss up her hair?" Armie challenged.

"I like to talk with my hands, Sheriff." Zep was completely unflappable when it came to this. Which was good because she'd lost the power of speech.

"Yeah, I bet you do. And Roxanne apparently likes to

talk with her shirt untucked in the back," Armie said with a sly smile.

Zep hurried her out.

Maybe life would never really go back to normal.

Two hours later she sat in his truck as he drove toward the B and B.

He was completely quiet, his eyes on the road. He'd been thoughtful the whole time they'd gotten ready. He'd had to stop by his place for clothes, and while he'd picked up what he needed, she'd had a pleasant conversation with Delphine. They'd sat on the front porch, a glass of sweet tea in her hand, and talked while they'd waved to anyone walking by.

It had been a nice moment.

"Are you worried I'm going to kick you out tomorrow?"

He was quiet for a moment. "Well, I probably should go back to my place. There's no real reason for me to stay. Don't think I don't want to. I do, but we've only been dating for a few days when you think about it."

Her heart sank a bit. She'd thought he would fight her on it.

She wasn't sure she liked reasonable Zep. But he was right. They'd only been "dating" for a few days, though they'd been circling around each other for so much longer. She held on to the one thing she knew that might forgo logic. "I'm hoping you'll still help with Daisy. I've never trained a dog before."

"I will certainly not let Miss Daisy overwhelm you." He seemed to relax. "Maybe we can go see a movie next weekend. Or go into New Orleans and have dinner."

She breathed a sigh of relief. "I think that would be

nice." There were an awful lot of cars in the parking lot. And out of it. There were cars lined up down the road. She caught sight of Lila's crossover. "Why is Lila here?"

"I need you to understand that your mom made me promise."

She groaned. "God, is this a birthday party?"

"She wanted to make it pretty big," he admitted. "I didn't actually know about it until this morning. It's something she worked out with Sera and Harry when she scheduled the trip. I know she's obnoxious, but she loves you."

Or she was trying to make a point. Her nerves were right back on full alert. "Did she invite everyone?"

"According to Sera, it's just forty or so people. Everyone you work with and some of the people from city hall. My family got a late invite, but Remy and Lisa promised to be here to make sure Momma doesn't do anything too crazy."

"They're throwing me a birthday party." She'd planned to do next to nothing for her birthday. She hadn't had a party since she'd left New York. Family birthdays were a big deal to her mother. Of course she also celebrated because, as she put it, she'd done all the work. Her father gave her mother a present every year on her and Brian's birthdays. "You should know my mom is going to act like it's her day."

"She told me." He pulled the car into a space that had been left open. "That's kind of weird, but it seems harmless."

She would see about that. "Let's get this over with."

He reached for her hand before she could open the door. "Hey, what can I do to get you to go into this with a positive attitude?"

"You can turn the truck back on and take me to New Orleans and we'll hide until they're gone," she replied, and then sighed because he was really trying. "Okay. I'll put a smile on my face and get through the evening. If nothing else, this hopefully has been good for Sera and Harry."

She liked the B and B. It had been nice to spend time out here.

"Has it been a total waste of your time?" Zep asked.

"No." If she was really honest with herself, there was only one answer. "It was actually sort of nice to see them again. For the most part, it was good to catch up."

"Then why the bad mood? I can promise you Sera's cake is going to be delicious, and the rum punch is going to be extra rummy."

That made her smile. She wanted a night with him where they stayed in and listened to music and drank all they liked until they fumbled into bed together after telling each other all their secrets.

Being with Zep was the best thing that had happened to her in a long time. She had her parents to thank for it. So why did she still have that terrible feeling in the pit of her stomach like something was going to go wrong? Like the bottom was still waiting to drop out.

But she was going to try to enjoy the evening, she vowed as Zep kissed her and moved to get out of the truck. He was around and to her door before she'd gotten her seat belt off. He opened her door and held out a hand.

"You're in heels," he said before she could protest. "I'm perfectly aware that you can get out of the car on your own, but the gravel can be hard to walk on."

"And you're a gentleman." It had been weird at first. She wasn't used to the gentleman routine, but she'd rapidly discovered that helping was his love language. Service. Sacrifice.

She'd learned they had so much more in common than she could have imagined.

She put her hand in his and let him help her down. She walked hand in hand with him across the lawn and toward the back, where she could hear music being played and people laughing.

How long had it been since she'd gone to a party where she wasn't going to do anything but enjoy herself? Years.

She walked through the flower-laced arbor that led to the back of the B and B, where the patio overlooked the bayou. It was a spectacular space made more beautiful by Harry's gorgeous work. He'd built the arbor with his own hands, and Sera had planted the flowering vines that gave it color.

It would be a gorgeous place to have a wedding.

She shoved that thought aside because she wasn't even close to being able to process it. She wasn't planning on ever getting married again. She hadn't been good at it, hadn't enjoyed it.

"Surprise!" Her mother was standing by a big gorgeous chocolate cake.

And she wasn't alone.

Roxie's ex-husband was standing right beside her.

At least the other shoe had finally dropped.

# *chapter thirteen*

"Who is that?"

Zep knew something was wrong the minute Roxie had stopped and gone stone still. Her hand had been in his one moment and she'd dropped it the next. He could feel the distance between them, though she hadn't taken a single step away.

And then there was the fact that everyone he knew was watching him as though they realized something had gone horribly wrong.

Maybe he should have checked his phone. It had buzzed as texts had come through, but he'd ignored it because he'd wanted to focus on her.

"That's my ex-husband," she said, a tight expression coming over her face.

"Roxanne, come here. Don't be shy," Pamela was saying. "He came all this way to see you."

He. As in her ex, the police captain. He was a blandly attractive man in a suit that looked like it had been made for him. He probably hadn't been forced to go through his entire closet to find two outfits for nice nights out because everything he owned was jeans and tees. He was a good eight to ten years older than Roxie, though they would make a handsome couple.

What had Roxie been like with this man? What had he given her that made her want to marry him and spend her life with him?

"Do you want to leave?" He suddenly wanted to leave very badly. He wished he'd done exactly what she'd asked him to do and turned the truck around and booked it straight to New Orleans. But no. He'd wanted to fit in with her family, and her mom had asked him to do something. He'd wanted to show her that together they could get through everything.

Now all he could see was her past, and it was definitely clouding up their future.

Pamela made her way across the green lawn, her heels not holding her back for a second. She was in a stunning cocktail dress that looked a bit out of place with the rustic charm of his sister's entertainment space. Her hair was in an elaborate updo and her makeup flawlessly done. All she was missing was a tiara because she was obviously dressed to be the queen of this party. "Come on and say hi. He came all this way, Roxanne. Now, don't be rude."

"Nobody asked me if I wanted a surprise," Roxie said in a quiet voice that let him know how upset she was.

"Well, it wouldn't be a surprise if I told you about it." Her mother's mouth became a flat line of irritation as her voice went low. "Can't you be gracious? Didn't I teach you better than this?"

"We can walk right now," Zep offered since she hadn't replied the first time.

She glanced up and her expression shuttered. "Oh, no. I think I should definitely find out why my mother thinks springing my ex-husband on me is an appropriate birthday gift."

Joel strode up with the confidence of a man used to respect from those around him. "Roxanne. It's good to see you. It's been a long time. This is . . . a very interesting place you've landed."

"What are you doing here?" Roxie asked in a blunt manner, though there was a friction to her words that was unusual.

"Why don't we get you a drink, dear." Her mother acted like there was nothing at all wrong. The smile on her face was back the minute she realized her ex-son-in-law had joined them. "It's your birthday, and that is a very special day for both of us. I had our host make your favorite. A beautiful rack of lamb."

"I don't like lamb, Mom. I haven't since I was a kid. You like lamb." Roxie's shoulders were straight as an arrow. She looked over to where Armie stood with his wife. "Is this what you were talking about earlier today?"

"I spoke to him on the phone. I didn't know he was actually here in town," Armie admitted.

Her ex-husband had called Armie? He was confused and the feeling unnerved him. Something had been in play for a while now, and he and Roxanne had been on the outside.

"I told you she wasn't going to take this the way you thought she would." Brian stood to the side with his fiancée. "And just for the record, I do enjoy a good rack of lamb, and the one in the kitchen smells delicious."

It was good to know her brother was on top of things. Zep was at a loss. Should he scoop her up and take her out of here? Hold her hand and help her through it, despite the fact that she'd completely shut down and distanced from him?

"Oh, Roxanne." Her father stepped in. "Don't be difficult. This is exactly what got you in trouble in the first place."

"I was hoping that I would be a pleasant surprise. I have to admit that I was looking forward to seeing you again." Joel stared at her with a curious expression on his face. "I would have thought after all this time that you would have forgiven me. The fact that you have such an emotional response is interesting. Perhaps we should talk."

"Or we can leave." Zep didn't want her being forced to talk to her ex. He wasn't about to stand by and let her family bully her.

"No, I definitely think we should talk," Roxanne agreed, her eyes on Joel. "Why don't we go into the library. If I recall, that's where Sera keeps the booze. I definitely could use a drink."

"It's good to know you haven't changed your habits," Joel said with a wistful smile on his face. "I might have brought a bottle of your favorite Scotch along as a gift. And I knew you didn't like lamb."

Pamela shook her head, looking genuinely confused. "She always loved it as a child."

Tony put a hand on his wife's shoulder. "I guess her tastes have changed, dear. You know that can happen as a child grows up. We just have to hope her good sense hasn't changed."

"Let's get this over with." Roxanne ignored her parents.

"All right." He was going to follow her lead. He could use a drink, too, but he wasn't going to get one. Someone had to be sober, and he wasn't putting that on her. Not tonight.

She turned his way. "I'd like to talk to him alone, Zep."

He hadn't expected that at all. "I don't think that's a good idea."

"What exactly do you think I'm going to do to her?" Joel's brow had risen. "She accused me of a lot of things at the end of our marriage, but I assure you, domestic abuse wasn't one of them."

"He's not going to hurt me," Roxanne said with a sigh. "Just stay here with your family. I'll be back in a little while."

Zep watched as she walked away with the man she'd married. Why would she want to be alone with him? He didn't think she was still in love with the man. Not at all. She'd made it plain who she wanted in her bed.

But this was about her life. Was she going to make decisions that didn't involve him?

She'd stood in front of the whole town and basically fought to get him a job that would occupy the majority of his time and make him important to these people. Had she done it knowing she would leave him behind? Had it been a parting gift? Or had she wanted the sacrifice he would have to make to keep him here?

She had no idea what he was willing to sacrifice for her.

"Why would she be upset?" Pamela asked, her hands on her hips.

Tony watched as his daughter and ex-son-in-law disappeared into the house. "She won't be once she figures out why he's here."

It struck him forcibly why the man would have come all the way across the country. "He's offering her a job."

"An important one," Tony replied. "I would like to talk to you about it. Can we take a little walk?"

Nope. He didn't want to walk anywhere except into that house to pick up Roxanne, throw her over his shoulder, and run. "Of course."

The rest of the party milled around the buffet Sera had set up, talking to each other. Soft music played and the whole patio was lit by twinkle lights, giving the space a romantic feel. It would be perfect if he were standing beside Roxie, her hand in his.

He wasn't ready to let her go. And they hadn't had enough time for her to ask him to go with her.

Would he?

Yes. He would leave everything behind. He would drop it all and walk away with her.

He loved Roxanne King, and that was all that mattered.

His mind was going a thousand miles a minute as he walked with Roxie's father down the path that led toward the water.

"I need to talk to you about my daughter."

Zep stopped right before the walkway that led down to the dock. They were far enough away that they couldn't be heard, and not so close to the water that he would be tempted to throw the man in when he inevitably turned nasty. Before he could do that, Zep was going to lay it all on the line and hope for the best. "All right. You should know that I'm in love with her."

Tony sighed, a long-suffering sound. "Actually, I was hoping that wasn't the case."

"Well, I'm sorry you feel that way. It's the truth and it's not going to change because you bring her ex back into her life. We're together and we're not planning on breaking up." She'd seemed surprised he was going back to his place, but he didn't want to move so fast that he scared her.

And offering to move to New York with her would be going slow? He felt himself being shoved into a corner and wasn't sure how to get out.

Tony turned to him. "Look, Zep. I have to be brutally honest with you. Roxanne has wanted to do one thing her whole life."

"Be a cop." She'd told him. When other girls had played

princess, she'd preferred taking the bad guys down herself. She'd never dreamed of a knight saving her.

"Yes."

"She *is* a cop. She's very important around here." People had come to depend on her steadiness. He'd noticed in the last week that women opened up more around her about their problems. Moms would bypass Armie to complain to Roxie about their worries for their kids.

"It's not the same here, and you know that very well. You have a department of what? Six people? Seven or eight if you count support staff. It doesn't even compare to where she came from. There's very little opportunity for her out here. Roxanne's dream hit a hiccup, but it's time to get her back on the right path. The question is, are you going to make this hard on her?"

He'd already made his decision about this. "No. If she takes the job and moves back to New York, I'll support her."

"Good," Tony said. "But I need you to do more than that. I'm hoping she does the right thing for herself and her future, but I'm worried she won't."

"And what would that be?"

His gaze went steely with pure will. This was likely the look he had on his face when he was dealing with subordinates. "Break up with you. You can't come with her. It's clear you have a life here, and a long-distance relationship won't work."

"I think that decision is up to Roxanne." He was willing to be reasonable but only to a point. It didn't matter that he was already going over everything she'd done in the last day and a half looking for clues that she'd known her time here was almost up.

Hadn't she told him what she'd wanted to do in the first place? Screw him out of her system. She'd been talking to

Armie when he'd walked into the office today and it had been a serious conversation. Armie had looked upset.

Had she been telling her boss it was time to move on?

"My daughter is about to be offered a position that will lead her into the upper echelon of the world's premiere police force. This job could open doors that will lead her to amazing places."

"I get that." He wanted to be excited for her, and he promised himself he would shove down his anxiety if she came out of this meeting bubbly with plans for her career. He wasn't going to bring her down. "I think it's great. She'll be amazing at whatever job she wants to pursue. That's just who she is."

"Yes, I believe that as well. She's always been serious about her career and she's worked hard to get the opportunities she's been offered. Which is precisely why I'm worried about this one."

"I thought you had already set everything up. It seems like you did."

"I can set everything up and it could still go wrong. She's still got to interview and go through a vetting process. Do you honestly believe no one will vet her partner? Do you think having a convict for a boyfriend, or worse a husband, is going to help her? It's not. It's going to hold her back. It could even be an obstacle she won't be able to overcome."

He felt his gut twist. It happened whenever someone brought up his conviction. He should have known her father would look into his background, and there was no hiding the brief time he'd done.

Tony was right. What had happened in Arizona when he'd basically been a dumb kid didn't mean anything here, but it could be a huge problem for Roxanne as she made her way up the ladder.

She was ambitious. She worked hard. Would he be the reason she didn't get where she wanted to go?

"I can see you haven't thought about this." Tony's voice was softer now, almost sympathetic. "You made a mistake a long time ago, and it seems like something you've gotten through. I admire that. But you have to understand that it wouldn't matter if your conviction was thirty years ago. It would still hurt her. It could cost her a lot of opportunities. Do you think she won't come to resent you for that? She divorced a man she loved because he hurt her career."

"And then you brought him down here to see if he could do it again?" It was an irrational question, but he wasn't really thinking. He was responding like someone had kicked him in the gut.

If the question bothered him, Tony didn't show it. He simply checked his watch and smoothed down his shirt. "Joel made a mistake. I did, too. We're going to make it right and get her where she needs to go. We're going to do everything we can to support her. All you can do is drag her down. I want you to think about that before you try to convince her to let you come along. My daughter can be very loyal, and I'm afraid this time it will cost her dearly. If you care about her, you should let her go. Now, I've said my piece and I'll have to leave it up to you. I'm going back to the party and I'm going to hope Roxanne is reasonable about all of this. It would hurt her mother to have a scene at a party she planned so carefully."

He stepped away and Zep got the point. *Don't mess this up. Go away quietly.*

"Hey, you okay?" Remy passed Tony as he strode down the path.

He should have known his brother would show up. His brother was usually around for the humiliations of his life.

He took a deep breath. It was time to put his mask back on. "She's getting a big job offer."

Remy glanced back to the patio, where the party seemed to have started up again. "Yeah, I wondered if that wasn't the case. Armie wouldn't talk about it, but I can tell he's upset. Lila told Lisa he'd gotten a call about Roxanne earlier today."

And Roxie hadn't mentioned it to him at all. When they'd gotten home, they'd taken Daisy for a walk, then hopped in the shower to get ready. He'd made love to her there and not once had she talked about the possibility of a job offer.

"Good for her. This is what she wanted." He put a smile on his face.

"I would assume this job would take her to New York."

"Yes, but she's wanted to go back for a long time." She'd made a home here. She'd found a life here, but he couldn't force her to see it. Who was he to keep her from her dreams? He'd lost enough chances to not want to be the reason she lost hers.

He loved her. Didn't that mean he should do everything he could to ensure she got what she needed? Even if that meant letting her go?

Remy's eyes narrowed. "I thought you would be upset."

"I don't want her to go, but I also have to be reasonable. Why would she let a dream job go to hang out with a guy she's basically only been dating for a week?"

"I understand that the formal relationship hasn't been long, but there's been something between you since the moment you met. Don't play this down, brother."

"What am I supposed to do? Ask her to stay? She never meant to stay, and it doesn't make sense for me to go." He had to find a way to get through this without breaking down. He couldn't. Not now. If she stayed for him, she would likely come to resent him, and that would be worse than never having her at all. If he found a way to let her go, at least she would have fond thoughts of him. He would spend the rest of his life loving her, but at least she wouldn't hate him. "Hey, we're borrowing trouble here. We don't know she'll even take the job, and she'll have to put in some notice, so there's still plenty of time."

It was a lie. His time had run out.

Remy nodded but managed to look unconvinced. "You're right about that. But you need to talk to her."

He started to walk back toward the party, where he would do what he did best. Put a smile on his face and shove every feeling he had down deep. For her.

She'd hated the look in Zep's eyes when she'd told him she needed to talk to Joel alone.

Had he thought she wanted to be alone with her ex? That there were feelings still between them? That was the furthest thing from the truth. Well, not any good, happy feelings.

"You said you wanted a drink." Joel looked his normal, elegant self. Every inch the bureaucrat who believed looking good made him good.

She shook her head. "That was an excuse to do this in private. I think I'll stay sober for the moment. What are you doing here?"

He frowned, a sure sign that he was displeased with her abruptness, but she didn't care. She didn't have to please him anymore, and honestly, she was embarrassed that she'd ever tried. It was odd. Now that she was in a relationship with a man who accepted her on pretty much every level, it was easy to see how much of herself she'd shoved down for her ex.

"I'm here because I thought it was past time for us to

talk," Joel announced. "After all, once you decided to break up our marriage, you cut me off without a word."

It hadn't been that hard. In the beginning her life hadn't even changed that much, and that had been the moment she'd known the divorce was truly the best move she could have made. They'd spent the majority of their marriage working on their careers, completely unfocused on the other person. "I have a phone. You could have called. I'm going to assume since my parents brought you all the way down here, that they would give you my phone number."

"I wanted to see you, Roxanne."

"Why?"

"Because we were married at one point in time, and I still care about you. I can see plainly you don't feel the same way about me."

She took a deep breath. They *had* been married, and it hadn't all been bad. Joel had helped her through some rough times. If he hadn't been right for her, she hadn't been right for him, either. "I'm sorry. I was surprised to see you. It's been a week full of those, and you know I'm not a person who likes surprises."

He poured himself a drink. "I told your mother you wouldn't be happy about them springing this on you, but you know how she can be. She's been planning this for a while. I was hoping by the time I got here, you would be used to the idea of seeing your family again. I know we're divorced, but I still think of them as family."

"Yes, you see them far more often than I do." She'd had a couple of pleasant nights while her parents had been here. She'd almost thought it had been a successful trip.

"I'm not the one who felt the need to put thousands of miles between us. Was that about me or them?"

"Both, I suppose," she allowed. "I needed to be away from everything I knew before. I know you won't believe it, but this place has been good for me. The sheriff is a good cop."

"I understand you dated him for a while."

"The truth is I never dated Armie." It seemed so funny that she'd been desperate to keep up the lie in the beginning. "I told my mom that so she wouldn't lecture me on how old I'm getting and how I'll never get a man. Somehow it was easier for her to deal with me being gone if I had a man in my life."

"Or it was easier for you," he countered. "Your mother can be quite aggressive about defending her traditional family views. I know you think I had it easy with her, but I was given many a lecture on how I failed to get you pregnant."

She groaned at the thought. "Why didn't you tell me?"

"Because you had enough to deal with when it came to her." He leaned against the side of the big leather couch. "I know I wasn't the best husband, but I did try."

Her heart softened a bit. She'd spent the majority of her adult life married to this man. She'd gotten over him, but perhaps it was time to truly forgive him—and herself. "We weren't right for each other. We were far too alike, and I've come to realize that some differences are good for a relationship. We can both blame that one incident, but we would be wrong. It would have fallen apart eventually. I was never going to be what you needed, and I honestly didn't know what I needed then."

"But you do now?" he asked softly. "You've found it with that kid?"

"He's not a kid. He looks younger than he is."

"I'll be honest. I didn't take you for the type to go for pretty boys. You always seemed to have more complexity than that."

She felt a grin cross her face. She was sure he'd had this

conversation with her dad, who'd probably chalked her attraction to Zep up to his abs. "He's ridiculously hot."

Joel's face scrunched up in obvious consternation. "You were never this shallow before."

She shrugged because now that she was in the same room with him, it didn't seem like such a scary place to be. Somehow she'd made more of him in her head, but they'd been friends once. Even though he was a pompous ass. It was odd because he hadn't seemed that way at the time. At the time, she'd seen him as serious and ambitious.

This was not a man who would spend hours of his life patiently training a puppy for no other reason than the puppy would be happier being trained than not. He wouldn't be genuinely excited about a job that would pay very little and require the world of him. However, Zep *was* excited, because his version of success was very different from Joel's.

Was it different from hers?

"What would be truly shallow would be to not look under his pretty face and see the real man underneath. He's a good man. He's a kind man."

Joel's eyes softened and he moved to sit on the couch. "Well, if you're happy with him, then I'm happy for you. I truly mean that, Roxanne. You seem different. More relaxed."

She took the chair across from him. "I assure you I wasn't a few minutes ago, but I've come to realize that I've got no control over this. So hit me. You're here about a job, I take it. Not to try to rekindle our romance."

One shoulder shrugged. "I can see that wouldn't work. But no, I came down to talk about a new position that's opening up. You would be back with your old team, and you would get a promotion."

It was everything she'd wanted in the beginning. "Tell me more."

"You wouldn't be leading the team, but you would be second in command," he explained. "The captain who took over is very enthusiastic about working with you, and you would have other duties."

"Other duties?"

"You would be offered a seat on the committee for dealing with sexual harassment claims." His expression had gone earnest. "I was wrong. I was shortsighted, and I didn't listen to you because it made me uncomfortable. I am sorry about that. I truly am. I'm working with brass so the next woman who faces what you did has an easier time."

Her heart constricted at the thought. It was everything she'd wanted for so long, but something was holding her back. Not something. Someone. Two months ago she would have jumped at this chance and now she was cautious because Zep was a part of her life. "I need time to think about it."

He sat back, his jaw dropping slightly. "That wasn't the reaction I expected."

He'd probably thought she'd cry in pure joy. "I've made a home here. I'm only just starting to realize that. This would be a huge move. I'll admit the job is something I've dreamed of, but I need some time to think about it."

"I'm afraid I can't give you much," Joel admitted. "They want to fill this spot quickly. I'm here to prep you for the interview, which is happening on Monday. It's another surprise from your parents. You'll fly back with us, and you have an interview Monday afternoon. Though you should know the job is yours if you want it. They'll go through the process, but I assure you, you're the one they want."

There it was. She'd briefly been comfortable, but the

low-level anxiety she'd been dealing with all day was back because the moment to choose was here and she wasn't ready for it. "When would I start?"

One shoulder shrugged. "It'll probably be at least two weeks before you get a formal offer, and then if you haven't put in your notice, they'll give you another two weeks, though I can't imagine you would need to put in two weeks here. I'm sure the sheriff can find someone."

"No, he can't. It's hard for him to find good staff out here." And according to him, it was nearly impossible to find women officers.

She'd helped three women leave their abusive partners. Lila had made it easier by opening a women's shelter, but would those women have gotten that far if the only officer they could talk to was a man?

It wasn't that Armie or Major or the other guys didn't care. They did. But sometimes it was easier for a woman to trust another woman.

What would Papillon lose if she walked away?

Her father and mother would say that didn't matter, that she needed to do what was best for herself and her family.

But Papillon had kind of become her family, and it was sad that she'd only started to realize that when the time had come to make this decision.

"Well, that's not going to be your problem because what I'm offering you is the best and brightest. The captain taking over is nearing retirement. He's going to groom you for his job. Within five years you'll take over, and from there the sky's the limit. Think about that." He stood up. "We should get back to your party or your new boyfriend will think I'm coming on to you. He looks like the jealous type."

He wasn't. Not in the traditional "no one touches my woman" way. Zep didn't get nasty if she talked to another guy. He trusted her.

Was she ready to let that go?

But the job was everything she'd worked her whole life for.

She stood and got ready to go back to the party. She needed to talk to Zep. He would help her figure this out.

# *chapter fourteen*

Three hours later, Roxie was frustrated beyond all belief.

The party had gone off without another hitch and everyone had gotten along. She'd even received a nice gift from her parents, a watch she'd been wanting for a long time. One of the high-tech ones.

Despite the fact that she wasn't fond of lamb, the meal had been delicious and the cake perfect.

Zep had been charming and sweet, but there was a distance between them she didn't understand, one that hadn't existed before she'd walked away with Joel. Despite the fact that she'd held his hand or wrapped her arm around his waist much of the time, she'd felt very alone.

She'd spent the entire drive back in confusion. He'd turned on the radio and hadn't spoken beyond making small talk.

She closed the door behind him and couldn't hold it in another second. "What's wrong?"

He moved toward the back of the duplex, where Daisy was already whining and crying about staying in the crate one second longer than she had to. "Nothing as far as I can tell. Everything seemed to go well. I'm sorry I didn't get you anything. I should have. I didn't know about the party and things have been busy, but I did know it was your birthday. That's on me."

He'd spent all of his time this week driving her to and from work, around town to get the things they needed for the pets. He hadn't had a spare moment to grab something he could call a present, but then hadn't the whole week been one long gift of his time and care and talent? "I don't need a present. You've done so much for me this week. But I think we should talk."

He'd avoided a long talk with her at the party. When she'd tried to pull him away from the others, he would drag her into the conversation he was having. When she'd told him about the job offer, he'd smiled brightly and told her he was happy for her.

But it was a mask. She'd seen that smile on his face a thousand times.

Or did she simply think she knew him better than she really did? After all, hadn't she thought she'd known Joel when she'd married him? Hadn't she gone into the marriage thinking it would be forever? Now she was in another relationship and she had to question everything.

Zep opened the crate and Daisy nearly tackled him. He picked the puppy up, though she was wriggling like mad. "Talk about what? I think it went much better than I expected after the way it started. Even your ex was pretty pleasant. I actually like your brother. He's cool. I can't get a read on the fiancée, though. She spent most of her time checking her nails."

"She's not as shallow as she seems. She's pretty shy, actually. She's better when she's one-on-one." She'd come to accept that sometimes relationships looked different to an outsider. People had thought she and Joel were the perfect couple. They'd been excellent in public. Bad in private. Shawna and Brian seemed to be the exact opposite.

"Well, I don't expect I'll see her much after this. I'm going to take this one out in the back. I suspect she needs to stretch her legs a little." He opened the back door and let himself out.

Why was he running away? She'd thought he would be disappointed about the whole idea of her leaving, but he seemed rather nonchalant about it all.

Sunny jumped down from her perch on the sofa and stretched, yawning.

Yeah. That was kind of how Zep was treating the whole thing. It was disconcerting. She had no idea how to deal with a Zep who wouldn't talk to her.

She followed him outside, unwilling to let it go. "I get offered a job that will take me a couple thousand miles away and you think it's great?"

Daisy was doing zoomies around the yard, and Roxie wondered how much the puppy had slept while they were gone and how hard it would be to get her back to sleep.

"It's the job you've always wanted." He stood staring at the yard. "Am I not supposed to be happy for you?"

There was the rub. He was doing exactly what he "should" do, and it hurt her heart. "Do you not want to talk about what happens if I take the job?"

"If? Roxanne, you would be crazy if you didn't take this job. It's everything you've wanted. Is this what Armie was upset about this afternoon?"

She hadn't mentioned her conversation with Armie because she hadn't wanted to ruin their time by upsetting him with something that might not even happen. Now she wondered if he would have been upset at all.

"Yeah. He asked me to stay."

"That wasn't fair," Zep replied in a perfectly reasonable tone. "You can't let him talk you into something that isn't good for you. I'm going to have a long discussion with him. He has no right to pressure you."

Every word hurt her heart. All her insecurities about this man bubbled right up to the surface. She'd expected a fight. Not for him to offer to fight to make it easier for her to go.

"Please don't. He wasn't nasty about it. He thinks I'm good at my job, and in this business, you want to keep essential people." It was becoming really clear that Zep didn't consider her essential.

"Still, you can't let him guilt you into staying." Zep went to one knee as Daisy stopped in front of him. "I might need to take her for a walk. She's wound up."

"It's fine. I'm not going to bed anytime soon." There was zero way she would sleep. "She can sit up with me. I need to get ready. Apparently I've got an interview on Monday."

His head turned at that. "Monday? This Monday?"

Finally she got a reaction out of him. Maybe he was viewing this as something that would happen a couple of months down the line. "Yes, Zep. I've got a ticket to go back to New York with my parents tomorrow afternoon. I interview on Monday, but I've been told it's a formality. I could be back in New York in less than a month."

He stood, his face falling before he managed a gentle smile. "I'm happy for you."

She felt tears behind her eyes, but she wasn't about to shed them. "That's great. What do you . . . what do you think this means for us?"

He went quiet and sank down onto the bench that had been here when she'd moved in. How many nights had she sat on that bench and listened to the sounds of the world around her? This was the place where she'd learned how to be still. Such a simple skill and yet it had made a world of difference for her.

"I don't think long distance is going to work for us," he said.

She sat down beside him but made sure they weren't touching. That distance she'd felt between them seemed intentional on his part. "I thought you wanted to try."

"We're not going to get a chance to try. If you leave tomorrow, when are you going to be back? Tuesday? Is that when you'll put in your notice? I don't think two weeks is enough time to try out something we both know isn't going to work. And you'll spend most of those two weeks getting ready to move."

"It could be longer. Even if I take the job, it could be a month or six weeks." That could give them time to figure out if he wanted to come with her. She could stretch it out, tell them she couldn't leave her department until they found a replacement. It might buy her another couple of weeks.

He turned to her, a faintly cruel expression on his face. "You need six weeks of stress relief?"

"Are we back to that? Because I apologized. It was a stupid thing to say and I was trying to protect myself. I never viewed it that way, and that's not what I'm asking for now."

"What are you asking for?"

That was the problem. She wasn't sure. She wanted for him to say that it would all be okay, that no matter what she decided, they would be all right. "I guess I want to talk this out with you."

"Really?" He turned her way, his handsome face in shadows. "Now you want to talk about it. How long have you known this was a possibility? You at least knew this afternoon and you didn't once mention it to me, though you had plenty of opportunities. You had all evening to say something. Maybe if we'd talked, I wouldn't have been so floored at what happened tonight."

"Were you? Because from what I've seen, it hasn't bothered you at all." He'd been the life of the party, making everyone laugh and charming her parents and all their friends.

"Of course it bothers me. I care about you, but I was also ready for it. I always knew you would leave. I didn't know it would be so soon. Isn't this what you've always wanted?"

It frustrated her, but there was only one answer. "Yes."

"Then tell me how I'm the bad guy for trying to not make this hard on you."

She wanted to cry but she couldn't. Not in front of him. She knew what he would do. He would hold her, and he might even tell her what she wanted to hear, but it would be pity. He was a deeply sympathetic man. "It almost feels like you want me to go."

"Of course I don't want you to go," he replied, his voice hoarse. "I don't know. Maybe I do because I know if you stay, you'll regret it. If you stay here for me, you'll resent me for the rest of your life because you'll never know what you could have accomplished somewhere else. You know in the end you're going to walk out that door and you won't look back."

She wasn't so sure about that. "Have you even considered the idea that you could come with me? I know it's probably way too soon, but we could try."

He stood, running a frustrated hand over his hair. "You would regret that, too. Look, this has been a real good time."

"Don't." She stood and faced him. "Don't you even go there, Guidry. I told you my feelings for you were real."

"I should go."

She'd thought he was staying the night, but it seemed like everything had changed for him the moment he'd found out there was a possibility she could leave. He wasn't even willing to try? She'd thought he at least cared about her. "I don't understand any of this. We were fine four hours ago."

He moved in and suddenly his hands cupped her cheeks and he leaned down, brushing her forehead with his lips. "I think it's best if I go now. I think . . . well, I should go."

She stepped back, completely gutted. "Yes. You should go. I've got things to do. If I'm leaving tomorrow afternoon, I should pack." Daisy was standing at her feet, looking up like she knew something had gone wrong. Oh, what would she do with Daisy?

"I'll take Daisy and Sunny until you get back," he said. "Can your landlady let me in tomorrow afternoon? I'll pick them up and take them to my place."

She watched as he started for the door.

How could this be happening? How could her heart be breaking like this? She hadn't hurt this much when she'd made the decision to divorce. That had been an almost easy thing to decide.

This felt wrong.

"I love you, Zep." It was the truth. It was simple and real and true.

He walked out the door. Had he even heard her?

And the tears finally came.

*I love you, Zep.*

He sat in the cab of his truck, the words he'd longed to hear echoing in his head over and over again.

He'd had to walk out or he would have stayed with her,

given her the words back and held her. He wouldn't have been able to leave her.

He would have become a millstone around her neck, dragging her down for mistakes he'd made in the past.

The look on her face . . . he might never stop seeing that look on her face.

A light shone in his rearview and he winced as he realized it was Remy and Lisa dropping off his mother. They'd stayed behind to help Seraphina and Harry clean everything up.

He should have driven around or gone straight up to his apartment over the garage. Not that it would have worked. The minute his mother saw his truck, she would have known something was wrong.

He shoved his pain down deep and did the only thing he could. He got out of the truck and waved his brother's way.

Remy rolled down his window. "Hey, I didn't expect to see you here. I thought you were staying with Roxie."

"She's got a flight to New York tomorrow. She's interviewing for a big job and I didn't want to be in the way." He managed to keep the words even, far lighter than he felt. "I'm going by tomorrow and picking up the puppy and the cat, and I'll watch them for her while she's gone."

Would she be able to take them with her? Or would they be left behind like he would?

It wasn't fair to think that way, but there was a tinge of bitterness that he forced back down. It wasn't her fault. She'd done exactly what her father had worried about. She'd asked him to come with her or to sit down and go over all the reasons for her to stay.

She would have stayed if he'd asked her to. He'd seen it in her eyes. She'd been looking to him to give her that reason, to say he loved her and wanted to build something with her here. With their dog and their cat and their two not-great-paying jobs.

But she could have an amazing future in the city she loved. She simply couldn't have it with him. What kind of a selfish ass would he be if he asked her to give it all up for him?

"I thought you were going to talk to her." Remy looked disappointed.

"Leave your brother be for the night," his mother admonished as she walked around Remy's big shiny truck. She waved to Lisa. "Thanks for a lovely evening, you two. I'll see you tomorrow. Love you."

His brother looked like he wanted to argue, but Lisa put a hand on his arm. "We love you, too, Momma. Zep, we'll talk tomorrow."

He waved as they drove away and promised he would find something to do tomorrow that didn't involve explaining to his brother how he'd lost the only woman he was ever going to love. He plastered a smile on his face for his mother's sake. "You have fun tonight? I saw you talking to Shawna. You seemed to be the only one she really opened up to."

"She's a sweet thing," his mother said as she strode up the yard. "We talked about her wedding. All brides like to talk about their plans. Roxie's parents are . . . well, they are different than I would have expected. Roxie's such a down-to-earth young lady. They're on the pretentious side. I thought a cop would be more blue collar. Not that there aren't perfectly nice white-collar people out there. But her mother seemed a little on the snooty side."

"I'm sure she thinks we're odd, too." Maybe he could get out of this without much deflection. It was late and his mother wasn't a night owl. In the morning he could dodge her, and after a couple of days, she would simply think he was back to his old habits. "You ready for bed?"

She stopped in front of him. "Baby, what happened tonight?"

Damn it. It looked like he would have to talk a little after all. "All that happened was Roxanne is getting an opportunity she's wanted all her life, that she's worked for and earned. She needs to go to New York and explore the possibility, and that means we're probably going to spend some time apart."

They would spend all their time apart.

Even in the shadows cast from the porch light and the moon, he could see his mother thinking. She studied him like she didn't believe a word that came out of his mouth. "Yes, I heard her ex-husband was some bigwig with her old department and he wanted to convince her to come back. Why did her father want to talk to you alone?"

"He just wanted to let me know that her ex-husband was strictly down here to talk to her about the job. Nothing more." Though he'd seen how the man had watched Roxie when she wasn't looking. Longing. It had been stamped on Joel's face. He was certain the same look had been on his own.

The moon shone down, illuminating the worry on his mother's face. "What did he say to you? Don't smile and lie to me, baby boy. If everything was all right between you and Roxie, you would be spending the night at her place, not coming back here when you don't even have your bag with you. You walked out without packing your things. You had a fight?"

"No. It wasn't a fight." Except it had been. She'd been willing to fight it out with him, but he'd always known he would have to lose for her to win. "She's leaving, Mom. She's leaving and I can't go with her."

"Why not? Zéphirin, you love her. Don't try to tell me you don't."

"It doesn't matter how I feel. Long distance won't work."

"Then go with her. Baby, if she's the one, then you can't let her go," his mother implored. "You have to try with her."

"She's a cop and I . . ." His mother didn't know where he'd been for those months he'd been gone when he was eighteen. Remy had been the one to find him and come get him. Remy had kept his secret all these years. His mother should have run a trace like everyone in Roxie's family.

"You what?" she asked. "You don't think you're good enough for her? Because you are."

"I think I would drag her down. She can't do what she needs to do if I'm with her," he said.

"Why? I know the idea of moving to New York might seem scary at first, but it's just a city. It might even be exciting. And you can always come home and see us. I know you have that new job, but this is more important than any job. A job won't hold your hand. A job won't grow old with you."

He wasn't getting out of this, and maybe it was time for his mother to truly understand how badly he'd screwed up in the past. "Stop. I can't go with her because when I was eighteen, I went to jail for writing a hot check. When you thought I was in LA, I was actually in a prison in Arizona."

His mother's jaw dropped, her shock easily apparent. "What? You were in jail?"

"He was in jail?" a soft whisper echoed.

He glanced over and realized they weren't alone. Armie and Lila lived next door and they were sitting out on their porch. Lila had a mug of something steamy in her hand, and Armie was dressed in sweats and a tee.

Great. His humiliation had an audience, and now the sheriff would likely tell him he wasn't interested in him working part time for the sheriff's office. Of course, once Sylvie found out, she likely wouldn't want him heading a department.

"Yes, Doc," he replied with a sigh. "I was in jail, as my momma just found out. My first attempt at adulthood landed me in the pen."

"What happened? You didn't even call me." Tears slipped from his mother's eyes. "You were all alone out there and you never called me."

"I was ashamed," he admitted.

"And dumb as dirt because I read those case files and I'm pretty sure he got set up," Armie offered.

Zep stopped, utterly shocked that Armie knew about his past. He thought he'd been so careful, but it turned out, he'd simply been a fool. Again. He couldn't show his mother his frustration, but he damn straight could take it out on Armie. "Do you mind?"

"I'm sorry," Armie said, getting to his feet. "We were sitting out here enjoying some cocoa and then you were talking and we didn't want to interrupt you. Or we're horrifically nosy. Delphine, don't be upset. It was minimum security. It sucked, but he was released early for good behavior."

Zep laughed but it wasn't because he was amused. "Of course you've known all this time."

Armie stepped onto his lawn. "You should understand that if I'd been the sheriff at the time, I would have come out there and dealt with this myself. And I definitely would have called you, Delphine. Like I said, I learned about it years later and I was curious. I followed up. Did you know that girl of yours had three other boyfriends steal from her mother?"

"Who is she?" His mom had a look of pure rage on her face now. "I want a name and an address, Armie."

"She's in jail. Her mother finally turned her in after the last check cleaned out one of her accounts," Armie replied. "You don't have to worry about revenge."

"Is that why the dad hauled you off tonight?" Lila asked. "Was he giving you some bull about how Roxie can't possibly have a career with an ex-con for a boyfriend?"

"He said that?" His mother had switched her outrage to the next available target. "I will have a talk with that man."

"No, you won't." Zep had to put a stop to that right quick. The last thing he needed was his momma to show up at the Kings' doorstep, trying to put the whammy on them. Of course, if she wanted to make a voodoo doll of Roxie's dad, he might help stick the pins in. "He's got a real good point, and I've made my decision."

"It's the wrong one." Armie's frown was illuminated by the moonlight. "You did something stupid. It's not going to hold her back. It might cause her some ribbing from everyone else, but she won't be the first cop in the world to fall for a less than perfect human being. Look who I married. Do you know how many tickets she has?"

"I'm known for my lead foot," Lila said with a smile that quickly turned serious. "But Zep, he's right. This is something the two of you can overcome. Did she tell you she was concerned with it?"

He hadn't even opened up that argument because, while he'd been right, it was an argument he couldn't win. "She didn't mention it. She won't. She'll go into it not thinking about how I could hold her back. Maybe if we had more time, it would make sense. But she can't give up her whole career for a man she's spent exactly one week with."

"I moved from Fort Worth to be with your father after a week," his mother said. "He was in town negotiating for some equipment for the restaurant. I left with him when he went home, and I wouldn't have changed it for anything in the world. Nothing, Zep. Even knowing how it would end, I would go back and follow him time and time again because that man was half of my soul. I got to be whole for a while, and I know when I go, he'll be waiting for me and I'll be whole again. Baby, you don't want to go through your life without the person who can make you feel that way."

Emotion welled inside him. "I don't know what to do. If I try to stay with her, I hurt her. If I ask her to stay with me, I hurt her. If I walk away, I hurt her, but at least she has a chance to find what she's always wanted."

"What if what she's always wanted was you?"

He turned because Lila had asked the question. The nurse practitioner had joined her husband on the lawn. She always looked professional at work, but she was wearing pajama bottoms and a T-shirt that showed a slight rounding of her belly. She rested her hand there as she stared across the grass at him.

"That wasn't what she said. I assure you Roxanne King didn't spend her childhood dreaming about finding a man," he pointed out.

A mysterious smile curved Lila's lips up. "Neither did I, and I'm not saying she would take any man. I'm not saying she would give up her career and settle down into some perfect gender role. I never thought I would be here, and if you'd told my younger self I would find what I needed in Papillon, Louisiana, I would have laughed at you. But I found myself here. I found a me I like, a me who wants a family and who wants to raise them here. It was about more than falling for Armie. It was about finding myself. Have you asked her if she wants to stay?"

"No, but only because I know she'll regret it," he insisted.

Armie pointed his way. "Then her dad got to you and he's living in your head rent free, brother. If there's one thing I've learned about women, it's that we don't get to choose for them. That's not what a marriage is. You can't make this decision for her."

"There's no decision to be made." He wasn't sure they were listening to him.

"No, there isn't because you're not allowing her one," Armie replied. "You're not giving her a choice because you don't think you're good for her. You're wrong. You are good for her. This place is good for her. I knew her before she moved down here. She's more relaxed than she's ever been. She's softer than she was, and she's started to really find her place here and not just at the stationhouse. But I can't force you to see that she needs more than a job. Look, she's coming back. She won't simply quit. She'll work out a notice. My suggestion to you is to take this time and decide what you want."

"I want her to be happy." It was all he'd ever wanted.

"Then find out what will make her happy," his mom said, stepping back. "From her. Armie and Lila are right. You're treating her like her opinion doesn't matter, and I didn't raise you that way. Lila, I'm making biscuits and gravy in the morning, and I'll have too much because I won't be feeding my son until he treats his lady like I raised him to."

"I will be there," Lila vowed. "This baby likes gravy. Lots of gravy."

His mother nodded and walked to the front door. She didn't bother to close it quietly.

Armie sighed. "Think about it. You've got some time, but if you don't talk to her, you'll make the biggest mistake of your life."

Zep heard the door to the house he'd grown up in lock, a fateful sound.

He would have to go around the back to get to his space.

It looked like he'd be doing everything the hard way from now on.

# *chapter fifteen*

Roxie looked up at the big board that listed all the departing and arriving flights at Louis Armstrong Airport.

Had Zep already gotten Daisy and Sunny? Had he moved all their stuff over to his tiny apartment?

She'd packed his bag, taking out the clothes he'd brought over that had somehow wound up in her closet or in the empty drawer next to hers. She'd picked up his razor and toiletries that had sat beside hers for a week, packed them in his duffel, and placed them next to Daisy's crate along with a note.

Thanks for everything.

Like he'd simply done her a favor. Like he hadn't changed her life. She hadn't signed it with love. Hadn't mentioned love at all since he didn't seem to want hers.

"Hey, sweetheart, your father and Joel found the lounge, and Brian and Shawna are grabbing something to eat." Her mother was dressed for travel in her chic slacks and wrinkle-proof blouse, her most comfortable heels on her feet. "I thought you might want to join us for a drink. We've got an hour before we board and get back to civilization."

"It's perfectly civilized here." She turned away from the board with its times and gate numbers.

Her mom's nose wrinkled up. "Some of it is nice, but I don't understand all the nature stuff. Our backyard is more than enough nature for me."

The backyard of their brownstone was a postage stamp of green, though her grandfather had managed to grow tomatoes and strawberries every year. Her landlady had fig and Meyer lemon trees that blossomed and dropped fruit over into her part of the yard. Lately she'd been thinking about a small garden. She'd helped Darlene with her planter boxes this year, and it had been surprising how much she'd enjoyed watching them grow and then sitting down with her neighbor to eat a salad she'd basically raised.

She would miss Darlene. She'd rarely known her neighbors when she'd lived with Joel. Everyone worked odd hours or all hours. Neighbors had been people she nodded at briefly as they passed in the hall.

She would miss Sera and Harry and Armie and Lila. She would miss town halls and watching the kids she'd met grow up.

God, she was going to miss Zep. The idea of not seeing Zep was a hole in her heart, but she was surprised by how much she would miss that tiny town.

"Roxanne? Have you been listening?"

She shook her head because obviously her mother had continued talking and she hadn't noticed. "I'm sorry. I've got my mind on other things. What did you say?"

"I said that when we get back, I'm going to make some dinner plans with a couple of your father's more influential friends," her mother explained. "I want you to be able to hit the ground running. How much time do you have to give the sheriff?"

"I don't know. At least two weeks. Probably more like a month, but I don't know that I'm going to take the job." She'd sat up all night with Daisy asleep on her right side and Sunny nestled on her left. She'd taken Zep out of the equation. He hadn't replied to her declaration of love, and he wasn't one to lie or hold back.

So he wasn't going to be a part of her rationale.

Did she want to leave Papillon?

The question wasn't if she wanted this job. She did, and she knew somewhere in the back of her head she would always wonder what she could have done with it. But wouldn't she wonder the same about Papillon? Wouldn't she wonder what her life would have been like if she'd concentrated more on living than merely working? There were possible futures in front of her, two potential versions of herself. One was full of success. That Roxanne would likely have the admiration of everyone around her.

The other might have a shot at being happy.

"What do you mean, you don't know if you're going to take the job?"

She shouldn't have started this conversation. She wasn't sure why she had. Maybe it was being around the Guidrys that had made her want some kind of connection with her own family. "I said I don't know."

Her mother's eyes widened. "Roxanne, don't be ridiculous. Your father and Joel pulled a lot of strings to make this happen."

"But they didn't ask me if I wanted it, and honestly, I don't know what I would have said if they had."

Her mom stared for a moment as though trying to figure out what to say. "I was so sure this was what you wanted."

"I've changed a lot since I left New York, Mom. I'm not the same person. I'm starting to think I don't want to leave this place."

Her mother's lips firmed as though she was trying to hold something in. The words spilled out anyway. "Are you doing this to spite me? Are you thinking about staying in that town because you hate me?"

Was she even ready for this conversation? She could simply walk away and go join her dad, who definitely wouldn't ask her any emotional questions. Wasn't that exactly how her mom usually handled things? Ignore them and they go away. They'd been doing it all her life. Maybe it was time to stop. Maybe it was time to see if there was any hope for them. "I don't hate you. I don't understand you."

Her mom sank down on the nearest bench, clinging to her handbag like it was a lifeline, and for a moment Roxie worried she was going to do what she'd always done. Instead she took a deep breath and forged into new territory. "I don't understand you, either, sweetheart. I never have. I try to connect with you but I always seem to do it wrong. I wanted this week to be special. I wanted to get my daughter back. I miss you."

Something softened inside Roxie at the sight of her mother looking utterly forlorn. All of her life she'd felt like she'd let this woman down by not being the daughter she'd wanted. She'd let it close her off, and that disappointment had flavored every encounter with the woman who'd given birth to her.

What she'd learned, whether it be from the people around her, the place she'd found herself in, or simply by growing up, was that there was always another side to every story, always a connection to be made even in the most opposite of humans.

Did she always have to win? Some arguments were meaningless.

"It was special. Thank you for thinking of me, Mom. And for the birthday party."

Her mother's eyes were suddenly sheened with tears. "But you don't like lamb. I swear you liked it when you were a kid. At least I thought so. I didn't . . . I wanted to please you but sometimes I don't know how and I am not good about asking. I feel like I should know and that if I have to ask, I'm already failing. It's what my mother taught me. A mother should know what her children need."

Roxie sat down beside her mom, setting her carry-on to the side. "And I often get frustrated and stop trying. How can you know what I want or need if I never tell you? So let's talk. I never dated Armie. I lied to you so you wouldn't know that I basically ran away because it was too hard to stay in New York, where I knew I'd disappointed everyone."

A little gasp came from her mother's mouth. "That's not true. Oh, Roxanne. I wasn't disappointed in you. I didn't understand the situation and I didn't want to. I wanted things to be the way I saw them in my head as a kid. I wanted a happy family with grandkids and big meals together. I wanted what my parents had."

"I'm sorry I wasn't the daughter you wanted me to be."

She shook her head. "What I wanted was an illusion, and I worry I'm still trying to find it. My parents weren't perfect. Far from it. Neither is your father. Lord knows I'm not. I'm struggling with getting old and feeling like life has passed me by, and I worry that you rejecting the life I led means you don't value it."

She reached out and held her mother's hand. "I do value it, Mom. You can be a lot, but I'm guilty, too. I didn't fight for the relationship I wanted with you. I didn't even tell you

I wanted a relationship. I want to be able to call you, but you have to stop pushing. You have to support me even when you think I'm wrong."

Her mother's fingers entwined with her own, like they had when she'd been a child. "I will always tell you my opinion, but I will try to stop saying I told you so. And I will absolutely stop talking about how much better your life would be with a man. I think you understand that now. The relationship with Zep was real, wasn't it?"

"Yes."

What had Zep said? Sometimes he asked his mother's opinion not because he needed it, but so she would know he valued it. Life didn't have to be a contest between her and her mother. It didn't have to be some checklist where she finally measured up to what her father expected.

"It was real for me. I don't know about him, though."

A brow rose over her mother's eyes. "What do you mean?"

"I told him I love him and he didn't say it back," Roxie confessed. "He told me he was happy for me and I should take the job and acted like it was over even though I hadn't made any kind of decision. It wasn't like him. I expected him to sit down with me and talk it out, but he wouldn't. I don't know what to do. My instinct is to walk away, but I think he's important."

The hand in hers tightened. "There's something you need to know. Your father talked to him while you were with Joel. He basically laid it out to Zep that he would hurt your career if he stayed with you. He told Zep he knows about his record. Please don't be mad. Your father thought he was doing the right thing, but I can see now that he wasn't. We were being selfish because we want you home. I didn't think you were in love with him. I would have fought your father if I'd known how you felt. What I did know was he was in love with you."

The world went a little watery. "How can you know?"

"Because of the way he looks at you. He looks at you like you're the brightest star in the sky. And he broke it off with you because he didn't want to hold you back. The fact that you're here at the airport with us shows that."

He was doing what Zep did. He was sacrificing. "So what do I do? Go and have the interview and talk to him when I get back?"

"Do you honestly want the job if it means you have to leave this place? You've changed, sweetie. I didn't want to admit it, but you glow here. You have a light in your eyes I've never seen before," Pamela said, tears flowing freely. "Darling, I don't completely understand what you see in him, but after seeing you with him here . . . I do know you're in love and if you're very sure about this—about him—then don't even get on the plane. It will only waste time. Zep was trying to do what he thought was best for you. He was sacrificing his own happiness."

"He was making decisions for me."

Her mother's shoulders straightened. "Then let him know he can't do that. Tell him if he's going to be your partner, he's got to respect your part of the relationship. Be strong enough to tell him he made a mistake and he should correct it. I've been married to the man I love for almost forty years. He is a flawed man, and more than once I've given him the opportunity to correct a mistake. You can't love someone and let your pride be the only thing that matters. Give him another shot."

She wanted to. "What if you're wrong and he doesn't want me?"

"Would that change your mind about coming home?"

"No." When she looked deep down, she knew. Perhaps it had been the act of standing here in the airport getting ready to leave that made it simple. "I live here now, Mom.

There are at least ten women I know of in New York who will be amazing at the job they've offered me. But I'm the only one here. They need me, and there is something beautiful about that. I won't get the recognition I would in New York, but I'll make a difference here in ways I can't there. I'm going to stop pretending like this is a stopover. Papillon was always the destination."

Her mother reached up and ran a hand across her cheek, brushing away her tears. "Your father is going to be upset, but I need you to know that we are both very proud of you. You always found your own path. Just remember to light it for the rest of us. So we can find you. So we can be a part of you."

"What's going on?" Her father was suddenly standing in front of them. "Is everything all right?"

Her mother smiled at her and nodded, giving Roxie permission to do what she needed to do.

Her mother was difficult and she always would be, but they could connect when they both let their guard down. She didn't need the walls she'd built. They could come down now.

"Thanks, Mom." She hugged her mom and stood up because her father would need time. "Dad, thank you, too. Thanks for everything you've given me, including this opportunity. But if you ever try to come between me and Zep again, I won't be able to forgive you. I love him. I'm probably going to marry him and raise little bayou babies who will drive me insane, and we'll do it all as two overworked and severely underpaid civil servants. I hope you'll be a part of that, but if you can't, know that I love you."

"Roxanne," her father started in that tone that meant business.

Her mother stood. "No, Tony. She's made her decision

and we're not going to say another word except to express our love for her and to let her know when the time comes, Zep will be welcome."

"Pamela, we can't let her throw it all away," he said.

"She's not throwing anything away. She's building a life for herself, and she's going to do it now." Her mom nodded. "Go on. I'll deal with your father, and I expect to see you and that man of yours at the wedding this fall."

A light joy shoved out all her insecurity. The decision was made and it was the right one. And her mom was behind her. "Tell Brian I love him. I'll call you tomorrow and let you know how it goes."

Roxie grabbed her bag and ran for the exit.

It was time to go home.

Zep stared at the beer in front of him and wondered why he'd bothered. It wasn't like he was thirsty, and he definitely couldn't drown his sorrows. After all, he had a puppy to deal with. Roxie's cat would be fine, but Daisy would need him to take her out in the middle of the night, to wake up in the morning and take her for a walk. He couldn't do that if he was blitzed out of his mind, though it sounded like a really good thing to be. After all, if he passed out, he wouldn't have to think about how he'd wrecked the best thing that ever happened to him.

"Something wrong? I don't usually see you in here by yourself. You usually have a friend or two." Cain Cunningham worked the bar at The Back Porch. Not that there was much in the establishment besides the bar. There were a couple of pool tables in the back and a small dance floor. And the man was right. He usually sat at one of the tables with his friends. Sometimes he came out with his brother and shot some pool. He rarely sat at a bar and drank.

"Just didn't feel like company tonight." Yet he hadn't been able to sit in his little apartment, either. And while his mother was perfectly happy to let Daisy and Sunny into her house, her own son had been told he wasn't welcome until he brought back her other baby, as she was now calling Roxanne.

Had he made a mistake? Had he treated her as less than she truly was? He'd thought he was sacrificing for her happiness, but what if it was really his fear that had reacted?

"So you decided to come to a packed bar that seems to be hosting not one but two girls' nights?" Cain looked out over the bar toward the tables where a bunch of young women were partying. Raucous country music thrummed through the place, and there were several groups out dancing, their boots shuffling across the hardwoods.

"Well, if I went to my family's place, I would end up having to explain my screwed-up life to my brother. Here I thought I would find the company far less nosy," he said pointedly.

Cain merely shrugged one big shoulder. "Nah. It's been slow up until now, and I have help this evening. They finally hired a couple of waitresses. And all anyone wants is beer, wine, or shots, so my talents are wasted and I can focus on my customers. I hear the deputy is leaving. Now, what I can't figure out is if that's good for you—because she arrested you a lot, man, and for very little provocation—or bad for you because you're obviously in love with her. Which one?"

Did anyone in the world not know about his trouble? The gossip mill had worked quickly. "How the hell do you know she's gone?"

Cain leaned over, putting his big hands on the bar. "Let me see if I can put the chain together. Major talked to one of the girls at Miss Marcelle's while she was cutting his hair earlier today. According to her, he doesn't like the way the barber shop does it, but I think he's sweet on the hairdresser. Anyway, her sister is one of my waitresses, and according to her, the deputy is on her way back to the city, never to be heard from again. Or as she put it, she got away. Did she get away from you?"

"She's not gone forever. She'll be back in a couple of days. She just has a job interview." Nosy people were always talking. Usually he was one of them. It wasn't like there was much else to do, but he had to admit it felt different being on the other side.

"Yeah, but she would just be working out a notice because she would be crazy to not take a job in New York."

It was perverse but Zep felt the need to argue. "Why? Why is New York so much better than here? She wouldn't be crazy for staying in a job she loves, even though it's not the most high profile. Some people don't want to live to work. They work to live. Some people want to have a life outside of the office."

"But not the deputy? Well, I suppose our lifestyle here isn't for everyone."

But it had been good for her. "She's been happier the last few days than I've ever seen her. Happier and more relaxed despite the fact that her parents were in town causing all sorts of trouble."

Cain backed off. "Then I wonder why she's leaving. I always liked the deputy. She seemed smart and fair, although obviously not when it came to you. She was pretty rough on you."

"She was never rough. She was . . . It was her way of staying close to me." He sighed and stared at the beer. Was he actually unhappy he might never get arrested in this town again?

"Well, she won't be close now."

"Don't you have customers to serve?"

Cain shrugged. "Like I said, my waitresses are on top of things. It leaves me with all kinds of time on my hands. So what do you think made the deputy run? Was it dealing with Otis, because he does have a particular smell."

"She's not running." He bit back a groan. "Except maybe she is because I didn't tell her what I should have."

"What should you have told her?"

He stared, unwilling to say the words he hadn't said to her.

"Ah," Cain said with a nod of his head. "You love her but you didn't tell her. You know you have a phone. You could tell her now."

Call her from a bar? That didn't seem like the best idea. He'd sat up all night thinking about what he would do when she came back, how he would handle it during those two weeks before she left again. Should he be friendly or just leave her alone?

Or should he ask her to stay? Should he get on his knees and beg her to give him another chance to show her how good life could be if they were together?

He glanced at his phone. All afternoon he'd watched the app that gave him all the information about the flight she was taking. Her flight was around three hours, so she wouldn't have landed yet. She would still be in the air.

He could text her so it was waiting. Or leave her a voice mail.

He chose to text because she would at least see part of it on her notifications. She might not listen to a voice mail.

I love you, too. Please call me.

It was all he needed to say, and the minute he sent it off, it was like a weight had lifted and he could breathe again.

That had been his true mistake. Not what happened back when he was barely old enough to vote. His real mistake was not being open with her, not trusting them enough as a couple to get through whatever came their way.

"Good for you, man," Cain said with a smile that quickly turned down. "There's some trouble. Did I mention all those girls' nighters? You're one of the only men in a bar full of women who've had a few. Do you know what that means?"

It meant he should probably go home and wait for his lady to call.

"Hey, Zep," a feminine voice said. Debra Griffiths slipped onto the barstool beside him. She was dressed to kill in a short skirt and a barely there tank, boots on her feet, and her hair teased halfway to heaven. "Happy to see you out in the world again. I'm partying with some of my friends. Maybe you want to come join us? Misty and I have been talking for a real long time about how hot you are."

Dear god. "I have to get home. I've got a call I'm waiting on."

He slid his beer toward Cain, but Debra reached out and stopped him. "Come on, Zep. Don't be like that. I know all about the deputy and how she's leaving. There's no reason for you to play the good boy now. We've missed the baddest boy in all of the parish."

"I'm going to need to ask you to move along, ma'am."

His heart jolted at the sound of the voice. He turned and Roxanne was standing just past the doorway looking like the most gorgeous thing he'd ever seen in khakis. She was here. She was standing close enough that he could almost touch her.

"How are you here? You're supposed to be on the plane to New York by now," he said, taking her in like she was the sunshine and he'd been in the darkness forever.

"And you're supposed to be at home watching our dog and cat," she replied, her eyes narrowing. "I suppose Delphine got that duty."

"Hey, now." Debra stood up and faced Roxie. "I heard you were gone and that means he's fair game, and we aren't even on parish land so you can't tell me what to do."

"I said move along. I'm not saying it in a police capacity, Debra. I'm telling you plainly to get your hands off my man. Unless he's been doing something he shouldn't," she began, sending him a look that had him answering in quick time.

Zep held his hands up. "Nope. I was crying into my beer because I love you and I couldn't stand the thought of you leaving, and I didn't even drink the beer."

"He's been perfectly innocent, Deputy." Cain backed him up. "He was, in fact, pathetically lovelorn, and I think you'll find he's left you a text. Debra here was getting handsy. You know, Deb, that whole sexual harassment thing works both ways."

Debra glared at Cain and snorted. "Yeah, sure. Because men don't like it when you come on to them first."

"Should I change?" Roxie stepped in, her hands on her hips. "Because the ass kicking I will give you if you hit on him again will not be parish approved. Do I make myself clear? Or should I say it again?"

Debra lost every bit of her courage at Roxie's words and close proximity. "I am moving along, ma'am. Nothing to see here."

She scampered back to her friends.

"Have you been drinking, Guidry?" She had on her stone-cold cop face.

"I had a few sips of one beer."

"And were you planning on driving?" she asked.

Why was she asking him cop questions when they needed to talk about real things? "Rox, what are you doing here? You're supposed to be in New York. Why are you in uniform?"

"Major's father had to go to the hospital," she explained. "He had a fall. He's fine but no one else could take his shift and I happened to walk into the stationhouse at the perfect time to take over. As for why I'm here, you should understand it's not for you. I'm here because I want to make this place my home. I don't want the job in New York, and I've informed Armie that I will be staying for the foreseeable future. Now, I came out to this bar because I heard there was trouble. I know this is technically not parish land, but I can still handle my business."

He needed to make her understand. "Roxie, baby, I made a mistake."

A brow rose over her eyes. "I would say you did. You're parked in a fire zone."

"We have a fire zone?" Cain asked. "I didn't think we had any of those. Our parking lot is made of gravel and there are no actual spots. People just kind of park."

Roxie shook her head. "His truck is blocking what would obviously be used as a fire escape should the building catch on fire. So I'm going to have to take him in. Mr. Guidry, put your hands behind your back. You know the routine."

He was being arrested? He stared at her, bewildered, as she touched his arm, turning him around gently. "Baby, just look at your phone."

"I don't look at my phone while I'm on duty," she replied, and he felt the cold cuffs snap around his wrists. "Cain, I'm taking him down to the station. He'll come by in the morning and get his truck."

"But what if we have a fire?" Cain yelled the question over the thump of the music.

"Don't," she called back as she guided him toward the door.

What the hell was happening? "I made a mistake. Can't we please talk about this?"

She pressed him through the door and out into the parking lot, where his truck was parked in a perfectly respectable place. "I've decided you're a dumbass. But you're my dumbass, and if this is the only way I can keep you safe from your own dumbassery, then this is how it's going to be. What do you want for dinner? I'll call it in on our way."

He was so confused. "What?"

"Dinner. Your mom didn't feed you. You're too smart to eat at that bar. So what do you want to eat? You're going to need your strength because when I get off my shift, we've got to pick up the pets, and Daisy will definitely need a walk."

He stopped when he hit the gravel and refused to move any farther. "Roxanne, what are you saying?"

She tilted her head to look up at him, and the sweetest smile curled her lips up. "I'm saying I'm staying in Papillon and I'm not doing it because I love you. If I wanted to move back to New York, we would go. I wouldn't leave you behind because I love you, but I'm not staying because I do. Do you understand?"

He thought he did. "You're making this decision and it's yours and you're going to own it. You won't blame me."

"Good. You can learn. Now, what do you want for dinner?"

He wasn't interested in dinner. He needed to make things plain. "I am madly in love with you, Roxanne King, and I had already made the decision to come after you no matter what your father said. I should never have made the decision for the both of us. If we're in this together, then we decide everything together. And your father better understand that I'm not leaving, because no matter what he says, I'm good for you. I love you, and if you'll forgive me, I promise I will do my best to never let you down again."

She went up on her toes and brushed her lips against his briefly. "See that you don't. And your mom packed some clothes for you, but she told me that she's already got a renter interested in your apartment and she needs you out by the end of the week."

"My momma's kicking me out?" It appeared a lot had changed since he'd decided to go get a beer.

"I explained to her that you were moving in with me." She winced. "Though now that we've agreed to make decisions together, I see I probably should have talked to you about that."

"Nope. I'm good with that one." She was here and she wasn't leaving, and he was going to get every chance he needed to show her they belonged together forever. "Say it again, Rox."

The sweetest smile curled up her lips. "I love you."

"I love you, too, baby." He kissed her again and really wished he had use of his hands. "Now let me out of these cuffs and we'll grab some dinner."

She shook her head with a smirk. "I've decided this is really the best way to keep you out of trouble."

He allowed her to steer him toward her SUV. "But how can I get my hands on you if they're cuffed behind my back?"

She opened the rear door. "Get creative, babe. I know you can do it."

"At least let me ride in the front with you," he said even as she was pushing him into the back.

"Can't do that. But I will do something I don't do for any

other person I put in the back of my car." She kissed him. "Now be a good boy and I'll put you in the comfy cell."

He would only be comfortable if she was in there with him, but he might be able to make that happen. "Drive fast then."

As she pulled out of the parking lot and flashed her lights, he knew he was finally heading into his future.

# *epilogue*

***One year later***

"I've made a monster," Roxanne said as she watched her brand-new husband arguing with the mayor about funding for the first phase of his shelter plans.

Did he have to do it at their wedding?

"I like how passionate he is," her mother said with a happy sigh. "He's eager for life, and that's a beautiful thing. Your father thinks so, too."

Her parents had come down three days before, though it hadn't been their only meeting. Pamela had come down a couple of times to help with the wedding plans, and now she was thick as thieves with Delphine and Miss Marcelle. They were planning a girls' trip to the city, where Pamela intended to introduce them to all the best psychics.

It was weird, but like everything in life, now it seemed perfect.

"I think Dad's just happy to get all the weddings over with," Roxie said as she saw her father sitting at a table with Armie and Lila and their two kids. Noelle was back home after her first semester in college, and she seemed fascinated with her tiny baby brother.

"He's particularly happy that you're settling down." Her

mother sipped on the champagne she'd nabbed from a passing waiter. "I know he was upset at first, but he's had time to reflect. He won't ever tell you this but you remind him so much of his father. Your grandpa would have loved this place."

Roxie wasn't so sure about that, but she knew he would have loved Zep. "Thank you for talking to him."

Her mom's eyes got misty. "I don't think it was me. I think it was our granddaughter."

Roxie looked over at the table where her brother, sister-in-law, and their new daughter sat. Little Constance was three and she had some special needs, and she had become the light of their lives.

"I didn't think it would be the same," her mom said quietly. "I thought I would feel differently about a child who wasn't your brother's blood, but the minute that baby girl held her hands out to me, I realized how little blood means. I love that child with every bone in my body, and so does your father. I think it's made him realize that who he is isn't nearly as important as how he loves."

Her father had danced with her out on the patio of the B and B, with the sounds of music and the hum of the cicadas all around them. The father-daughter dance wasn't as awkward as she worried it'd be. Her father had told her how beautiful she was. He'd told her he was proud.

Her wedding day had been an emotional one.

"I told Sylvie I would protest the mayor's office until she gives me the money I need to microchip every pet who comes through our shelter," Zep announced as he walked up. He'd ditched his jacket and tie and looked perfectly scrumptious with a bit of his chest on display.

"Hey, all protesting better wait until I've had my honeymoon," Roxie said. They were headed into New Orleans for the night, and then in the morning they would catch a flight to Hawaii, where she intended to do nothing but lie on the beach and love her man.

"Hey, Deputy, Mr. Guidry." Ashlyn Travers had worn all black to the wedding, but then she hadn't really been a guest. She'd been working. The now high school senior turned out to have far more skill with a camera than common sense, but then Roxie was certain she would say an artist needs no common sense. "I got some great shots of the reception, and I'm letting you know that next month I will be premiering *The Rougarou's Revenge* at the senior center. I would really like to include some of the footage I took from the wedding, if you don't mind. After all, you two are my romantic leads, and apparently people like a happy ending. Unless you would let me set something up where just before you say *I do*, the pastor turns into the rougarou and kills you both. Because that would be a great way to end the film."

Zep's eyes lit up, and Roxie realized she was going to have to cut him off.

"You can absolutely use the footage of the wedding. A happy ending sounds like the right way to go," she said firmly. After it had gotten out that Ashlyn had been making a film, the people of Papillon had all caught the acting bug. Now, months later, Ashlyn was almost ready to show off her masterpiece.

Ashlyn huffed. "Fine, but it won't be the same. Thanks for helping me out."

"We can't wait to see the movie," Zep said, his arm going around Roxie.

"I'm applying to film school in California," Ashlyn announced.

"I'm going to give you a word of advice," Zep said gravely. "Fly out there. Don't drive."

That made Roxie laugh. "I think she'll avoid your mistakes."

Ashlyn waved and went back to work.

"It's so nice to see all the young people being ambitious," Pamela remarked. "Though you should know now that you're married, it's time to give little Constance a cousin. Your eggs aren't getting any younger, Roxanne." Her mother stepped away.

She groaned. "I should have known I was only getting a temporary reprieve."

Zep's arms went around her waist, and he pulled her back against him. "We'll decide when we're ready. Sera hasn't told anyone, but she and Harry are going to give Luc a sibling in about six months."

Roxie turned her head so she could kiss his cheek. "I'm glad. I know they've been trying. And we will, too. Hey, we've managed to keep a dog and a cat happy. We should be able to handle a small human."

Once, she'd given up on the idea of having a family. Now she wanted nothing more than to add to the one she'd found. One day they would have a kiddo and he or she would follow after Dad, learning how to take care of the world around them. And they would follow Mom and she would teach them how to protect it.

She would also teach them how to enjoy it.

"What do you say we knock off early and head to the hotel?" she asked.

"I like the way you think, Guidry," Zep said with a chuckle.

"Well, I like the way you love me, Guidry. So let's get started."

He leaned over and she was in his arms.

They weren't going to waste another minute.

# *acknowledgments*

Special thanks to my editor, Kate Seaver. Thanks for believing in this project! Also thanks to the whole Berkley team, including Fareeda Bullert, Jessica Brock, and Mary Geren. Thanks to my agent, Kevan Lyon. I love working with you. To my whole team—Kim Guidroz, Maria Monroy, Stormy Pate, Riane Holt, Jillian Stein, Jenn Watson and Social Butterfly, Margarita Coale, and Kori Smith.

Look for the next Butterfly Bayou novel

***Bayou Beauty***

Coming from Berkley in summer 2021!